THE PAST IS TOMORROW

Also by Liz Ryan

Blood Lines
A Note of Parting
A Taste of Freedom

THE PAST IS TOMORROW

Liz Ryan

With warmest wishes

Liz Ryan

Hodder & Stoughton

First published in hardback and paperback editions in Great Britain in 2000
by Hodder and Stoughton
A division of Hodder Headline

10 9 8 7 6 5 4 3 2 1

British Library Cataloguing in Publication Data

ISBN 0 340 76870 3 Hardback
ISBN 0 340 79237 X Paperback

Typeset by Palimpsest Book Production Limited,
Polmont, Stirlingshire

Printed and bound in Great Britain by
Mackays of Chatham PLC

Hodder and Stoughton
A division of Hodder Headline
338 Euston Road
London NW1 3BH

Yes, miraculously you're all still hanging in here, helping this fourth book see daylight with all the enthusiasm you brought to the first, and I can't thank any of you enough: Annie, Mary, Jeannette, Gerry, Sheila, Sarah, Sharon and Philip – I'd have gone round the bend years ago without your absolutely determined, unflagging, fantastic friendship!

And then there are the readers I've never even met, who take the time and trouble to write from everywhere from Aberdeen to Australia. When the going gets tough I take out your letters and read them and think of you all and tell myself, hey, get this show on the road, get this book out there this minute!

You all mean so much. Much more than it's in my power to express. I can only hope you know the difference you make.

Chapter One

It was ten weeks since the hospital installed its swish, impressive new security system. And ten hours now since Baby Kilo Finnegan went missing.

Shivaun Reilly ran through the drilling midsummer rain to her Mazda hatchback and let herself into it as if into a cocoon, a private bubble in which she could finally strip off the blithe, brisk mask she had worn all day. People always felt somehow invisible in their cars, safe to scratch their noses or sing off-key or, in this instance, howl. It was a huge relief to let the tears flow freely and she didn't bother groping for a tissue as she started the engine, because she knew she was going to bawl most of the eight-mile, seventy-minute way home. The car was her space and she could do what she liked in it.

Kilo Finnegan was *her* baby. Her scrawny, writhing, fabulous first-born, over whose birth she had triumphantly presided only five weeks ago as a newly promoted staff midwife. To be technically accurate his mother was Fionnuala Finnegan, and he'd been delivered by Dr O'Hara, but that was mere detail, paperwork. Kilo was her spiritual soulmate, a fragile little fighter battling, and beating, the odds.

A preemie, he'd weighed in at just one kilo, and as Dr O'Hara lowered his mask she'd known from his briefly bitten lip that young Kilo Finnegan was off to a dodgy start. Dodgy and scary, just as her own start had been twenty-four years before.

His name was officially Danny. But his exact birthweight

instantly earned him his nickname, and there was a communal feeling of campaign to get him up and running, kick-start him on the rocky road to his target weight of two and a half kilos, at which point he would be allowed to go home with his anxious but optimistic young parents. Shivaun had fallen in love with him the moment she saw his wrinkled, puzzled little ET face, and followed every inch of his progress thereafter. Each morning she ran to the intensive care unit to beam down at him, or at what bits were visible amidst the tubes and wires: he was in an incubator, on oxygen, a ventilator and an antibiotic drip, with a naso-gastric feed line running up his nose. He looked wired to the moon, a micro-Martian. He was her *project*. She cheered when he put on two grams, exulted when he gained five, even brought his mum Fionnuala a demented-looking Donald Duck toy 'for when he gets big and goes home'. Slowly he had got big, grown into a squishy, yummy baby and been on the brink of going home when, suddenly this morning, his cot had been found empty.

Empty! It was incredible, nobody could believe it, there had almost been hysteria until Matron rolled up like a Saracen tank, gazed into the cot as if commanding Kilo's reappearance by sheer force of determination, and marched off to call the police. As she departed, the ward sister who'd been on duty stammered tearfully: 'May – maybe he just—'

Matron whirled round. 'Maybe he just what, Orla? Popped out to the pub for a pint? Ran round to the bank to cash a cheque?'

This was unusually sarcastic of Matron, who was famously loyal to her nurses and supportive of them. But Matron had been under pressure lately, with perpetual budget meetings and a complete moron of a health minister to deal with – a minister who thought overworked, underpaid nurses in understaffed hospitals were a perfectly 'productive' way to run a health service. Matron loathed this man, who insisted on calling her Director of Nursing as if she were running a business, and everyone knew the babbling goon intended to close down St Jude's at the first opportunity. A hundred and twenty years old, the hospital had been the birthplace of virtually the entire community, of their grandparents as well as today's children, but the minister didn't give a stuff about that; he would merge it with one of the big hypermarket hospitals because small ones were no longer 'viable'.

Well, Kilo Finnegan had scarcely been 'viable'. But he had made it, thrilling his parents, nurses and doctors as he swarmed his way up the weighing scale to the point – *yes!* – where he could be taken off the hardware and put on the breast. Shivaun knew she would never forget that first sight of him nuzzling into his mother, lolling in her arms like a drunken sailor. My bambino, she whooped to herself, has done it! Although she had delivered dozens of others since (with doctor's assistance, as she liked to think of it), Kilo Finnegan held pride of place in her heart.

And now, he was gone. Missing. AWOL. Distraught and distracted, Shivaun became aware she was in the wrong lane, and signalled to the driver on her offside that she wanted to change. But he nudged deliberately forward, wouldn't let her in. Bastard! She swore as she cut in front of him, and raised two fingers for good measure. In return he hooted fiercely, and she felt an almost uncontrollable urge to slam on the brakes, leap out of her car and run to his, crash her fist through the window.

Road rage. Oh, Christ. Was this how it happened, was this country becoming completely impossible to live in? Making a serious effort, she signalled a grudging apology and turned left, into a static gridlock that looked as if it had been there for hours. On rainy evenings this road was always tied in knots, except for the free-flow bus lane. But there was no bus to St Jude's in time for her eight o'clock start, so she had to take the car . . . sighing, she dropped it into neutral, her mind refusing to let go of Kilo Finnegan. What if some looper had taken him, someone seriously dangerous even to a tiny baby? *Who* would take him, *why*?

Some instinct told her that the police were wrong in their glib assumption that some grieving mother must have done it, one of the ones whose babies had died or been adopted. Only three babies had died at St Jude's in recent years, but several had been adopted, and the female of the two cops who'd arrived to investigate had demanded a full list of all the mothers' names and addresses.

'Hormones,' she'd said in an automatic, know-all tone, 'haywire. Some mixed-up mama, but means no harm . . . we'll find this child in no time, have him back by close of play.'

Yeah. Right. But the day had worn on with no word of Kilo, and Shivaun thought bitterly of that slick new security system. How much had it cost? Fifty grand? A hundred? Whatever the figure, it was money down the drain. One person could swipe open a door with their ID card and politely hold it open for fifteen others to walk through. Brilliant. Nothing like this would ever have happened in the days of Stan the hall porter, who'd never in thirty years let so much as an unauthorised mouse into the building. The money for the system should have been spent on doubling his salary – or on medical equipment, instead of expecting the parents to fund it with cake sales, karaoke nights and sponsored trudges through Thailand. A hundred and fifty parents had literally slogged their way through that country, in addition to paying the taxes that were supposed to buy all the things they apparently did not. Shivaun was far from alone in wondering what exactly her taxes did buy, apart from a nice Mercedes-Benz for the health minister.

The parents were wonderful. Always loyal to St Jude's, they threw their weight behind every new fundraising drive, did all sorts of voluntary work and sent in private, secret cheques . . . but their faith in the hospital was going to be seriously hammered when they heard about the missing baby. It would look like negligence, maybe the Finnegans would even sue Matron despite her overruled opposition to the new electronic security?

Shivaun fumed as she thought of the uphill battle Matron was now facing, and fumed some more as she thought of those poor women suspected of the abduction. As if they hadn't enough to contend with, without opening their front doors to find the police 'diplomatically, sensitively' demanding to search their homes! It would come to a search, she supposed, when they denied all knowledge of Kilo's whereabouts . . . the nerve of it, the outrage!

Meanwhile, a counsellor had been rushed to the side of Fionnuala Finnegan, who naturally had screamed aloud on being informed her baby was missing. She was electrified with horror, as any parent would be, but not in the least irrational; Shivaun had privately given a clenched-fist salute to hear her tell the well-meaning counsellor to fuck off. Despite her youth Shivaun was an old-fashioned nurse, knew that pain and grief were things you had to work through in your own way at your own pace. Drugs could alleviate them but they couldn't cure their source; sooner or later you had to tackle that yourself. In any event, Kilo's father Martin had come storming in to gather Fionnuala into his arms and lead her to a private room for the far more intimate comfort she needed. Love and hugs were, in Shivaun's opinion, far more productive than any smartass shrink spouting Californian psychobabble. Vividly she still remembered the clever-clogs counsellors who'd been drafted in to give her 'therapy' after her own 'trauma', five years ago . . . she'd listened to them, but she'd never spoken to them, because what was there to say?

All the counselling in Christendom wasn't going to change anything, and it was only when she realised that fact that she'd taken the first shaky step to recovery. Not that she had recovered, or ever entirely would, but at least today she could function, she could absorb the nightmare into reality and get on with her daily life.

That's not too bad, she thought, is it? I'm not in care, I'm not institutionalised or supervised, I'm coping, surviving, doing my best.

But suddenly she realised, as she turned on the radio to hear whether there was any news of Kilo, that she was exhausted. It had been the worst day of her career, she hadn't eaten since six this morning, barely been able to concentrate on the Hughes baby who entered the world with a twisted wrist or the Killeen infant who, after one piercing screech to announce her arrival, had suddenly stopped breathing. Both were doing fine now, but – but where was *Kilo*?

Nobody knew, the radio said. A baby had been abducted from St Jude's hospital at seven this morning but the police were not yet following any definite line of enquiry . . . the parents had declined counselling . . . Shivaun cheered to hear that Martin was supporting Fionnuala on that score, that both parents were united with Matron in rejecting a counsellor whose services had not been requested. The counsellor had been frogmarched in by the authorities, and now the Finnegans were socking the authorities one in the eye. Good.

There was only one useful thing a counsellor could do, and that was produce Kilo Finnegan, intact, pristine and safe. As yet, nobody had been able to do that. Snapping off the radio, Shivaun gazed into the gnarled knot of traffic, up at the surly sky; God, she couldn't wait to see Ivor, talk to him! And meanwhile, get home to Alana who'd have dinner ready and something wry to say, no doubt, about the missing baby being only a very small one.

Alana Kennedy was indeed cooking dinner, putting on some water to boil for the rice to go with the chicken masala. Even allowing for the Friday evening traffic and rain which mysteriously doubled it, Shivaun should be home soon. Home panting with anxiety about the Finnegan child, fretting and worrying and refusing to unplug her mind from the work that consumed her. Alana was a nurse too, but for her it was a job – poorly paid at that – whereas to Shivaun it was a vocation. A true vocation, in the sense that the babies were forever calling, crying out to her. Any minute now she'd dash in with her hazel eyes looking like she was drowning in them, tugging at the tawny hair which had developed split ends as a result. She'd need persuasion to pick at her food and let it go cold while she rattled on, raging about the mismanagement of the Irish health service; then there'd be a rant about the dreadful weather everyone else said was beautiful – in Ireland, a 'beautiful' day meant it wasn't actually raining as you spoke. Then there'd be the bit about the taxes and the traffic and the crime rate, the nation's rapid and comprehensive slide into Babylonian venality . . .

Really it was a wonder Shivaun didn't go into politics, she took it all so much to heart, just as she did her work, perpetually tilting at windmills. Prosperity didn't encourage decency, she said, it was her belief that Ireland's new affluence was fostering corruption, the country was turning into a vain, violent little thug.

Alana had to admit that yes, some of the latest scandals did make the Mafia look like the Legion of Mary by comparison. There were lies and thefts and tribunals, the clergy seemed to be sex-crazed almost to a man, drugs, deals and bribery simmered under the shiny new surface. People were getting into debt with the collusion of the banks, chasing rainbows . . . but you couldn't carry it all on your own shoulders, not when they were as bamboo-slender as Shivaun Reilly's. She was so fragile, under the skin.

Of course it was that dreadful shock, five years ago, that had got her started down this road. Alana hadn't met Shivaun until after the event, but after living with her for over four years, she knew where she was coming from. Shivaun had got her life and her emotions back under control, but she still hadn't forgiven what had happened or understood how it could have happened. Down in her depths she still howled and lamented, beat her fists against the truth, denied the nightmare and tried to drive it from her. When she married Ivor, as she surely must some day soon, she'd be better off moving out of Dublin, settling in some relatively peaceful rural place. There'd be a cottage hospital to work in and Ivor could work anywhere, all he needed was a computer and the internet.

And then children would come along to distract her. Alana was in no doubt that Shivaun would have several – four, five, even six. She craved a family, would barricade herself into it, and Alana knew the reasons why. Kids, security, Ivor's devoted love; Shivaun needed all of that in a way that she,

Alana, sometimes found alarming in its intensity. Like the rain it sometimes subsided, but always came flooding back, engulfing her. It wasn't a question of romance or domestic bliss, it was virtually a question of survival. Spiritual survival and, Alana sometimes thought uneasily, even physical survival. It was imperative that Shivaun marry Ivor, now that he had graduated, and have children with him, and have them soon.

As she waited for the water to boil, Alana found herself thinking of the first time she'd met Shivaun, one unpromisingly wet March day back in 1994. She'd been twenty-two then, fresh up from midwifery training in Ardkean, and Shivaun had been only nineteen, a student nurse who mysteriously owned this house and was looking for someone to share it. Alana answered her ad on the staff noticeboard at St Jude's and was amazed to discover a prospective landlady even younger than herself, a mere teenager asking a ridiculously low rent for a double room with full access to garden, kitchen and laundry facilities. But only on probation, at first; Shivaun said she wanted to be sure they'd get on together and Alana had wondered, frankly, whether they would.

Shivaun had seemed jumpy and edgy as she ludicrously conducted that first meeting, completely different to Alana's own tumbling, teasing horde of brothers and sisters. In the Kennedy home in Waterford things were relaxed to the point of horizontal; it was crammed with so many people that nobody ever knew where anything was, who owned anything or who that extra person sitting at the table might be. The Kennedys were a bunch of slobs, cheery chatty slobs: eight kids, two parents, three dogs, a donkey and a fistful of scuffling chickens. Alana was the eldest and the first to leave for Dublin, not at all sure she liked it when she reached it, or whether she liked Shivaun's unnervingly tidy, well-organised house. It seemed sort of – *fortified*, somehow, as they sat there discussing domestic details over cups of tea. Proper cups, with saucers.

'What about the third bedroom?' she'd asked, thinking maybe the more the merrier, 'are you planning to rent that out too?'

'No' Shivaun had replied without hesitation, 'my boyfriend sometimes stays over weekends and he likes to have somewhere of his own to study. He's a trainee accountant.'

Alana was surprised and rather cheered to hear there was a boyfriend. He might be fun, put a grin on Shivaun's face and soften its slightly combative angles. It wasn't that Shivaun didn't smile – she did, several times – it was just that she was somehow making Alana feel junior to her despite being three years younger. She seemed terribly grown up for nineteen.

She wondered why the boyfriend didn't live here with Shivaun, since living together was so common in Dublin, but as if reading her thoughts Shivaun added something about his mother being widowed, his needing to spend time with her. She was, Alana gathered, the kind of mother who couldn't be left alone. So Shivaun was alone instead, offering a room in this clean fresh house at the absolutely bargain rate of fifty pounds a week. Earnestly, she leaned forward and asked Alana what she thought her 'best and worst' personal habits might be.

Alana, who'd urgently needed somewhere to live, decided on an exercise in damage limitation.

'Well' she said, 'I am a bit untidy, but on the other hand I'm a good cook and I have a sense of humour . . . we might have a bit of craic together?'

Shivaun looked, she thought, like someone who could use a bit of craic, youthful fun, midnight giggles over pizza and plonk. Even though midwifery was the brighter end of the business, nursing could be a sometimes sad, wearing job, with huge responsibilities. Had something gone wrong for Shivaun already, had there been some tragic mistake with drugs or dosages? But then, she wouldn't still be working at St Jude's, her career would be over before it had properly begun.

'Yes' Shivaun nodded thoughtfully, 'we might. I have to warn you that I'm not the disco type, I don't want you playing loud music at midnight or throwing parties, but if you think you can handle that then why don't you move in for a month, let's say, and see what happens?'

And so Alana had moved in, and there had been instant friction over the wet towels she left strewn around the bathroom, unrinsed dishes piled in the sink, a hairbrush she borrowed when she couldn't find her own. At the end of the month, when she produced her rent money, she fully expected to get her marching orders in return. But Shivaun simply looked out the kitchen window, and pointed.

'When are you going to mow that grass? It's your turn and we agreed to take turns, Alana.'

Surprised and somehow chastened, Alana resolved to make an effort. Shivaun was a bit prickly, but she was fair and honest, there was a kind of tenacity about her that was engaging. But another full month passed before Alana dared ask her how she came to be living here alone, and to own the house.

'My parents died' Shivaun replied matter-of-factly, 'and I inherited.'

'Oh. Oh, wow. What a bummer. You're awfully young to be orphaned.'

'I was orphaned,' Shivaun replied shortly, 'at birth.'

Alana gasped, could still hear her gasp as she thought of it today.

'What? Y – you mean you were only a baby when your parents died?'

'No. The parents who died were my adoptive parents. My birth parents left me in a church doorway when I was a few hours old.'

Speechless, Alana stared. In the same blank tone, Shivaun went on dispensing the information as if it were a bus timetable: 'I don't know whether my mother took me there, or my father, or both, I don't know whether she recovered from the birth or not, or what happened next . . . but now *you* know, OK?'

Her look was so defiant that Alana recoiled. But it was most certainly not OK. Alana was appalled, yearning to know how Shivaun had lost the second set of parents as well. But she couldn't summon the courage to ask, only to enquire when it had happened.

'It happened eight months ago. I don't really want to discuss it.'

Alana nodded dumbly, and the subject was dropped. But from that moment their relationship changed, they were no longer mere landlady and tenant. Alana felt a shaft of protectiveness for Shivaun, and a surge of respect: most people would be in tatters, on crying jags, reeling from such recent bereavement. Double bereavement – what in God's name could it have been? A car crash, plane crash? Some even worse thing that hardly bore contemplation? It must be something pretty bad, judging by Shivaun's face and tone . . . and yet she was so composed. She never inflicted her pain or moaned about her misfortune, and Alana had to admire her for that as they gradually inched their way forward to friendship. Not a chummy, matey friendship, at first, but some form of raw communication.

What did Shivaun see in her? Sometimes Alana wondered. She knew she was messy, a slob in both kitchen and bathroom, she was overweight and absent-minded, had to be chivvied into doing the boring bloody housework. But one day as she sat roaring with laughter at some comedy on television, she'd sensed a presence behind her, and turned to find Shivaun smiling at her.

For her part, she saw standards to be lived up to in Shivaun Reilly. There was something almost stern about her, she didn't take any prisoners or mince her words, but she was so forthright and candid you just had to admire her, and she did turn out to have a sense of humour. She was bloody attractive too, looked good even in her nurse's uniform, when she dressed up for a date with Ivor she radiated beauty all around her. Yet she never flaunted the fabulous Ivor, never poked into Alana's own sex life which was, demonstrably and embarrassingly, non-existent. Alana was stunned when she met Ivor, completely captivated by his sporty physique, edibly delicious looks and friendly charm, a charm that hooked her like a floundering fish. From the start Ivor was always nice to her, often turned up with flowers which he gallantly said were for them both, even as he embraced Shivaun and complimented her appearance.

But it was Shivaun's provocatively perfect appearance, oddly, that cemented their camaraderie. When the third month's rent was due, Alana was forced to go cap-in-hand and mumble a mortifying confession.

'Shivaun . . . I'm really sorry, I'm a bit short this month, my cheque might bounce . . . could you possibly give me a few days' grace?'

She'd dreaded this conversation, felt like a child apologising to teacher for not having its homework done. When Shivaun smiled, she nearly fainted.

'Let me guess. The money for the gym, huh?'

Yes. It was. Alana, in her increasing desperation to lose weight, had joined such a horrendously expensive gym that she would have to use it to justify it.

'Yes. I feel so guilty – but Jesus Christ, Shivaun, you're barely eight stone, you don't know how it feels to—'

'To have adorable dimples and rosy skin and baby-blue eyes? I'd imagine it feels as lovely as it looks.'

Alana was astonished, as much by the unexpected compliment as by the sudden sting of tears in her eyes. Nobody had ever commented favourably on her appearance since she was five years old.

'Well, I – I'd much rather have racehorse legs and gorgeous auburn hair like yours, I've always thought red is fabulous—'

Shivaun's hair was in fact a dark umber shade that only showed its true colours when the sun was on it, and she fiddled constantly with the ends of it, but it was certainly glossier than Alana's mangled mop which had originally been strawberry blonde, and virtually every colour since. The hairdresser was always luring her into experiments with fresh promises of beauty and glamour.

Shivaun looked candidly at her, with the hazel eyes that dissimulated but never lied. 'Alana, I know you're a bit touchy about your appearance, but can I tell you something frankly?'

Alana quailed. 'What?'

'You're lovely. Not because you spend a ton of money on cosmetics and hairdos and gyms and clothes, but because you smile so much. You laugh and you make me laugh and I love you for it.'

Alana gaped. She knew her family loved her but none of them ever bothered saying so, and no outsider had ever said it. Now, she hardly knew how to handle it.

'Oh, come on! I just try – try not to take life too seriously, that's all.'

'Yeah. Imagine if everyone were like me, always on the warpath! You're laid-back and, what's more, not a bit nosy. When you moved in I was afraid you might snoop into my affairs, but you didn't.'

'No . . . well, I come from a big family, I know how valuable privacy can be. I know you've had a hard time, too. Losing two sets of parents is really pretty – pretty careless, Shivaun!'

Cynicism was her way of coping with things and she cringed as she spoke; dear Christ, she'd gone too far, Shivaun would kill her.

But Shivaun grinned, twistedly. 'Yeah. I'll try to be better organised in future.'

Phew. Alana returned the smile with relief, and suddenly they were friends. They'd shared the house in harmony ever since, and shared all their secrets too, slowly, gradually, in full. Every secret, except one.

Shivaun pulled into the drive, switched off the ignition and sat for a minute taking deep, concentrated breaths. Thank God Alana hadn't been the ward sister on duty this morning, couldn't be blamed like the luckless Orla! She'd phoned Alana to tell her about Kilo's abduction, but today was after all Alana's precious day off, so she didn't want to walk into the house now with the woes of the world on her face.

Still, it was a goddamn disgrace! If only that brain-dead minister had listened to Matron, there'd be no security lapse now, no missing baby. Chewing her lower lip – hard – she jumped out of the car and went to clean up the junk lying in the front garden, the litter the local kids flung over the wall every day en route home from school. She felt like grabbing every little brat and ramming its face into its personal, scrunched-up cola can.

Trying to keep the garden as Jimmy had kept it was a losing battle. But she tried, because this house was her home, her haven. Architecturally it was just one more suburban Lego block, but it was where she'd come running to Mum when she fell off her bike or out of the Devitts' apple tree, she could still feel the sun-warmed porch tiles under her bare feet as she ran to Dad on summer evenings, welcoming him home from work, leaping into his outstretched arms. It had been a secure, happy home, smelling of washed cotton and wood wax, Mum's Tweed perfume and Dad's sneaked pipe. Later, after . . . after that Alana had arrived, Alana the experiment everyone said she must make. She couldn't live here alone, not after what had happened. She must have company.

And so Alana had come barrelling in, and almost got thrown out again, and then didn't get thrown out. At first Shivaun had hated sharing with her, resented this total stranger, but gradually Alana's cushion-comfort qualities had become a fixture. Of course Alana had changed since then, lost a good deal of her puppy fat and shaped up in many ways, but she was still always ready with a teapot and a smile. Besides, they worked together, were united in their fight for St Jude's, a far more socially valuable institution than any state-of-the-art monolith. Maybe the parents did have to trudge to Thailand to keep it going, but the fact that they were prepared to do so spoke volumes. Its threatened status gave herself and Alana plenty to talk about.

Shivaun waved to Fintan Daly next door, put a smile on her face and turned her key in the hall lock.

'Hi Ally! I'm home!'

Something smelled good. Dumping her bag in the hall, she picked up the post and went into the kitchen where Alana stood stirring some steamy, fragrant concoction.

'Indian? Yum.'

They smiled at each other, and Alana picked up a glass, thrust it at her.

'Here. G & T. Doctor's orders.'

Shivaun thought she could drink twenty G & Ts. But she was meeting Ivor later, didn't want to pass out halfway through *Titanic* at the Omniplex. As she raised her glass, she was aware of Alana's unvoiced question.

'*Sláinte*. Here's to Kilo's safe and speedy return.'

Standing sideways at the cooker, Alana eyed her.

'You OK?'

No. She wasn't OK. But – 'Yeah, fine. He's come this far, he'll go the extra mile, do a Cinderella and be home by midnight.'

Alana grinned. 'ET, phone home!'

Shivaun sipped her drink, longed to gulp it only she knew that gin was a trigger, would start her on a thundering speech about the mess this bloody country was in.

'Ivor ring?'

'Yeah. You just missed him. He said he'd pick you up at nine, but if you don't feel like the cinema that's OK, he'll bring round a video in case you'd rather stay home.'

Shivaun thought she would rather, was grateful for Ivor's foresight. He could always read her thoughts and moods. They'd all watch the video together, the three of them, and then when Alana left them – as she would – she could simply talk to Ivor, see what he made of this whole business. He'd been aghast to hear of Kilo's disappearance.

'Have I time to shower and change before Madhur Jaffrey serves her masterpiece?'

'If you're quick.'

She stood up and put down her drink as another thought struck her, one hopefully unconnected with Kilo.

'Any word of that girl in Kildare?'

Alana groaned to herself. Another young woman was missing in Kildare, one of a series missing all over the country. It had been going on for years, and some bodies had been found, but nobody knew whether it was a serial killer, or dozens of unrelated cases, or what. Shivaun watched and worried every development like a terrier.

'No. Nothing. But look, Shivaun, I really think you have enough on your mind for one evening. Why don't you just go have your bubbles and then we'll eat, huh?'

'Yeah. Right. Five minutes.'

It was only when Shivaun reached the bathroom, and saw herself in the mirror, that she realised her mascara had run, she looked like a panda. Cleansing it off, she stripped and got into the blissfully hot, powerful shower, reaching for her favourite fragranced gel. Oh, heaven! The foaming water made her feel better immediately, and she'd look better for Ivor, too. Ivor her man, her rock, her one remaining vestige of her former life.

Ivor Lawlor and Shivaun Reilly had known from the start that they would get married. They'd agreed on it the very first time they met, over a disputed KitKat bar, but decided to announce their engagement not quite immediately. She was only four at the time, he was nearly five.

'That's mine' she'd informed him, firmly. He pouted at her.

'Is not.'

'Is so.'

He thumped her. She thumped him back. They thumped each other, harder. The bar had flown out of reach and been grabbed by Shorty Maxwell, never to be seen again. Teacher had arrived to find a whirling dervish spinning round in the dust, spewing blood and gravel in all directions. Teacher had hauled it upright, separated it into its component parts, both of which continued to shriek and kick at each other.

'Stop that immediately! You are two very bold, wicked little – Ivor, I said *stop*!'

He delivered a last triumphant thump, and gazed tragically up at teacher.

'She stole my KitKat.'

'And who is she? The cat's mother? Has she not got a name?'

It was only their first day in kindergarten, and they had not been introduced. Ivor shrugged.

'I dunno.'

'Well she has, her name is Shivaun Reilly and she is a very nice little girl, I cannot believe you would hit a girl, Ivor.'

'But she stole—'

'Apologise. Right now.'

Ivor considered. She *had* pinched his bar. Still . . . he was bigger than her, and his father had warned him against hitting anyone smaller than himself. There might be trouble if . . . oh, all right.

'Sorry' he muttered.

'That's better. Now go and get cleaned up, both of you, here's a hanky, go and run it under the tap – oh, dear God, look at the cut of you, I don't know how I . . .'

Mumbling to herself, teacher had evaporated and both infants had tottered to the tap in the school yard where, as he soaked the hanky, Ivor had seen that Shivaun's forearm was really grazed, bleeding in a way that was as satisfactory as it was unnerving. Suppose she told her mum – or worse, her dad – that he'd done it?

He'd better find some way of redeeming the damage. Thoughtfully, he looked at the girl with her rusty little ringlets.

'I'm going to marry you when we grow up.'

She was about to protest when he took her arm, quite gently, and held it under the cooling, gushing water.

It felt good, and she looked at him in turn. He was quite a big boy, but he had a cut over his eye. She'd made her mark on him. She giggled.

'OK.'

'But we won't tell teacher yet. Or anyone.'

'No. We'll have a secret.'

'Yup.'

As the water poured over their shoes they both laughed, and punched each other's shoulders amicably. A secret engagement. Well, it wasn't quite the kind of thing you shared with your fellow junior infants.

* * *

From that day forth Ivor had claimed possession of his fiancée, taken her under his protection and sat beside her in school until, to their mutual outrage, they were segregated into boys' and girls' classes. But love knew no barriers, they always met up at break in the yard to swop their sandwiches, plastic horses and stickers. Nobody else ever got a look-in, and when Shorty Maxwell once threw a gym shoe at Shivaun Reilly, Ivor Lawlor beat him to a howling pulp. Ivor got into serious trouble over that, was pulled from the school picnic in Glendalough, but he didn't care. Shivaun Reilly was his girl and nobody messed with her.

'We'll have babies' she informed him when they were ten.

'Why?' he asked, not unreasonably.

''Cos – 'cos we haven't any brothers or sisters. So when we're big we'll have babies instead.'

She knew he'd say yes. He always got her whatever she wanted, because he was her best friend for ever and ever, until death do them part, amen.

'OK. Babies.'

She beamed at him, and the deal was sealed with a kiss. Ivor and Shivaun, and bundles of babies. On this happy note their childhood continued, in the days before childhood ended early, with designer goods and pre-teen pregnancies. Neither of them even knew how babies were made. But they were too busy to care at ten, eleven, twelve; their innocent days revolved around bikes, school sports, swimming at Red Rock on summer days, dissecting insects and camping in tents in their back gardens. Her dad Jimmy built them a tree house and it was their secret hideaway, they climbed up into it and spent whole days holding private pow-wows, discussing things that were never revealed to anyone else. Nobody else would be interested, they said loftily when questioned, and nobody else was allowed up into the tree house; when they got there they pulled up the rope ladder and shut the real world out. Over time, their toys were thrown down to the grass below, gradually replaced by books, atlases, maps and Ivor's compass; they loved looking at illustrations of foreign countries, seeking out places with crazy names that made them giggle: Allahabad, Cyangugu, Ryukyu, Sverdlovsk. Together, their minds set out into uncharted territory.

Ivor said he'd go to see all these places when he grew up, and he would take Shivaun with him, they'd get rucksacks and run off and be nomads. They'd dye their faces blue and travel with a Tuareg tribe for a while, then maybe raft white water through the Rockies, ride a husky sled to Antarctica . . . of course he supposed they might need a bit of money for sleds and rafts and stuff, but Shivaun needn't worry about that, because he'd get some first, he didn't know how yet but he would. He'd take care of everything, he said, and she laughed as she fell, without the least awareness of it, in love with him.

Their days felt full of fun, of sun and grass and skinned knees; they were always falling out of things or into things, exploring, trekking, growing. They were best mates. And then, unexpectedly, there was a hiatus.

She thought he went funny, and he thought she went funny. She said the tree house was for kids and started hanging out with girls instead of climbing up to it with him. She began listening to music and reading magazines he said were 'stupid', while he collected 'stupider' football posters and talked in a voice that went from squeaky to gruff and back again, so that she could no longer ever be sure what mood he was in. Yet he said she was the one who was moody, said she went up and down like a yo-yo and refused, incredibly, to hear her hint about taking her to one of the hops at the tennis club he'd joined. It was only a junior hop, but he wouldn't take the slightest interest in it.

It was the first time he'd ever refused her anything, and she was devastated. She made up her mind to find another boyfriend and instructed her mother Viv, in the quavering but resolute tones of a young Ophelia, to tell Ivor Lawlor she was out the next time he rang looking for her. It was a major body-blow to find that he did not ring for nearly a week, by which time she'd decided to put the cart before the horse and divorce him prior to their marriage. When Viv laughed at this she threw her first pre-teen wobbly, a major wobbly starting with trembling lips and ending with slamming doors, a bellowed accusation that nobody, *nobody* understood her.

But of course they did understand her, her mum Viv and her dad Jimmy. They were the greatest parents on the face of the earth, Jimmy with his quiet, constant good humour and Viv with her endless books, classes, projects and flow of peculiar information. Jimmy tended to his garden and his work as a tree surgeon, which sometimes took him away around the country although he rarely stayed overnight, always tried to get home in time for family dinner with his tales of toppled oaks and ravaged elms, huge forests which, when she was small, were inhabited by elves and wayward pixies. Viv would contribute to these pixie tales, embellish them scandalously, give the pixies squabbling offspring and stolen diamonds and invading monsters to contend with, making everyone laugh with her perpetual imagination.

Viv Reilly was what her friends called 'a card'. Dark and petite, she smoked cigarillos and played poker on Thursday nights, read three books a week and was renowned for serving up casseroles with such offbeat questions as 'Do you realise Amelia Earhart is still missing?' or 'I wonder if French secret agents sank the *Rainbow Warrior*?', questions that caused Jimmy to throw his eyes to heaven and made Shivaun think. Viv was a quirky character and life was never dull with her: she worked in a crafts shop in Dublin where she assured the bemused tourists that they'd need metal detectors if they wanted to find gold at the end of rainbows, on one occasion actually sending someone off to buy one in Lenehan's hardware store. Viv was, as Jimmy frequently and affectionately remarked, 'half cracked'.

But boy was she a good mother. Shivaun couldn't remember a time when Viv hadn't been there for her, working only part-time until she started school and even then dashing to pick her up, ferry her round, read stories or make them up as she went along. Ivor, a fixture at their house, was included in these stories, invited to contribute his opinion on how 'logistically, Santa can get down the chimney' or whether 'by rights, the Indians should be running America'. Viv wrote incendiary letters to the newspapers, rang up chat shows to denounce things, considered marijuana perfectly harmless and once famously threw herself under a bulldozer that had been sent to demolish a Georgian house on Mountjoy Square. Ivor thought Shivaun's eccentric, lively mother was great and Shivaun absolutely adored her.

And then, one day a few weeks after Shivaun and Ivor had had their 'coolness', Viv put her hand on Shivaun's across the kitchen table and said no, don't do the dishes just yet, sweetie, there's something your dad and I want to talk to you about.

Shivaun had assumed it must be about secondary school, about which of the three mooted ones she'd prefer. They'd been discussing the matter on and off for ages. But as Jimmy drew up his chair and leaned forward in his tweedy, bottle-green old sweater she'd seen from his expression that it was something more serious, and wondered what trouble she'd inadvertently got into.

No, they assured her. No trouble. It was just that she . . . was . . . well, old enough now to know something important, something that had happened when she was only just born. It was a long story, Viv said, a big story, but for once she wasn't going to embroider it, she was just going to tell it to her straight, and then they could all talk about it, she could ask as many questions as she wanted, OK?

Even as she nodded solemnly Shivaun had been conscious of wishing Ivor was there beside her, there to share whatever it was going to be. But he wasn't, and so she sat stock-still alone between her parents, her blood going ice-cold and her whole body rigid as they gently, quietly told her the truth: they were not her parents. Not her real parents, at all. Her real parents, she slowly grasped, had given her up for adoption.

'G-g-gave me *up*?' she gasped. 'G-gave me up to who? Why? Who were they?'

The kitchen was whirling, she couldn't breathe, couldn't make sense of a word of it. She felt Jimmy's hands on her shoulders, holding her tight, felt his kiss on her hair as he stood behind her while Viv spoke slowly, carefully, not letting go of her hand as she sought to explain, sought the right words. Viv was good with words, but this seemed to be a struggle even for her.

'Your dad thought maybe we should start letting you know, little by little, when you were small. Thought it might be better to explain piece by piece. But I thought that could confuse you, it was better to let you be secure as a toddler, wait till you started to grow up . . . I can only pray that you are old enough now, sweetie, that we reached the right decision . . . we love you so much, you know, that's why we wanted you in the first place.'

But why, Shivaun stuttered, had her parents not wanted her? Her real parents? The words felt like glue in her mouth as she uttered them.

'We're sure they did want you. But we think they were very young, too young to be able to keep you.'

'You *think*? But don't you know? Who *were* they?'

Shivaun's world reeled and tinkled as Viv drew breath and carried on: they were an unknown couple, one or both of whom had taken her to a church warmly wrapped up, with a note pinned to her blanket asking whoever found her to look after her, and get her a family. Her name, Shivaun, had been written on the note.

It wasn't until years later that Shivaun realised why her name was spelled as it was, instead of the usual 'Siobhán'; her parents hadn't known how to spell it properly.

But the rest of that May night in 1986 was a blur, a welter of tears and questions, questions, questions. By the end of it she was more certain than ever of Viv and Jimmy's love for her, and certain of nothing else. Had the sun failed to rise the following morning, she would not have been in the least surprised. When it did rise, she rose pale and shivering with it, while Viv and Jimmy slept exhausted, scrubbed her face violently, ran out to the garden and seized her bike, tore off on it heading instinctively for Ivor's house, and hammered the door down when she got there.

'Mrs Lawlor! Let me in, let me in, I have to talk to Ivor, where is he—?!'

Racing past the open-mouthed, dressing-gowned Mrs Lawlor she flew up the stairs to Ivor's bedroom and threw herself on top of his sleeping shape.

'Ivor! Ivor, wake up, wake up, it's me, I – I – I'm *adopted*!'

She couldn't remember a single word of the conversation that had followed, all she could remember was that Ivor, in blue striped pyjamas, had held her, held her and held her, for hours, for ever after.

It was a defining moment for them both. As they entered their teens their bond deepened, gaining a sexual dimension as well somewhere around the age of sixteen, although they would not sleep together for another three years. After the shock wore off, Shivaun felt a need to query and investigate everything she could about her birth parents, and Viv answered her questions to the fullest extent of what knowledge she had, which was not much. Slowly, sadly, Shivaun came to accept that she had no family of her own, would never have cousins or nephews or nieces, no blood ties at all, and the hollowness of that thought drew her even closer to Ivor, who would one day father the children she began to long for. Viv and Jimmy liked Ivor, but worried that Shivaun was 'putting all her eggs in one basket'. Would she not date a few other boys occasionally, she was so young for such an exclusive attachment? To please them she dated a few, but always went back to Ivor, knowing he would be there for her. Naturally his eye wandered occasionally, but he never strayed, was utterly dependable.

Viv and Jimmy were utterly dependable, too. As she grew up Shivaun thought a great deal about their constant, generous love for her, drew into it as if it were a protective garment, had far fewer rows with them than most adolescents had with their parents. It was difficult, in any case, to get angry at quiet, thoughtful Jimmy, who was always slipping her fivers and telling her to 'enjoy herself.' When sparks flared between Shivaun and Viv, the conflagration nearly always burst into laughter in the end; Viv had an endearing way of seeing the funny side of things. Her quick, agile mind darted every which way, encouraging Shivaun to learn, read, study, and they became close friends, often going to a concert, film or play together. Shivaun gave heartfelt thanks that she had been adopted by such a wonderful couple, appreciated that everything they did for her was voluntary and did her best to reciprocate.

When Ivor was seventeen, his father had a heart attack, and spent an agonising week in hospital before dying of complications. Ivor was shattered, and as she held him to her, comforting him as once he had comforted her, Shivaun began to think. The staff at the hospital had been fantastic, done everything humanly possible to save his father's life . . . although they had not succeeded, their efforts were both moving and impressive. It came to her that nursing could be a very rewarding career.

'Not doctoring?' Jimmy asked when she talked to him about it. 'We'll send you to university to do medicine if you think you have what it takes.'

She was touched. Medicine was a long, expensive course and his offer was munificent. But for some reason it was nursing that attracted her – nursing new mums and bringing babies into the world, in particular. A field with a lot of loving and caring and joy to be found in it, plenty of rewards and challenges and what Viv called 'positive energy'. Six months before her final exams, she enrolled to train at St Jude's, pending her exam results which turned out to be more than adequate. She was accepted, she was in.

That first year was exhilarating, and she loved every minute of it. In turn Ivor embarked on his accountancy studies, and they had to start planning their time together, fight for it, but they were happy, each fulfilled in their different ways, beginning to talk now sometimes about their marriage. It was a long way off, but it was in distant sight.

God, they were happy that year! As Shivaun emerged from her shower and her reverie she smiled to herself, thinking of the fun they'd had, the first holiday they'd taken together – not a trek with a Tuareg tribe, after all, because you needed months for that, instead they'd spent a couple of weeks in Portugal, combining beaches with villages and excursions up into the mountains, laughing and drinking and dancing, still teenagers, still madly in love.

But, despite Ivor's eagerness, they hadn't slept together on that trip. Not yet, not even when Viv had openly suggested it 'because you need to know whether the man you're going to marry is any use in bed, just take precautions young lady and don't make me a granny.' Shivaun couldn't say what held her back, but something did, and she was glad of it afterwards because, a year later when the moment was right, it was dramatically right.

It was the only thing that was right, when it finally happened. The one solitary thing, the single light burning in the blackness that so swiftly slammed down on her youth, her world, her life.

Pushing the memories away, Shivaun towelled her body and her hair, dressed and put on fresh make-up, clamped a smile on her face and went downstairs ready for Ivor, who would show up at nine as promised. He was always on time, always true to his word, and she loved him dearly for that besides so much else. Loved him just as Viv would have wanted, with her whole heart and soul.

Chapter Two

Alana drew in her breath, as she always did, when Ivor Lawlor walked into the room. Drew in her stomach too, for all the good it ever did her. He had his own key to the house and simply sailed in, gathered Shivaun into his usual affectionate hug and twinkled at her.

'Hi. How's my girl?'

Shivaun murmured something as she kissed him and stopped eating; Alana was forever fascinated by the way she could simply stop. She couldn't leave her own meal unfinished, but neither could she take her eyes off Ivor, who seemed to be in his usual sunny mood. She'd once told Shivaun he looked like a young Pierce Brosnan, and often jokingly called him Baby B although his eyes were a different colour, a deep dark brown like Belgian chocolate, irresistible. But Alana never told him this, didn't want him to get a swelled head. A guy could, with looks like his and now a lucrative career to boot . . . of course he'd only just joined his firm, accountants didn't get rich at twenty-five, but as her mum down in Waterford would say, his 'prospects were good'. Shivaun was a lucky girl, extremely lucky in Ivor if in nothing else. Even as Alana thought about it, Ivor winked at her, in that fraternal way he had, as if she were his kid sister. Or a pet. It was a casual, pally wink, but it was enough to turn her bones to butter.

He turned back to Shivaun, eyed her as he stacked the plates, helped to clear the table.

'So. What's the latest on Kilo Finnegan? Is the little bounder back yet?'

Shivaun kept her voice even. He'd had a long day too, plus dinner with his mother which, as she knew, could be a trying experience.

'Not a dicky-bird. I guess he must have run away to sea . . . Ivor, would it be all right with you if we gave the movies a miss tonight? Unless you're really keen—?'

'To see *Titanic*, and drown in floods of weeping women? I look on it as a merciful reprieve. I picked up a video on the way over, *Some Like It Hot*, how's that?'

That was great. Trust him to choose a comedy, something to cheer her up. Gratefully, she grinned at him.

'You are a gem, and someday soon I am going to lasso you with a giant-size wedding ring, before Pamela Anderson swipes you from under my nose.'

Momentarily he looked quizzical, and then he laughed. 'If anyone's doing any swiping, I'd prefer it to be Winona Ryder or the late, lovely Lady Di, if she were still around.'

He'd always been a Diana fan, the three of them had made a full day of watching her funeral on television and he'd roared encouragement at Earl Spencer – 'yeah, you tell 'em, sock it to 'em, attaboy!' Alana was an admirer too, but she'd learned something from Diana's life: beauty didn't necessarily make you happy. After her death, she'd let her hair grow back to its natural strawberry blonde and no longer leaped on the bathroom scale with quite such bated breath.

They moved into the living room with the video and a six-pack, Alana popped corn and they shared it while they watched. One of the things she liked about living here was the way she was included in evenings like this, there was never any question of 'the lodger' creeping away to leave the lovers alone. In return she tried to gauge things, clock the moment when, after the video and half an hour's chat, they might want to be alone. Shortly before midnight, she stood up and yawned.

'Well, I'm getting the train to Waterford tomorrow, so I'd better get my beauty sleep.'

They wished her good night and she left them, thinking as she did so what a wicked pair of jeans Ivor was wearing, how well that cable-knit sweater suited him . . . he really was dishy, she couldn't help feeling a little forlorn as she plodded up the stairs to bed. As soon as she went, Ivor zapped the television and put his arm around Shivaun, kissed her with more concern than passion as the embers of the fire banked down in the lamplight.

'You haven't mentioned Kilo once, which I presume means you're really worried about him, huh?'

Plucking at the ends of her hair, she curled her legs up on the sofa and snuggled into him.

'Yes. I am. But I don't want to bore you.'

'Oh, come on. Spill it all out.'

'Well . . . it's just that . . . oh, Ivor. He was my first – *is* my first. I couldn't bear it if anything happened to him, you know how much he means to me.'

Yes. Ivor knew. Kilo's birth had brought a huge flush of pride and joy to Shivaun's features, the features that sometimes still looked as if they were pinned together, bolted somehow, ever since her parents died. Her animation had been tremendous.

Wriggling closer, she laid her cheek on his chest, and closed her eyes.

'Things like this upset me so much, they remind me . . .'

They reminded her, understandably, of her own terrible loss. Closing his eyes in turn, he stroked her hair and thought back, all the way back to August 1993.

Jimmy Reilly was a peaceable man, known for minding his own business, living and letting live. Nobody knew what had made him stop his car that night as he drove home, unusually late, from his day's work on an estate near Maynooth. Taking a short cut back through one of Dublin's dodgier suburbs, he had come across a street fight between two youths, and stopped his car.

A girl was screaming. At first Jimmy possibly thought she

was in danger, the one being attacked. But the two youths were fighting each other, silhouettes in the dark, wielding knives. It might have been the street light overhead that glinted on the knives, brought them to Jimmy's attention. At any rate, he pulled in and jumped out of his Volvo station wagon.

'Stop it! Stop it, you'll kill each other!'

No response from either youth, only from the girl who, later, told the police she'd tried to push him away, known his intervention would be useless at best.

But it was worse than useless. Much worse. One of the youths, crazed with drugs, lashed out at him. In one clean sharp sweep, the knife drove into Jimmy's heart, and killed him.

Ivor thought it would kill Shivaun too, the pain in which she phoned him sometime after midnight.

He raced to meet her at Beaumont hospital, where Jimmy was already lying dead in the morgue. Together, gripping each other, they stood over his body in silence, and Shivaun bent to kiss her beloved dad goodbye. As they were leaving, a doctor came up to say how sorry he was, how Jimmy was a hero, one of the few brave and decent citizens unafraid to confront this depraved metropolis, and Viv thanked him for his kindness. But Shivaun stood silent, iced into her anguish, and Ivor clutched her, sharing her grief but unable to assuage it. She looked split open, as if she were the one who'd been knifed.

After Jimmy's funeral he visited the Reilly home every night, sat with Shivaun, struggled to comfort her shattered mother. Viv, for Shivaun's sake, was doing her best to sound calm and look normal. She wore make-up, he remembered, and smart fresh clothes, shirts and trousers with plain gold jewellery as usual. But he sensed her tautness, as did Shivaun; they felt that like cracked glass Viv might disintegrate at the touch of a feather. She seemed suspended, as did life itself; nobody even bothered to turn on the news, which was unprecedented for both ever-curious women.

In slow motion, time went by. Both Viv and Shivaun returned to work, tried to regroup and downsize from being a threesome to being only two. And then, a few weeks after

Jimmy's death, Viv's friend Maura phoned from Roscommon, invited her to come visit for a weekend. A few days in the countryside, Maura suggested, might help: do come, Viv, and bring Shivaun with you. To this day, Ivor gave thanks that Shivaun had been working that weekend, unable to go.

But she'd encouraged Viv to go.

'Maura's such an old pal, Mum, you'll be comfortable with her. She'll take you out walking, pour whiskey and sympathy into you . . . go on, ring her back and tell her you'll drive down after work on Friday. Ivor will look after me, I'll be fine.'

Viv held out. But Ivor, Shivaun and her friend Maura continued to work on her. She needed the break badly, they pointed out, needed to see that Shivaun could manage without her for a few nights and to get a grip on her sudden surge of over-protectiveness. Eventually, reluctantly, she agreed to go. Ivor remembered watching mother and daughter embrace on the driveway before Viv got into the Volvo. Jimmy's Volvo.

'Try to enjoy it, Mum. Just go with the flow, and call me when you arrive, OK?'

Viv nodded, hugged Shivaun tightly and got into the car. Two hours later she phoned to announce her safe arrival, said that Maura had welcomed her warmly and everything was fine.

And so it was. Reassured, Shivaun let Ivor take her bowling with a group of his student friends that night. The friends knew what had happened to her father but studiously didn't mention it, except for one guy who said he thought Jimmy was great and it was a shame Dublin didn't have more like him. Shivaun had flushed, but agreed with him too, thanked him for his comment.

On the way home she seemed to be in as good form as could be expected, she'd enjoyed the game and Ivor was heartened, felt a glow of tenderness for the way she was trying to cope. When they reached her house he came in with her, took her in his arms and kissed her, looked her in the eyes.

'Do you want me to, Shivaun? Do you want me to stay with you tonight?'

She understood what he meant.

'Yes, Ivor, I do . . . only not in that way . . . would it be too much to ask if you could just sleep here? Sleep in my bed with me, I mean, without . . . you know?'

It nearly strangled him, but somehow he did it, gave her the platonic comfort she needed without any complications. They shared the bed the way they used to share tents and sleeping bags when they were little kids, warmly and innocently. He knew she was emotionally confused, didn't push things, but felt they were drawing close to consummating their relationship. Some other night, he thought, some night soon now.

And that was how he'd come to be with her when, at five in the morning, the phone rang. She jolted awake instantly, leaped up and ran to answer the extension in her parents' – mother's – room.

It was a neighbour. A neighbour of Viv's friend Maura, who'd been delegated to find Shivaun's number and make the call. A motherly woman, she'd done all she could, but there was no way to soften it.

There had been a fire. Viv and Maura, in their joint attempt to blur the jagged edge of Jimmy's death, had had a few drinks. They'd gone to bed late and Viv had apparently fallen asleep instantly, forgetting to switch off her electric blanket. The bed had caught fire, then the house, and the house was remote, the nearest village had no fire station. By the time fire engines arrived from other, distant towns it was too late. Maura had extensive burns, lung damage and injuries from the window she'd jumped through, and Viv was dead.

The events that followed spun round and round in Ivor's head even today. Shivaun's screams, her translucent face were imprinted on his mind like fossils on an ancient sea-bed, branded, sealed. She had gone completely rigid, been unable to move or speak, he'd had to call a doctor and his mother, and it had taken them hours to prise it out of her, get her to disclose what had happened. The doctor sedated her, Ivor put her to bed and there was an eerie silence; he hadn't discovered the still-dangling phone until noon, abandoned in mid-sentence somewhere amidst it all.

He moved into the house, then, to be with her round the clock. There was a procession of people: policemen, priests, friends, neighbours, Viv's only brother Cormac who flew home from Australia for his sister's funeral. Nobody wanted Shivaun to go to it, so recently after Jimmy's, but she'd insisted, stood there like a marionette, watched her mother buried in the still-fresh grave.

Matron, Ivor remembered, had been very good to her afterwards, virtually commanded her to take extended leave. Everyone else had rowed in behind the police, who produced counsellors and advised her to 'talk her feelings through' with them. Obediently, in deep shock, she had listened to what they had to say, but she had not talked to them. Nor had she uttered Viv's name again, or Jimmy's, for nearly five months. She was a zombie, and he was heartbroken for her.

But he stuck with her, tried to help in every way he could think of. He wanted to move in with her altogether, at that point, only she said no, she couldn't handle it. Couldn't switch so fast from living with her parents to living with him, he wasn't to be any kind of substitute. He should stay with his mother for the moment, in fact; after all his mother was widowed and older, less able to cope alone.

He felt maybe this was an excuse, that for some reason she was pushing him away. But she wasn't pushing him away, she was simply clearing space. Space to grieve, to stalk the house night after night, to cry more tears than there was salt in the ocean. She didn't want to inflict it all on him.

But she did want him. Not immediately, but several months later, round about the time she began to be able to talk, to say 'Viv' or 'Jimmy' in coherent sentences, normal tones. That was when she pulled him fiercely to her one night, dug her nails into his back, clung to him and dissolved into him.

It was a baptism of fire. He'd never imagined anything so violent, so intense in his life, was astonished to discover later that neither of them actually had any broken bones. It went way beyond sex, he felt as if they'd been welded together with a flame-thrower, merged like molten metals in a furnace. Afterwards, Shivaun looked at him as if from another planet, light years away.

But it had drawn them closer, infinitely closer; the line had been crossed. 'Now,' he said, 'I'll move in with you now.'

No. Not now. Now, they would consume each other if he did that. What she'd prefer, for the moment, was that he should only stay with her for weekends, would that be all right?

'But you can't be alone. You can't, Shivaun, you're not really well yet, you need someone to keep an eye on you.'

Yes. She could see that herself, admitted she did. So she would get someone, some calm relaxed outsider, a girl, someone around her own age. A tenant, a lodger who could have her room now that she'd moved into the main bedroom. Her parents' bedroom; she didn't feel that Viv or Jimmy would mind that she was sharing it with Ivor, had started her own sex life in it. They would, she thought, understand. They talked to her sometimes at night, did he know that? They guided her, helped her to know what to do.

And so Alana came on the scene, and he was immensely relieved to see her nonchalant, smiley face. She was a pudgy girl, but she was a weight off his mind, he felt Shivaun would benefit from her company. Conscious of some pressure lifting, he was able to return to his studies at last, play tennis again, resume normal life.

Shivaun resumed it too, in many ways. She went back to St Jude's and rediscovered her interest in nursing, she even passed her exams that year. She started socialising, reading, talking about life with Alana in a reassuring way after their briefly faltering start. By the following summer, she was his girl again, lively, even laughing.

But she was not the same. Never the same, again. Her beauty returned, she regained her animation and lost her skeletal look. But in its place she found new depths within herself, became more reflective and intense than he had ever known her. When her interest in current affairs returned it returned with a vengeance, she took to walloping the newspapers as she read them, banging the table and saying things were a 'disgrace'. She grew almost into Viv's ghost as she wrote provocative letters to the media, overtook Viv's obsession with the state of the nation. Well, naturally; her father had been murdered by a drug addict and her mother had died because a rural village had no fire station. She'd been abandoned by two unknown parents who hadn't the means or skills to keep her. She had survived, but she had suffered. He felt that her soul was damaged, pulsating with pain under the scar tissue.

He did all he could to draw her out, let her talk, exorcise it all. Her passion sustained her, her anger cleansed her, she looked fabulous when fired by something like political bribery or environmental vandalism, a warrior queen riding into battle. Sometimes he got embroiled in these battles, dragged along on marches, protests, pickets; one memorable day she even got arrested and he had to bail her out despite her insistence that she *wanted* to go to jail, make her point. They had a row over his intervention, she was upset by his 'interference' and he was upset by the cavalier way she shrugged off his protection. But they made it up after a brief sulk, and gradually he learned to live with the new Shivaun.

In many ways she was still the old Shivaun, his friend and lover, future wife even though she didn't want to marry just now, said she was too busy – too confused, in his opinion. Sometimes she cancelled dates to attend rallies or meetings, sometimes she was so immersed in campaigns for justice that he felt he was losing her full attention. She was – was harder work, now, than she'd ever been before, he had to fight for her time and interest. But he did fight, and he did get them, kept her love despite everything that clamoured for it. The only thing he could not get her to do was discuss how she felt about the man who'd killed her father. That subject was taboo, she fended it off by defending other people who'd been hurt, by embracing life instead of death.

And that, tonight, was why she was so concerned about Kilo Finnegan. She cherished all the babies she helped bring into the world, valued every last little scrap of human life. Ivor scarcely dared think what it would do to her if Kilo was not found, if he came to any harm. And later, what of their own children? How closely would she cleave to them?

He looked down at her, and she raised her lips to him, kissed him.

'Ivor?'

'Mmm?'

'You remember, when I was kidding you earlier about getting married?'

'Uh huh?'

'Well, I wasn't entirely kidding. I've been thinking lately that maybe it's time now to set a date. You've got your job and I've got my promotion, we have this house . . . what do you think?'

He didn't know what he thought. Their marriage had always been out there somewhere, happily anticipated, a distant sunny day. Meanwhile, they'd been happy together for the past four or five years, semi-detached, enjoying the small degree of independence which, until now, had suited them. After her parents died he'd have married her instantly, but the timing would have been wrong, and so they'd drifted pleasantly, securely.

He kissed her nose and peered down at her.

'Would it be right for you now, Shivaun?'

'Yes. I think it would. You know, Ivor, apart from you I – I feel so alone, sometimes.'

'But Alana is here, even when I'm not.'

'Yes, but that's different. Alana isn't family. I mean I feel alone in the sense of not having anyone who's mine, belongs to me. I'd like to start a family, I'd like us to be a unit. Mr and Mrs Lawlor and lots of baby Lawlors.'

He laughed. 'How many?'

'How many d'you think you could stand? I wouldn't mind twins or triplets myself, to get us started, then we could start working on the full soccer team.'

'Ha! You forget, I play tennis.'

'So you do. OK then, a Davis Cup team.'

He wrapped his arms around her as she lay stretched alongside him, and started thinking about it, seriously for the first time. Children. Troops and hordes of children, that Shivaun would love to death.

Later, lying in Ivor's arms, feeling cherished and protected from the wind that tore through the trees outside, Shivaun nestled into his sleeping body, savouring his presence, his warmth. He understood her, loved her, cheered her. He weighted and balanced her life, was so good for her, in the same way that Jimmy had been for Viv.

Jimmy and Viv. She always felt closest to them here in their bed, sensed the pleasure and joy they had long shared. But they'd been dead for five years now and sometimes she felt she was losing her grip on the memories she treasured of them; she had to concentrate to hear Jimmy's voice in her inner ear, conjure up Viv's gestures and expressions. People told her she'd never fully lose them, but that they would become absorbed into her consciousness, a part of what they had made her. She'd fought that thought at first, but now she had to accept it, let go the hard edges and concede that the images would blur and fade. But only physically. Spiritually she'd stored up the best of both beloved parents, the legacy of Jimmy's calm generosity and Viv's questing curiosity . . . but still, the stab of pain, sometimes! How could you get over such loss, how long did it take? Could you ever enjoy Christmases and birthdays again, really laugh or celebrate, sing or dance without remembering, without that sudden stab? Did life really go forward, could memories be packed away in your heart without leaping back out, like muggers from alleyways? She'd known her memories to seize her in the weirdest places, in nightclubs and labour wards, pubs and shopping malls, grab her so hard she gasped.

Alana said you could. Alana said the throb would turn to an ache, it would dull, recede, until one day the memories would be filtered into happy ones. Ivor said so too, after eight years his father was only a soft-focus photograph now, someone he'd loved but lost very young. Dead people wouldn't want the living to mourn forever, he said, they'd want them to get on, go forward, do all the things they'd missed themselves. You owed it to them to survive, make the most of your own days; after all your own days could be suddenly ripped from you too.

Jesus. Scary. But in a way that was a positive thought. It jolted you, drove you forward, made you determined. It was driving her forward now, into thoughts of marriage to Ivor at last, the long deferred marriage that would replenish her world with stocks of new people.

Suddenly she almost yelped aloud in the dark. Kilo Finnegan was a new person. An absent, missing new person. She'd let Ivor distract her from her thoughts of the infant, knew he had done it deliberately, but now the baby's red rumpled face came back to her, vivid and disquieting.

Where was he? Who had taken him, and why?

Willing the night on, she lay close beside Ivor, her mind roaming in search of him.

The wild weather calmed overnight and Shivaun was glad to wake up to a warm sunny morning, to hear Ivor whistling cheerfully in the bathroom where he was shaving.

'What time is it?'

'Time you got up,' he called, 'and made us a picnic. It's looking like summer, we could go to Howth or Lough Dan for the day.' Emerging from the bathroom, tying a towel round his waist, he came to kiss her, his eyes sparkling, his body young and firm, cedar-scented from the shower.

'Get up there out of that bed, wench, and into the kitchen where a woman belongs!'

Laughing, she kissed him back, leaped up and threw on a robe. Last night's conversation, about marrying and starting a family, lay unfinished between them, but it was a bit early in the day to pick up where they'd left off, and Ivor's mind seemed to be elsewhere at the moment. Meanwhile, it was Saturday, and Alana was leaving for Waterford. Shivaun decided to run downstairs to say goodbye to her, grab some coffee and then discreetly call St Jude's for any news of Kilo without telling Ivor, unless by any miracle the child was back. On their days off, Ivor preferred to talk about anything and everything except work, was always telling her to relax and forget about it.

Alana was in the hall hefting her weekend holdall over her shoulder, had only time to say a quick hi before running out to her waiting taxi.

'The train's at nine, I'm off – call me if there's any word of Kilo, OK? And don't worry in the meantime. He'll turn up.'

'Yeah. He will. Have a great weekend, Ally, and give your lot my love.'

Alana nodded and vanished, leaving Shivaun thinking wistfully of the family she was going to visit – so many of them, so warm, so close, always looking out for one another. Lucky Alana! Alana had always agreed that yes, she was blessed with her big readymade gang, was great friends with all her siblings.

'I might not have a fab figure or a gorgeous guy like you, Shivaun, but I do have them. Everyone has something, huh?'

Yes. Everyone had something, someone. Shivaun padded into the kitchen and poured coffee, sipping it while she waited for Ivor to come and join her. But she heard his mobile phone ring upstairs, and his voice sounding impatient as he answered it; his weekends were often plagued with calls from one or other of his colleagues, and as a junior partner he was expected to be permanently available. Mobile phones, he maintained, were a curse from hell, he hated having to have one. But it was umbilically attached to him.

Eventually he came briskly into the kitchen, gulped the coffee she handed him and ran a hand through his wet hair, looking purposeful. 'So, are we ready to roll? Drive down to Lough Dan, ten-mile walk and then a late lunch in some pub? How's that?'

That sounded as if he'd been reading her mind. She was dying for some fresh air and exercise, wanted to walk and talk – but just then her own phone rang on the wall beside her, and she was on it in one breathless bound. The hospital!?

'Shivaun here, yes, hello?'

'Shivaun, it's Orla – it's Kilo, we've got him, he's back!'

She felt her knees go weak. 'He – he's back? Safe? Unhurt?'

'Yes. Safe, fed, watered. Not a scratch on him.'

Her relief was so vast it felt oceanic, engulfing her. She was barely able to speak.

'Oh, thank God . . . but . . . how? Who, what . . . ?'

'Well, that's the strange story. You're not going to believe who, or what.'

'Tell me – for God's sake Orla, tell me, quick!'

'It was Stan.'

'Stan – what? Stan our old hall porter? But—'

'Stan, as you well know, who wouldn't hurt a hair of a baby's head. But Shivaun, he's gone a bit funny . . . it seems that losing his job unhinged him a bit.'

'What do you mean?'

'I mean he felt redundant, apparently – well, he'd been made redundant. But he says it was more than that. Says St Jude's was his whole life, he missed the company as well as the work, the chat and activity . . . he lives alone as you know, and he kind of felt his whole life had caved in with no job to go to any more, nobody to talk to.'

'Oh, Orla, oh, no . . . poor old Stan.'

'Yes. Well, anyway, he must have flipped, because he decided to stage a protest. Decided to demonstrate the uselessness of the new security system. So he took Kilo. He's talking to the police as we speak, explaining how he did it. Says it was as easy as falling off a log, he just walked in on somebody else's card, he was such a familiar face nobody questioned him, he was able to get into the nursery and bundle Kilo under his coat while nobody was looking. In a way I'm hardly surprised, we were so busy yesterday, short-handed.'

'But – but Orla, how could he do that to you? He must have known what trouble you'd get into – and what about Fionnuala

Finnegan? Did he not think of her, of Martin, how distraught they'd be?'

'Shivaun, I don't think he could have been thinking rationally at all, or he'd never have done it. He looks and sounds to me as if he's having some kind of nervous breakdown. I'm absolutely furious with him, we all are, but everyone feels a kind of pity as well. Even the Finnegans have said they're not going to press charges.'

Shivaun sank down on a chair and closed her eyes, vaguely aware of Ivor listening, watching her intently.

'Oh, God, Orla. I can't tell you how relieved I am to hear about Kilo, but this is a nightmare. Terrible. Stan was always so . . . so *reliable*.'

'That's exactly his point. He feels he was a lot more reliable than any amount of demonstrably useless hardware, and look at the thanks he got for thirty years of devoted service – a pittance payoff, or kiss-off as he calls it. He's babbling away to the police, made absolutely no attempt to apologise for what he did, only for the worry to the staff and to the Finnegans. Apparently he kept Kilo at home in his own house overnight, looked after him like a – well, like a baby. He had no intention of harming the child in any way.'

Shivaun exhaled a deep breath.

'What does Matron say?'

'She's furious. Ranting like a demon. Says it's outrageous such a thing could happen, it never once happened before in the entire history of St Jude's . . . between you and me and the wall, I think she's kind of taking Stan's side. Not that she couldn't kill him, but she does seem to see his point. Of course the main thing is that Kilo's all right, everything else is secondary to that.'

'Yes. It is. But still . . . Orla, would you do me a favour?'

'Sure. What?'

'Will you tell the police that I'll vouch for Stan if need be, give a statement that he was always completely honest and dedicated? And then, will you tell him I'll come to see him later this evening? Are they going to release him or what? Surely they won't take him to – to *jail*?'

'No. I don't think so. Not for the moment, anyway. He'll have to go to the station to make a statement, but I gather they might release him then, if Matron goes bail which she says she will. She thinks everyone should have a cup of tea and calm down – including the Finnegans who can't wait to take Kilo home. Doctor says they can, under the circumstances.'

'Home? Now? Oh, Orla – you mean I'm not going to see him again?'

'Doesn't look like it.'

Shivaun was conscious of Ivor's gaze still on her as she took a long deep breath, steadied herself, tried to sound crisp and professional. Oh, Kilo! My beautiful baby, safe now, but gone for good?

'W – well of course he would have been going home soon anyway. If he's well enough and permission has been given, then – then he'd better go. The Finnegans have been through hell.'

'Yeah. We think it's the best thing. They really need to bond with their little boy. The police will leave and the storm will die down, Matron wants everyone to underplay the whole thing and get back where they belong, even Stan . . . I'll tell him you'll visit him at home tonight?'

'Yes, do. He must be in an awful state. It doesn't sound as if he should be left alone at home.'

'No. The police are causing a bit of hassle about that, Matron's trying to persuade them he's just a bit overwrought and there's no danger of him taking another baby. I don't think there is myself. He's made his point.'

'Yes. He certainly has. Look, Orla, thanks for letting me know all this. I was worried sick, and you must have been too.'

'We all were. In a weird way it's been good for morale, everyone's been pulling together, supporting each other . . . but it was an awful fright, an awful thing to do. I'm going to go and talk to Stan a bit when the police are through with him. I'll tell him you – you sympathise.'

'Yes. In a way . . . when I get over . . . I'll talk to him tonight. Bye, Orla, and thanks.'

Hanging up, Shivaun turned to Ivor, sensing the concern and tension in him. He was frowning, waiting for her to fill in the unheard half of the conversation.

'It's OK. Kilo is back. Safe. Unhurt.'

'So I gather. Did my ears deceive me, or did Stan the porter take him?'

'Yes. It seems he's more upset about being made redundant than anyone realised. Gone a bit off the rails.'

'A bit? Jesus, Shivaun, he must be barking mad! To take a child – it – it's *abduction*, it's kidnapping, a serious crime!'

She sighed, fiddled with a coffee spoon.

'Yes. I know. But he – oh, Ivor. The poor man.'

'What? First it's the poor baby, now it's the poor man . . . did you say you actually intend to go and speak to him, visit him?'

'Yes. Of course I do, Ivor! He lives alone, and he can't be well, he needs to talk this out . . . it's completely unlike him. He's a good man, a kind man.'

Ivor stared at her, and flung himself down onto the chair facing her.

'You're so wrapped up in your work you can't see the wood for the trees.'

She was stung. 'Well, you're wrapped up in yours too, I heard you taking that call upstairs. You know how important some things are.'

'But I – oh, Christ, Shivaun, look. Why don't you finish your breakfast and get dressed, then we'll go to Lough Dan, you can tell me the full story on the way, and then let's put it out of our minds, OK? It's over and done with, the baby is safe, let's try to have some part of this weekend to ourselves now.'

She bit her lip, turned to look out of the kitchen window at the garden.

'Yes. We will have. But Ivor, I must go to see Stan tonight. And I – I'd like to see the Finnegans too. Just call in on them for five minutes to say hello and give Kilo a kiss. They only live over in Rathnew, we could do a quick detour—'

'Shivaun, they have their friends and family! They won't

want to see anyone from the hospital, they'll want to batten down the hatches and just be alone in the bosom of their family.'

Yes. He was right. But . . . but just five minutes, please? Just one last glimpse of baby Kilo, before he vanished forever? She'd put so much into him, surely that wasn't too much to ask?

'Well . . . all right, Ivor. We'll go for our walk and I'll try not to bore you too much talking about any of this. But I am going to see Stan when we get back this evening, and I'll drive over to visit the Finnegans by myself tomorrow. In the morning. We'll still have Sunday afternoon together. How's that?'

He caught her tone, sensed that she was somehow disappointed in him, shutting him out a little. It wasn't very nice to feel shut out by a baby.

'Oh, knock it off. You know you won't bore me. Talk all you want. Visit anyone you like. All I'm asking, Shivaun, is that you make room for me too. It's been a long busy week and we're surely entitled to some rest, some time together. Is that OK?'

She stood up and smiled at him.

'Yes. Of course it's OK, Ivor. Don't worry. We will have our walk and our weekend.'

He knew she'd keep her word, shelve the baby episode now for long enough to give him some time, some thought. Relief might even make her a bit euphoric. They could have a great night, later . . . if this man Stan didn't get in the way, if she didn't stay talking with him for hours and forget all about him.

God, no wonder she was in a 'caring' profession! She cared so much about everything and everyone. Sometimes he felt he was the only one taken for granted . . . yet he was her childhood sweetheart, her future husband. Wasn't she supposed to care that bit *more* about him? Was he always to be crammed in between babies and parents and politics, Alana and now some crazy kidnapper?

Suddenly irritated, he rummaged for his keys and pulled them out.

'Come on then, let's go before it rains again, the forecast says it might.'

She looked at him, her eyes widening in wonder at his impatient tone. And as he looked into them something caught him, something maddening, something moving. She was so beautiful, standing there with the sun illuminating her rich red hair, bringing up its true colours, bringing him back to the school yard and those rusty, bouncing little ringlets. He loved her so much, had loved her for so long.

The countryside was wonderful in June, foaming with hawthorn and apple blossom, the light swivelling from behind the clouds like a torch, highlighting each green field in turn, emerald, jasper, olive, pistachio, every shade exuberant in the ripening crops and glossy leaves. Lough Dan was sometimes called a 'Guinness lake' because of its black bottomless depths, but it was blue today, violet, azure, teasing as the sky changed hue. Ivor took Shivaun's hand and they set out as they'd so often done before, in all seasons and all weathers.

But somehow today was different. They both sensed it, but neither of them said anything as they walked in intermittent silence, punctuated only by idle remarks, carefully neutral bits of conversation. She wanted to talk about Kilo and Stan, he didn't, and the result was a vacuum.

A long vacuum, that she suddenly couldn't stand.

'Ivor, you know I was worried about that child. And now it's normal to be worried about an unfortunate man who's lost his marbles because he's lost his job. Why are you making such a big deal of it?'

'I'm not making any deal. I didn't say a word.'

'No, you didn't – that's the bloody point! Do you not care, or what?'

He heard her voice rising, and it triggered an almost automatic reaction in him. He knew how sensitive she could be, and it had always been his role to protect her from things that upset her. She'd suffered so much, his embrace had been her haven from that day she was only twelve, came flying to him crying that she'd been adopted.

He tightened his grip on her hand.

'I just don't like to see you worrying so much, Shivaun. I want you to be carefree and happy – for us to be happy.'

'Are we not happy?'

He thought her tone contained a challenge. Did it?

'I think – hope – we are. But sometimes I wonder whether you are.'

'Me?' She was nonplussed. She had no idea whether she was happy, whether real happiness was possible in the real world. All she knew was that it was a dangerous, frightening world, one she wanted to improve. She *could* make it a little better, make some tiny difference. You had to try.

'I – I'm doing my best, Ivor. I'm sorry if that's not good enough.'

He stopped walking, stood stock still, looking at her.

'I know you are. I know what you've been through – I was there, remember? But Shivaun, it's over now. You have to let go of Viv and Jimmy and your birth parents, you have to live *your* life.'

'I'm trying to live it! I put my heart into everything I do!'

'I know you do. That's just the problem. You put too much in.'

She was incensed. 'Don't be ridiculous! How can anyone ever put too much into anything? If only everyone would put *more*, it would be easier all round! Maybe then things would be better, fairer, happier—'

'Jesus, Shivaun, you're not Mother Teresa! There's only so much you can do! The world always has been a mess and always will be.'

She was shocked. Absolutely appalled by his pragmatism. He'd never sounded like this before, said anything so callous. She stood back and stared at him.

'Ivor – are you by any chance turning into a real accountant? A money-man, a calculator, one of those heartless men in suits?'

Heartless. After all he'd done for her, all they'd endured together. He was very wounded. But until now she'd always been the wounded one, it was his job to shield her from wounds.

'I am an accountant, yes! But that doesn't mean I have no feelings, it just means I have a lick of common sense. You're such a crusader, Shivaun, I can't fight all those battles too! One of us has to keep things in perspective. If I didn't keep my feet on the ground we—'

'We'd sprout wings and fly off the face of the earth? No, Ivor. I don't think we would. Frankly I'm beginning to wonder whether you have the imagination to fly anywhere, rise six inches above your spreadsheets and balance exercises.'

He found her unfairness completely unreasonable, exasperating.

'So what do you want me to do? Turn into a tree-hugger? Go to pot, smoke pot, become a total flake? Raise our kids in a caravan? Well, I'm sorry Shivaun, but that's just not me. I'm a solid, sensible guy and if that's not enough for you then that's a bloody shame.'

Furiously, he let go of her hand and dug it into his pocket, strode ahead of her looking suddenly stony. She was taken aback.

'Are we having a row? Are you mad at me, just because I try, I care?'

No answer.

'Ivor! Don't just march off! I want to know!'

He stopped dead, turned back to her.

'I want to know too, Shivaun. I want to know whether you really love me, or whether you love the whole damn universe, and I'm just the guy you turn to, lean on, when the going gets tough.'

'Y – you – yes, of course you are! That's what relationships are for, they're all about support and – Ivor, you're my *rock*!'

'Your rock, huh? Well, I reckon rocks are cold comfort, Shivaun. They don't sprout wings, as you say, and fly off on your flights of fancy with you, your missions of mercy.'

There was bitterness in his tone. And sadness, she thought, in his eyes. She had not thought to hurt him, but perhaps she had. Perhaps she was more wound up about Kilo Finnegan than she realised, was taking things out on Ivor that were not his fault. A little sheepishly, she reached out her hand to him, but he did not take it, so she put it on his shoulder and reached up her lips to kiss his cheek.

'A rock is a good thing to have, Ivor. A great thing. You've always been there for me when I needed you. Don't pull away from me now.'

He had never pulled away from her, not even in their darkest days, when she'd been a shivering speechless wreck. He'd given her everything she needed. Done one hell of a lot of giving, he thought with irony. She wasn't the only one who gave, she just spread her net wider. If he hadn't protested, she'd be with that Finnegan baby and its parents at this very moment, all concern and sympathy, leaving him to wait for her to throw him what crumbs were left of the day. The thought was very galling – and tonight, he was to be fitted in around her visit to Stan.

He stood thinking a moment, and then shrugged.

'It's getting a bit chilly, Shivaun. Let's go find that pub and have some hot soup.'

Something warned her to go along with his proposal, say no more. She'd never seen him so touchy.

'All right. Maybe we're just hungry, we didn't eat much breakfast.'

It struck him that he was hungry. Not for food, but for her undivided attention, for pure uncomplicated love that had nothing to do with need.

'You're right, Shivaun. I am starving, actually.'

Alana came back from her family reunion in Waterford, beaming. She always enjoyed going home, reclaiming her place among the people who loved her for herself, didn't care whether she bit her nails or hung her clothes in their proper place. Toting her weekend bag, she collapsed into the house in a hot red-faced heap.

'Hi! I couldn't get a taxi, had to lug this bloody thing from the bus stop – it weighs a ton, I'm whacked!'

Shivaun looked up from the book she was reading, alone on the sofa. 'So how was Waterford? Did you have a good time?'

'Yeah, great! I went fishing with my brother Malachy, we caught a smashing salmon and – hey, where's Ivor?'

'He's playing tennis.'

'Oh. And Kilo Finnegan? I heard on the radio—'

'Yes. He was found. I called a couple of times to tell you, but the line was busy.'

'As usual! Ten people, one phone – but Shivaun, who took Kilo? It didn't say on the radio, only that a man was helping the police with—'

'Alana, it was Stan who took him. Stan Murray, hall porter turned babysnatcher.'

'What?!?'

'Oh, look . . . let's make a pot of tea and I'll tell you the whole story.'

As Shivaun made the tea and told the story, Alana gazed at her, baffled. She couldn't get her head around the bit about Stan, nor around Shivaun's expression, almost detached.

'But aren't you thrilled? Kilo could be dead in a dustbin, it's a miracle!'

'Yes. Of course I'm thrilled. I went to see the Finnegans and they're thrilled too, everyone is – except Ivor Lawlor, who couldn't give two hoots about any of it.'

Oh. Uh, oh. Alana twigged a subtext. 'Ivor? Surely he's not – you're not—?'

'Yes. We're having a bit of a coolness, actually.'

Alana snorted, choked into her tea with laughter.

'Oh, Shivaun, don't wind me up! Romeo can't be scrapping with Juliet!'

'Romeo? Alana, I think you've been watching too much television.'

Shivaun looked sceptical, a bit frosty, but Alana couldn't take her seriously.

'Oh, come on, what did he do, steal your KitKat again?'

Alana knew the story of how the two had met, knew also that they had very few chilly patches, because they were joined at the hip, made for each other. She'd have done jail for a shot at Ivor herself, long ago, if she didn't know it was useless. Ivor had eyes only for Shivaun, belonged to her in some exclusive, fundamental way.

Not that she would ever tell Shivaun such a thing. Her admiration of, and longing for, Ivor Lawlor was the one secret she would never dare speak of, to anyone. Ivor was unattainable, and she would look a fool. Ivor was the dream that haunted her in the night, and evaporated by day.

'He – he didn't do anything, as such. He just wasn't very – he didn't seem to understand – but Jesus, Alana, *you* know how important that damn baby was to me! How important they all are – and now we have Stan Murray, Ivor nearly threw a fit because I went to see him last night, couldn't care less what fix he's in or how he feels. I'm starting to think Ivor is a cold hard man, that new job has done something to him—'

Alana gaped. 'Cold? Hard? *Ivor?*'

'Yes – well – oh, hell, Alana, I don't know what to think. He just seems to be changing in some way.'

Thoughtfully, Alana sipped her tea, reached for a biscuit and then pushed the packet away. For once Shivaun seemed to have forgotten about niceties like plates and saucers.

'Well, he is a grown man now. He's hardly the same person you fell in love with when you were four!'

'No. But I thought we were changing together, grew up together. Now I wonder whether I might be mistaken.'

Alana considered, didn't answer until she was sure what to say.

'Well, everyone grows and changes at their own pace, I suppose. Maybe you and Ivor have reached different points at different times. But he is – he is your only family, Shivaun, in every way that matters. I know you're not actually married yet, but don't lose sight of everything he's been to you, or everything he will be.'

Shivaun stared into her tea, thinking in turn. Alana was right. Ivor had always been everything to her. Only two nights ago, they'd been talking about getting married. Talking about having children . . . only he hadn't been so enthusiastic, now that she remembered it, about a whole soccer team of them. The conversation had drifted off somewhere, undecided.

'Alana – I – I'm not even sure any more whether he wants us to have kids. I mean, he does, but I don't know whether he wants as many as I do, or wants them as soon as I do.'

Alana frowned. This sounded like a more serious disagreement than she'd realised at first. Things were emerging from the woodwork.

'H'mm. Well . . . I know kids matter to you, Shivaun, so maybe you should discuss that question a bit more with him. You don't want to end up a divorced mother-of-six.'

Divorced! Shivaun felt an electric shock at the very word. It had never before entered her head, she'd never thought of such a thing. She'd always simply assumed . . . assumed too much, maybe? She felt she might be losing her grasp of this whole situation, that Ivor could go spinning out of sight. But—

'Alana, don't say such a thing! You're panicking me!'

'Am I?' Slowly, Alana smiled her rosy, reassuring smile. 'But Shivaun, there's nothing to panic about. You've just had some minor tiff with Ivor, that's all. Don't let it grow bigger than it is. Is he coming back here when he finishes playing tennis?'

'Y-es, I think so, he said he'd eat with us, but he might go for a pint with his partner first.'

'Really? Well, he doesn't go drinking very often. Let him enjoy it, and don't say anything if he comes back late, just give him a big kiss when he gets here.'

Shivaun blinked. Now that Alana mentioned it, Ivor did not go drinking very often.

Chapter Three

It appeared to Shivaun, in the days and weeks that followed, that her misgivings were unfounded. Ivor regained his usual good humour, produced a very beautiful bouquet of yellow roses and said she was even more lovely, he was sorry if he'd been a bit off form. She apologised in turn, conceded that maybe she did get a bit too caught up in things that were none of her business at times and promised to be more attentive to him. That brought a smile to his eyes and a kiss to his lips, and they made love that night with a sense of being very special to each other, in tune again, in love.

But their brief dispute had been bitter while it lasted, and it gave Shivaun a fright, caused her to examine the relationship for the first time. Was it solid, was it what they both wanted? Somehow she couldn't raise the issue of children again, not yet; instead she asked Ivor about his feelings for her, probed the depth of his commitment to her and his joy in her. Did she still make his blood tingle? Yes, he said, she certainly did, she was one sexy lady and he was aflame with lust for her, sometimes he thought of her while doing somebody's accounts and got his maths all wrong, had to wipe the smile off his face and start again.

And did he think they were, well, compatible? Could he live with her battle for a better world, her causes and outbursts? His answer to that was that she could be exhausting, but exciting too; she'd inherited her attitude from Viv and would make a wonderfully weird old lady some day. Meanwhile, since she felt so strongly about everything, why didn't he give her a computer and set her up with e-mail? Then she could fire off rockets to everyone, the blasted health minister and the entire world for that matter, there were lots of people who'd love to share and discuss her views. The computer, he said, would be his way of apologising for the little row they'd had.

So it was installed, and she was delighted with it. Now she could air her opinion of fiscal mismanagement and hospital closures and missing women, scams and scandals of all descriptions, to a much wider audience! She could vent her fury and save her sunnier side for Ivor, Alana too, everyone who wanted to relax in her company, not joust. Socially it took the gusting wind out of her sails, politically it gave her more clout; Ivor had given her a louder voice and he was great, she didn't know why she'd ever doubted him. He had empowered her to shake the whole world by the scruff of the neck, instead of targeting only himself and Alana, driving them demented.

In a burst of contrition she redecorated her bedroom one weekend, steeled herself to throw out all that had marked it as Jimmy's territory and Viv's. Their William Morris wallpaper was torn down and she painted the room an ivory colour, stencilled designs from some book about Mexican adobe houses, patches of vivid red and green that made Ivor laugh and say she was mad, was he supposed to wear a sombrero to bed now or what? She made amends to Alana too, told her to keep a month's rent and buy a new outfit with it, or put it towards a holiday, whatever she wanted. Surprised, Alana looked at her quizzically.

'I know it was no fun to lose your parents, Shivaun, but it must be great to be an heiress, not have to worry about money.'

'No, I don't have to worry about it, so I'm trying to worry less about other things as well. Lighten up a bit, you might say.'

But she did still sneak off to see Stan, befriended him and took up his cause. She did not want him to be punished for kidnapping Kilo, she wanted him to find another job, and eventually she found him one, caretaking in a community school. It was full of rowdy teenagers and it was, she felt sure, the right place for him. He had company again, a purpose, people to keep him balanced on the rails. At the hospital there was a conspiracy of silence, nobody ever told the press who stole Kilo, nor did the police, nor did the Finnegans. Their communal goodness cheered Shivaun greatly.

She was less heartened by news of another missing woman, in Wicklow this time, and the discovery of her battered body a week later. What a horrible thing, what an awful country! Sensing that she might be going to rant about it, she gritted her teeth and decided to get out of it instead, with Ivor, for a summer holiday.

'Where'll we go? Somewhere sunny, or somewhere interesting?'

He hesitated. A flash came to him, of their tree house and their hatching gleeful plans for river-rafting, husky-sledding . . . but he only had a fortnight's freedom, and if they went somewhere like that Shivaun might get into controversy about defoliation or pollution or God knew what.

'How about Italy? We could mix sun with culture, see some old masters and stuff, what about Florence, or Venice?'

She eyed him from the floor where she sat surrounded by brochures. He sounded a bit – what? Restrained?

'That's what you'd really like?'

'Yes. It'd be great. It's just that things are so busy at work right now, and Italy will be so hot – how about September?'

She wanted to go now. But that didn't seem to be what he wanted.

'OK. I'll book for September. And dig out Viv's art books, bone up on all the Italian painters!'

'You don't have to do that. Holidays are meant to be relaxing.'

She sighed and nodded. They were. It was just that the skill of relaxing did not come easily to her. In fact she was finding it difficult to learn. But she was doing her best, for his sake.

She was succeeding too, to a creditable extent. She'd

dropped the question of children for instance, and was letting it lie until Ivor chose to raise it. Alana said she shouldn't rush or push him, and Alana was able to see such things clearly, not being involved in them. On the other hand, Alana had never been involved in a real relationship of her own . . . why was that? After all Alana was twenty-seven now, far more attractive than in her puppy-fat youth, and she was so easy-going, even Ivor occasionally remarked on what pleasant company she was. Surely she must find herself a nice man some day soon? It would be fun to be a foursome, they could do things together and she wouldn't feel so guilty any more when she went out with Ivor, leaving Alana alone when by nature she belonged in a group. She surely did, coming from that big family in Waterford.

Was that why Alana was such a good listener, able to whittle things down to their proper perspective? She was used to hearing confidences from her siblings, helping with their problems and jollying them up . . . Alana was being helpful to her at the moment, and Shivaun was grateful. It was good to be able to discuss Ivor freely, over a glass of wine late at night, confide the insecurity she sometimes felt. It wasn't that she didn't trust Ivor – of course she did – but there were moments when she still regretted that small row they'd had, felt it had done some damage.

'Shivaun,' Alana responded equably, 'you're not a saint, and neither is Ivor. To fight is human, to forgive divine.'

Yes, Shivaun said laughing, but it wasn't really a fight, as such. It was – more of – a – divergence. She wasn't sure whether Ivor really understood how strongly she'd felt about Kilo, and Stan, whether he was on her wavelength in these matters.

'Well, he wasn't born on a white horse, was he? He might be your knight in shining armour, but he doesn't have to fight by your side in every trench . . . why don't you just give the guy space?'

Space. Did Ivor really feel he needed some? Apparently he did. So she was doing her damndest to give him space, pulling back on her talk of work, crime, politics, and it seemed to be working . . . even if communication was slightly strained as a result, at least they were communicating, weren't they?

She thought they were. Still, Shivaun was looking forward to going to Italy and being alone with him, getting a bit of romance back into things. Maybe Italy would do the trick, Ivor would sweep her off her feet, tell her to chuck her pills in the Arno and make her a mama! They'd marry in a gondola and the holiday would turn into a honeymoon . . . She grinned as she confided the thought to Alana.

'Yes, well – don't rush round to Richard Lewis for a wedding dress just yet, Shivaun. I don't think Ivor would do something so serious so lightly. Not unless the sun goes to his head.'

The sun? To his head? But the sun had gone to both their heads years ago, they'd got engaged when they were only four for God's sake! It was just a question of logistics now, of their future coming together in the right place at the right time. Of course Alana meant well, but she really shouldn't be such a doubting Thomas. She hadn't been around from the start, she didn't know the depth of Ivor's love and commitment, the powerful bond of twenty years.

One evening late in July Alana lay in a deep warm bubble bath, wearing a face mask and painting her nails. She looked good these days, but she had to work at it. Still, the warmth and scent of the water felt good, she should let herself relax a little . . . but she could not relax. Something felt coiled inside her, some taut thing waiting to open out and blossom. It was a good feeling, an exciting feeling, but her mind was swirling with conflict.

Ivor was not going to marry Shivaun in Italy, nor impregnate her. She knew he wasn't. He still spent weekends here at the house, was around most other days too, but something was different. He was as friendly and chatty as ever, but he was not quite the same. His look had something very fractionally guarded about it. If Shivaun chose not to see it, or face up to it, she was deluding herself. She, Alana, could see it clearly from her viewpoint on the outside.

The outside! She'd been there for so long, ever since she came to this house, watching from the sideline. She'd known the couple for four years, and Ivor had known Shivaun for twenty. If he wasn't prepared to marry her now, if he didn't sense her needs . . . well. But she thought he did sense them. She thought Shivaun's needs were, in fact, the problem.

Shivaun was a good friend, and Alana was very fond of her, as such. She wanted her to be happy. Much as she ached for Ivor, she would never try to steal him away from Shivaun. That, in any case, had always seemed a futile aspiration – until now. Now, she thought she might not have to steal him at all. She might, if she got lucky, simply happen to be in the right place at the right time. If Ivor broke up with Shivaun he would be consumed with guilt, he'd need comfort and reassurance. He'd be like one of the patients at St Jude's, only male of course, he'd turn to Nurse Kennedy who was so well used to doling out comfort and reassurance. Only this time, she might get some thanks for her efforts, might get a bite at the cherry for a change.

The prospect of that first sympathetic touch, that brush of her hand on his, thrilled Alana to the bone. Ivor was the most beautiful creature she'd ever seen in her life, sometimes she had to clench her fists in his presence, she was so hypnotised by him, so frustrated by the way he looked at Shivaun, spoke to Shivaun, hugged and kissed Shivaun. He'd always been so devoted to his fiery fiancée. But was he devoted now? Or was he starting to tire, just a little, of his supporting role?

Alana thought he was. He hadn't given Shivaun that computer merely as a gift, he'd given it to her to divert some of her emotional energy, to channel her perpetual concerns away from him. He was weary of her 'state-of-the-nation' stance, her crusades. She could see the change in his eyes, in his body language. He was in conflict.

Shivaun was going to be in conflict too, if he found the strength to make the break. More than that. She was going to be devastated. Totally, completely annihilated. Ivor was the only person she had left in the world, it would be like an amputation, she would be crippled. It would be a nightmare, the house would be in chaos and uproar for weeks, for months.

Poor Shivaun.

Alana felt real pity for her, sympathy already rising. Shivaun had looks and money, her car and her house, some people even envied her – but Alana knew her history, her insecurity. And knew, too, that she didn't have any luck at all. If something could go wrong in Shivaun Reilly's life it always did, and it was about to go wrong again now.

On the other hand, something might be about to go right, for the first time, in Alana Kennedy's life. Alana Kennedy might be about to get a man, at last. A lovely man, a real stunner, to show off to everyone. Nobody thought she could do it, she was sure, but she could do it. She could have Ivor Lawlor, if she set her mind to it.

But she must do nothing to hurry things. Her conscience would have to be clear on that. She would have no hand in precipitating the split, not even give Shivaun any deliberately bad advice. She knew Shivaun trusted her, and that her trust made her vulnerable. But Shivaun was her friend, had always been good to her, and fair was fair. She'd be standing by, armed with teapots and tissues, when her world collapsed.

But then, if Shivaun were crying and grieving, Ivor would not come here. He'd promise Shivaun his friendship, undoubtedly, but he wouldn't want to hang around the scene of his crime. Wouldn't come near the place if it was full of tearful weeping women, if Shivaun went to pieces.

He'd wait until Shivaun regained her composure. Which might take a long time. Meanwhile – horror! – he might even meet someone else. He could have any pretty face with a snap of his fingers. It would be a sorry thing, Alana felt, to be secluded here with a sobbing Shivaun while Ivor went off and consoled himself elsewhere.

Something would have to be done about that.

Alana stretched her leg and turned on the hot water tap

with her toe, replenishing the bath while she considered the problem. Ivor would have to be kept in sight somehow . . . but how?

He'd need someone to talk to. Men didn't talk to each other, not about this kind of thing. It would be natural for him to turn to Alana Kennedy, who was an old pal as well as an intermediary. She'd be in a position to reassure him that Shivaun was recovering, coming along fine. She could salve his conscience.

But only if he was physically available, not driven away by Shivaun's despair. If that could be managed, everything else would follow. There must be a way to do it.

Frowning, Alana swirled the hot water to revive the bubbles, and lay back thinking. This was a dilemma. But it was one well worth solving, because the prize for figuring it out was absolutely inspirational. Some day she might even be a patient in St Jude's herself, if it wasn't closed down by then, having Ivor Lawlor's babies. It would make such a huge change to partake in all the joy, instead of merely facilitating it. What a pleasure, to be on the receiving end of the flowers and congratulations and kisses! It wasn't so much to ask, but it would mean so much, to someone who'd felt invisible all her life. The prospect lit up Alana's face, her whole body, made her feel like a new person. It would be wonderful!

If only it wasn't all going to be at Shivaun's expense. She wished things didn't have to be that way. For a nurse it went against the grain, to be the cause of suffering. But she mustn't let herself start thinking that way.

She was *not* the cause of it. It wasn't her fault that Ivor's love for Shivaun was waning, she had said or done nothing to weaken it in any way. She would not do anything now.

But it was waning. She could feel it. All she had to do was be ready when the time came, looking as good as she possibly could, waiting to catch Ivor in her open arms. This perfumed bath was a start on looking good, but it was not the reason why her face was glowing, her body tingling.

* * *

Ivor strode from his office through to the secretary's station and poured himself a cup of coffee from the perker. It was scalding, and it burnt his tongue.

'Damn! Sally, surely to Christ this coffee doesn't have to be molten lava? Can we not keep it at a drinkable temperature?'

Sally raised an eyebrow. It was unlike Mr Lawlor to be grouchy.

'You could add a drop of cold water. In your cup I mean, not the pot. The partners like it to be hot.'

The partners. Was the woman being smart, reminding him that he was not yet a senior one of them? Well, the way things were going today he didn't want to be a senior one of them, not ever. He wanted to get out of this sweltering office, go home, tear off this bloody suit and tie, get into his shorts and go hit balls. Dozens of tennis balls, hundreds of them, bam bam *bam*!

The day was far from over, but already it was filled with idiots. First there'd been that stupid chemist whose idea of keeping records was a welter of indecipherable squiggles on the backs of envelopes, all solemnly carted in in a shoebox. Then there was the moron who'd opened an offshore account three weeks before the revenue lads did a sweep of offshore accounts and caught him red-handed. There was the dingbat who hadn't paid any VAT for three years, didn't believe in it, now looking to be bailed out without actually coughing up. There was the farmer with the double set of books and the sly grin, the woman who whipped out her handkerchief and wept at the mention of tax audits . . . was he really going to have to endure such a procession of lulus for the rest of his days?

Did he really want to be an accountant? No. Today he wanted to be a boxer, a mountaineer, an André Agassi or a Pete Sampras. He wanted something to eat, too. But nobody seemed to believe in lunch around here, they all worked right through, he'd be conspicuous if he went out even for half an hour to grab a sandwich and walk round the block. He was hungry, and trapped.

Trapped. He couldn't get rid of the feeling lately; this entire firm seemed to hum with tension, stress, everything had to be done in a rush and a panic. A trolley would come round with sandwiches eventually and he'd buy one to eat at his desk, but he wouldn't get to eat it because the phone would ring and he'd spend the time explaining to yet another idiot that yes, you could go to prison for running a business that way. It would serve the lot of them right to all be thrown in prison – some of the civil servants too, they were so righteous, no wonder the clients were so adversarial. Everyone seemed to hate everyone else, everything was filled with suspicion and resentment. It was a horrible job, now that he thought about it.

But he was stuck with it. Stuck with going home to his mother this evening too, who'd want to know whether he was eating properly and why he hadn't put up those shelves for her yet. He was tired of living at home, twenty-five was far too old, but you couldn't very well walk out on a widow.

But his mother would just have to adjust, get over it if – if he married Shivaun Reilly. That would hardly be a shock to her, it had long been on the cards, and it was time he made up his mind about it. Shivaun was keen and there was no reason, now that he had a job, not to go ahead. In fact they could have done it last year or the year before, she had her house and the legacy from her parents, she'd have supported him while he was still a student, an articled clerk. Only he hadn't wanted to be supported. He was the one supposed to do the supporting.

But at this moment he felt he could use a bit of support. He felt some burden weighing him down, some crushing thing that made him keep wanting to loosen his tie – not that such a wildly radical breach of the dress code would be permitted in this prim sleek office. He should have gone into the stock end of the money market, been a dealer, then he could have rolled up his sleeves and shouted and jumped up and down, worn no tie at all. Then he could have had a heart attack on his twenty-fifth birthday and it would all be over.

Jesus. Did he really feel that bad?

Yes. As a matter of fact he did. His head was pounding, the air was stifling and it was unnatural to be working in this glass box on a summer's day when, for once, the sky was blue and the sun blazing outside. All he'd ever get now, for the rest of his life, was two lousy weeks out of every summer, to breathe fresh air and do the things he wanted to do. Work was a complete pain in the ass.

He was twenty-five years old and he was a prisoner. He didn't love his job the way Shivaun loved hers, you couldn't get emotionally engaged with a screen full of figures for chrissake . . . funny, he'd thought until today that he did love figures. Maths had always been interesting when they were conceptual, he enjoyed working out problems. But now, working out problems was all he ever seemed to do, for dimwit clients who thought two and two added up to eleven and a half. The only thing that could be said in their favour was that they . . . they kept his mind off Shivaun. He'd scarcely thought of her all morning. But he was thinking of her now. He didn't have time to, he didn't want to, but he was.

He banged down his coffee cup and turned to the secretary he shared with five other people. He wouldn't get his own secretary for years, and then only if he behaved himself, kow-towed his way up the corporate ladder.

'Sally. Field my calls, will you? I'm going out for half an hour.'

Her mouth all but fell open. '*Out?*'

'Yes. Out. You can tell anyone who cares to ask that I've gone out for a bite and a breath of air, that I'm practising to become a human fucking being.'

Brona Mulcahy was having a hell of a time producing her whopper of a ten-pound, kick-boxing son. She was yelling blue murder, shrieking and swearing on every Bible that she would never do such a thing again. Next time – not that there would be one – the father could do all the roaring and struggling and yelling. Shivaun grinned as she wiped Brona's forehead with a cold cloth and murmured encouraging things, aware that in some perverse way she was enjoying this ghastly experience.

The baby was a massive bruiser, but that, in its way, made his delivery as exciting as Kilo Finnegan's had been. Brona would have something to show for all her shouting and swearing, a literally huge reward at the end of it. She would embrace her strapping son and forget all the pain in a flash of love, of pride; in years to come she would beam up at him when he engulfed her in his arms, he would be 'my son, the lumberjack' or farmer or whatever he turned out to be. Well – hardly a ballet dancer or a jockey, although you never knew. Whatever it might be, he would be worth every minute of this gruesome day. There was a point to it all.

Besides, Brona was barely sixteen. She wasn't quite alone – her partner was out in the corridor tugging his earring and scratching his tattoos – but he didn't seem to be much help, and at this moment everything was up to her, and Shivaun felt an affinity with her.

Had her own mother endured all this? Had she too been sixteen and scared stiff, screaming that she wanted to die and yet afraid to die, because who, then, would care for her newborn baby? Had her own father paced up and down, had he been a strutting, petrified youth like the one outside? Was she, in some weird timewarp, reliving her own delivery? Not that hers had been in a hospital – she was sure it had not – but she thought the emotions must be very similar. Fear and anguish and then a pure surge of . . . of joy?

Yes. If only for one fleeting instant, her parents must surely have felt joy. No matter what came later, they must have felt that single instant of relief, triumph, achievement . . . her mother must have, anyway, even if her father hadn't been there. Her mother must have gone through what Brona was going through now, and for that reason if nothing else she was going to make sure Brona came through. Brona and Buster, both of them.

Someone touched her elbow and whispered in her ear.

'Shivaun. There's a phone call for you. A man. He says it's personal.'

She nodded acknowledgement, but didn't move.

'Thanks, Evie. Could someone get his number and tell him I'm busy, I'll call back later?'

'Sure. But Shivaun, maybe it's important.'

'Maybe. But so is this.'

Briefly, she wondered. Was her house on fire? Had someone been in an accident? A tremor flashed through her. But she was already embroiled in a matter of life and death, one she could do something about. She couldn't leave young Brona now, not when Brona had bonded with her and was trusting her. Brona was a very vulnerable kid, and she was going to stick with her. Whatever the phone call was about, it would just have to wait until this baby was born.

But, when he finally was forty minutes later, she didn't wait to share in the celebrations. She washed, weighed, wrapped him and handed him back to Brona at speed, beamed at them both and ran out into the corridor. The tattooed teenager was still pacing it, smoking in flagrant disregard of the notice over his head.

'Mr – er – um – Benny, you have a son. He and his mum are doing fine. You can see them now if you like.'

In fact he could have seen them long ago, been with Brona through it all. But he had chosen not to. He was a big beefer, but behind his bulk Shivaun thought she detected a wimp.

She hadn't time to worry about wimps. She ran to the nurses' station and grabbed the message pinned to the board for her.

'Shivaun, ring Ivor on his mobile ASAP.'

She grabbed the phone and stabbed Ivor's number into it.

'Ivor? I couldn't talk earlier, I was in the delivery – what's going on? What is it?'

It was unlike him to call her at work. He knew the nature of the hospital, knew that even high-priority calls might have to wait.

'I – Shivaun, I just need to talk to you. Could you possibly get away now?'

'Now? But Ivor, it's only three o'clock, I'm on until six . . . are you not at work yourself?'

'No. I took the afternoon off.'

'Off? Why? Are you all right?'

'Yes. No. I – Shivaun, I just want to see you! Please try to get away. It's important.'

'Ivor, *what* is important? We're up to our ears here.'

She heard his sigh, sensed what he seemed to be thinking, that her work came before him. But that wasn't true. If he was ill or injured or – but he couldn't be, if he was here on the phone. He sounded agitated, but coherent.

'I – look, I'll try to get away at five. That's the best I can manage. The Laheen baby looks like arriving by then and I'll – where are you, anyway?'

'I'm at Portmarnock beach.'

Huh? *Che*? Portmarnock beach was miles from his office, from home or the hospital, any of their usual haunts.

'What the hell are you doing there?'

'I'll tell you when I see you. At the kiosk, you know the one where they sell ice-cream . . . if you leave at five you could be here by six.'

She wished she had time to delve further into this. But she hadn't.

'Yes. All right. Six at the kiosk.'

Hanging up, she retraced her steps down the blue-tiled corridor, intrigued to note that the father of Brona's baby had vanished. Whether into the maternity ward to see his new family, or into the blue yonder, she couldn't tell.

Had her own father vanished? Had he too been sixteen and terrified, by what he had created? Had he ever held her, had he sat on the steps of the church and cried as he gathered his resolve to go, to leave her? Had he . . . had Ivor . . . had Ivor taken leave of his senses? She'd never known him to desert work before, end up on a beach in the middle of the afternoon.

She went back into the delivery room and smiled brightly at Mrs Carol Laheen, who at the age of thirty-eight was about to bring her ninth child into the world.

Everyone fervently prayed it would be her last, although she was rejecting the suggestion of 'getting me tubes tied' during the Caesarian delivery. She didn't want that, and she was none too keen on the Caesarian either, which was necessary now that her heart had begun to register the strain. By the time Shivaun reached her she was ready for pre-med, but alert and vaguely suspicious.

Shivaun said hello and squeezed her hand encouragingly.

'Hi, Carol. I'll be looking after your baby when it arrives . . . don't worry now, everything will be fine.'

Carol looked at her, sceptically.

'Is that so? And tell me, Nurse Reilly, how many chisellers do you have yourself?'

'Uh – well, none actually, not yet! But I hope I will soon.'

Carol nodded. 'Aye. Well, missy, when you have a squad the size of mine, you can tell me then whether to worry or not.'

Shivaun laughed, and squeezed her hand again. Carol was a career mother, having kids was what she did best, but this one was likely to be her last. Shivaun wanted her to wake up feeling it was her finest hour.

The evening was still warm, but had turned cloudy by the time Shivaun reached Portmarnock and parked parallel to the beach. Knotting a rain jacket around her waist, she waved to Ivor as she got out and locked the car. He was standing by the kiosk with his hands in his pockets, still wearing his suit from work but without a tie, looking windblown and ruffled.

'Hi. Sorry I couldn't make it any quicker. I was on a Caesarian.'

He took her hand and looked at her.

'Yes. Very important. I understand.'

His tone made her wonder whether he did. But it *was*, for chrissakes, she couldn't just abandon ship! Deflated, she decided to say nothing about it, nor about the bouncing Buster Mulcahy either. Instead she snuggled against him as they set out onto the beach, miles of white sand stretching all the way to Howth, with the mountains beyond in the distance. Looking vaguely bleak, Ivor gazed at them.

'Beautiful, huh?'

Yes. Dublin was in a lucky, lovely location, with the sea and the mountains on its doorstep. Yet Shivaun knew she couldn't safely walk in such places alone, and the theft of such freedom angered her. It also angered her to see a couple of jetskis zooming through the water now, buzzing like mosquitoes – and yet, horses were banned. Horses galloping through the spray had once been a joy to behold, but now the city fathers only allowed aquaplaning motorbikes.

She bit her lip. Ivor's expression said he didn't want to hear about it.

'So, what's up? Why haven't you been at work this afternoon?'

'I called in sick.'

She looked at him with concern, noting his pallor. He didn't seem quite himself.

'Why? Are you sick?'

He shrugged, and she smiled.

'Or did you get sacked? Fired out of the mouth of a cannon?'

He didn't reply immediately as they walked across the soft sand, sinking into it, making rhythmic footprints in tandem. Romantic footprints, Shivaun thought, even if the tide would soon come in and wash them away.

'No. I didn't get sacked. But I was sick.'

Something clenched in her with fright. Was something really wrong with him – some awful incurable thing that he'd held off telling her? She hadn't noticed anything amiss, but now every drop of blood sluiced from her face. Checking her stride, she gripped his arm, and he smiled sidelong at her.

'Nothing physical. I was just suddenly sick of that office, sick of the system.'

'What? But Ivor – you've only been there a few months – I thought—'

He nodded, rather grimly she thought. 'Yeah. So did I.

Thought I should get what my mother calls a "proper job" so I could be a "proper husband". I seem to recall promising you once that I would provide for you.'

She was baffled. 'Oh, Ivor! I don't need providing for! I have all I need! What are you talking about?'

He stared ahead of him, far down to the end of the beach where the sky met the horizon.

'I'm talking about . . . about rafting through the Rockies and husky-sledding through Antarctica.'

He turned his face to hers, enquiringly. But she had long buried that childhood dream, among the nightmares that followed it, couldn't remember it. She didn't know what he meant.

'Antarctica? The Rockies?'

'Yes. Well. Or wherever. Somewhere big and free and open, somewhere you can breathe and live by the sun, not have to clock in or worry about your pension scheme.'

She only vaguely followed, but enough to make her laugh. 'It's my fault, then, isn't it? I accused you of turning into a real accountant, so now you've decided to rebel. You want prairies and deserts and wild wilderness.'

He nodded, grimaced wryly.

'Yeah, okay, so maybe it does sound bloody stupid from a grown man, a hot-shot accountant. But I – I do want space, Shivaun. Physical and spiritual space. I can't breathe where I am.'

'Really? But Ivor, why didn't you tell me before?'

'I'm telling you now. I've only recently been thinking about it.'

She considered. 'So just how miserable are you? Do you want to quit your job?'

'Yes. I do.'

She didn't hesitate. 'Then go ahead! Go for it. I hadn't realised you weren't happy, but if you're not, then you mustn't go on. You must search for something else, something that's right for you . . . I don't want you stitched into a strait-jacket, Ivor. I want you to be happy.'

He eyed her with an expression she couldn't read.

'Do you, Shivaun? At all costs?'

'Yes! Of course! I know it might be expensive, but that's not the point, is it? The point is your welfare, your joy in life.'

He stopped walking, pulled at her sleeve and spun her round to him.

'Shivaun – if I quit my job, would you quit yours too?'

His eyes were so dark and intent, the question so sudden, she was punched by it, breathless.

'Quit mine? But Ivor, I love mine! Why would I want to leave it?'

'To come away with me.'

'Away? To Antarctica or . . . ?'

'To wherever our instincts take us. Wherever we can just be – be ourselves.'

'But I am myself! I'm doing what I love to do.'

'Yes. Perhaps. Your work nourishes you. But I wonder whether you really are yourself.'

'What do you mean?'

'I mean . . . you give so much of yourself away. To everyone, everywhere. And yet you sometimes give so little, to me . . . you've never told me, for instance, how you feel about that man who killed your father.'

She froze. 'I feel nothing. The law dealt with him and that was that.'

'That was five years ago. He'll be released by the end of this year.'

Her voice rose. 'Ivor, I do not want to talk about that man. You're changing the subject. The subject is whether or not I could give up my job to travel with you and the answer is . . . is that I'm a midwife! That's what I always wanted to be, it's what I love.'

He didn't answer. It was a few moments before his silence became eloquent, and spoke for him.

'Do you think I love it more than I love you? Is that what you think?'

He paused, bent to pick up a shell, turn it over and examine it.

'I don't know, Shivaun. All I know is that you're very wrapped up in it. Sometimes I feel so . . . shut out, by your babies and your lame ducks and your eternal causes. I feel that – that if we marry and have children, they might take over, matter more to you than I do.'

She thought he must be mad, wondered whether he'd been drinking. He didn't appear to have been, but – but he must know how important he was to her, how much she loved him!

'Ivor, I will always love you. No matter how many children we ever have, I always will. It's as simple as that.'

'Then – then will you prove it, Shivaun? Will you give up nursing, say for a year, and come away with me?'

Her heart lurched, felt somehow stretched, pulled in different directions. Part of her wanted to simply be with him, do whatever he wanted; part of her saw the squished-up face of Kilo Finnegan, heard the lusty cry of Buster Mulcahy, smelled all the silken baby skin.

'But . . . Ivor . . . I thought we were going to start a family.'

'Yes. I did too, Shivaun. I wasn't pretending or lying, I genuinely thought we were. But now I – I think I need some space, first. I really think I do.'

He was still looking down at the sand, still turning the shell in his hands, and the look on his face, the implications in it, were like icy water rising up around her.

'W – what exactly do you mean by space, Ivor?'

He lifted his face to hers. 'What exactly do you mean, Shivaun? You haven't answered my question. Will you give up nursing, throw it to the wind for a while, or not?'

No! Oh, no, oh, Ivor, don't ask me to do that. Please don't ask that of me, she thought.

She wished there was something to steady herself on, some solid object she could grip while she caught her breath. For the first time in her life, she was unable to lean on Ivor.

'I . . . oh, God . . . Ivor, I can't give it up. But I can support you if you give up your work, if that's what you want. You can lean on me for a change, move into the house, I'll pay the bills while you . . .'

'Shivaun, that's not what I'm asking you.'

No. She knew it wasn't. But it was the best she could offer. The thought that it might not be enough made her feel as if she were drowning. Ivor had always been her rock, and now she felt as if the sea were closing over him, washing him away.

But she couldn't leave her work, drift away directionless. If he needed space, she equally needed purpose.

'Ivor, I – I'm sorry. I'm so sorry.'

He put his hand under her chin, tilted it up to him, saw how very sorry she truly was. The pain in her face made him feel like an axe murderer. But her pain was – had been for five years – part of the tight band that made him feel he couldn't breathe. Her pain was all bound up with her babies and her causes and everything that rivalled him, fought him everywhere he turned.

'Then – then you must stay on at the hospital, Shivaun, and do what you have to do. I don't expect you to give up what you love most.'

That caught her full on, straight through the heart.

'Ivor – it isn't – I don't—'

She had never seen him look so sad, and he had never felt so sad.

'Oh, yes, Shivaun. It is, and I think you do.'

She could find no words. He was wrong, but how could she prove that? Only by doing what she could not do. Immobile, stricken, she looked at him.

'But – but what—?'

He smiled tightly, fractionally.

'What will we do? As a couple, we won't do anything, because I don't see how we can continue to be a couple. Not now, not until – Shivaun, this is the last thing I want, but I think it's the only thing – if we . . .'

Oh, God. Oh, Christ. He forced the words out like stones.

'If we split up for a while.'

Her face was whiter than the sand.

'A while?'

'Yes. A few months, a year . . . if we love each other then surely we can survive that? We've been together all our lives, maybe that's part of the problem, we've never . . .'

'Never what?'

Jesus. This was like having bone marrow extracted by force.

'Never – explored! Never deviated, never wavered, never tried or tasted any of the freedom you give up when you marry! To marry would be to make a commitment we don't fully understand!'

She kept her gaze fixed level with his chest.

'I see. Then you'd better taste your freedom, Ivor, before you give it up. Maybe you'll find you don't want to give it up.'

He knew she was gathering her forces, pulling into the mantle that always camouflaged her deepest feelings, until she could cope with them. He touched her face, attempted to smile.

'I will want to give it up, eventually. I do know that, for sure, because I know I want you. I just wish you . . . you could travel with me, first, literally and figuratively.'

She wished so too, wished it with all her heart. Maybe St Jude's would be closed down and she wouldn't even have that left, for all her devotion. But she had to stay, she had to fight for it, for the children and the community who were the one constant thing in her life. Her birth parents had abandoned her, Viv and Jimmy had died, and now Ivor, it seemed, was leaving her too. Even Ivor.

Steeling herself, she put her hand on his arm.

'I can't, Ivor. I can't go with you. May God go with you instead, and lead you to wherever you need to be.'

The look in her eyes held him at bay, stopped him from speaking as she broke away from him, turned and began to stride back towards the dunes, her hair gleaming like beaten copper as her figure receded.

He had not expected it to be like this, so sudden, so swift. He had known she would be shocked, but thought she might rally after some tears, some debate would ensue, reasons would be found not to do this. Instead he was the one shocked, stabbed by the finality of her words, her tone. For once, she was not putting up a fight.

None. Not for him. For other people, she fought like a tiger; for him, she walked away. Something coiled and clenched in his chest as he stood immobile, watching her until she was lost to his sight.

But it had to happen, he thought. I love Shivaun Reilly with every bone in my body, but we could not have gone on as we were. I was losing her already, to all the needy people. I thought she needed me, but she needs them even more. She has chosen them.

The thought was agonising, yet he stood holding it, examining it for a long time, facing out to the grey, empty ocean. For some reason a memory came to him, of the old building Viv had once defended on Mountjoy Square, listed for demolition, and reconstruction.

Chapter Four

One day, Alana thought, was permissible. Two days were, well, understandable. But three days were really stretching it. She knew Shivaun was alive, because she had heard her moving about in her room, but she didn't know what was keeping her alive. It could hardly be the half-dozen cups of tea she had accepted before shutting her door again.

Alana decided the time for sweet reason was over. She was going to have to go about this more forcefully. Grimly, she marched up the stairs and banged loudly on the door.

'Shivaun! I've had enough of this! Get up and get out here this minute!'

No answer. Alana banged again.

'I'm telling you, if you're not downstairs for dinner in ten minutes' time, you're toast! Take a shower and come down before I turn you in, tell Matron you're just moping over your bloody man!'

She turned on her heel and marched back down, thinking maybe she'd hit on a good strategy. Shivaun wouldn't want Matron to think her 'flu' was anything other than that. Matron's respect, like everyone else's, mattered to her.

Back in the kitchen Alana tinkered with her beef stroganoff, flinging cream and lemon juice irritably into it. Really Shivaun had no consideration, was just being a drama queen. After all Ivor had only said he wanted a temporary break, hadn't he? It wasn't even a proper break, final and forever. It was just one bloody hell of a mess.

She turned as she heard a shuffle, and there stood Shivaun, wrapped in a green kimono which had, apparently, once belonged to Viv. Her hair was wet, her eyes were like two chunks of quartzite, and she looked about twelve years old.

Alana grunted. 'Right. Well, at least you're here. Now sit down at that damn table and tell me the full story.'

'I told you already. Ivor and I have broken up.'

Shivaun sank down at the table and Alana thrust a steaming plate of food under her nose.

'Eat that. And explain yourself. It had better be more than that he wants to go to Italy by himself for a fortnight. If he's just catching his breath I—'

'No. He doesn't want to go to Italy. And he isn't catching his breath. He said – he said he wants a year. A whole year.'

Shivaun's voice trembled, and Alana paused to think, to weigh her words.

'A year . . . ? Well, that is a long time. Why does he want it?'

Wretchedly, Shivaun took up her fork, and put it down again.

'He wants it because he's not sure about marrying me. He says he can't compete with my work and other interests, thinks I'd put them before him.'

H'mm. Alana permitted herself a cynical glance.

'Well, wouldn't you? I mean, let's face it Shivaun, you are virtually married already, to St Jude's and your political hobbyhorses . . . you can't have everything.'

No. Everybody had something, but nobody had everything. Shivaun stared into her stroganoff. She literally could not eat one mouthful.

'Oh, for God's sake Shivaun, I've gone to trouble to cook your favourite thing, and you have to get back to work tomorrow, you can't go on an empty stomach . . . did he say he'd stay in touch then, or what? Are you still friends?'

'No. He said nothing about staying in touch.'

Alana felt a surge of something, glanced down into her plate.

'Nothing? Not even a weekly phone call to make sure you're OK?'

'No! I told you, nothing – not that I want anything. If he doesn't want to marry me and father our children, then I don't want a – a weekly bloody phone call!'

She burst into tears. But Alana merely handed her a table napkin, thinking that this sounded promising in one way, ominous in another. She didn't want Ivor Lawlor disappearing into the sunset entirely.

'But – but he's your best friend.'

'Not any more.'

'What? Why not?'

'Because he wanted me to give up my job, and I wouldn't.'

'Give up your job? Why did he want you to do that?'

'Because he – well, he said he wanted us to have some adventures before we got married, but I think the truth of it is that he resents my job. He's jealous of it.'

Yes. Alana could well imagine why he might be. 'So what did you tell him?'

'I told him I wouldn't – couldn't.'

Alana felt suddenly exasperated. 'Well then, it was you who made the choice, not him!'

'But Alana, you surely don't expect – he can't expect – if he loved me, he'd never ask such a thing! He knows how important it is to me.'

'Shivaun . . . that's exactly the problem. It's too important. You don't seem to be seeing this from his point of view at all.'

Suddenly Shivaun felt weary, exasperated in turn. Nobody seemed to be seeing this from *her* point of view. They seemed to think St Jude's was just a job, nothing more. All the other activities, too, that focused her mind and kept her sane.

Oh, God, if only Viv and Jimmy were here! At this moment she missed them desperately, the way a small child might miss its parents, run to them for love and comfort. Alana was doing her best, in her way, but it wasn't Alana's problem, she was having no difficulty eating everything on the plate in front of her. Abruptly, Shivaun stood up.

'Thanks for cooking dinner, Alana. I'm sorry I can't do better justice to it. I'm going to go back to my room, but I'll be OK, go to work tomorrow and get my game together.'

In her face Alana could clearly see that she would not be OK. She'd cry all night and . . . oh, well. She might as well get it all over with, let Shivaun have the full whammy in one fell swoop.

'Shivaun . . . about the hospital.'

Shivaun turned back. 'What about it?'

Alana cleared her throat. 'Look, I know this is a bad time, but you would have heard from Matron or someone tomorrow anyway . . . while you've been off work, the hatchet has finally fallen.'

Shivaun looked blank. 'Hatchet?'

'Yeah. The closure order. We're being merged with St Peter's. In January. Nobody will lose their job or anything, but we'll be shunted over there. The building is to be put up for sale at the end of this month, and we have until Christmas to wind things down.'

She cringed inwardly as she said it, wondering how Shivaun was going to react. She'd fought the battle so hard, for so long. It was going to hit her almost as losing Ivor had hit her, full in the face.

And indeed Shivaun did sway slightly, seemed to nearly buckle as she gripped the door frame to steady herself. There was a long silence.

And then something seemed to slam shut in her face.

'I see. Well, that is a shame. I had hoped – but I take it there isn't any point in hoping any more, is there?'

'No. I'm sorry, Shivaun, but there isn't.'

The computer sat in its corner, and Shivaun gazed at it as if it were made of lead, of concrete. Before Ivor – before she'd broken up with Ivor, things would have been different. She'd have hurled herself on it the moment she heard about St Jude's being closed, bombarded the minister and his entire department with abuse, arguments, every weapon at her disposal. She would, as Alana put it, have rallied the troops and blown the bugles, stormed the citadel and scaled the walls. But now . . . now, she felt unmanned. She was, literally, unmanned. Ivor was gone and with him every drop of her drive was gone, she didn't care if the minister shut down every hospital in the country.

'Maybe,' Alana remarked acerbically, 'Mr Minister will have an accident some day, be rushed to casualty only to find the staff too busy to treat him. Maybe he'll be left lying on a trolley in a corridor for hours, with a fractured skull and no painkillers, not so much as an aspirin to clutch for comfort.'

Shivaun smiled vaguely, but didn't answer. Her mind kept drifting back to the beach, to Ivor, standing where she'd left him. She *had* left him . . . but only because he wanted to leave her. Even now she couldn't comprehend, couldn't get her mind around it, knew only that she'd had to walk away before she crumbled, wept and collapsed and said she couldn't live without him, he couldn't do it, please, Ivor, *no*! In those few moments she had used up a colossal amount of strength, put everything into holding up. She couldn't relinquish her pride or her dignity, it would only have made the situation unbearable for them both, without helping at all.

That was her way of coping with things. He must know her well enough to know she faced things square on, had the wits to recognise finality when she saw it, accept it not willingly but with as much grace as she could muster. Ivor had not really been himself at all this summer, and she was a fool not to have read the signs earlier. He was disenchanted with her as well as with his work, only she'd been too busy to see it. He'd been right that day at Lough Dan, about taking him for granted. God, why hadn't she listened, listened properly to him? *Why?*

Because she'd been all wrapped up in Kilo's kidnapping that day, and then afterwards in the sorry saga of Stan Murray, who'd needed her help . . . now, she needed help herself, but who was there to turn to? Alana was trying, but some of her help was worse than useless.

Alana had said, for instance, that Ivor probably did mean what he said about only breaking up temporarily, that he 'wasn't just letting her down gently', didn't intend the split to be permanent at all. Until Alana said that Shivaun had not thought of this aspect of things, but now it came to her that men often did suggest a short break from their partners when they meant a long one, because they didn't want to face the scene that might ensue if they confessed the truth. They wimped out. They left your life with empty promises of return some day . . . she had not thought Ivor was like that, but was he? Was she too close to him to see him in perspective, warts and all? He wanted to leave his job too he'd said, but there was no mention of going back to that. On the contrary, he intended to quit for good. So why should he not intend to quit her for good, too? He had been just trying to let her down gently. Alana, in her way, was trying to wise her up, make her face reality. She had, after twenty years, lost her best friend, her lover, and her future. St Jude's, now, as well. Her entire world had been torn from under her.

She knew she was losing weight, not eating, looking exactly as she felt, barely even concentrating on the babies when they came, pell-mell it suddenly seemed, everyone in the entire world was having babies, starting families. Everyone except her – and Alana, of course. Everyone except the two of them.

The gaping space where Ivor had been in her life felt like a crater, swallowing her up. Without him her life felt pointless, everything was pointless.

'Don't be ridiculous,' Alana retorted briskly to that, 'you'll live to fight another day. Meanwhile, why don't you click on that computer and shake a stick at those developers building the new shopping centre . . . you know they're knocking down the old stone cottages on the site? Thatched stone cottages, over a century old – you should e-mail their head office and complain.'

'Why? Why does it always have to be me? Why don't you do it?'

'Because – because you're the one who does this stuff! I wouldn't be any good at it. But somebody has to stand up and be counted or we'll all get stamped on. Flattened, pulped.'

But Shivaun felt pulped already. She was sick of struggling, fighting lost causes and other people's battles, crushed by the futility of it.

'No. It's somebody else's turn, Alana. What goddamn thanks do I ever get, only people throwing their eyes up to heaven and thinking I'm a crank?'

'But you won lots of rounds before, achieved lots of things.'

'Yeah. You win some, you lose some. And then the next lot comes along, another avalanche of crappy laws, crappy planning, crappy bloody everything. I've had it with the whole caboodle. This country can bury itself alive under an avalanche of crap for all I care. Go hang itself, take a hike to hell. I don't give a goddamn.'

She saw that Alana was surprised, even shocked. Alana, like so many of the people around her, had got into the habit of relying on her, turning to her to take up cudgels on their behalf. And it was her willingness to do so that had cost her Ivor . . . now, all she wanted was Ivor.

But Ivor didn't want her. He had not even phoned, and she was certainly not going to phone him, not lower herself to explaining what he surely knew, that she loved him and missed him desperately. Desperation only frightened people, drove them further away.

She was trying not to let anyone see hers. At work she told nobody what had happened, because the last thing she wanted was pity: 'oh, poor Shivaun Reilly whose parents died, now her boyfriend's gone too . . .' Alana was under orders not to breathe a word, not even to Matron. Shivaun knew that Matron would understand, be sympathetic and supportive, but Matron had her own problems. When St Jude's closed all the medical personnel would be 'deployed elsewhere', according to the blasted minister, but Matron was classified as administrative staff and to be made redundant. Shivaun could clearly see the strategy behind this; the minister feared and hated Matron and was, therefore, getting rid of her. This one aspect of things would have fired Shivaun to send the minister a rocket via e-mail, if she thought it would do any good, but she knew it wouldn't. The system had won, and society had lost. People like Matron were an undervalued, vanishing breed.

Meanwhile, despite Alana's comforting cups of tea and well-meant words, what was going on with Alana? Shivaun sensed some new, nervy mood in her; she jumped every time the phone rang and seemed to be sitting constantly on the edge of her seat. She was losing weight, too, at a rate even faster than her own, only it was deliberate in Alana's case, she had taken to weighing everything she ate and counting calories with a fervour that verged on the pious.

'What's all this about?' Shivaun asked her one evening when she came home with a stash of Weightwatchers from the supermarket, 'you don't need to take things this far, Alana, you know, you have a perfectly healthy figure already.'

'Well, maybe . . . but I can never be too careful. I don't want to go back to my puppy-fat days, not at the age I am now. Anyway, you're a fine one to talk, eating nothing yourself, moping round the house in those old jeans . . . why don't you go out and do something for a change, get some fresh air? Even a walk might perk you up a bit.'

She was right, and Shivaun did go out for a short walk, but she didn't enjoy it. Walking alone wasn't the same as walking, talking with Ivor. And besides, she felt somehow *pushed* out, almost as if Alana wanted her out of the way. Wanted her out of her own bloody house, as if *she* were the tenant and Alana the owner. But why would Alana – God, was she getting paranoid, imagining that everyone suddenly wanted her out of the way, out of their life?

No. That was surely nonsense. She'd have to get a grip, stop imagining such a silly thing. Stop crying herself to sleep every night, too, because as a result she was getting no sleep, twisting and turning and yearning for Ivor, going to St Jude's next morning looking like hell and feeling even worse. In turn this was affecting her confidence, and it would be only a matter of time before she made some potentially fatal mistake. Drugged a patient in error, dropped a baby, wrote the wrong information on a chart? Never before had she felt unfit to be a midwife, but she felt unfit to be one now.

'Well, Ivor, now that you've thrown up your job, perhaps you'd have time to put up those shelves for me? God knows I've only been waiting about a hundred years.'

Mrs Cynthia Lawlor glared at her son, and Ivor glared back. He'd only left the accountancy firm a few weeks ago, she should know him well enough to realise he wasn't the type to laze around. Was she upset that he wasn't contributing money to her household budget at the moment, was that it? Since he'd resigned voluntarily, he wasn't entitled to any benefits, he hadn't a penny – but he would have, soon, he'd make it all up to her as soon as he figured out how. Meanwhile, his father had died well insured and left her comfortably off, there was no danger of anyone starving.

Stung, he got up, went out to the garage, gathered up the wood he'd been planing, finished it and carried the smooth, rounded boards back into the house. There he applied a coat of sealer and assembled a ladder and his toolbox, measured the space while he waited for the sealer to dry. He'd better get it exactly right, Cynthia would have a stroke if her shelves were one millimetre out of kilter. Perfection, that was what Cynthia Lawlor wanted out of life. Not a son who'd chucked accountancy for – what? His mind ran over the possibilities as he worked, wondering what kind of qualifications you needed exactly to be an adventure tour guide, or a long-distance courier or . . . weren't there people who paid guys to drive cars from one side of America to the other? Even that would be a start, and the sooner he got out of Cynthia's house the better. She couldn't have her cake and eat it.

It was, of course, Shivaun who was holding him up. Shivaun who'd stayed on his mind long after she walked away down the beach, haunting him with her hazel eyes and her head held high, her tenacity even in this. He'd thought she might relent, phone him to say she'd been too brusque and maybe they should discuss things further, but she had not. About fifty times a day he reached to phone her, but never did, because what if she said yes, he'd been right, he should get on with his life and leave her to get on with hers? She hadn't seemed to understand at all about him only wanting a temporary break, time to think and regroup. She was so damn *definite*, the way she'd walked away, so decided in this as in everything.

Yet he worried about her, wondered how she was. Up to her eyes, no doubt, with her hospital and countless activities, out chaining herself to some disputed railing or picketing some government office . . . she was so dynamic, such a survivor, probably surrounding herself now with so many things she hadn't time to think about him at all. Hardly at all, after all their years, all their closeness; hardly at all.

Should he call Alana, perhaps, to get some information? Alana wasn't a squealy, fussy kind of woman, she'd give it to him straight without elaboration or recrimination. It was a bit sneaky, perhaps, but they were pals and it was worth a shot. Alana would let him know Shivaun's state of mind, put his own at rest to some extent. Yes. He'd call her now, actually, when these shelves were up.

It wasn't easy single-handed, but at length they were up, and looked damn good if he said so himself. The shape, the size, the battens that would take the weight of whatever Cynthia planned to put on them. For an accountant, he wasn't quite as bad with his hands as he would have thought. In fact he'd rather enjoyed the job, not that Cynthia was to know it. Now, for his reward, he'd go phone Alana, and pray that Shivaun did not answer. If she did he would hang up, because to hear her voice, to find it cool and dismissive, would be more than he could bear. He who'd known her since she was four, with her little sausage ringlets.

Bracing himself, he summoned his mother to inspect her shelves, and went to the phone extension upstairs out of earshot. As he dialled the number, something constricted in his throat.

'Hello?'

It was Alana. But for a moment, he still couldn't speak. He hadn't expected anyone to answer so quickly.

'Alana? Hi. It's Ivor. I – I just thought I'd give you a ring—'

'Give *me* a ring? Or are you looking for Shivaun?'

What was wrong with the woman? She sounded as twitchy, as nervous as he did himself.

'No. I'm looking for you. I just wondered – whether you—'

'Hold on.'

He held on, and there was the sound of the phone being put down, a door closing. Then she picked up again, sounding better this time he thought.

'Sorry, I was just shutting the door, there's an awful draught. Now, what can I do for you, Ivor?'

He cleared his throat. 'Well, I'm sure Shivaun has told you about – our – that we – we've decided to take a bit of a breather? I was under pressure at work, needed to—'

'Yes, Ivor. I know all about it. I'm really sorry to hear that the two of you have split up. But maybe it's for the best. Shivaun seems to think it is, anyway.'

What? 'Sorry, Alana, I didn't catch that, what did you say?'

'I said maybe it's for the best. Shivaun says you wanted some space, and so did she.'

'She – did?'

'Yes. So she tells me, anyway. I reckon she could be right.'

'Why, Alana? Why do you think that?'

'Oh, well, you know, she . . . look, Ivor, this is really a bit delicate to discuss over the phone. I don't want her to come in and think I'm talking about her behind her back.'

'Uh – no. No. Of course not.'

'But I suppose you – look, I tell you what. If you want to talk about it, I could maybe meet you down at the pub for a drink.'

'Yes. The pub. That's a much better idea. Are you free now, tonight?'

There was a pause. 'No. Not tonight, Ivor. In fact I'm a bit busy this week. But I could meet you – say next Sunday night, if that suited you?'

Next Sunday? Damn! He wanted to talk now. But he didn't want Alana telling Shivaun that he sounded too eager, sounded desperate. Didn't want her telling Shivaun anything, in fact. With effort, he lowered his voice into what he hoped was a casual tone.

'Yeah. Sure. Sunday sounds fine. Meanwhile, Alana, I'd appreciate it if you – if you'd keep this just between the two of us, for the moment?'

She sounded nonchalant in return. 'Yes, naturally, Ivor. I understand. Mum's the word.'

'Great. Thanks. I'll see you in the Horse and Hound then, at say nine Sunday evening.'

'Right. And meanwhile, Ivor, don't worry. Shivaun is fine, everything is grand.'

He didn't know how to feel. But there was one other thing he wanted to know.

'Is she at home at the moment?'

'Er – no, actually. She went out, said something about meeting . . . let me think, who was it now . . . oh, I remember! It was just Fintan Daly from next door. He asked her to go to some community meeting about something or other.'

Fintan Daly? Freckled, six-footer Fintan, who was single and notorious for the number of women he brought to stay overnight at his house? That Fintan?

'I see. Well, I'm sure she'll come to no harm with him. Thanks, Alana. See you Sunday.'

He hung up, and stood rooted to the spot.

* * *

Three weeks later, one charcoal-cloudy morning at the beginning of September, Alana came into the living room where Shivaun sat filling in a form. It had a travel agency logo on it, and she guessed what it must be: an insurance claim for the money Shivaun and Ivor had paid for their abandoned Italian holiday. Her heart somersaulted.

'Are you going to contact Ivor about that money, Shivaun? Give him back his half?'

Shivaun looked up, and Alana was struck by how strained she looked, how pale in her cream silk shirt and faded denims. One word with Ivor, she thought, would be enough to catapult Shivaun back into his arms, just as one word from her would have the same effect on him. The two were at the worst stage of a break-up, aching acutely for each other, far more than either of them knew. Or would ever know, if she could help it.

'If we get a refund, I'll just post his share to him.'

Phew. Alana felt faint with relief. Above all she must keep the pair apart, and so far she was succeeding. She had met Ivor three times now, at the pub where he had poured out his heart to her, demanded to know everything about Fintan's fictitious attention to Shivaun, confided things she never would have expected. It was clear to her that he still loved Shivaun enormously, also that he was extremely restless, but she felt that all she needed to do was hold fast. There had been some shocks and setbacks – she was appalled by the news that he had quit his job and was thinking of moving abroad – but thus far she was staying one step ahead of him, even managing to circumvent him whenever he mentioned maybe getting in touch with Shivaun.

He couldn't possibly leave the country, nor would he if she could help it. He would stay here and they would get to know each other even better, more intimately, as she continued to provide her shoulder for him to cry on. Not that he had cried on it, literally, but he had appreciated her concern, thanked her for her time and her help, done everything she hoped he would do – except embrace her, so far, or kiss her. But it was early days. That would come in time, when he realised how he had come to depend on her, know her, admire her. Want her. It would all fall into place, if only she could keep him convinced that Shivaun was now involved with Fintan. She knew that had been a major blow to him, to his pride too, a really inspired idea that was having a restraining effect on him. He would never crack, never rush round to see Shivaun if he thought Fintan might open the door to him, and she had given him to understand that Fintan might well open it.

But it was a terrible strain, and Alana really wasn't sure how long she could hold everything together, or hold everyone apart for that matter. Ivor was a wonderful guy, and she was beginning to feel he was noticing her a bit now, paying attention to her in her own right, not just for what comfort she could offer him. In a little while longer they would have said everything there was to be said on the subject of Shivaun Reilly, start talking more about themselves, if only she could somehow carry him through to that point. If only she could get Shivaun – not to put too fine a point on it – out of the way.

That was the only solution, long-term. Too many lies had been told now, too many things said which, if discovered, would ruin her. Ivor would hate her for what she had done, or tried to do, and Shivaun would go ballistic. Shivaun would, at the very least, throw her out of her house and never speak to her again, maybe tell everyone what an evil bitch she was.

But Alana did not think she was a bitch. She thought she had simply made the most of an unexpected, God-given opportunity to have, for once in her life, some love, some affection. Shivaun had had that all of her life, and now it was Alana Kennedy's turn. She ached for Ivor's brown eyes to look her way, really look properly, see everything she had to give him. She would make him a fine wife, devote herself to him, earn his attention, respect and love. But she could never fully enjoy any of those things as long as Shivaun continued to exist, continued to threaten her. She needed to see her way clear through to clinching Ivor and keeping him, and that was why Shivaun would have to go. That was why she was holding, this rare morning when they were both off duty, a scrap of paper in her hand. One small scrap, that could change both their lives.

Sitting down in an armchair opposite Shivaun, Alana smiled and looked enquiringly at her.

'No make-up? No breakfast either, I'll bet?'

'I'm not hungry now. I'll have something later.'

'Oh, Shivaun . . . you know, you're not making much progress at all, are you? Eating, or sleeping, or working, taking any interest in anything.'

Shivaun frowned, curled a strand of hair round the biro in her hand.

'I'm doing my best, Alana, in my own way at my own pace.'

'H'mm . . . well, you know what I think you need?'

'What do you think I need?'

'A break. A complete change of scene.'

Shivaun looked wounded. 'That's what I would be having at this minute if we'd gone to Italy.'

Alana met her gaze, but didn't flinch. 'Yes, but Italy was only for a holiday. What I'm talking about is more than a holiday. It's an adventure! After all, if Ivor can have adventures, why can't you?'

'What do you mean?'

Enticingly she hoped, Alana held out the piece of paper. 'This is the name of a woman who lives in America. In Massachusetts, to be exact. She's had a mild stroke and she's looking for someone to nurse her.'

Shivaun sat forward, looked startled Alana thought, but not combative as she took the piece of paper, read it with her eyebrows raised.

'Marina Darnoux? Gloucester, Mass? Alana, who is she, what is this?'

Alana drew a deep breath, recognising the moment as one of the most potentially important of her life. Somehow, she must hook Shivaun on this proposal.

'Marina Darnoux is, I hear, an architect. A radical architect who designs controversial houses for people all over America.

She's famous. She's even been on *Oprah*, talking about the environment and forests and stuff – mad as a hatter, I reckon, but you might like her.'

'But – Alana, where did you get this? Where did you hear about her?'

Alana had, in fact, gone to a great deal of trouble to find out about Marina Darnoux. She had first bought a stack of American publications, gone through their medical recruitment pages noting down the names of numerous nursing agencies. Then she had contacted them all, from a pay-phone in a post office, to enquire about vacancies. From there she had narrowed down the jobs on offer to half-a-dozen, thought them through until she decided, finally, that the one in Massachusetts sounded most likely to entice Shivaun. Calling back, she pursued her enquiries further and was told by an obliging secretary that Marina Darnoux was 'a lively patient looking for an energetic nurse in a beautiful area'. Furthermore, Ms Darnoux was an architect, very well-known apparently, slightly eccentric but a charming lady who would be 'most rewarding' to nurse. Saying she'd think about it, Alana had hung up, gone to a bookshop and added several American guidebooks to her arsenal. She felt, now, well armed.

'Oh, one of the babies' fathers at the hospital mentioned her to me. He'd heard about St Jude's closing down and thought I might be looking for a job! I told him I wasn't, but that I had a friend who might, got him to write down the name and address – he saw an ad in an American newspaper or something, and put it in his pocket when he was coming in to visit his wife. Wasn't that good of him?'

Shivaun frowned, perplexed. 'Yes, but – it all sounds a bit vague. Besides, I already have a job.'

'Yes, but not at St Jude's any more. You'll be moving to St Peter's, a big hospital you say you don't want to work in. I thought this could be just the break you need, Shivaun. One-to-one nursing with somebody who sounds interesting, sort of on your political wavelength.'

Still frowning, Shivaun peered at the paper again.

'H'mm . . . but where or what is Gloucester? Do you know anything about it?'

'Nothing at all, but I asked my sister Shona – you know she spent a summer waitressing in Massachusetts – and she says it's gorgeous, a little village community near the ocean, kind of arty and bohemian, they're all painters and sculptors and whatnot.'

This was perfectly true, according to the guidebook, and Alana's conscience was clear on this count. It wasn't as if she were trying to shunt Shivaun off to anywhere she wouldn't like; on the contrary, she'd picked somewhere she might very well love, because she didn't want Shivaun coming back disenchanted after a month or two.

Idly, struggling to sound indifferent, she shrugged.

'Anyway, it's just a thought. You seem so fed up lately, not just about Ivor, but about the hospital too . . . about everything, really. A change of scene might perk you up more than you realise, Shivaun.'

A change of scene? Exactly what Ivor had suggested? Shivaun smiled almost bitterly as she recalled her firm refusal to leave St Jude's for the Rockies or Antarctica . . . and then, only two days later, St Jude's had got its closure notice. Christ, if only she'd known in time! The bloody health minister couldn't even get that much right.

And then a thought hit her.

'You know, Alana, Ivor wanted me to go to the Rockies with him. I wonder – I wonder if I called him—'

Alana's jaw dropped. 'If you what?'

'If I called him to tell him about this, to say I'd changed my mind . . . I know the Rockies are nowhere near Massachusetts, but it's still America, isn't it? He might be interested. He might come with me, find some kind of work in the area – Jesus, Alana, you're a genius! This is a brilliant idea!'

Shivaun jumped up, her eyes sparkling, and Alana felt as if she'd been impaled on a skewer. Oh, God – oh how – oh, *no*!

How she got a grip on her whirling mind she had no idea, but somehow she did. Somehow, she managed to stay vertical, sound normal as she said the first thing that came into her head.

'Oh, Shivaun . . . I'm so sorry . . . I thought you knew.'

Shivaun paused halfway, it appeared, to the telephone.

'Knew what?'

'Knew that Ivor – Ivor has gone away.'

Shivaun whitened, stood like a statue. 'Gone? Away? To where?'

'I don't know – someone down at the pub just mentioned that he chucked his job and – and bought a one-way ticket to somewhere. I think it may have been Australia. He left a week ago or more, I hear.'

Not answering, Shivaun stood pinned to the floor, and they stared at each other in mutual shock. Alana felt her legs trembling, but even then she held on: If Shivaun investigated, and found that Ivor had not gone anywhere, she could simply say oh well, it was only hearsay.

But Shivaun stood transfixed. So. Ivor had gone away, had he? Left the country, without even bothering to tell her, to say goodbye, to make one last effort? Their twenty years weren't even worth that much?

Trembling, she sank back down on the sofa, the insurance form still in one hand, Alana's scrap of paper in the other.

'I didn't know' she whispered. 'I never knew that.'

Alana mustered what she hoped was a comforting smile. 'Maybe nobody wanted to tell you. You were upset enough, already. Or maybe you just haven't been out enough lately to hear the local gossip. I heard it myself, but I was just trying to be tactful. I thought you must know but you weren't mentioning it, so I didn't either.'

Shivaun couldn't reply. Her mind was blank with shock, her heart was missing beats. Alana gazed at her.

'I think I'd better make you a hot cup of tea.'

The afternoon was shading into evening, turning stormy, by the time Shivaun felt sufficiently recovered to pull on a jacket, go out to her car, and drive away to no particular destination. All she knew was that she needed somewhere quiet, someplace to think, piece together the shattered pieces of her existence and examine them.

Eventually, after an hour and a near miss with a hurtling hay lorry, she found herself up on Dublin's north-east coast, unfamiliar terrain somewhere around Lusk, Skerries, Balbriggan. Spotting a lay-by overlooking the sea, she pulled in and sat in the car, thinking.

Ivor was gone. Really gone. Her mind played on that for as long as she could bear. And then she thought of St Jude's, her hospital . . . gone, also, in a few weeks' time. Viv and Jimmy . . . gone. Her other parents, her blood parents . . . long gone.

She felt as if her entire world had collapsed, vanished from between her two hands. In its place she was holding empty air, grasping at nothingness. The faces of all the babies she had delivered smudged and melded in her mind, warped into a caricature; the hopes she had had, the battles she had fought . . . all useless, all chimera, all for nothing.

The only thing she could clearly see was the ocean, churning and stretching away to Wales, far up to the violet hulk of the Mourne mountains. Her home was here in Dublin, but she felt adrift, alienated from the city that was becoming so corrupt, violent, greedy and snobbish. She'd resisted these things for as long as she could, spoken out and taken action, but she'd encountered hostility in return, from many people happy to ignore the ugly underbelly in exchange for designer labels and ritzy restaurants. Turning to her right, she could see the city from where she sat, looking heartbreakingly beautiful as the evening lights began to twinkle all around its horseshoe shape, glittering like a fairy necklace. In this city people were dressing up for a night out on the town, while the homeless cast about for doorways to sleep in. Some child was playing with a thousand pounds worth of computer equipment, while some old lady died alone in a rat-infested hovel. Some politician was sipping his first claret of the evening, while a young mother watched her child die for lack of medical resources.

That was Dublin, today. That was her home town, her birthplace, changing out of all recognition, and she felt isolated in her disquietude, which was shared by so few. Clenching her fists, she forced herself to think of the good things as well: the sense of fun, the friendliness and the wonderful neighbourliness. Just when you thought you could throttle everyone, someone would turn around and do you a great goodness. There was still much warmth, so much kindness in many people.

And there was always the craic, the music, the lovely natural setting around the bay below the hills. Today, for the first time in living memory, Dubliners had work and money, employment was at full capacity and life was sweet for those with the strength to ransack its rewards. People had more than the necessities now, they had multiple holidays, exotic food, enormous cars, landscaped villas, prizes once only glimpsed on American or British television.

So why, then, was it necessary to bake cakes and trek to Thailand to keep your local hospital open? Why was it necessary to close it? Why were public monies pumping into tribunals, investigations of endless frauds and rackets? Even those convicted of corruption never went to prison, while criminals lolled in luxury hotels . . . including Jason Dean, the youth who killed Jimmy Reilly. He was a murderer, but he'd only got five years in a detention centre, plus counselling and sympathy for his drug problem. His problem wasn't as great as Jimmy's though; he wasn't buried in Deansgrange cemetery, dead of a stab wound through his heart.

He was very much alive. He was due, as Ivor had said, to get out soon and get on with his life. With every ounce of her force Shivaun wanted to grab him by the wrist as he left the centre and drag him all the way to Jimmy's grave, shove him right to the edge of it and shout 'Look! Look what you've done! This was my dad, my dad who I loved, and my mum is buried with him, she died too because she was distraught, and you've never even said sorry, you bastard!'

No. He had never even said sorry. He had shuffled and mumbled in court and let his lawyer explain to the jury what a fine young man he was really, no previous convictions, came from a fine family . . . but he had destroyed the Reilly family, stabbed all three of them through the heart. To this day she had never spoken to anyone of her feelings for him, because she hated him so much for what he had done. She was consumed with pain and fury, the more she tried to push it down the more it surged up in her. God *damn* him! Five years after her parents' deaths she was no nearer to forgiving, and would never forget. But these were thoughts you couldn't voice, because they sounded anti-social; besides which there were enough whining voices everywhere today, moaning about miserable childhoods and grievances going back into infinity, what was to be gained by joining their wretched ranks? Self-pity was pointless and she would not contribute to its rising tide.

But she knew Jason Dean was the reason why she was sitting here now in the twilight, shivering, her life lying like dust in her lap. She was not the same person she would have been had her parents lived, she was marked and changed. After they died she had tried to channel her anger into diversionary activities, but she had been driven by that anger nonetheless, it gripped her and seethed in her heart. And now, the prospect of Jason Dean's freedom was suffocating her, she could not endure the thought of him roaming loose. Without Ivor she felt exposed, emotionally naked and vulnerable.

Alana's idea of going to America had sounded strange to her; once again she had the sensation of being somehow manoeuvred, propelled out of the way – of what? But she hadn't rejected it outright, because she saw that, whatever the reason, it had merit too. Her life in Ireland was at a crossroads, it had taken a wrong turning five years ago and now she was lost. Everything, her relationship with Ivor, her work at St Jude's, even her friendship with Alana and other people, could all be traced back to Jason Dean, to the enormity and influence of what he had done. In a way she was his prisoner, his one action dictated her entire direction, her development in the years that had followed.

Now, she knew, she had to break free. Even as he came

back into society she had to get away from him, exorcise him, cleanse herself of the pain and the fury which, otherwise, would consume her. She would belong to him, be his prisoner for ever, if she didn't resist, didn't act. Somehow she was going to have to reclaim her life, live it as Viv and Jimmy would wish her to live it, reconstruct the entire edifice.

America? What she knew of it was conflicting: fabulous landscapes and terrible massacres, blazing sun and lethal blizzards, huge wealth and horrendous poverty. Like any country, it was a kaleidoscope. But it was a new country, a new horizon, and as she thought of it she felt something stirring in her, responding. She could do it, if she tried. She could go.

For an hour, perhaps two, she sat looking out over the city and the sea, thinking of Ivor, and Jimmy, and St Jude's with its cots full of milky babies. Babies she had once thought of as templates for the ones she would have with Ivor, and now never would. Babies destined to replenish other lives, enrich other families. She could barely remember, any more, what it felt like to have a family.

'The first of October?' Alana gasped. 'But that's hardly a month away.'

'That's right. I'll be just in time to see the autumn foliage. They said it's absolutely spectacular. Out on the coast it goes right on until Hallowe'en . . . look, I picked up this bumpf from a travel agency, let me tell you what it says.'

Simultaneously exhilarated and shocked by the speed at which Shivaun was suddenly moving, Alana waited while she rummaged in an envelope, extracted a brochure and began to read aloud.

'Hike, cycle, canoe or ride a horse through the farms and hillsides tinted with gold, crimson, pink and scarlet . . . wade through the crunching leaves to a roadside stall piled with fat orange pumpkins . . . match the colours of the leaves to the species of the trees.'

'Huh?'

'You get yellow leaves on elm, beech, birch and maple trees. Scarlet leaves mean it's a cherry or oak. The berry bushes turn crimson . . . doesn't it sound beautiful? I can't wait to get there!'

Alana was left breathless by the speed of it all. She wanted Shivaun to go, go soon before she ran into Ivor and discovered the awful, massive lie she had told, and she wanted Ivor to herself at last, once and for all. But surely it couldn't all happen just like that, snap, decision taken, bags packed?

'What about getting a visa? How do you do it?'

'You apply to the embassy. You need a sponsor – Marina Darnoux, obviously, is mine. Her secretary says there won't be a problem.'

'Uh-huh. And what about the house? You're not going to sell it, are you?'

Shivaun looked at her, somewhat accusingly.

'It's my family home. I have no intention of selling it. Instead I'm going to leave you in charge, you can have the whole place to yourself for a year.'

Wow. Alana could scarcely believe her luck as Shivaun clutched her 'bumpf' and thought for a moment, speculatively.

'I tell you what. Marina Darnoux is offering a good salary, so I'll waive your rent if in return you'll look after the house for me. But I mean look after it properly, Alana, OK? I don't want to come home to a shambles.'

What? No rent? But then – then she could even buy a car! Alana was so thrilled she actually felt a twinge of guilt.

'No way. No shambles. You can rely on me, Shivaun, I'll keep this place looking like a five-star hotel.'

Shivaun nodded. 'I hope so. I hope I can rely on you in everything, Alana.'

Crikey. What did she mean by that? Nothing, probably; it was just guilt that was making her feel as if Shivaun could see clear through her. But Shivaun couldn't possibly know, or remotely guess, that Ivor Lawlor was soon going to be living here. Living here by Christmas if she, Alana, had anything to do with it.

'Will you be coming home for Christmas, d'you think?'

'No. Ms Darnoux's secretary made it clear that I'm expected to stay for a full year. That's how long it'll take her to be independent again, her doctor reckons.'

'H'mm. How did you clinch the job anyway, with your midwifery experience? I was afraid – I mean, I thought that might hold you back.'

'I simply explained to the agency that I had full general training, and invited them to contact Matron as well as Dr O'Hara and two referees from my student days. If I say so myself, my references are pretty good. I'll still have to bone up a bit on neurology, of course, but most of the work will involve basic nursing and – and common sense! After all the woman is out of hospital now, only seeing her doctor once a week, I'll mostly be doing rehab therapy. She can walk and speak pretty well, but she's still not fully co-ordinated. Needs help dressing, bathing, eating, that kind of thing.'

'Was she able to read that e-mail you sent her?'

'Yes, of course! She's convalescent, not incapacitated. Actually I think it was the e-mail that clinched the job. We got on really well when she wrote back – took her ages, mind you, because her left arm is banjaxed so she had to write one-handed. But she was funny about it, said she could still pick off a poacher at forty paces if she had to, with her shotgun!'

'*Shotgun?* Jesus, Shivaun, I didn't think Massachusetts was the wild west.'

'Oh, she was only joking! She's an architect for God's sake, barely an hour from Boston. Hardly a hillbilly.'

'I suppose. Did she mention what the weather is like?'

'Yes. It sounds like a real bonus. Four clear distinct seasons, hot in summer, cold in winter, no more endless grey cloud.'

'So – so are you looking forward to going, then?'

'Yes. Now that I've made my mind up, I am. I know Americans are different, don't have our sense of humour in some respects, and I'm vehemently opposed to their gun laws, but I'm going with my mind wide open. After all, they think Ireland is a quaint little farmyard full of piglets and pixies, so maybe our image of America is equally crazy. It'll be interesting to find out.'

Alana almost hugged herself. This was going great. Shivaun seemed genuinely enthusiastic, even eager to depart for Massachusetts. But then, there was so little to keep her here. She would be better off.

'Are you going to have a party before you leave?'

Shivaun reflected. And then she grinned unexpectedly, hugely.

'Yeah. Let's do that. Let's celebrate new places, new faces. You can do the food and Larry Macken can bring his guitar, let's have some laughs – hey, Alana, tell me straight, have I been a pain to live with lately?'

Alana thought Shivaun looked truculent, suddenly, her eyes were glinting and her colour rising. There was a new verve to her voice she'd never heard before, as welcome as it was surprising.

'Oh, who cares – a party's just the job to cheer you up. Who'll we invite? Will we do a big spread, or just pizza stuff?'

Shivaun waved her hand. 'Anything. Just so long as there's lots of music and booze. I'm getting a shot at a new country and a new life, let's go for broke – Jesus, I can't wait to go!'

Alana was startled, and delighted. 'Lucky you! I've never been anywhere near America.'

'Well, it's out there and it can only be better than this hellhole. Go on, answer my question – have I been driving you round the twist? I know I'm out of tune with Ireland and I'm shattered about Ivor . . . has it all been gruesome, have I been a nightmare?'

She laughed challengingly, and Alana decided to pull her punches. Shivaun sounded so weird, so giddy, it was like watching a banked ember explode into flames.

'No. You haven't been that, because I know what's wrong with you. You're worn out. This year in America is going to be very good for you, Shivaun. Therapeutic. You'll forget all about St Jude's and Ivor and have a great time, maybe even find yourself a new man.'

Privately, Alana prayed that she would. That would be ideal. Perfect. But Shivaun picked up the cheese knife and traced little figures with it on the cheeseboard.

'Oh, no. That's the one thing I won't do, Alana. I will give Marina Darnoux my best shot and give America my best shot, but I won't find any new man. I loved Ivor Lawlor with all my heart for twenty years and nobody will ever replace him.'

'But—'

'But what?'

'But – I mean – he treated you so badly! You should forget all about him and find yourself some nice American. Some hunk in cowboy boots and a Stetson.'

Shivaun looked at her quizzically. 'But Alana, you don't seem to understand. I still *love* Ivor.'

Yes. Yes, of course she did. Shivaun Reilly had the tenacity of a mule. Stubborn to the bitter end. But it needn't be bitter, if only Shivaun would yield a little, not cling to Ivor until her last gasp, in that – that *adamant* way of hers.

'So, you love him still, huh? And what has your love got you, only a broken heart and a ticket to America?'

Abruptly, Shivaun grasped the knife by its hilt and plunged it into the wooden cheeseboard, so hard it quivered.

'Maybe! But that's my business! You don't know the first thing about how I feel, Alana, you really don't! I knew Ivor long before I knew you, knew him since he was a little boy in short pants and I tell you—'

Alana quailed. 'Tell me what?'

As suddenly as it had hardened, Shivaun's face softened again. But her tone did not.

'I tell you I love him. In spite of everything, because that's what love is. It doesn't change with circumstances or with moods or with external things. It simply *is*.'

They faced each other, but neither spoke. Shivaun, as she thought of Ivor, was unable to speak. And Alana, as she also thought of Ivor, began to glimpse for the first time a vista of just what she might be up against. If Ivor felt as fixedly about Shivaun as she evidently still did about him, it would be no easy matter to divert him, make him focus on her.

But then, Shivaun had always been the serious one, Ivor the sunny one. He was made of lighter, brighter stuff, didn't mope over things or pine for them, didn't *cling* to them. His grip on Shivaun, on her memory, would soon be prised loose, or relax of its own accord.

It was merely a matter of time, of continuing the strategy which so far was working like a charm. And how furious Ivor would be, when he heard that Shivaun had gone to America! She wouldn't go with me, he would say, and now she's gone by herself? What kind of logic is that, where's the loyalty there? As she envisaged his face darkening, Alana's brightened to its rosiest.

'All right, then. You love him. If you say so. I think you're a fool, Shivaun, but let's not quarrel. He's not worth it. After all he didn't even live here full-time, whereas you and I have shared this house for over four years. I'd hate for you to leave on a bum note. I'm going to miss you, you know. I want us to part as friends.'

She not only felt she could afford to be magnanimous, she wanted to be. Now that Shivaun was about to leave she was conscious of how fond of her she'd actually become over the years; even though she sometimes thought Shivaun was a mad crank and nicknamed her Victor Meldrew, she looked up to her and craved her approval. Her affection, too, which had warmed her bleak life in Dublin for so long. It was a shame about the Ivor situation, and already some part of her was trying to work out ways of making amends for that; meanwhile, she truly hoped that Shivaun would enjoy America and find some happiness there. It dawned on her that she could never be fully happy herself, if it was to be at the expense of someone she liked and admired, who even now was being so good to her.

Chapter Five

It was raining daggers as Shivaun hoisted her luggage into her car and handed the keys to Alana.

'Here. You may as well drive, it'll be practice for coming back.'

Alana nodded nervously and got into the Mazda with more than a little trepidation. Being given the use of this car for a year was terrific, and her brother Ciarán had taught her to drive years ago, but she was very rusty. What if she reversed into the pillar behind her, or made a horse's hash of the M50? Worse, what if she returned from the airport to find the house burgled, or flooded or in flames?

'Jesus. This is scary.'

'Oh, just do it!'

Hastily she started the engine, and Shivaun swallowed. She didn't mean to bark at Alana, but she did want to get out and go, right now. She couldn't bear to sit looking at the house while Alana fumbled and stalled, left her to gaze at the roses Jimmy had planted, the hall door Viv had painted a once-shocking shade of scarlet . . . Shutting her eyes, she did not open them again until they had travelled half a mile, and the house had disappeared.

Alana glanced at her. 'You OK?'

She would not cry. She would not. She nodded vehemently. 'Yeah. I'm fine.'

'Good. I know it's a wrench, but it really is for the best, Shivaun. You'll have a ball in the States.'

Yes. America was, in every sense, another country. It was new, it was fresh, it was hers to make of it what she could and would. She felt weepy, confused and absurd, and laughed suddenly. Shakily.

'What's funny?'

'Oh . . . I just sort of feel like a pilgrim setting out in the *Mayflower*! It landed at Plymouth Rock you know, not far from where Marina Darnoux lives.'

'I tell you what. If I ask – someone – to show me how to use the computer, will you send me an e-mail? Tell me all about this place when you get there?'

'Yeah. But I won't write every day. For one thing I'll need to concentrate on work a lot at first, and for another, I want a clean break. I don't want to look back over my shoulder at all.'

'No. You have to look forward. Forget Ivor and St Jude's and everything else, move on.'

Shivaun didn't reply, wanting desperately to move on, get through the traffic and reach the airport, *go*. The trip took well over an hour, but eventually they reached it, and she gathered her strength.

'Well, here we are. I think – I think it's better if you don't come in, Alana. Just let me get my stuff and get on with it, we won't have any weepy goodbyes, OK?'

Alana found she actually did feel emotional, and swallowed.

'Yeah. OK. Just – just c'mere and give me a quick hug.'

Shivaun turned, embraced her briefly but hard.

'Take care of yourself – and that house of mine, all right?'

'Yeah. And you take care of yourself too, kid.'

Shivaun jumped out, grabbed her bags and whirled away without another word. For a few minutes Alana sat with the engine running, looking after her until she vanished into the departures area, thinking how sassily confident she looked in her new blue linen duster coat – and how vulnerable, under it, how alone. It must really be a dreadful thing to have no family, no relatives at all to wave you off. Poor Shivaun.

Biting her lip, she drove away, not knowing what to make of her mixed emotions. It had all happened so fast, but now the reality of it dawned on her, the realisation that she was on her own . . . very much on her own, for at least a year, if she did not succeed in seducing Ivor Lawlor. Her mind flew to him immediately and, as she struggled to cope with the unfamiliar car, she had a thought. She would go to the parking area over near the Naul, alongside the runways where you could watch the planes taking off.

Why, she hardly knew. But an incoming plane indicated the direction the flights were taking today, and she drove to the other, outbound runway, parked the car amidst a bunch of bincocular-equipped aviation buffs. On their short-wave radios she could even hear pilots talking to air traffic control, there was a kind of surreality to the scene.

But there was nothing surreal about the huge plane that glided out, over an hour later, onto the runway. Alana knew it must be Shivaun's flight, it was the right time and the right airline, and it stopped almost in front of her for its final check, awaiting take-off clearance. Then, with a massive surge of power, it unleashed the full force of its engines and raced down the tarmac, lifted up into the sky with the majesty of a magnificent eagle.

Alana's hands clenched, her whole body grew taut as she watched it swoop up and away, up into the clouds that would reveal brilliant blue above, the rain all gone and the sun beckoning. It was time, she thought, that the sun shone for Shivaun.

And for her. At long last the coast was clear, Shivaun was gone and nothing stood between her and Ivor Lawlor. Nothing at all. With a huge smile she started the car and drove off, already wondering what to wear when she phoned him tonight to invite him round for dinner.

Dinner! With candles, with Ivor, at last! *Yes!*

As the plane reached Canadian landfall and began the final stage of its journey down America's east coast, Shivaun pulled her seat upright and gritted her teeth, making decisions.

At this moment, leaving her country and gaining a new one, she felt reluctant in some ways, eager in others, a mixture of apprehension and optimism. But she had set her course and she would stick with it, give America a chance and give herself a chance. At her farewell party everyone had warned her she would feel lonely at first, until she met local people and made new friends. But she would meet them. As for Marina Darnoux . . . private patients had a reputation for being difficult, nursing them was rarely easy, but she was resolved to smile one long relentless smile at the woman until she won her over. After all she would be living in Marina's house, it was vital that they get on together. As for America itself . . . at this moment it was far too busy worrying about Bill Clinton to care less about her. Personally she thought Clinton should be impeached for the lies he'd told about Monica Lewinsky, but that was America's business, not hers. For once she must zip her lip and let other people do the shouting. America was not her country and she was not responsible for it in any way . . . that in itself was a liberating thought. Instead of engaging in public battles she would be free to repair and reconstruct her private life, learn somehow to live again, eradicate the constantly resurgent memory of Ivor Lawlor.

I will not think of Ivor. I must not think of him, at any time, in any way. He's gone, gone for good, I don't even know for sure what country he's in. He doesn't know I'm on my way to this one. Our paths have diverged and I must break free of the memories, put him behind me.

Oh, *Ivor.*

With resolute effort she turned to look out the window, caught her first sight of Massachusetts as it came into view below. Here and there she could see patches of gold and yellow, tinged with rich shades of chestnut and ochre . . . the autumn foliage, that she'd been told would be beautiful. And it was beautiful; her heart lifted as the plane dipped through the bright blue sky, heading into Logan airport where 'someone' was to meet her. Marina's secretary had been a bit vague about who exactly, said only that it was a man and she'd know him when she saw him.

And then buildings came into view, massed chunks of grey and white, crowded together along the edge of the sea. She was glad Massachusetts was a maritime state, like Dublin, she would be able to breathe salt air and walk on the sand whenever she wanted to. You could see the beach, Marina had said, from the upstairs windows of her house, there were gulls and fishing boats, headland walks all round the tip of Cape Ann. It was an invigorating place, she would love it.

Shivaun made up her mind to love it, buckled her seat belt and went with the flow as the plane banked, dropped and came in to land with a roar of engines, a sense of arrival and anticipation. It had been a long flight, but here she was, ready to meet America halfway and make the most of the renewal it offered. Gathering up her bag and coat, she joined the disembarking throng and took her first step onto American soil.

The airport was vast and crowded, but she made her way through immigration, retrieved her luggage and headed out into the arrivals area where, to her relief, she almost immediately spotted a dapper black man holding a neat white card with her name on it. She went up to him, and he held out his hand, shook hers enthusiastically.

'Ms Reilly? I'm Joe Santana. I'll be taking you to Ms Darnoux – here, let me help with that baggage! My, you ladies bring plenty, don't you?'

She grinned and let him take charge of her four suitcases, one for each season. With an air of knowing his way around, he wheeled the trolley to a parking area outside and clicked his keys in the direction of a sleek grey car. Immediately, the lid of its boot lifted up.

'I can put everything in the trunk? Nothing fragile in these bags, no?'

No. Not in the bags. She shook her head, and he indicated the back seat of the car.

'OK. You get in there and make yourself comfortable.'

Obediently she slid in, and registered a degree of comfort verging on opulence. Was this car from some kind of taxi service, or was Joe Santana Marina Darnoux's personal driver, or what?

As he got into the front, started the engine and swung the car with quiet ease towards the exit, he looked back at her in the mirror.

'This your first visit to Boston, Ms Reilly?'

'Yes.' She wanted to tell him to call her Shivaun, but wasn't sure whether it would be appropriate. He was wearing a suit and had a vaguely formal aura despite his friendliness.

'Well, you won't see much of the city today, but you can come back in on your days off, it's a fine sight when all the yachts are out on the Charles river, you have to visit Quincy Market and do the Freedom Trail . . .'

Freedom Trail. She liked the sound of that, and said so.

'Oh yes, you can walk it, you'll see Faneuil Hall and Paul Revere's house, Old North Church . . . then you can do the Black Heritage Trail as well, that'll take you up Beacon Hill where my folks come from.'

She looked around her as they made their way into traffic, feeling a surge of interest and excitement although he said they were in east Boston, not the centre; wherever it was, it looked lively and attractive, the day was crisp and bright, with autumnal warmth still in the sun. Driving slowly, with attention to speed limits and traffic lights, Joe indicated distant points of interest and gave her a potted history of the city, punctuated with little anecdotes that made her laugh. He smiled back at her in the mirror.

'Glad to see you've got a sense of humour, Ms Reilly. Ms Darnoux's got one too.'

'Has she? Tell me more about her, please – do you know her well?'

He nodded. 'Oh yes. I do. I've worked for her ever since she came to Massachusetts fifteen years ago.'

'Oh. So she wasn't born here?'

'No. She came from California, right after her divorce. Said she'd had enough of all those West Coast picallilies and was ready for civilisation. She's a very civilised lady, though not everyone might say so. She speaks her mind, and I like that in a lady. You'll find her very fair and honest to work for.'

He chatted on, with candour and yet discretion, and it struck Shivaun that this man seemed very loyal to his employer, that she inspired admiration in him, even affection. She hadn't known Marina was divorced, but he filled in the picture for her.

'Her husband was an architect too, and she started out as an interior designer originally. They had a joint practice in L.A., made a lot of money. But then she got interested in architecture and decided to study it herself at UCLA – he didn't like that at all. When she graduated and started getting her own clients, her own commissions, he got jealous. Saw her as his rival instead of his partner . . . anyway, they split up. It wasn't what you'd call amicable. Matter of fact it was World War III.'

He winked at her. 'But I'd better let her tell you the rest herself, if she chooses to. You comfortable back there?'

Yes. Shivaun was comfortable, and curious, increasingly eager to meet Marina Darnoux, the apparent survivor of a break-up like herself. Not that she and Ivor had broken bitterly, or *divorced*, but she felt as if they had. The pain must be much the same for everyone, whatever the circumstances.

The car was leaving the city now, gliding out into gorgeous countryside dotted with grey clapboard houses and small white churches, the trees massing into a vivid flame-coloured canopy under the cloudless blue sky; here and there children jumped and raced through piles of leaves, shaking the branches for chestnuts, laughing, their faces glowing. Little villages came and went, one clustered around a duckpond, others spread out in a way that suggested that land was plentiful. Shivaun was struck by how clean they all were, not swish or fussy but comfortable-looking, cosy and tended, with bikes and rocking chairs out on verandahs as if no-one would steal them. Many of the houses were built entirely of wood, either whitewashed or left to weather naturally, turn to a pale ash tone set off by shutters painted mostly blue.

'This is so pretty! Is Gloucester one of these villages, Mr Santana – I mean, does it have houses like these?'

'Yes, up to a point. It has a lot of shingle houses, some quite big ones, but it's right on the ocean, the atmosphere is different . . . you like fried clams, Ms Reilly?'

She laughed. 'I don't know! I've never had them.'

'Well, you will. I tell you, there's nothing to beat the taste of a fried clam, straight out of the ocean. Dorothy may well serve some for supper tonight.'

'Who's Dorothy?'

'She's the cook. Been with Ms Darnoux nearly as long as I have myself.'

Cook? This household sounded larger than she'd realised.

'How many people work for Ms Darnoux, altogether?'

'Oh, just us two, and Azalea her secretary—'

'Azalea? Like the flower? I never heard it used as a name before.'

'No, well, I guess in Ireland the girls are all Moiras and Brigids, huh? Azalea is Native American, from Mohawk territory up north.'

Shivaun had spoken to this secretary on the phone, but not known her exotic name or origins, and now her interest was piqued.

'Anyone else?'

'Only Patrick the gardener, but he's part-time, sort of a consultant, has his own landscaping business over in Lowell. There are a couple of dogs too, big boxers called Jiffy and Daffy – I hope you like dogs, ma'am, because these two are the household gods.'

'I'm glad you warned me. I'd better get to like them.'

Shivaun sat back, thinking about all these unexpected people she hadn't known she'd be living amongst, while Joe drove through rolling open farmland, unhedged, not dark green like Ireland's but golden, sun-warmed, full of recently-harvested fields and orchards bobbing red with apples.

Some line from an old school poem came to her, something about 'the alien corn' – but, although it was different, this land did not feel alien. It felt warm and welcoming and so far she was experiencing none of the disorientation she'd expected. Joe was kind and sociable and, for a newly-arrived immigrant, she was getting off to as good a start as could possibly be hoped for.

Of course, she had yet to meet Marina Darnoux. Their first meeting – in cyberspace! – had gone well, but still something told her Marina was the kind of woman you either loved or hated. She could only pray it would be the former.

Expecting something in keeping with a 'radical architect', Shivaun was astonished when, finally, the car turned into the driveway of an old, enormous house, built of what Joe called shingle. Surrounded by lawns and trees, it was three storeys high, with many white-shuttered windows and a walkway running the entire length of the top storey, from which white wood pillars ran down under a grey-shingled porch. Although she could not see the ocean she could hear and smell it, knew that it could not be more than half a mile away . . . but what a house! Despite its size it fitted completely into the landscape, was bigger than many but no different in design. Far from being radical, it looked traditional, almost historic, the kind of place where smugglers and sea-captains might once have burned the midnight oil.

And there, standing on its porch, stood a woman who could only be Marina Darnoux. Supporting herself on the rail with one hand, she was waving with the other, shouting something as Shivaun got out of the car and waved back.

'Hello! Darling child, come up here and let me look at you!'

Taken aback, Shivaun gazed up at her. Whatever greeting she had expected, it was not 'darling child'. Nor had she expected to hear it uttered with such clarity, outdoors, from a woman who did not look at all like an invalid. Far from being frail, Marina Darnoux was an utter vision of beauty and vigour.

As she came closer, her trained eye did detect the signs of Marina's stroke; the waving but damaged arm she couldn't raise higher than her shoulder, the slightly lopsided tilt to her face. But Marina was a tall, elegant, vibrantly beautiful woman. Somewhere in her mid to late forties, she wore her abundant dark hair piled high off her face, exposing magnificent cheekbones, a long slender neck and large, quick eyes that seemed to be assessing everything, keenly and humorously. From her earlobes dangled two miniature violet waterfalls – amethyst earrings, each a good two inches long, tinkling in the breeze with an almost rakish air. Her commanding frame was not so much dressed as draped in a long navy velvet robe, with a crimson silk scarf floating down to its crimson cuffs, matched by her crimson lipstick. As Shivaun mounted the steps she could smell perfume, too, some exotic spicy fragrance such as, perhaps, Opium.

'Hello, Ms Darnoux! I'm Shivaun Reilly.'

'Marina, darling, call me Marina! Come inside, Joe will look after your things, Dorothy has your room ready – but first you must come and have a sherry, relax after your long journey.'

Marina embraced her lightly and then turned, looking for something that Shivaun immediately spotted, a brass-handled walking stick hanging over the porch rail. Picking it up, she gave it to Marina and automatically put her hand under the woman's elbow to help her. Walking, she could already see, was not easy for this dramatic-looking lady. But Marina grimaced impatiently.

'Oh, never mind, never mind, come along, you must be dying for a drink!'

Leading the way with a somehow regal air, she moved slowly but purposefully through the huge hallway of the house, which was both floored and panelled in wood, imposing in size but cluttered with books, papers, beach boots, fishing rods and a pair of oars leaning bizarrely up into one corner. Its atmosphere was nautical, but a huge vase of fresh wild flowers spilled softly under the light streaming through a window, a green-shaded banker's lamp illuminated a glossy oak table, and from where

Shivaun stood she could see through into a big, bright lounge filled with sunlight. As she looked, two gigantic dogs shot out of it and hurled themselves on her, barking wildly.

Jesus! If she hadn't known to expect them, she'd have been petrified; as it was she managed an idiot grin as she tried to peel the paws of the larger, darker one off her shoulders. It was licking her face, slobbering all down her linen coat. Marina raised her stick a fraction, and barked at it.

'Jiffy! Get down immediately!'

Looking abashed, Jiffy got down and joined the other dog, which was racing around Shivaun's ankles in frantic circles.

'The smaller one's Daffy, they're quite harmless – sorry about your coat, but don't worry, Dorothy will see to it. Now, young lady, come in here to the library, sit down and tell me, how are things in Gloccamorra?'

Shivaun sat, in a chintzy flowered armchair, and laughed. 'Things in Gloccamorra are insane. Ireland has lost the run of itself completely.'

Also sitting, Marina raised an eyebrow. 'Is that so? What's happened to it?'

'Oh – crime, fraud, taxes, tribunals, a new scandal every day. It's a circus. I think America might actually be calmer by comparison – what little I've seen so far looks lovely.'

'Yes. This is a very nice part of America – you must go down to the beach, later, and take a stroll through the village, the fishing boats will be coming in. But first, a drink, a welcome toast – will you have sherry, or do you prefer something else?'

Marina's accent was quite distinctly American, but it wasn't a drawl; under the slight slur that Shivaun recognised as the result of the stroke, it was crisp and cultured, pearly. At her feet, the two dogs settled panting, giving her a matriarchal air.

'Sherry would be great, thank you. If I'm not on duty yet – I don't drink when I'm working!'

Marina laughed. 'Well, maybe you will, after a few weeks of nursing me! My current nurse is leaving, as you know, that's why I needed you – not that I want any nurse at all to be perfectly frank, this whole business is a colossal bore.'

Shivaun surveyed her. 'Well, I must say, you don't look too bad to me. It's what – ten weeks now, since your stroke?'

'Yes. It was only mild, but – oh, good, here's Dorothy. Dorothy, this is Shivaun, the poor girl is gasping for a drink.'

Dorothy, apparently the housekeeper as well as cook, smiled and shook hands with her. A large woman of about fifty, she had a capable aura and a no-nonsense handshake.

'Welcome, Shivaun. Let me take your coat while you settle in and get acquainted with Marina. Dinner's not until seven, but if you're hungry I can fix you a snack.'

'Oh, no thanks, I ate on the plane—'

But Marina was peering at her as she took off her coat, inspecting her with a look that verged on horror.

'Good God, girl, you're thin as a pin! Dorothy, make her a sandwich right away, and after that she'll have a big bowl of Ben and Jerry's.'

Ben and Jerry's what? Shivaun had no idea, but she decided not to cavil. Marina was being hospitable, and Dorothy had already poured their drinks, gone bustling off to the kitchen. Shivaun lifted her glass and looked to see whether Marina needed help with hers. But she didn't.

'No, my right arm is fine, I only have trouble with the left. I'm sorry I can't join you in a sherry, but the damn doctor rations me to one glass of wine a day, so I save it for dinner in the evenings. However, here's to you, Shivaun, welcome to Chederlay. This has been my home for fifteen years and I hope you're going to be happy here.'

Shivaun sipped and smiled. 'Chederlay is a beautiful house, Marina. But it's totally different to what I expected.'

'Yes. Let me guess. You envisaged some modernist monstrosity in glass and steel? Or a chunk of concrete with windows the size of pinpricks?'

'Well – I'm not sure what! Something less traditional, less – less homey.'

It was very homey. The room in which they sat was hung with numerous oil paintings, photographs in gilded frames, there was a fireplace with tartan footstools strewn in front of it, the armchairs were deep and comfortable, an old dresser stood by the wall piled with rose-patterned china, candles and bric-à-brac. Despite its length and high ceiling, Shivaun felt at ease in it.

'Well, you see, I design a wide variety of houses for my clients. Some are really extraordinary, they vary from the innovative to the truly spectacular. So I need a restful home myself, one that doesn't distract me or make my mind work overtime. People are always surprised when they see Chederlay, but I find it a necessary contrast to all the madness around me. Half of my clients are barking mad, you know.'

Shivaun laughed. Marina certainly looked eccentric, in all her flowing fabrics, but she sounded quite sane. When Dorothy came in with her sandwich, she suddenly realised she was hungry, and accepted it gratefully, blinking at the size of it. An entire mini-deli seemed to be packed inside. Taking a bite, she looked around her.

'What beautiful bits and pieces you have!'

'Yes. They're called *objets d'art*. Some are family heirlooms, others I picked up at auctions or markets on my travels. I normally travel quite a lot . . . one of the few benefits of being grounded is that I get to see the full fall this year. Aren't the trees stunning?'

Yes. They surely were. Shivaun gazed out at them, thinking how Jimmy would love them, be able to tell her each species . . . but she had come here to work, not daydream.

'Please tell me more about your stroke, Marina. How restricted are you exactly, how are you feeling generally?'

'Oh, it's just a nuisance, that's all! I have to work on my arm, get off this damn stick and learn to stop talking like a drunk. I can't do up zips or buttons or lift things, or drive, which is making me crazy. But I feel fine and do not wish to be treated like an invalid.'

'OK. You're not an invalid, then. We'll look on you as an athlete who needs to be got back into peak condition. After I've met your doctor we'll set up a training programme, as rigorous as you like and he permits. Or is your doctor a woman?'

Marina's eyes twinkled. 'No, he's a man – a Harvard hunk who would be upstairs tied to the bedposts if he were not unfortunately encumbered with a wife.'

Shivaun stared, and giggled. 'What?'

'He's a dish. I could do him serious damage if – oh, well, never mind. You'll meet him on Monday. And you'll meet my current nurse, Lena, at dinner tonight, I suppose you'd better have a chat with her before she goes. Awful woman. I'll be glad to see the back of her. But I don't expect you to start work straight away, you must spend this weekend just settling in. Ah, here's your ice-cream.'

Shivaun turned to find Dorothy placing a glass dish on the table beside her, filled with flavours that looked like chocolate, cherry, maybe honey or banana, spiked with a long spoon.

'This looks amazing! Thank you.'

Despite the sandwich she found she was able for it, enjoyed it thoroughly and emptied the dish at a rate that surprised her. Thoughtfully, Marina watched her.

'I'm glad to see you have a good appetite, despite being so thin.'

'Yes, well, I – maybe it's the sea air.'

'Maybe. You'll have a view of the sea from your bedroom. It's a bit cool for swimming now, but the pool will stay heated until the end of the month, you can swim in that.'

Pool? Shivaun was delighted. She hadn't yet seen any pool, but if the weather stayed as warm as it was today, even for a few more weeks, it would be a joy to swim. In fact she was eager to explore now, see the rest of the house and the grounds, the beach and the village . . . distracted, she realised belatedly that Marina was studying her.

'You say you used to be a midwife, Shivaun? But your hospital was being closed down?'

'Yes. That's right.'

'Well, I don't want to be treated like a baby! But won't you miss them?'

Shivaun thought about it. 'No. Not for the moment, I – I'd kind of had enough of babies.'

'I see.'

Marina said no more, and Shivaun wondered whether she might be getting tired, want to be left to rest a little. She was the type of patient, she guessed, who needed to be made to rest, under protest. Putting down her glass dish, she stood up and looked at Marina.

'That was delicious! But I must look a mess after all the travelling, maybe I should find my room and freshen up?'

Marina nodded, in her queenly way, and tinkled a little glass bell by her side. Almost immediately, Dorothy appeared.

'Dorothy, would you show Shivaun to her room? She's had such a long trip – we won't expect to see you again until dinner at seven, Shivaun. Take a nap for the rest of the afternoon, or go out for a walk if you'd rather . . . dinner will be informal, by the way, there's no need to dress up.'

Shivaun nodded and smiled as she took her leave of Marina, thinking that she wouldn't wear jeans tonight all the same. There was just something about this woman that set a certain tone – not formal, but definitely civilised. She'd wear make-up and nail varnish and maybe Viv's gold earrings . . . As Dorothy led her out through the hall and up a winding oak staircase, chatting cheerfully, she had a sudden sharp sense of déja-vu.

What was it? Nothing she could see or hear, not the distant sound of crashing waves or nearer sound of rustling leaves . . . what, then?

A smell. As her hand rested on the polished banister, it came to her. Wood wax. The same yellow wax, out of an old green Fiddes tin, that Viv used to use on the woodwork at home.

When she reached her room, her legs were trembling under her.

In the days following her arrival Shivaun became conscious of something new and yet familiar; a sense of serenity came to her as if retrieved from the depths of an old storage chest. Dinner on that first night was an enjoyable affair, around a circular table set with crystal glasses which Marina encouraged herself and Lena to fill with mellow Californian wine; she was a generous, genial hostess and asked many questions, savouring Shivaun's tales of shenanigans in Ireland, of fraudulent officials and missing public monies. But she excused herself early, leaving Shivaun to talk to Lena in the library over coffee, glean the information she needed about physio and speech therapy. Lena, a stocky sandy-haired girl not much older than Shivaun, was not overly helpful, but she yielded what facts were necessary with the sceptical hope that Shivaun would get further with Marina than she had.

'She's impossible. A witch.'

'Maybe she's just frustrated? It must be maddening for such a lively person to be ill, as well as having to repeat every second word she says.'

'Oh, you'll get used to her speech problem. I couldn't understand what she was saying at first either, but your ear will tune in. You'll know when she's swearing at you, don't worry!'

For a nurse only in her mid-twenties, Lena sounded exasperated. Shivaun asked her why she was leaving.

'I'm going back to New York. I'm a city girl. It's too quiet for me up here.'

It was quiet, when Shivaun went up to bed later, but she liked the stillness in which she could hear the distant waves, and opened the long windows which gave from her room onto the balcony outside, which was apparently called a widow's walk. There she stood for some time, looking up at the stars out over the sea; without the rivalry of city lights they were very clear. She did not return indoors until the air became chilly, but its ozone tang must have done her good, because she fell asleep almost instantly in her wide comfortable bed with scarcely a thought of Ivor, or home, or any of the things that had plagued her nights in Dublin.

Next day, a Sunday, she walked around the grounds after breakfast, exploring the house that stood on five acres including the pool with its bleached wooden deck, a tennis court and numerous outhouses. In one of them she found Joe Santana polishing two cars, the sleek grey Oldsmobile in which he had picked her up from the airport, and another zippier car, a little red Toyota with a convertible top. Joe looked up and grinned at her.

'This one's for you. Lena had the use of it, and now Ms Marina wants me to shine it up for you.'

'For *me*?'

'Yes. She says you'll need it to visit Boston or go sightseeing – you can have it today, if you want.'

Shivaun considered, and laughed. 'Well, I never knew a car came with the job! But today I'd rather just explore on foot, walk round the town and the coast a bit. Anyway, I've never driven on the right before.'

'Oh, that'll come easy. After the first half-hour you won't even think about it. This car's an automatic, much easier than your European ones with gearshifts. Anyway, just let me know whenever you want the keys.'

'Are you in charge of cars?'

'Yes. Cars, security, maintenance . . . I'm normally off on Sundays but it depends what's happening, today I've to drive Lena to the airport for her flight back to New York. Hey – d'you mind if I call you Shivaun?'

'Of course! And I can call you Joe?'

She wasn't sure, because he was older and somehow polite, even today in his casual clothes. But he grinned and nodded.

'That'd be nice. I live in town but I'm here most days, if you need any help with anything I'm your man.'

Much taken with his friendliness, she walked on until she found a pathway leading out through the trees, with a high wooden fence behind. Following it, she came eventually to a gate which was locked on the inside, so she climbed over it and dropped down onto what turned out to be a grassy headland, with dunes in the distance below. It was a bright, windy day, and she plunged her hands into her pockets, determining to walk as far as possible.

The path meandered for some time, but eventually she turned a corner and found herself looking down over the little town, with the sea on the right, channelling into a harbour filled with fishing boats. It looked like a busy harbour, she could see cars and bikes, buildings that looked like shops, maybe restaurants . . . with the breeze in her face she continued with interest, realising that she felt safer here than she would have walking through unknown sand dunes in Dublin. Why, she didn't know, but it was sunny and she was enjoying herself, feeling fresh after her long deep sleep. A hot shower, too, in the large luxurious bathroom; she had been given plenty of space to call her own at Chederlay.

The town was very quaint when she reached it, built of blue, grey and white shingle, with a bustling air even on Sunday morning. By the quayside some sailors were loading equipment into their small yacht, weekend sailors by the look of them, and two kids grinned as they passed by her, carrying a large live crab gingerly but triumphantly between them. Further back, some of the shops were open, a bakery and two art galleries amongst them, one filled with marine paintings and the other seeming to specialise in sculpture. Pausing, she gazed in the window, and a woman with dark curly hair waved out at her invitingly.

'Hi there! C'mon in! Browsing's free!'

She went in, and looked around at the sculptures, made from wood, metal, marble, stone; they were mostly abstracts and one was so outlandish it made her laugh. The dark woman laughed in turn.

'Yeah, well, people see different things in it I guess. The guy who did it takes his work very seriously though . . . you on vacation, or just up from Boston?'

'I – I live here, actually, as of today!'

The woman cocked her head quizzically. 'But you're not from around . . . I can't place that accent. Where are you from?'

'I'm Irish. From Dublin.'

'Oh? And you've just moved here?'

'Yes. For a year. I'm a nurse.'

The woman beamed. 'Oh, I get it, you must be Marina Darnoux's new nurse! Well, you'll have fun with her.' She extended her hand. 'I'm Kathy.'

Shivaun shook the hand. 'Hi. I'm Shivaun. Do you know Marina?'

'Oh yes. Everybody knows Marina. But we've hardly seen her since her stroke . . . how is she?'

'Well, I only arrived yesterday, and don't start work until tomorrow, but she looks and sounds quite strong. I'll be meeting her doctor tomorrow so I'll know more then.'

'Oh, right! Dr Dishy! He came in here once, bought a little onyx piece – he's quite a sculpture himself. If I didn't have a husband and two kids I'd . . . um, well, the man would not be safe. Say, how do you like Gloucester?'

Shivaun found herself smiling hugely. 'So far, it's gorgeous. Not that I've seen much yet, or spoken to anyone except you.'

'Really? I'm your first native? Well, what do you know.' Kathy paused, glanced at her watch. 'I tell you what – have you ever tasted fried clams?'

'No! I thought I might be going to last night, but it turned out to be duck for dinner, with pumpkin soup to start. I hear the clams are great, though.'

'Yeah. They are. And if you'd care to come back here at lunchtime, say around twelve-thirty, I'll give you your first taste of one. There's a little place on the other side of the harbour does them . . . I only have forty-five minutes for lunch, but if you're free why don't you join me?'

'That'd be great! I'd love to!'

'OK, then. Clams at high noon! See you later.'

She turned her attention to a middle-aged couple who seemed taken with a chunk of round polished stone, and Shivaun left the gallery, as surprised as she was pleased. What a nice lady, what a warm welcome. She was beginning to think Alana's idea of coming to America had been really inspired.

Shivaun had lunch with Kathy, loved the clams and discovered that, already, she'd made a friend. Kathy was thirty, a 'mom, most of the time', but she worked in the gallery at weekends 'just for the heck of it really, it's fun and it gets me out.' When her children were at school she painted, she said, with more enjoyment than talent: 'Everyone does around here, we're all real artsy. Some are *very* artsy. But I just find it relaxing, hang my work at home or give it to friends. Nobody's going to hang it in the Isabella Stewart Gardner or anything.'

The Isabella what?

'It's a big gallery in Boston. Have you seen anything of Boston yet?'

No, Shivaun said, not a thing. Not one inch of Massachusetts, apart from the drive from the airport.

'Oh, well then, we'll have to do you up a list. Harvard, Cambridge, Sturbridge, Plimoth Plantation, Louisa May Alcott's house in Concord, Lowell Park – and I tell you what's real good. The cranberry bogs, and the Blaschka glass flowers in Harvard botanical museum.'

Kathy wrote it all down on the spot, on a table napkin, and handed the scribbled sheet to Shivaun, delighted to hear she had access to a car and offering, when time permitted, to accompany her on some of the trips. Lunch was rounded off with blueberry pie and mutual enthusiasm, an invitation to visit Kathy's house if Shivaun could 'fend off the fighting monsters – only two, but they sound like dozens'.

Afterwards, when Kathy returned to her work, Shivaun continued her long ramble round the town, peering into shops and houses with interest, smiling at the many people who smiled at her, feeling a sense of community amongst them. Gloucester, she thought, was just the right size, small enough to be friendly, big enough to command attention. She spent a long time listening to fishermen chatting on the pier, and then went on round the headland for miles, revelling in the warm breeze and wild flowers, making plans to visit as much of the area as she could. When she got back to Chederlay it was nearly dinnertime, and a bicycle lay up against the side of the house with a note from Joe: 'I dug this out of the garage, thought it might come in handy for you.'

She wanted to go off and do more exploring on it the very

next morning. But instead she put on her nurse's uniform and went to greet Marina, start work officially.

Marina burst out laughing. 'Darling child! What is this?'

Shivaun looked down, and back up at her. 'It's my uniform. My whites.'

Marina gestured impatiently but indulgently. 'Well, since you've gone to the trouble, today . . . but there's no need. You can wear whatever you like in future, whatever's comfortable. Now, Dr Hunt will be here in a minute, so please ask Dorothy to make some coffee and the three of us will have a talk about our strategy. I want to be rid of this stick by Christmas.'

Dr Hunt came sailing up in a very large car, and Marina seemed to perk up on the spot; Shivaun saw her check her reflection in the mirror and had to suppress a giggle. This doctor seemed to have a devastating effect on women.

'Good morning Marina, how are you!'

In he bounded, both hands outstretched in greeting, and Marina almost simpered as he kissed her on either cheek.

'Steven, how lovely to see you. Do come in, my new nurse has arrived and you won't believe what she's wearing – Shivaun, this is Steven Hunt. Steven, Shivaun Reilly.'

They shook hands, and Shivaun had to admit that rumour was not exaggerated: the man was very handsome, blond and tanned, immaculate in a navy suit, with a voice that had Kennedy-style overtones.

'Ah. Nurse Reilly. Nice to meet you.' He surveyed her with ice-blue eyes, and unexpectedly nodded approval. 'Excellent. I like to see a nurse dressed for the job.'

Shivaun was about to say Marina didn't, when he swung away from her and returned his full attention to Marina.

'Wonderful game of golf yesterday, wonderful – when are we ever going to get rid of this tiresome stick of yours, Marina, and put a club in your hand instead, h'mm?'

In a flash, Shivaun got the picture. Steven Hunt was the kind of doctor to whom nurses were invisible. She had met others like him, less handsome but equally patronising. Since arriving in America, he was the first person to whom she took a faint dislike. But she was aware of Marina's sudden keen look at her, and forced herself to smile as all three of them sat down and Dorothy brought coffee.

'So, first of all, how's the speech? Can you say *she sells sea-shells on the sea-shore* yet, or do we still have our charming lisp?'

Yes. A smarmy bedside manner, Shivaun thought, and huge bills. I hope Marina's insurance covers an ego as big as Steven Hunt's. But Marina merely inclined her head.

'Oh, I think you understand me well enough, Steven. And Shivaun will learn to, I'm sure.'

All three of them seemed to catch each other's eye, and Shivaun was aware of some mutual – what? For some reason she was glad she'd worn her uniform despite Marina's amusement, appeared professional to Steven Hunt when he turned to her and began questioning her about her experience. She'd taken the precaution of reading up on everything she needed for this job, and felt she was acquitting herself creditably as the meeting progressed. After about an hour, they were able to agree on a programme satisfactory to everyone, and Steven's square classic face registered approval if nothing more. He stood up.

'Well, your new nurse seems quite competent to me, Marina. I'll leave you in her capable hands, and come back to see you again next week.'

What? Wasn't he even going to examine Marina, check her out physically? Shivaun thought he wasn't, and forestalled him by also standing up.

'It was nice to meet you, Dr Hunt, and now I'll just leave you to examine Marina. If you need me for anything, I'll be in the kitchen with Dorothy.'

He blinked at her, and she left the room with the sensation that Marina was watching her as she departed. Had she been too hasty? Maybe. But she couldn't take chances. Marina was in her charge now, she was responsible for her.

Fifteen minutes later she heard the doctor leaving, and returned to Marina.

'So how's your blood pressure? Your heartbeat, reflexes? Did he check everything?'

Marina smiled, rather wickedly. 'Yes, he did. Everything's fine – except his bruised self-esteem. He always does check me out, but nobody's ever put it up to him like that before.'

'I'm sorry if I was a bit premature, then. But better safe than sorry – I hope you're not offended?'

She laughed. 'No, I'm delighted! I see you care about your patients. I also see you're not smitten by Steven Hunt.'

'Uh – does it matter? He seems to have plenty of other admirers. It's just that I've met so many doctors like him—'

'Vain, you mean? Arrogant?'

'Yes, well, it doesn't matter so long as they're good at their work.'

She didn't want to say any more, since Marina seemed to be a fan of Steven's. But Marina looked candidly at her, with a twinkle.

'Yes. I'm not a fool, Shivaun. I know Steven has many shortcomings. But he is a very good doctor in fact. That's why I employ him. His pretty face is just a bonus, and his charm, even if he does sell it by the yard. However, I see you're no more bamboozled by charm than I am myself.'

Shivaun felt some relief. So Marina wasn't entirely captivated by Steven Hunt, after all. She was simply choosing to play a game that amused her, brightened up her convalescence. Shivaun laughed.

'So you're just a flirt!'

'Of course! I'm forty-eight, flirting is as much fun as I get!'

They laughed in unison, and Shivaun felt herself warming to Marina, who was regarding her with interest.

'You know, Darnoux is my maiden name. I reverted to it after my divorce. My grandfather was French. Flirting is in my blood. You have to keep in practice when you're divorced, even when you're ill, otherwise life would get so dull and flat. You're not by any chance divorced yourself, are you?'

Shivaun was surprised, because divorce was uncommon

amongst Irish women of her age, but she realised it mightn't be in America.

'No, I'm not – why? Do I *look* divorced?'

Again they both laughed, but then Marina sat back in her armchair, thoughtfully.

'Yes. In some odd way, I think you do. I can't put my finger on it, but – well, when somebody leaves their country, travels three thousand miles for a change of scenery, it makes me wonder.'

Shivaun sat back, wondering in turn. She didn't want to talk or think about Ivor, she certainly didn't want to bore Marina with her personal affairs, but . . . the woman almost seemed to be inviting her confidence.

'I wasn't married. But I thought I was going to be.'

'Ah. A bad break-up, was it?'

'It was a – a shock. A shock to both of us, I think. We'd been together since we were small children, we took each other for granted . . . which turned out to be the problem.'

'I see. Well, that's a major problem, and a good reason for splitting up. Nobody should ever take anybody for granted. It's a lazy, unfair thing to do.'

Shivaun was jolted. She'd never thought of herself as lazy in the slightest degree, nor unfair. On the contrary.

'I worked very hard. But Ivor thought I worked too hard.'

'Did he? Then he was concerned for you.'

Yes. You could look at it that way. But there was more to it than that.

'It was almost as if he – he was jealous. Jealous of my time and my commitment and my other interests, as well.'

Marina sighed. 'Yes. I know all about jealousy. My own husband was horribly jealous when I became an architect like himself . . . I thought we were partners, he thought we were rivals. Of course, it was all a long time ago.'

Interested, Shivaun leaned forward. 'And now? How do you feel about it now?' It was a very personal question, especially of someone she was only just getting to know, but curiosity let her risk it. If Marina told her to mind her own business, well – she would.

'I feel sad, if you want the truth. Sad that he didn't understand, that we didn't both try harder, communicate better – I was very driven at the time, ambitious, consumed by my passion for architecture. I couldn't have given it up, for him or for anyone, but maybe I could have listened more closely, tried to understand his fear. Men are so easily threatened . . . unlike women, they think their careers are all they have. It ended up being all I have.'

'But – but you love it, don't you? I'm told you're quite a famous architect.'

'Oh yes. I adore it. Everyone thinks the design is the fascinating part, but I love the actual building work too, going out on the site in my hard hat and my boots, overseeing those first girders go up, first stones settling . . . the joy on the clients' faces. Their homes matter so much to them. It's an almost primal thing.'

Shivaun empathised instantly. Not that babies might seem to have anything to do with building, but in a way they had, it was all about creating, setting up home, investing in the future – for a split second, she wondered how Kilo Finnegan was getting on, and Buster Mulcahy . . . they, too, were a primal joy.

'Well then, Marina, I think you have quite a lot.'

'Yes. I do, and I'm not complaining. I'm extremely fortunate, and I know nobody can have everything. The one thing I don't have is children. It didn't seem to matter at the time . . . but . . . tell me, would you have liked to have children with this Ivor?'

'Yes. I'd have loved to. We assumed we would. But then he – I don't know what happened. He suddenly seemed to get very unsure about everything. He even chucked his job.'

'Really? For what?'

'For travel, adventure! He didn't want to settle down. He did ask me to travel with him, but I was very involved with my hospital then, not just with the babies but with a battle to save it from closure.'

'Which turned out to be a losing battle?'

'Yes. Only a few days after I'd told Ivor no, I couldn't go with him. It was the last straw. That's why I thought America . . . well, a friend of mine said a break would do me good. I think she was right actually.'

'H'mm. And what did your family think?'

'I – I haven't any family. My parents are dead.'

Although she appreciated Marina's interest, and sensed she could trust this woman, Shivaun stiffened slightly. She wasn't ready to discuss Viv or Jimmy or – or Jason Dean. None of that, yet.

'Oh. I'm sorry to hear it. And you have no brothers, sisters, cousins?'

'No. None.'

'So your friends are important to you, then, to a perhaps exceptional degree?'

'Ye-es. I shared my house with Alana, who suggested coming here, and I relied a lot on Ivor. Too much, perhaps.'

'H'mm. But you did have a wider social life, as well?'

'Oh, yes. I was involved with CND and an East Timor lobby and all sorts of political movements, always out at rallies and meetings . . . my crusades, Ivor called them.'

'What got you interested in those?'

Marina frowned, and so did Shivaun. Maybe some day she would tell Marina about the catalyst, the deaths. But not today.

'My mother was an agitator before me! I guess I just picked it up from her.'

Oh, God. Please don't let Marina start asking about Viv, start picking and peering into . . . but suddenly Marina sat up straight.

'Your mother, I'm sure, would be horrified if she could see how thin you are. When you were out in the kitchen, did you happen to see what Dorothy is making for lunch?'

Shivaun blinked. 'She – I think she said something about roast peppers, and arugula, whatever that is.'

'It's a green, and you'll have another bowl of Ben and

Jerry's after it. But let's do a little work on this arm of mine first. Even though I draw right-handed, it makes me nuts . . . I'm designing a house for clients in Utah at the moment and it's way behind schedule – they've been very understanding about it, but I do want to catch up. Steven lets me do some work in the afternoons, so you can go for a swim or a cycle if you like, after lunch. Then we'll do the speech therapy this evening. That OK?'

'Yes – of course! You're the boss.'

But, even as she went to Marina and began gently manipulating her left arm, Shivaun found that she could no longer think of her as just 'the boss'. Some closer connection than that had been made, and it felt good.

Chapter Six

Ivor felt a few flowers were the least he could offer Alana, since she was cooking dinner for the third time in as many weeks. His budget didn't currently stretch to a fancy florist's bouquet, but his mother's garden boasted beautiful roses even coming into November, and he cut a bunch of pink ones without bothering to consult Cynthia, who might object. As he wielded the secateurs he found he was hungry, looking forward to Alana's promised roast beef even though he didn't know what he was doing to deserve it. Alana must be lonely, he thought, to invite him yet again; undoubtedly she was missing Shivaun, albeit hardly with the same intensity he was missing her himself.

America! Just like that, with a snap of her fingers, before St Jude's had even formally closed? After all she had said about staying put, all the energy she had invested in her career, the firm way in which she had refused to travel with him, it was a mystery. A hurtful mystery, as if he were not hurting already . . . sometimes, when he saw her long-loved face in his mind, heard her voice in his head, it was almost more than he could bear. Last night, watching a video starring Sigourney Weaver, he'd had to switch it off, because Shivaun looked a little like Sigourney, and the resemblance made him ache, physically throb with pain – pain made all the more acute by the sudden distance now between them, three thousand miles of bleak steely ocean.

That was why, he supposed, he'd accepted Alana's invitation

to come to dinner yet again; it was somehow a small comfort to return to the house he'd been visiting all his life, see Shivaun's things in it, sit on the sofa where they'd so often embraced and kissed . . . he should return his keys now he supposed, give them to Alana or simply leave them discreetly on the hall table. But he couldn't bring himself to do it. There was a finality in the gesture that he could not, would not accept; it would be like saying 'yes, Shivaun is gone, I no longer belong in her home, everything we once shared is over. There is no hope.'

Realistically, it did not seem that there was any hope. Even if Shivaun changed her mind, came flying back and said she was sorry, I made a mistake, Ivor, let's make it up and try again, reconciliation would be neither automatic nor, perhaps, even possible. Since their agonising parting on the beach he had done a great deal of thinking, and planning; now it was time to act. Should Shivaun be standing here with him at this minute, there was still no guarantee that she would approve of his plans, or want to join him in them. As dearly as he loved her, he recognised that they had reached a fork in the long road they had travelled together. Their needs had diverged, their interests and aspirations had – oh, *damn*! Why couldn't he bring himself to ask Alana for Shivaun's new e-mail address, why couldn't he make contact, throw some kind of rope ladder across the Atlantic?

Pride, he supposed. Stupid male pride. He'd been rejected, he wasn't going to beg, admit to his terrible feeling of loss, hear what a great time she was having without him, how she'd been right to make the break . . . if she said that, he would crack completely. At least this way there was still some tiny glimmer of hope, he didn't know for sure whether she was happy in America, he could console himself that maybe she was feeling as wretched as he was himself. Maybe she – or maybe not?

It was better not to know. Better to turn down a dimmer switch on the memories that glowed so brightly, snap them off altogether and get on with – with dinner tonight, and his life thereafter, his future. At least Alana seemed to understand how he felt, she was soothing company, would make no demands on his tortured emotions. They'd simply share a companionable meal, talk over some wine, not about Shivaun because Alana seemed to know he didn't want to do that, but about other people, activities, anything and everything except Shivaun Reilly.

Christ! Ivor swore as he pricked his finger on a thorn, gathered up the roses and threw the secateurs into Cynthia's garden shed. Not even a phone call, not even one lousy postcard? Did he really deserve to be cut off, cut out of her life, as sharply as that? But of course that was typical Shivaun: all or nothing. Nothing, it seemed in this case, nothing whatever to indicate she missed him, or gave a fiddler's about the years they had shared, the life they had lived together, the endless support he thought he'd given her. *Had* given her.

With a surge of something he reluctantly recognised as anger, he went indoors, flung the roses into water and went upstairs to get ready for Alana's dinner. He should shower and shave, he supposed, dress up a bit to acknowledge the trouble she was going to, the food she was buying and cooking . . . but he didn't feel like dressing up, or even shaving for that matter. He felt like throwing himself out the bathroom window, and if the glass slashed his wrists as he fell to perdition, so much the better.

Except that then he – oh, bloody hell! He wanted Shivaun but he wanted other things, too. He was going to do other things, with her or without her. Yanking some clean clothes out of the wardrobe, he threw them on his bed and went to take a shower, wondering whether Alana might have invited some other guests tonight besides himself. Of course she meant well, with all this nurturing stuff, but at her previous two dinners he'd been the sole focus of attention, and wasn't entirely comfortable with it. Tonight he'd rather find a few other people gathered round her table, a bit of craic and even rowdiness that would take the spotlight off him, permit him to maybe get quietly sloshed. He didn't often get sloshed, but there were times, he told himself, when a man had to do what a man had to do.

* * *

'Ivor!'

Alana stood at Shivaun's hall door, looking nakedly surprised as he thrust the roses into her hands and walked in, feeling rather resentful that he'd had to ring the doorbell. He couldn't very well just let himself in, he supposed, now that she lived here alone. But then she plunged her face into the roses and smiled up at him, appreciatively; the pink petals became her very well, he grudgingly conceded, she'd always had a pretty complexion.

'Oh, these are lovely. Thank you!'

'Oh well, I always used to bring flowers, why stop now, huh?'

It wasn't a very gracious thing to say, but it was out before he could help it, before he noticed how dressed up she was herself in some kind of turquoise clingy thing, staring at him in his jeans and sweater.

'My God, Ivor, you look so different . . . is that designer stubble, or did you forget to shave?'

'I'm growing a beard' he replied with equal surprise; a beard had not entered his head until this moment. But he'd chucked his job, for God's sake, wasn't an accountant any more, she hardly expected him to turn up in a suit and tie reeking of aftershave? He was a tree-hugger now, he thought with grim satisfaction, or practising to become one anyway, turn into the kind of guy Shivaun apparently would have preferred. Better late than never.

Alana held up her face, evidently waiting for a greeting kiss, so he planted one rather irritably on her cheek, and looked around as she led him into the dining room. They'd always used to eat in the kitchen, but since Shivaun's departure she'd gone a bit more elegant, and it struck him that they seemed to be moving in opposite directions. Or was it him, was he moving on some path all of his own?

The table was beautifully set, with pale pink linen and the good glasses that had been one of Viv and Jimmy's wedding presents. Viv had always used them as carelessly as if they were Texaco tumblers, but now they stood lined up shiny as soldiers.

Motioning to him to sit down, Alana went to fetch a vase for the roses, trailing some perfume in her wake . . . suddenly he felt scruffy, a bit guilty too, which was annoying when he'd only had a shower an hour ago. Frowning, he inspected the table, which was indubitably set for two, no more.

'Nobody else coming?' he called out to her as she filled the vase in the kitchen, and returned to set the flowers on the table ceremonially.

'No – why?'

'Oh, I dunno, I just thought, you know, the more the merrier.'

She didn't look as if she thought so, raising an eyebrow slightly and handing him a box of matches; evidently he was to light the candles she'd taken to using when they ate. But she smiled when he handed her the bottle of wine he'd also brought – not a very good one, his funds only ran to supermarket Chianti.

'Oh, lovely. We'll have that with the beef. But I've made a scallop ceviche to start, there's some Pouilly Fumé in the fridge to go with that first – I'll bring it in.'

Pouilly Fumé? Ivor was bemused. They'd never drunk Pouilly anything when Shivaun was around. Beaming, Alana brought him the chilled bottle, with a corkscrew.

'Here we are – you may as well open the Chianti too, we'll let it breathe by the fire.'

Well, there was nothing new in that, log fires had always burned in this house in autumn and winter. But – as he uncorked the wine, Ivor felt a sudden unidentifiable shiver. What was this all about? Granted, Alana had always been a good cook, but there had never been anything formal or fussy about her meals before. Except the last two, now that he thought about it . . . it was as if she were revving up in some way, almost rehearsing for something. He laughed aloud.

'This is very ritzy, Alana! Have you been doing a hostess course or something?'

She blushed faintly. 'No, not at all, I just thought a civilised meal would be nice for you, since you're not entertaining clients at expense-account restaurants at the moment.'

'No, I'm certainly not! But I'd only ever done it twice anyway, I don't miss it.'

'Still, it's good for you to keep in practice.'

'Why? I'm not going back to my job. I've had it with all that.'

'Oh, never say never! You're hardly going to hang around in jeans for the rest of your life are you, making shelves and tinkering with bits of wood?'

He'd told her about the experiments he'd made, the enjoyment he was unexpectedly discovering in carpentry, the odd jobs he'd done for a few local ladies since making Cynthia's shelves. At first it had just been a way of earning pocket money and keeping himself occupied since . . . but now it was starting to get interesting. Starting, in his opinion, to have potential. He didn't know why he kept his next remark so brief.

'No. I'm not going to hang around for the rest of my life.'

She looked at him over the candles as she brought the scallops to the table, and in their light he couldn't help noticing what blue eyes she had. True blue, like a china doll's.

'Good. You – you can't let yourself go, Ivor, you know. This restless phase won't last forever.'

He felt she was eyeing his clean but old sweater as she sat down opposite him, disapproving in some faint way even though she smiled, took a delicate bite of the scallops and held out the smaller of her two wine glasses to him, just a fraction. Evidently he was expected to pour – and why not, he suddenly thought, she's gone to a lot of trouble with this meal and I'm being churlish. Gallantly, he filled her glass and his own, tasted the scallops and savoured them appreciatively.

'Mmm. Delicious.'

'Good. I'm glad you like them.'

She looked genuinely pleased, and he thought ruefully but affectionately how easy she always had been to please. A word or a smile, a casual hug, that was all it took, and unlike Shivaun she never took the conversation down political paths. There wouldn't be any friction about anything tonight, any infuriated outbursts or demands for support, no row over anything.

Which was unfortunate, he realised with a jolt, because he was spoiling for a row. Nothing physical or violent – although he was conscious of missing Shivaun sexually as well as in every other way – but something heated, engrossing, absorbing. Something he could get his teeth into, argue over. He was sick to the back teeth of being polite to his mother, he missed his energising games of tennis now that the season was over. Somewhat belligerently, he looked at Alana through the flowers and candles.

'Any word from Shivaun, damn her?'

'*Damn* her?' Alana gazed at him curiously. 'Are you angry with her, Ivor?'

'Yes! Of course I'm bloody angry – I have every right to be, haven't I?'

She appeared to be enjoying her scallops, considering as she ate them.

'Yes. Of course you have. I believe that's how it goes when people break up . . . first they're sad, but then they begin to realise how badly they've been treated, and then they get angry. I don't blame you in the least.'

Good. He was glad she saw his point of view. Settling more comfortably into his chair, he waited for her to answer his question. But she didn't. He was forced to repeat it.

'So – any word, then, or not?'

She put down her fork and seemed to deliberate, as if there were more than two ways of saying yes or no. 'Well, I did have a postcard, but it was very brief. She promised to send me an e-mail, only I don't know how to work the computer . . . would you show me some time, Ivor? It would be great, I'd really appreciate it.'

'Sure. I'll show you tonight, after we've eaten.'

Her eyes widened. 'Oh, there's no rush, you could come round at the weekend. I just want you to relax and enjoy yourself tonight.'

Enjoy himself? Well, the food was certainly very good, and

the wine; he was touched and flattered that she should go to so much trouble for him, but enjoying himself was another matter. How could you do that, when the woman you loved was gone? The woman you adored, were missing more and more with every passing hour? Christ, he should never have let Shivaun walk away that day, he was a fool! And furious, now, with himself. Picking up the bottle, he refilled their glasses, recoiling when Alana's fingers accidentally brushed against his.

She looked at him like a wounded doe, and he was mortified. Oh, God! It wasn't her fault, none of this was her doing – on the contrary, she'd been nothing but a help and a comfort since it all went wrong. Forcing himself to smile, he apologised profusely.

'Sorry, Alana! Don't mind me. I'm jittery with everyone lately.'

Nodding, she lowered her gaze, seemed to understand.

'Yes. Don't worry, Ivor. I know you've been having a hard time.'

She held out her hand to him, in a conciliatory way that obliged him to take it, hold it for a moment. 'I really don't know how you put up with me, or why you're being so good to me.'

She looked at him thoughtfully, fondly. 'We've always been good friends, Ivor, that's why . . . they say you only know your true friends when you really need one, and I think you've needed one these past weeks.'

Yes, he conceded, he had. He'd needed friendship and she'd given it to him, asking nothing in return. She was a warm, sweet girl. And an attractive one, too, with the candlelight illuminating cleavage he hadn't ever noticed before; her days of puppy fat and baggy sweatshirts were well behind her now. She was wearing some really nice make-up tonight, stuff that did wonders for her mouth and eyes, and it occurred to him that some day she would make some lucky man a lovely wife.

There was a moment's silence before she stood up and removed their plates, looking at him questioningly.

'Are you ready for your roast beef? Would you like me to bring it in now?'

Yes, please, he said, wondering that she should ask so demurely, like a geisha girl. It wasn't his role to sit here and be served by her. Standing up, he made to accompany her into the kitchen. 'Here, let me give you a hand.'

She waved him back into his seat. 'Oh, no, I can manage. Maybe you could just carve, though, at the table?'

Yes. He liked carving, and the beef was a pleasure to cut into when it came, meltingly tender, a million miles removed from his mother's burnt offerings. While he worked, Alana served vegetables, and brought the Chianti to the table, warm from the fire.

'So tell me what you've been up to lately, Alana – have you decided yet whether to go to St Peter's, or find another hospital?'

'Oh, I'll go to St Peter's' she said, but did not dwell on the subject that had so vexed and engrossed Shivaun. Instead she sat back down with him and talked of her brother Ciarán, who was building a new house, and a pub she'd discovered with a friend – great music, he should try it, maybe a few of them could all go together some evening? This led them onto the subject of music – he liked REM, she liked Simply Red, they both liked Mary Coughlan – and as the evening wore on he began to discover an Alana he had not known before. Not got a chance to know, he thought wryly, because Shivaun had always been the dominant conversationalist . . . but, if he could find nothing to argue over with Alana, he could find nothing to fault either. The wine went down, the fire banked down, and he realised that he was enjoying himself after all, mellowing out, thinking that Alana's home comforts were an excellent alternative to a night in a rowdy bar, or the joys of life with Cynthia.

Even better, Alana seemed to be actually listening to him, drinking in his opinions and agreeing with his views in a way that Shivaun rarely had, with no hint of confrontation or debate; even if he might not want such complaisance on an ongoing basis, it was a restful change. His desire for confrontation seemed to have melted away with the last of the food and wine . . . good Lord, had they actually drunk both bottles, already? And had he, by any chance, drunk more than she had?

Oh, well. Whatever. He felt agreeably sated, but did not hold out against a delicious crème brûlée when it came, nor protest when she suggested taking their coffees into the sitting room, where there was a comfy sofa and some music they could put on, a bottle of Cointreau in the cabinet she thought . . . he didn't seem to remember liqueurs after previous dinners, but what the hell, he was walking home after all, a danger to nobody. In fact the night air might do him good . . . what time was it, anyway?

'I think it's time,' Alana said, sitting down beside him in the light that had mysteriously dimmed, 'that you and I got to know each other a little better, Ivor.'

On any previous occasion, he'd have asked her what she meant by that. But tonight he thought maybe he saw what she meant, felt there might be slightly more to her than he'd always imagined. Before, for years now that he thought about it, there'd seemed to be a hard edge to her, a cynical tinge that enabled her to laugh and never take anything too seriously – God, Shivaun had taken some things so seriously!

But maybe he'd been wrong. Maybe Alana's laugh had been a defence, disguising a softer centre? It must have been tough for her, he thought as he sank back into the cushions and a piano began to play somewhere, always to be on the outside, watching himself and Shivaun conduct their romance under her nose. They'd tried to be nice to her, include her in as much as they could, but – still. It must have been tough, at times.

Even as he reflected on it, he became conscious of something changing. Alana was sitting closer to him than she'd ever sat before, she was – sweet Jesus – she was actually snuggling up to him. Yes, definitely snuggling, he knew a looming embrace when he saw it, and could hardly believe it was happening. *Alana?* He must be drunker than he thought, and so must she. With as much grace and haste as he could muster, he edged sideways, out of range, and grinned abashed.

'Uh – I think some more coffee would be good, Alana. Let me get it.'

He reached for their cups, but she forestalled him, put her hand quietly on his arm. Gently but firmly, he felt the sensation of a silken handcuff.

'Oh, don't bother, I'll get some in a minute . . . you look a bit flushed, Ivor, is the heating up too high for you? Here, why don't you take off that heavy sweater.'

Even as he grabbed at it, defensively, her hands slid under it, and before he could stop her she had lifted it up, off him, he was sitting astonished in his T-shirt.

Oh, God. Oh, *no.* He felt his face burning, strove to control his whirling mind. This *couldn't* be happening.

'Alana – I – look, I think things are getting a little out of hand here. Why don't we—?'

She curled closer to him, laid her palm on his stomach with a touch that was electrifying, all but purred with pleasure.

'Why don't we?' she whispered. 'Exactly, Ivor. Why don't we? There's nothing to stop us, nothing in the way any more. You're free now, free to do whatever you want.'

Her hand slid further down his stomach and he was appalled by the effect it had, as if a lighted match had been held to his skin – and other bits of him, too. Her face was so close his mouth was almost in her hair, he could smell its fragrance, feel the texture of its blonde mass – feel, he realised with sheer abrupt horror, lust for her. Lust for Shivaun's best friend, Alana Kennedy.

But – but it's practically incest, he thought wildly, Alana's like family, a sister! I have to stop this, end it immediately.

Wrenching away, he gripped her wrist, hard.

'Alana – no – I'm sorry—'

Instead of pulling free in turn, she leaned closer into him, used her proximity to put her lips to his cheek, her tongue just under his ear.

'But there's nothing to be sorry about, Ivor. Nothing at all. We're old friends who should be better friends, that's all . . . didn't you ever find me attractive before, just a little bit?'

No. He never had, never thought about her in this way

for one moment, and he was stunned by the undeniability of it now, the rapidly growing evidence that yes, he found her insanely attractive, with her eyes like big blue pools, her skin warm and soft as velvet. His face was tingling where her tongue had touched it, the blood was rushing to—

Jesus, he thought with a combined surge of rage, shock and desire, this is what Shivaun Reilly has done to us! She's gone off and left me here with this – this lovely lunatic! It would serve her goddamn right if I – if – oh, Shivaun. Oh, Christ almighty.

Alana's right hand was undoing his belt and his trousers, her left was tracing fingertip circles on the pit of his stomach, her lips were full and soft on his; he had the sensation of falling headlong over a crevasse, struggling in space, in vain. I will never forgive myself, he thought, I will never, ever forgive myself if I do this. Nor will Shivaun. If I want to throw Shivaun out of my life once and for all, slam the door shut on her forever, this is the way to do it, because there's no going back from here.

He gasped as Alana pushed his head back, forced his whole body back and moved hers on top of him, resting her breasts on his chest in a way that made him feel what he'd once felt when, as a child, he'd thrust the nib of a pen into an electric socket. Rigid, sweating, he shot sideways under her, summoned all his strength to lift her upright, hit her if necessary.

Never in his life had he hit a woman, not since he was five and thumped Shivaun in the school yard. He didn't want to do it now, but he was going to have to—

A shrilling noise suddenly exploded between them, hurled them apart like quivering molecules. It was so loud and unexpected they found themselves staring into each other's eyes with terror, panting and immobilised.

It was the phone. The phone sounding as if it was ringing from outer space, so urgent and commanding that they clutched each other, and lurched upright on the sofa.

'Answer it!' he barked, his voice crashing in his ears, relief making him feel close to violent. 'Answer the fucking thing!'

Tears gleamed in her eyes as she pulled at her clothes and

stood up, fighting for breath. Waves of recrimination seemed to flow from her, and something else too, something that made him realise she was in pain, throbbing with hurt and rejection. If he had been going to acquiesce, he would have ignored the phone. Picking it up, she turned her back to him, breathed huskily into it.

'H – hello?'

At speed he gathered his clothing, secured it and raced out to the kitchen. He needed cold water – not just to splash his flaming face, but to hold his head under, soak him through until he retrieved his wits. Wrenching on the tap, he ducked down and let the gushing stream pour over his head, his neck, erasing the scent and taste of Alana Kennedy.

How had this happened? How could Alana – had she always felt this way, or was it a snap urge, some crazed spur of the moment? Shaken as he was, he wanted to think it was the latter, it was the alcohol, because the alternative was unthinkable. The alternative was that she'd wanted him for years, had planned every move with slow cold calculation . . . but even as his mind moved around it, he saw it. The clothes she'd worn tonight, the perfume, the fine food . . . the previous dinners, the meetings in the pub when he'd thought she was only being a friend, a good friend.

But she'd been Shivaun's friend, far more than she'd ever been his, and he felt nauseated as he pulled himself up, reached for a roll of kitchen paper to dry himself with. If Shivaun knew about this – he must never tell her, if he ever saw her again, never let her know how she had been betrayed by the confidante she trusted.

What was it Alana had said, in the midst of her passion? '*There's nothing in the way any more . . . didn't you ever find me attractive before?*' His insides churned as the words came back to him, confirming what he did not want to believe: it was deliberate, he had been set up. Alana must have long been jealous – or worse, long been in love with him. Not just in lust, but in love. Her face came back to him as he stood irresolute, her look, her tears. This had not merely to do with sex, it was much more than that, and he was furious. Furious with himself, for not divining it, furious with Alana, for not only permitting but planning it.

And yet – in spite of everything, in spite of the anger and shame he felt, he felt something else too. It speared him to admit it, but he felt pity. And a wave of sadness. It was tragic, for all three of them. Screwing up the saturated paper, he kicked open the bin and aimed it into it.

And there, lying torn in half under a pile of carrot peelings, lay a card. A card with an American stamp and – with a violent lurch, he recognised Shivaun's handwriting. His heart felt as if it had been struck with a hammer as he reached in and retrieved the pieces, brushed the garbage off them. But the writing was in biro, it was still legible.

> Dear Alana – This is just to let you know I arrived safely and everything is great so far. Marina and I are getting on like long-lost friends and I can't thank you enough for sending me here. It would be totally fantastic if only I didn't miss Ivor so terribly.
>
> Let me know when you have an e-mail address, and we'll talk! Hope the house is OK and you're happy in it.
>
> Love, Shivaun

His whole body trembled as he read it and read it again, his breathing like bursts of gunfire: '*Thank you for sending me here . . . if only I didn't miss Ivor so terribly.*'

In a flash flood it all hit him then, Alana's assurances that Shivaun didn't miss him, that Shivaun thought their separation a good idea, that she'd gone to America of her own volition with no thought of him. Grasping the card, he crushed it and threw it back in the bin, anger pumping up in him like volcanic lava as he tore back through the house.

Incredibly Alana was still on the phone, her composure apparently returned as she turned to look at him, putting her hand over the receiver.

'It's my mother, in Waterford.'

He strode to the phone, grabbed it out of her hand and bellowed into it.

'Mrs Kennedy, this is Ivor Lawlor and I just want you to know that you have the vilest, most unspeakably evil daughter in all creation.'

Slamming it down, he ripped the whole thing from its socket and hurled it at the wall. Then, barely conquering the urge to slap Alana's face and hurl her after it, he left the house with a speed and force that rocked it to its foundations.

As autumn waned but lingered, the sun still bright but casting longer shadows, Shivaun developed the curious sensation that it was she, more than Marina, who was the recovering invalid. She'd been devastated about Ivor and St Jude's, but it had never crossed her mind that she might have been even more than that, physically affected in some way which, while not a diagnosed illness, could be some form of malady.

Was her mind playing tricks? Was it possible that the burdens she had carried from day to day, her thoughts of Jason Dean stabbing her father, her birth parents placing her small form in the church doorway, had affected her more profoundly than she realised? Was Ivor's failure to understand her fully no more than an extension of her own failure, to fully understand herself?

Whatever it was, it felt now as if it was all slipping away from her. Each morning she woke up to the sound of the ocean and the sight of the sun, she went out on her widow's walk to breathe deep lungfuls of the crisp clear air, she ate breakfasts that made Dorothy whistle with admiration – juice, muffins, pancakes, bacon, whatever was going. Then, feeling purposeful and invigorated, she went to greet Marina, who took breakfast in her bedroom and never appeared until she was fully dressed in velvets and bandanas, jewellery and make-up, the lot. While she accepted Shivaun's help in the evenings, she never accepted it in the mornings, and Shivaun was mystified.

'How do you do up all those clothes, Marina, apply those cosmetics – it must take forever, with only one good hand?'

Marina smiled rather enigmatically, but then more openly. 'Azalea helps me. It amuses me to vary my nursing a bit, you know, I don't like to depend entirely on any one person.'

Azalea, Marina's secretary, was only twenty-nine. But she had been with Marina for over ten years, and it became evident to Shivaun that she was more than a secretary, she was a trusted friend. When Shivaun met her, she almost gasped on first sight: Azalea was a breath-takingly beautiful Native American with an oval, copper-skinned face and deep sapphire eyes, hair and eyelashes of the lushest black she'd ever seen. She was transfixingly handsome, magnificent – and totally unselfconscious.

'Hi, Irish! So you're the new nurse? How're you settling in?'

'Great.' Shivaun replied when she caught her breath, her eyes pinned to Azalea's tall pliant frame; she looked as if she could run twenty miles without breaking stride. Her taste in clothes was almost as dramatic as Marina's; today she was wearing a billowing scarlet caftan and a purple skirt that appeared to have been draped around her by Michelangelo. Lots of jewellery, too, bits of leather, whisks of feather, bright points of silver and turquoise stone.

'Navajo,' she replied to Shivaun's unasked question, 'from Arizona, I went there for my vacation last year.'

Shivaun couldn't take her eyes off it, of the whole vision Azalea presented. It seemed bizarre to her that a woman as beautiful as this should be working, up to her elbows in correspondence and bills and the mundanities of reality; she should simply *be*. Painters would throw themselves at Azalea's feet, she thought, sculptors would whimper, men would – what men might do hardly bore thinking about.

'Do – do you live nearby?' Shivaun managed to articulate, wincing at the inanity of the question. But Azalea looked as if she should live on some celestial planet, surrounded by lotus blossoms and worshipping nymphs.

Azalea shrugged. 'Sure. I live in a commune. A dozen of us bought this derelict old grain mill and commissioned Marina to do it up. She turned it into a real enclave, added cabins and an amazing kitchen, all steel and chrome, huge windows so we could see the birch and maples outside. I love waking up to those trees, especially at this time of year.'

Trees. Shivaun thought of Jimmy, of his oaks and elms, and connected with Azalea instantly. More and more she was feeling at home in Chederlay, warming to everyone in it and everything about it. She felt as if some heavy mantle were sliding off her shoulders, sliding silently to the ground . . . it was so sunny here, there was a sense of such peace and companionship, everyone seemed in tune as if they were part of some organic entity. Her memories of suburban Dublin, of rain and traffic and scandals, of corruption and petty competition, were washing further away on every tide. There, she'd been aware that some people actually envied her, people who neither knew nor cared that her material possessions were the legacy of tragedy, whereas here nobody seemed to give a damn what she owned, or wore, or drove.

Here, there was a steady rhythm to life, an acknowledgement of nature and the forces that dictated that rhythm. Now, in autumn, everything wore the colours of autumn, smelled of autumn and tasted of autumn; it was a distinct season, as Marina had promised, filled with leaves and pumpkins and warm gusty breezes, the kind of weather that made her somehow enjoy everything sensory, from the woollen sweaters she wore to the golden sunsets she revelled in each evening. Inside, the house was spacious and cosy, vaguely tinged with the scent of sandalwood joss-sticks Marina liked to burn; outside the land glowed every shade of cedar, saffron, brass and flame, as if it were burning from deep inside.

But she was curious. She'd love to see a house that Marina had designed. She'd only just met Azalea, but—

'Could I go there, some time, do you think? It sounds fascinating.'

Azalea smiled; her white teeth were a work of art in themselves.

'Sure! We'd love to show you round. I share a couple rooms

with my boyfriend, but everyone eats together in the kitchen nights – why don't you come on Thursday? Pizza and beer, seven o'clock?'

She was so definite, so enthusiastic. Shivaun was delighted.

'That'd be great! I didn't mean for dinner, but—'

'Oh, you're new in town, Shivaun, you've gotta come for dinner! Do you know anyone yet, have you made any friends?'

She felt a happy flash to be able to say yes, she had, she'd met a lady called Kathy who worked in an art gallery and had given her fried clams for lunch.

'Kathy Shreve? The painter who thinks she can't paint? C'mere, let me show you something.'

Rising from her desk, Azalea took Shivaun by the sleeve and led her from her office through to Marina's lounge, where sunlight was washing through the bay windows onto the far wall.

'Here. This is the best time to see it, in the morning – isn't it terrific?'

Shivaun looked up, and was confronted with a huge oil painting, an abstract slashed with daggers of vermilion, needles of jade and navy, spears of black and a hue of ochre verging on gold. Little or nothing as she knew about painting, she was dazzled, not only by the vibrant colours but by the distinction of the thing, the firm confident strokes that were screamingly unique. Whether it was good or bad was, she supposed, a matter of opinion, but it certainly had identity. Loud, assertive identity.

Azalea grinned. 'Our Kathy has some quaint notion that she's a mom and a housewife who just paints for fun. Marina and I think she should be hanging in the Met. What do you think?'

Shivaun thought about it, focusing on the canvas because it refused to let her attention wander.

'My God. Kathy – I don't know! Kathy gave me to understand that she sort of – you know – just dabbled. I imagined seascapes or landscapes, gentle things, maybe flowers in vases or portraits of her children.'

'Yeah. That's what she makes everybody think. She won't assert herself at all, except on canvas – Marina's always on her case, telling Kathy she could sell her paintings to clients all over the country if only Kathy would go for it. She needs to go flat out, Marina says, but so far nobody has been able to persuade her. We keep trying, though . . . you must too, Shivaun! Kathy needs encouragement!'

Yes. Clearly Kathy did – and how great of Marina and Azalea to see it, think about her, try to help her. Their attitude was full of what Viv would have called 'positive energy'. So was this painting, too. She made up her mind to talk to Kathy about it when they went into Boston next weekend, where Kathy was dying to show her Blaschka's glass flowers. Whatever they might be.

But today was a work day – God, you could forget you were supposed to be working, around here! Reluctantly, she turned to Azalea.

'I'm supposed to be doing some physio with Marina at ten. I'd better go to her, Azalea – see you later?'

'Yeah. Have fun.'

Yes, Shivaun thought as she went off to Marina, she was having fun. Her working day was no longer fraught with crises over budgets or bed shortages, there was no tight-fisted health minister to fight with, no petty politicking – thus far she wasn't even missing the babies, only having occasional flashbacks to them. She'd done her bit, brought them into the world, now it was up to their parents to make the most of them.

Marina was sitting in state, waiting for her without apparent urgency, reading a book. Shivaun looked at the title.

'Sinclair Lewis? Who's he?'

Marina put down the book and stretched back in her chair, letting Shivaun start work on her arm in a way that seemed to say she trusted her, was gaining confidence in her nursing skills now.

'He's an American writer, specialises in satires on the bourgeoisie, the stranglehold of suburban conformity. He won the Nobel prize in 1930. I've only started *Cass Timberlane*, as you can see, but all his other books are in the library. Feel free to read them if you like. *Main Street* and *Babbitt* are absolutely wonderful.'

Marina's face lit up with a kind of enthusiasm that Shivaun recognised with sudden, startled clarity, a flashback that dug up old memories and tossed them straight to the surface. This was exactly how Viv used to look, and speak, about things that engrossed her.

With a kind of joy, she nodded, kneeling at Marina's feet as she worked on her arm. 'Yes, I'd love to read them, if you think I should.'

'It's not a question of should. Books are simply a pleasure I enjoy sharing. You don't have to read Lewis, but if you do I hope you'll find it a worthwhile experiment. It might keep you out of the bars at any rate . . . there's not a lot for a young woman like you to do round here at nights, is there?'

Shivaun was astonished. That was exactly what Viv used to say to her whenever she gave her a new book to read: 'Here, this might keep you out of the bars for a night or two.' And the strategy had worked; as a teenager she had never developed as much interest in pubs or alcohol as her peers. Now, without Ivor, she had little inclination to go to bars at all, they'd only ever used them as meeting places prior to going somewhere else. Reflectively, she looked up into Marina's face as she worked, noting that Marina was registering some pain in her efforts to raise the arm.

'Marina . . . may I ask you . . . how do you think you came to have your stroke? Have you any idea what might have caused it?'

Marina grimaced. 'Overwork, Steven says. Juggling too many balls. Mental meltdown.'

'H'mm. And do you agree with that theory?'

'Well, it's a better theory than the alternative, which is that my body is packing up! I guess maybe I was biting off more than I could chew – but dammit, Shivaun, I'm a busy woman, I can't be lazing round by the pool painting my nails.'

'No. But – I tell you what, if I experiment with Sinclair Lewis, would you experiment with something too?'

Marina eyed her suspiciously. 'Like what? Cocaine and toyboys? Group sex? Raw jalapēnos for breakfast?'

Shivaun laughed. 'No – I don't think we have any of the ingredients we'd need, have we? I was only going to suggest yoga. I think you might find it relaxing.'

Marina fingered her jet necklace and considered. 'Yoga as in Indian mara-whatsits? Old guys with long white beards, sitting on beds of nails chanting poetry to buffaloes? Gimme a break, Shivaun. I have my tarot cards and my I-ching, that's enough madness to be going on with.'

'Well, if you're into those . . . are you a feng-shui fan too?'

'No! I think anyone who expects their life to unfold according to the direction the teapot is facing should consider repositioning their brain. I just do the tarot and I-ching for fun, that's all. It's all complete nonsense.'

'Probably. But I don't think yoga is. It clears your mind and relaxes your body, that's all. I'm not an expert by any means, but I used basic yoga principles sometimes with women in labour . . . it didn't work for them all but it did help the ones who responded to it.'

Marina snorted. 'I'm not having a baby, darling girl. Forty-eight-year-old divorcées rarely do.'

'Oh, Marina! Come on! It could really be therapeutic for you.'

'Therapeutic, huh? Well, I guess it beats basket-weaving, which some moron at the hospital suggested. I told her I'd rather knit a two-mile scarf of steel wool and strangle myself with it. Strangle her, too. I hate the words occupational therapy, they conjure up gibbering wrecks crouching in corners, crocheting strands of spaghetti into coasters.'

Shivaun put down Marina's arm and laughed outright. 'God, you're stubborn! Yoga isn't occupational therapy, it's only refreshment and renewal – I could get you a few books on it, maybe a video? If you hated it, you could drop it. But

Marina, if mental overload caused your stroke, you might really find yoga beneficial. It's great for people who are wound up.'

Marina's mouth twitched, but involuntarily Shivaun thought.

'Why wouldn't I be wound up, with a business to run and this house to maintain, half a dozen employees and two design assistants – I created a monster the day I got into architecture, never would have if I'd dreamed I'd be so successful.'

'Right! You'd have stayed home and baked cookies! But being wound up is curable, Marina, you can do something about it.'

Marina eyed her narrowly, speculatively. 'Is that so? I presume you're into yoga yourself then, Nurse Reilly?'

'Huh? Sorry?'

'Oh, don't give me that innocent stuff. You were wound up tighter than a Swiss clock when you arrived here.'

She had to admit the truth of it. 'Yes. All right. I was. But I'm much better now, starting to breathe properly – besides, I hadn't had a stroke. All I needed was a change of pace and scene. You need – you need yoga, Marina!'

Marina flexed her arm, repeated an exercise Shivaun had shown her, turned the proposal round in her mind.

'OK. It's a deal. I'll start yoga if you'll start it with me.'

'Me? I thought I was supposed to be starting Sinclair Lewis!'

'You can do both. Why don't you run down to the supermarket right now and get us a couple of mantras?'

They both laughed, and Shivaun was pleased to find she'd won her small battle. Not that she needed yoga in the least, herself. She'd do it strictly for Marina's benefit.

Another thing that worked well for Marina, Shivaun discovered by accident, was music. One day she put on a CD in the kitchen for Dorothy, who'd expressed interest in hearing some Irish music. It wasn't hard-core Irish, in fact it was Enya, and Dorothy didn't look very impressed. But next thing Marina came hobbling in on her stick and asked what it was.

'Enya? Enya Who?'

'She's just known as Enya,' Shivaun replied, 'bit wishy-washy for me, I don't know why I brought it with me really.'

'Well,' Marina said firmly, 'I like it. Why don't you put it on the sound system when we're doing our physio tomorrow morning, it'll take my mind off your excruciating tortures.'

So Shivaun put it on, loud as instructed, and the room was flooded. From Enya they soon progressed to other music of all descriptions, and Shivaun discovered Marina's eclectic collection.

'Why is it gathering dust? You have all sorts of stuff here, and a smashing sound system too.'

'I don't know,' Marina mused. 'I used to listen to music all the time, but after I came home from the hospital I – I just seemed to forget about it.'

'Well, let's revive it then. We could work alphabetically. Abba, Bach, Chopin, Neil Diamond – you really have varied taste, haven't you?'

'I love music. Of all descriptions. I used to go to concerts in L.A. all the time with my husband. Why don't you put on some Bette Midler, there, Shivaun, and loud, give it some muscle!'

Bette Midler came on, singing 'The Wind Beneath My Wings', making Shivaun wince as she thought of Ivor; that's what he always was, she admitted sadly, the wind beneath my wings. But then she realised that Marina was studying her expression, and changed it.

'Well, you're fit enough to go to some concerts in Boston if you wanted, I could drive you—'

Marina brightened. 'Yes, why not? Tina Turner is coming in late November, we could get tickets for her. Do you like her?'

Shivaun loved Tina, for her gutsy attitude as much as her voice, and thought the night out would do Marina a power of good. She wasn't quite up to walking around Boston yet, but she could sit at a concert . . . and what about her friends? Marina had many, who often came to visit her, but none of them seemed to have thought of asking her out anywhere. The next time she met them she'd drop some hints, and start trying to get Marina out and about a bit. That was part of this kind of nursing, to activate things which, while not strictly medical, might be beneficial.

'Yes, I do! Let's book tickets.'

Marina smiled at her, with affection she thought. 'You're sure you wouldn't mind giving up your evening to be my minder?'

'Not in the least. I'd love it. Tina is fun and Boston is my kind of city.'

Shivaun was much taken with Boston, had been to see the beautiful Blaschka flowers with Kathy, to Harvard and Cambridge and Filene's for shopping. At Quincy Hall she bought bags of jellybeans in outlandish flavours for Kathy's kids, then they went to the Museum of Fine Arts where, she insisted, Kathy's paintings should be hanging amongst the Monets and Whistlers. Kathy laughed uproariously, but Shivaun was adamant.

'Azalea showed me the one in Marina's house – it was so strong, Kathy, so vibrant! Your painting should be far more than a hobby.'

Kathy ran her hands through her curls and dimpled a little, pleased but shy.

'Oh, maybe some day when the kids are grown . . . c'mon, let's go get a cappuccino.'

Shivaun couldn't prise her any looser on the subject, but she felt a sense of purpose and resolved to chip doggedly away at her. Unlike her 'crusades' in Ireland, this had no sense of urgency about it, no injustice to be redressed or law to be resisted, but it was interesting and ignited her imagination. Why was Kathy so reluctant?

Meanwhile, she went to Azalea's commune for dinner as invited, and was fascinated by her amazing house in the woods, built of blond timber with soaring ceilings inside, vast windows and fireplaces, communicating spaces that bespoke how much in harmony Marina had been with the project.

'She cost us,' Azalea said frankly, 'but she did us a good deal and between eleven of us we were able to afford her. This is such a great place to live, she was worth every cent.'

Shivaun supposed that somewhere in America there must be houses built like Irish ones, joined at the hip in straight rows, but she had yet to see any; meanwhile she was entranced by this one. It was quite different to Chederlay, newer and far more contemporary, ideal for the free-flowing group who lived in it. Several of them appeared for dinner, surprising her with their diversity: they ranged from a young guy who worked for a local real-estate office to a white-haired woman of sixty who made jewellery for a Canadian department store. They were all very friendly, hospitable – when Americans welcomed you into their homes, she thought, they really pushed the boat out, put their hearts into it.

Azalea's boyfriend Jeff turned out to be a tall fair-haired optician, frank and freckled, clearly happy in their comfortable, humorous relationship. Several times they touched or lightly kissed each other, he teased her about her inability to cook and she teased back about his myopic inability to see her other talents, and Shivaun sensed great warmth between the two. Yet there was nothing exclusive about it, nothing that made her feel an outsider even if she did think of Ivor with a pang. If only – no. Don't go down that road, Shivaun, concentrate on the here and now, enjoy these new people.

Jeff put a glass of chardonnay into her hand and grinned at her sociably.

'Hey, you're cute. We'll have to fix you up with an all-American guy . . . how about a baseball player or a rodeo rider? Or do you already have a boyfriend?'

Shivaun kept her expression bright and her tone light. 'No, I haven't. Brad Pitt sends me flowers every day, but he's just not my type, Jeff.'

He chuckled and winked at Azalea. 'Then I guess we're just going to have to find someone who is – how about Richard Gere? No? Bill Gates? I know – Bill Clinton!'

Azalea turned from the worktop where she was making a salad and waved Jeff's suggestion away with her wooden spoon.

'No way. Bill Clinton's taken a monastic vow of chastity, and besides he's fifty . . . what Shivaun wants is . . . h'mm, let me think.'

She actually did seem to think about it, looked Shivaun up and down several times with a contemplative air. 'I don't know why, but I get the feeling that somebody kind of mature would be good. Somebody who'd take care of her.'

Shivaun was surprised. She was well able to take care of herself. What vulnerability could Azalea possibly have intuited? For a moment she wished she smoked, so she could light a cigarette and assume a nonchalant glibness. Jeff, who was dishing out the delivered pizza onto hot plates, raised a speculative eyebrow.

'Did you have a man in Ireland, Shivaun?'

God, Americans were so direct! She took a slug of her chardonnay and laughed as airily as she could. 'Yeah. I had. When I lived in Ireland.'

Jeff and Azalea glanced at each other, and then Jeff grinned again as he brought the pizza and sat down with her.

'Ah ha. Broken heart, huh?'

Jesus! Was this guy telepathic or what? She determined to tough it out.

'Right. Broken, snapped like a twig.'

They must be just guessing, hitting the mark by accident. Her break-up with Ivor wasn't tattooed on her forehead in red neon, was it? She smiled when Jeff nodded at her, lifting his pizza under his palms, American style, and biting sagely into it.

'So tell us about him. Did he wear green britches and a stovepipe hat, was he a little leprechaun living under a rainbow?'

Relieved by his levity, she nodded back. 'How did you guess? He had a fluffy white beard and gold buckles on his shoes, smoked a clay pipe and told great yarns about fairy ring-forts.'

Everyone laughed, and then Emily, who made the jewellery, intervened to say she'd been to Ireland once, was it dinky or what, those tiny cottages and roads the width of shoelaces . . .

as the conversation widened and drifted elsewhere, Shivaun sat back thankful that the focus was swivelling off her.

The remainder of the evening was thoroughly enjoyable, interesting too; she discovered that some of the 'communists' held political beliefs akin to her own, others were sufficiently opposed that lively dialogue ensued. She contributed to it with pleasure but caution; this was their country and she'd made up her mind to stay out of trouble, out of anything that might lead her back to where she'd been in Ireland.

She managed to contain herself until someone raised the subject of the death penalty, which the state of Massachusetts was considering reintroducing, and then she felt one of her speeches coming on, had to bite her tongue and sit on her hands lest she start thumping the table. Jesus—! But she forced herself to shut up and listen, learn from the debate instead. Then Emily got onto the topic of the Kennedys, whose turf Massachusetts was, voicing her opinion that they were a dodgy bunch and that Bobby Kennedy had been mixed up in Marilyn Monroe's intriguing death.

'Cool it, Emily,' Jeff said, 'you'll offend Irish here.'

But Shivaun found Emily's candour a refreshing change from the idolatrous esteem in which the Kennedys were held in Ireland, and permitted herself to agree vociferously with her. The night seemed to gallop by, and at the end of it Jeff and Azalea offered to walk her back to Marina's house, ten minutes away under the swishing trees and peeping stars. Nights were getting colder now, and Azalea loaned her a huge warm scarf, patting her on the back as she settled it round her shoulders in a somehow sisterly way.

'I think I'm starting to get you figured' she murmured, out of Jeff's hearing. 'Something bad went wrong in Ireland, didn't it?'

Shivaun was so astonished she couldn't answer, a response that Azalea seemed to interpret as assent.

'Uh-huh. You have an expressive face, you know, it doesn't let you hide as much as you think . . . but don't worry, Shivaun. America is the land of opportunity and new beginnings. We'll get you sorted, you'll see.'

Horrified on the one hand, Shivaun was deeply touched on the other. How Azalea had managed to slip past her resolute bravado she couldn't imagine, but Azalea's tone was somehow intuitive, and very warm. Shivaun got back to Chederlay feeling that by her side walked the makings of a first-class friend.

Chapter Seven

It was over a week before Ivor could bring himself to return to Shivaun's house and confront Alana. But finally he went, steeling himself to find out everything he was determined to know.

She drew in her breath when he marched into the kitchen, assessing the look on his face before squaring up to him.

'Just because you have keys, Ivor, doesn't mean you can come in here any time you want.'

He threw the keys on the table. 'I know. Here you are. I won't be using them again.'

She bit her lip, looked at him uncertainly. 'Then why are you here now? Did you forget something, in your hurry to leave last time?'

He heard the bitterness in her tone, recognised the things she must be feeling despite the bravura in her stance. Without make-up, wearing a fluffy cardigan over a loose dress and her hair tied back, she looked almost childlike, and he was maddened to feel some sympathy for her. Whatever she had done, he suspected, had been done out of loneliness, the need for recognition and affection that everyone felt at times. If Shivaun had not been part of the picture, he might almost have been able to forgive her. But Shivaun was very much part of the picture, the reason why he was standing here now clenching his fists.

'No. I didn't forget anything, although you certainly forgot yourself.' He made his tone as frosty as possible, determined not to let her get to him, divert him from his mission.

She sighed, looked out the window in a way that made him suspect she regretted what she had done, was barely able to meet his eye.

'Yes. I did, Ivor, and I'm sorry. Can you forgive me, do you think?'

His resolve hardened. 'I could forgive your attempted seduction, yes, if that was all there was to it.'

Her eyes widened innocently. 'But that is all there was to it! What do you mean?'

'I mean, Alana, that while you were on the phone to your dear mother, I found Shivaun's postcard. In the bin. The postcard saying she missed me, but thanking you for sending her to America.'

She whitened, and he saw he'd hit the nail. 'I presume you sent her because you wanted her out of my reach, out of your way – is that right?'

She didn't answer. But he persisted. 'I'll take your silence as agreement, then.'

She lifted her head a fraction. 'So that's why you went ballistic! Not because I – I came on to you. I knew it!'

He was thrown. 'What?'

'I knew you weren't angry with me over – over that! I knew you couldn't be, not after – after the way you reacted!'

'The way I – what in God's name are you talking about?'

'I'm talking about you, Ivor, about the way you responded . . . you wanted to sleep with me, didn't you? You wanted sex and we would have had it if the phone hadn't rung!'

He was so shocked he had to grip the table, lean hard on it. She was so far off the mark – wasn't she?

'Alana, you're crazy. I'm sorry if that doesn't sound very chivalrous. But your imagination is running riot. There is no way we would have done any such thing.'

She smiled, almost happily he thought with astonishment.

'Oh, Ivor. Come on. Admit it. You were on the brink.'

The feeling came back to him, the feeling of falling into a

crevasse, and from nowhere a snatch of music came to him, something from Leonard Cohen's song 'Suzanne': '*You think that she's half crazy . . . just when you mean to tell her that you have no love to give her, then she gets you on her wavelength, and lets the river answer that you've always been her lover . . .*'

He experienced a horribly dizzy, sinking feeling. Oh, Shivaun! Where are you, when *I* need *you*?

'OK, Alana. Read it any way you like. I don't care what you do, so long as you tell me where Shivaun is. I want to contact her. I want her address, phone or fax number, e-mail, whatever you've got.'

She thought about it. And then she pouted. 'No. I'm not going to tell you where she is, Ivor, or give you any of those things.'

He was both baffled and provoked. 'But why not? For chrissakes, Alana, now that I know she didn't go to America of her own accord, I need to talk to her!'

'Well, I'm sorry, but you can't. You treated me horribly the other night, you said dreadful things to my mother and now you can go to hell.'

They stared at each other, and he realised that he was walking on glass. He'd been right about Alana; her former blitheness did indeed camouflage one lost, needy lady. Emotionally she was what the media had always called Diana Spencer, 'a loose cannon'. So this was how it felt, to be looking almost literally into the mouth of one . . . of course Shivaun had been needy too, but in a different way, she'd never looked at him in the yearning way Alana was looking now, hostility disguising desperation.

Deliberately, he stood back from her, and lightened his tone.

'OK. I apologise for what I said to your mother. And now, Alana, I am going to count to five. If you don't give me the information I want by then, I will tell Shivaun everything you did, and she will evict you from this house. You will be out on the street, have to find somewhere else to live at double the price, she'll take her car from you too. You will regret it, I promise you.'

He forced an ironic smile, one that suggested he was regretting having to say such things, but it was enough. It sobered her so sharply, so completely that she sank down on a chair at the table, and burst into tears.

'Oh, Ivor! How can you be so mean to me?'

'One. Two. Three. Four . . .'

'All right! All right, I'll give you her address!'

Relieved, he nodded grimly. It didn't seem to have struck her that he couldn't say anything to Shivaun, if she didn't give him Shivaun's address – or else she thought he might get it elsewhere, from Matron at St Jude's, perhaps? Somebody, somewhere, must know where Shivaun was – damn, why hadn't he looked at the postmark on the card?! Because he'd been so angry . . . but he'd find her now somehow, he had to know how she was and what she was feeling. God only knew what poisonous things Alana might have told her about him, maybe even that he was seeing somebody else or – a hideous thought struck him.

But he waited until she had found a paper and pen, written Shivaun's details on it and the paper was in his back pocket, before voicing it.

'Thank you. And now, I have another question.'

Dully, with something close to despair, she looked up at him. 'What is it?'

'It's about Fintan Daly. Was Shivaun really seeing him, or did you make that up?'

She groaned piteously, her eyes still full of tears. 'Yes. I made it up, Ivor. But only – only because I wanted you, so much. I've wanted you for years, Ivor, you can't imagine how much . . . you're so kind and so romantic, you have that little dimple when you smile, you had such a great future until you chucked your job – but you will go back to it, won't you?'

He heard the hardness in his voice as he answered her, but he felt a soaring sense of liberation.

'No. I won't. I'm going to Spain, actually. Tomorrow.'

She gasped, reached out to him in a way that made him

step back, thinking she was going to clutch him to her. 'Spain? Tomorrow? Oh, Ivor! Oh, no!'

'Oh, yes. I'm going to study carpentry with a craftsman in Seville.'

Her voice dwindled down to a whisper. 'But I – but Ivor, what am I going to do, without you?'

He was on the point of a brusque retort when something caught him, held him back. In spite of her terrible behaviour, he could see that Alana was genuinely lost, maybe heading somewhere neither he nor Shivaun would want her to go. He didn't dare sit down beside her, but he softened his tone.

'I think, Alana, that maybe you're going to have a long chat with somebody. Somebody qualified, I mean . . . someone who can help to make you feel better.'

He sighed to himself as he said it, remembering how Shivaun had once seen counsellors as per orders, but got nowhere with them. He could only pray that Alana was more positively disposed, because today's conversation indicated that she was really mixed up. Seriously mixed up. Sadly, he surveyed her, but was careful to hide the pity he felt for her. Despite her big family in Waterford, she seemed so isolated. Maybe dangerously isolated, when St Jude's broke up and her colleagues were dispersed – just as Christmas was coming up, too.

She turned to him, pulled her cardigan around her. 'Do you mean you think I'm mad, Ivor?'

He shook his head, forced a laugh. 'No! I merely think you're a bit stressed, that's all, emotionally overwrought. We've all been a bit overwrought lately, perhaps . . . that's why I'm going to Spain.'

It was far from the only reason, but he hoped it would soothe her. After a moment, it seemed to.

'Yes. Maybe you're right. I – I'm sorry about what I said earlier, Ivor. I don't know what I can have been thinking of. Will you forgive me?'

'Yes, I will – if you'll promise me to do as I say, and see someone?'

She nodded. 'Y – yes. OK. I will, if you think I should.

It's good of you to care . . . will you write to me, from Spain?'

Yes. He promised that he would, patted her gingerly on the shoulder, and escaped while the going was good. As he left her he felt her eyes boring into his back, following him all the way out of the house, and knew that she would weep her heart out when he was gone.

Poor Alana. But, when he was gone, safely out of sight, his heart almost did cartwheels, he exulted with joy. So Shivaun was missing him, was she? And now he had her address, he could say everything he needed to say, ached to say? She was not entirely lost to him, after all?

Yes! Way hey, way *hey*!

Marina grinned at Shivaun one morning and flatly refused to do any physio session.

'No. We're taking the day off.'

'We are? I don't seem to recall processing your application for a day off.'

'Oh, put a sock in it! And get your jacket. Joe is driving us into Boston.'

'Is that so? And why would we be going to Boston?'

'We'd be going – we *are* going – to have fun. A girls' day out.'

Shivaun grinned in turn. Marina was twice her age, but she was never conscious of it, in fact she was the one who felt rejuvenated when Marina twinkled as she was twinkling now.

'OK, you're the boss! Steven will kill us both, but—'

'But,' Marina replied serenely, 'I have other plans for Steven. First, you and I are going to get our hair done. Then a manicure, facial and massage. Then lunch at the Bay Tower. Then shopping at Saks and Neiman Marcus.'

'Shopping? Marina, are you sure you—?'

'Yes. I'm quite sure. My treat. Besides, Christmas is coming, I want to get some things. Do you have plans for Christmas, Shivaun?'

Something in the way Marina looked at her held her back, stopped her from saying yes, Kathy Shreve has invited me to spend it with her.

'Nothing definite yet.'

'Good. Then I hope you'll be spending it here with me. My brother Max and his kids will be flying in from California – three teenagers, but no wife. Divorce seems to run in our family, I'm afraid.'

Without further ado Marina got up and walked, quite briskly Shivaun noted, to the waiting car outside. She still leaned on her stick, but she looked distinctly stronger, visually arresting in jade and ruby crushed velvet with buckets of jewellery. As she threw on her jacket Shivaun felt real satisfaction; her patient was improving, definitely.

In Boston they were deposited at an extremely swish hairdressing salon called Simon Bratz, where Shivaun sank into a luscious leather seat thinking the place should be called Spoiled Brats.

'Now darling,' Marina trilled at Simon, 'you know what to do with me. The question is, what are we going to do with young Shivaun here?'

Simon lifted up a strand of Shivaun's hair, peered and tutted at it.

'Tsk. Split ends. A good cut to start with—' Abruptly, he seized Shivaun's chin and chucked it first upwards, then sideways. 'Layers. And shorter. Much shorter, yes?'

He raised an enquiring eyebrow, and Shivaun was about to say no way, pal, hold it right there, when suddenly she thought of Ivor. Ivor had loved her shoulder-length hair, had always run his hands through it when— She was astonished to feel an irrational, searing flash of fury.

'Yes. Much shorter. Do your worst.'

Delighted, he clicked his fingers for some illustrated styles to be brought and looked knowingly at Marina. 'Let me guess. Your friend has had a little tiff with the boyfriend, yes?'

'No,' Shivaun interjected before Marina could answer, 'not

a little tiff. A huge tiff, the mother and father of all tiffs. The bastard has gone to Australia.'

There was a shocked silence, and then Marina burst out laughing. 'Ah! So we're getting to the angry stage, are we!'

Yes, Shivaun thought fuming, it seems we are. Taking the illustrations, she selected a feathery crop with a fringe and stabbed her finger at it.

'I'll have that.'

Simon beamed. 'Oh yes, that will be stunning. And then some gold lowlights perhaps—?'

'Gold, diamond, emerald, whatever you think.'

Marina purred with pleasure. 'Gold will be gorgeous on you, Shivaun. I feel rather staid settling for just plum myself!'

Their hair was duly washed, and then Shivaun was startled to see a tray arriving with two glasses of champagne on it. Christ. They were into big-bucks territory here for sure. But so what? Even if this wasn't Marina's treat, she didn't have any family to worry about, did she? No school fees to pay or rosebud mouths to feed – abruptly, she knocked back half the glass in one gulp, and nodded at Simon when he brandished his scissors.

'Go for it.'

He went for it, all right, and two hours later Shivaun beamed transfixed at her transformed reflection.

'Wonderful! I love it!'

Everybody loved it, and Marina paid for it, squashing Shivaun's protests like insects. 'No, I'm the boss as you say and I insist. Today is on me, darling.'

Shivaun looked again at her gleaming new reflection, and was suddenly moved by Marina's generosity, so moved that she threw her arm impulsively around her and hugged her.

'You are so kind! Thank you!'

Briefly Marina looked moved in turn, but then she gathered her forces. 'Now, our beauty treatment next, come along!'

A memory stirred in Shivaun, a distant delicious memory of her thirteenth birthday, on which Viv had marched her into Dublin with just such enthusiasm for a 'teenager's makeover', treating her to her first taste of beauty and glamour and femininity. They'd had a fabulous day out, giggling and gossiping, and laughed themselves senseless at the end of it when Jimmy gasped horrified, saying they looked like a pair of prize begonias. But, whatever they looked like, she'd felt very special that day, cherished and loved and nurtured.

That was how she felt now, too, as Marina steered her into a perfumed beauty salon for more pampering, which this time resulted in make-up that made her feel and look shimmering, starry-eyed. Marina was thrilled with it.

'You're reborn! A real Renaissance beauty!'

She certainly felt reborn, and there was no denying the captain's glance of admiration when they arrived for lunch at the Bay Tower, where Marina regally seated herself at their window table overlooking the city.

'What a view! My God, Marina, this is amazing.'

'Yes. How refreshing to see it through your new eyes, too. This was my regular table for years, but I hadn't been back since my stroke . . . *hello,* Charles, how *are* you?'

Charles, their waiter, seemed genuinely delighted to see her, and champagne cocktails arrived as if by magic. Shivaun gazed askance.

'More champagne? I'll be under the table.'

'Yes, and I may very well be under – oh, never mind, let's look at the menu, d'you like lobster?'

In fact Marina ate and drank very sparingly, gave Shivaun her cocktail because it might 'screw up my medication, darling', but Shivaun ate an entire lobster and had a wonderful time.

'Oh, Marina, this is the best day I've had in ages.'

Marina nodded approvingly. 'Good. I'm glad to see you eating well, too.'

'I've put on five pounds since I came to America! You're force-feeding me, fattening me up for Christmas!'

'You needed it, you were positively ravaged when you arrived here . . .' looking thoughtful, she stopped, and then put her hand on Shivaun's. 'Darling child, may I ask you a personal question?'

Shivaun hesitated, but then said yes, she could, although she wouldn't promise to answer it.

'What happened? What really happened to you, apart from losing Ivor?'

A door swung shut in Shivaun's mind immediately. But then, to her surprise, it swung open again, like the swing doors the waiters were coming through.

'It – it – oh, Marina. It's a long story. You really don't want to hear it.'

'Yes, I do. Will you tell me, or am I intruding?'

'No. You're not intruding. You're being incredibly sweet and caring and I . . . I will tell you, if you're sure you want to know. But not now. Not here in public.'

'No.' Marina considered, and Shivaun thought how well she was looking today, with her own revamped hair and make-up, her large eyes bright and animated. Steven Hunt would be impressed when next he saw her. So would Azalea, when they got home this evening.

Home? Was she really starting to think of Chederlay that way? Was she not pining for Ireland, not homesick in the way she'd expected to be? Sometimes she had visions of it, memories of friends and colleagues, mothers and babies, random things like Ken Hammond reading the news, the theme music of *Glenroe*, banks of fuchsia and aubrietia lining the roads of Kerry where she'd once gone hostelling with Ivor . . . she was missing Ivor, crucifyingly at times, but increasingly she felt that this, for the moment, was where she was meant to be. Was he too where he was meant to be?

Marina patted her hand, and she realised she was day-dreaming.

'You're quite right. This is not the place for intimate conversation. I'll leave it up to you, Shivaun, to choose when and where . . . if it would help to tell me about it, you know, I'm listening. Maybe I could even help in some small way.'

Shivaun looked at her, and found herself taking Marina's hand.

'Oh, Marina, you are helping, already. You have no idea

how much I appreciate being taken out and treated like this, how glad I am that you're my – my patient! You've been so welcoming, everyone at Chederlay has, you make me feel almost like – like part of your family.'

Marina touched the amethyst brooch at her throat, and smiled at her in a way that was somehow wistful.

'I hope you do feel a part of it, Shivaun. I feel – I feel a great deal better, since you came to nurse me.'

Eagerly, Shivaun smiled in turn. 'Do you? I was just thinking how well you look today. Steven will be chuffed with you.'

Unexpectedly, Marina roared with laughter. 'Chuffed! What a quaint expression! But I hope he will be chuffed – oh, I've had enough of being ill! I want a brandy and a cigarette!'

She looked around her as if she were about to order both, but Shivaun waved away the waiter who stood ready to spring.

'No! Like that parking sign said downstairs, don't even think about it!'

With a sigh, Marina subsided. 'Oh, all right. You're the boss, Nurse Reilly.'

Shivaun laughed at the petulant pout she affected, but she resolved to watch Marina now that she was getting well enough to start wanting things that would harm her. She devoutly did not want Marina Darnoux to come to any harm.

'Come on. I'd better get you out of here. Let's hit Saks.'

Diverted, Marina stood up. 'Yeah. Let's. I want to buy Max's kids some razor blades for Christmas.'

'What?!'

'Well, Max has called me several times since my stroke, sent cards and flowers, but they never did. Now they're probably expecting a thousand bucks' worth of gifts apiece for Christmas. I think some cute little nasties would be a nice surprise for them, don't you?'

Again Shivaun found herself laughing, and thinking of Viv, who would wholeheartedly agree with Marina.

* * *

Boarding the train at the Gare d'Austerlitz, Ivor caught sight of himself in its window, and was satisfied with what he saw. Ivor the accountant was entirely eradicated now; in his place stood a bearded man dressed in denim jeans, hiking boots, a flannel shirt and a scruffy leather jacket, carrying a rucksack, packed sandwiches from the station buffet and a paperback copy of Ernest Hemingway's *For Whom The Bell Tolls.* He'd never read Hemingway before, not been as avid a reader as Shivaun, but the friend who'd found him the craftsman in Seville, through his job at the Spanish embassy, had thrust the book into his pocket as he was leaving.

'Read this, Ivor. Read as much as you can, about Spain. It can be a harsh, cold country, you won't find it easy to crack.'

Ivor thought this friend was being unduly pessimistic. Admittedly, he did not speak Spanish, knew nothing about Franco or Picasso or the Spanish civil war, but . . . what did Frank mean, about Spain being cold? Did that refer to the physical or the spiritual climate? Well, he didn't expect blazing sunshine in late November, but – throwing himself onto the train as it began to move off, he made his way through its unexpectedly crowded carriages until he found himself a seat, and handed his ticket to the inspector who materialised almost immediately. It had been a bit embarrassing to have to borrow the price of it from Cynthia, and haggle for an under-26 fare with his birthday imminent, but hey, here he was at last, on his merry way.

As the train crossed over the border from France into Spain tonight, he would turn twenty-six, and the synchronicity of it pleased him. A new day, a new year, a new career, a whole new life if he chose to embrace it . . . if he did not hear from Shivaun, after he'd written the letter he'd been composing in his head since leaving Alana, and would romantically post from a border station. In fact he might as well get started on it right now, because although this long journey would give him plenty of time, he wanted to compose it more than once if necessary, get it absolutely perfect. So much depended on it . . . as he thought of Shivaun opening it he could see her astonished face in his mind's eye, the way she would twirl her hair around her finger or a pen in that way she had, her hazel eyes drinking in every word – he prayed – while she thought of him in turn, and decided she'd made a mistake after all. He'd better turn up the heat a bit, pour all his passion for her into every word and make sure Alana's lies were fully obliterated. Even now he didn't know the exact extent of them, but he could guess at their general thrust, which was that he, Ivor, was a very bad bet and Shivaun was far better off without him.

God *damn* that bitch Alana! The more he thought about her meddling the more infuriated he became, not least because he'd been so taken in by her. And if he'd been duped, Shivaun almost certainly had been too – Christ, what if she threw his letter away unopened, without even giving him a hearing? What if she'd met some bloody American . . . ? The thought of his girl touching or kissing another man was absolutely unbearable, excruciating, he felt he'd punch the guy's lights out whoever he might be. But worse than anything was the simple fact that he didn't know, had no idea whatsoever what she was doing, how she was feeling or whether, finally, she still loved him at all.

If she did truly love him, why had she not quit her job when he asked her to, why was she in America instead of here on this train with him? Or had that been too much to ask? Or might she have changed her mind, if he'd persisted, insisted? Or – as the train chugged out into the suburbs of Paris, gathering speed north of the Loire valley, Ivor began to mull over all the ifs and buts, the mights and maybes, and found it a very unsatisfactory exercise. Unlike mathematics it had no definite answers, no strategy that would produce a final solution; all he knew for sure was that Shivaun felt like a missing limb, and the pain was getting worse, ghosting horribly. In his mind's eye her vivid face flared up, in his head he could hear her challenging all the things that made her so mad, so beautiful, in his bones he ached for every inch of her body – and then with a jolt he remembered Alana's body, to which he had so nearly succumbed. That's the truth, he thought; I was on the brink. I am a worthless louse. I am going insane without Shivaun Reilly. I am going to Spain and what the hell am I going to do about sex when I get there? *What* am I going to do, without Shivaun?

Rummaging in his rucksack, he extracted a pen and paper and positioned them on the swaying table, resolutely shutting out the chattering adults and rampaging children around him. Then he chewed on the end of the pen, gazed at the blank page and chewed on the pen some more. He had never before written a love letter, and now when faced with it he found it extremely difficult to transport the words from his head to the paper. Dear Shivaun? Dearest Shivaun? Darling Shivaun . . . ? Christ, how did you go about this? How did Shakespeare and all those lads just knock this stuff out, could he remember a single poetic line he'd ever learned at school?

No. Not one word. Cynthia and his father might as well have saved their money and sent him to a hedge school, for all the good his expensive education seemed to be when the chips were down. The train was coming into Bourges before he came up with the first three words, and hurled them onto the page with the exhausted triumph of a mother delivering triplets.

'My beloved Shivaun.' Well, that was a start. She was his beloved. Only a couple of hundred more words to go. Perspiration began to bead on his forehead as he clutched the pen and groped for the next bit.

And then suddenly the dam burst and the words flowed like Niagara Falls, poured out onto page after page, took on a life of their own until he felt as if he were actually talking to Shivaun, as if she were there in front of him. So much depended on this, he *must* convince her that he still loved her! But Chambon sped by, Neuvic and Cantal and Villefranche, the train was almost in Cordes by the time he felt the letter was coming right, oblivious to falling dark and shunting carriages, passengers boarding and alighting around him, voices taking on the rich soupy accent of the south. Only when they reached Toulouse did he finally sit back and read what he'd written, frowning as he scanned every word, checking and double-checking for mistakes, misunderstandings, any traps he might inadvertently have laid for himself or for her . . . but he could detect nothing.

It was, he thought with pride, a fair and honest letter, not as elegant as he might have wished perhaps, but clear, direct and full of hope. She would certainly understand it.

My beloved Shivaun,

I am on a train en route for Spain. I am beginning the adventure that caused our separation. And I am missing you more than I have ever missed anyone or anything in my entire life.

That's the price of selfishness, so I deserve it, deserve all the pain I inflicted on myself the day I said I wanted us to separate. But I *did* only mean temporarily, do you believe and understand that? The last thing I want is for you to be feeling the pain I'm feeling, even if I do hope you're missing me and thinking of me – just once in a while, tell me you are?

Oh, Shivaun! You drove me mad so often, you scared me in so many ways, but I adore you and always will adore you. And now, with that firmly established I hope, there's something I have to tell you, because you must wonder why I never contacted you. The truth is that I wanted to, needed to talk much more about what happened on the beach, beg you to keep open our chance of a future together. But Alana stopped me. She told me you were glad we'd parted, that you felt it was for the best and, worst of all, she told me you were seeing Fintan Daly.

I was gutted. But I believed her, because you're so beautiful, any man would be eager and lucky to get an hour of your time . . . meanwhile, I don't know precisely what she told you, but it seems she went to great lengths to keep us apart, even initiated your visit to America, may have given you to understand I'd left the country long before I did. I only left Ireland yesterday!

The reason for my going to Spain is the reason I can now understand why you couldn't give up nursing to travel with me. I've taken up carpentry, discovered a real joy in it, the kind of joy that makes me feel I'm doing the right thing in going to Seville, to study it there with a local craftsman who makes furniture. It has become a kind of passion, and you wouldn't recognise me if you saw me – Ivor the accountant has vanished without trace. Now I feel the same way about something that you always felt about nursing and the other things that consumed you . . . I couldn't *not* go to Spain, but now I know why you went to America. Alana sent you, she set the whole thing up. Set us both up.

Her reason for doing that is embarrassing to explain, but I have to tell you: she is – or was – apparently infatuated with me. She wanted you out of the way so she could have me for herself. It's a horrible thing for you to hear, you will feel deeply betrayed by the friend you trusted and I only wish I could be there with you, for you, when you reach for someone trustworthy to buffer the shock. I *am* with you, in spirit – Shivaun, please tell me you still love and trust me, that you haven't met any American man? I want you to make friends, to be happy in America, but I cannot bear the thought of you getting any closer than friendship to anyone.

Will you write to me? Please say you will, tell me everything about what you're doing and who you're with? The thought that you might be lonely or homesick is killing me, I had absolutely no idea that Alana was capable of driving you so far away. But, dreadful as her actions were, I don't think you should rush into any row with her, do anything rash or drastic, because she doesn't seem entirely well. For now, it might be best to just leave her as she is and things as they are. She's kind of fragile.

I asked her for your phone number but she said she didn't have it, only this address I'm writing to – I'm enclosing my own new address in Seville and I swear I will not *breathe* until I hear from you. I never realised I was going to miss you as much as this, I was a fool to think you'd wait a whole year for me and now I can only pray it'll be a worthwhile year for us both and we'll fall into each other's arms at the end of it. Our sex life had been suffering, I think, we'd both got distracted, but now I can't wait to rekindle it, to hold and love you for the rest of our lives. If you tell me there's no other man – Jesus, Shivaun, *please*! – I will be totally faithful to you until we see each other, not even speak to a Spanish woman except on business. You're my girl and I want you desperately, not just physically but in every way that truly matters.

The train will be entering Spain in about an hour and I'm going to post this from the first place it stops. Write back the minute you get it, promise me? I need to know – have to know – that we still love and understand each other, care for each other as deeply as ever if not more. I can't *wait* to talk to you.

Meanwhile, don't let anyone steal your KitKat, OK? If anyone tries, I'll kill him. I love you with all my heart.

Ivor

Yes. That was as good as he could possibly make it. It wasn't flowery, but it said all the essentials. Shivaun would know how he felt and respond with the passion she always put into everything that mattered. He didn't care what she wrote back – anger would be fine, or amusement, she could shout at him or laugh at him, anything she liked – just so long as she did write back and confirm that yes, she was still his girl. Putting the pages into his pocket, he left them there to burn a hole in it until, under a starry, chilly night sky, the train finally slowed into the Spanish border station of San Sebastian, where he jumped out to buy stamps and envelopes from a kiosk, found a postbox and pushed the letter securely down into it with a throbbing mixture of tension and relief. Then, completely drained, he got back on the train, folded his arms on the table in the darkened carriage and fell fast asleep.

As it carried him on to Madrid, he had no inkling of what an inexorable grip Alana Kennedy still held on his life and Shivaun's, what power she still wielded over them all the way from distant Dublin. He did not know that she had given him a false address, and that his letter would never be delivered.

The morning after their Boston spree, Shivaun went to greet Marina purposefully, resolved to make up the time they had lost yesterday. First yoga, then physio, then speech exercises . . . as if in sympathy, the house was busy today, she could hear Azalea whistling in her office and Dorothy vacuuming in preparation for anticipated visitors tonight. Marina was getting more visitors, Shivaun noticed, now that her speech was starting to improve and people could understand it better. Making a mental note to recruit people to get her out more, she went to Marina in the library, where she sat resplendent in an amber ensemble and full make-up, listening to Pavarotti belting out 'La Donna È Mobile.'

'Good *morning*. Watch my lips! What a racket!'

Marina smiled serenely. 'Good morning, darling girl. Are we ready to start?'

'Yes, let's get going, we have a lot to catch up.'

'Indeed. And I want to be finished by noon. Steven is coming to see me.'

'Is he? I didn't think he was due today.'

Marina admired her new manicure, which featured subtly silver nail polish, and smiled again as she gazed at her hands. 'Apparently he has another patient only a few miles away, so he called to say he'll drop in. Tell me, what are your plans for the afternoon?'

'I was going to steer you out for a good walk – if you can manage Saks and Neiman Marcus, I reckon you can make it into town. We could drop in on—'

'Oh, not today, darling. I did quite enough walking yesterday. Why don't you take the car and go out for a nice drive? You've been meaning to visit Sturbridge for ages, haven't you?'

Yes, Shivaun had, but not on a working day, she didn't want Marina giving her so much free time she'd feel guilty about it.

She didn't want Marina lounging around this afternoon either, she wanted her active.

'I can go to Sturbridge on my own time. Today I'd really rather you—'

Marina sighed, rather impatiently she thought. 'Shivaun, look. I'm giving Azalea the afternoon off as well. Why don't you two girls get together and amuse yourselves, h'mm? It's perfect weather for a fun jaunt somewhere. So let's agree on that and say no more about it, h'mm?'

Shivaun thought she smelled a rat. What was going on here?

'Marina, what are you up to?'

Marina laughed, making Shivaun think what a lovely laugh she had, deep and throaty. 'Shivaun, you're my nurse, not the police! I have some private business to attend to this afternoon, that's all.'

'Well – if you insist – but—'

'Shivaun, you're forever telling me that I'm the boss. So today I *am* the boss, OK?'

OK, then. Somewhat sceptically, Shivaun cut Pavarotti off in mid-bellow and got down to work.

Azalea knew the Mohawk Trail up in the Berkshires intimately, and Shivaun set off with her to visit that. As they drove through the now bare countryside Azalea dispensed information about the sights to be seen, but eventually Shivaun interrupted her.

'Azalea, why does Marina want us out of the house today?'

Azalea turned her head long enough to grin at her. 'Oh, Shivaun! Can't you guess?'

Shivaun thought for a moment, and then an awful suspicion came to her. No. Surely not. It couldn't be that.

'It – you're not going to tell me it's Steven Hunt, are you?'

Azalea laughed aloud. 'Give the girl first prize! Yes, it is Steven – I'm pretty sure it is, anyway. She's had her sights on him for ages.'

'But she doesn't even like him!'

'Yes, well, I think that's beside the point. Our Marina moves in mysterious ways.'

'But – but she's ill! Her health won't stand up to—'

'A little gentle exercise? But isn't that exactly what you wanted her to get, this afternoon?'

Shivaun spluttered. 'Jesus, I meant a walk, not *that* kind of exercise! Besides, Steven looks like a stuffed shirt to me, I don't think—'

'No. Don't think. Better not to. It is a horrible thought. Betcha fifty bucks I'm right, though.'

Shivaun could scarcely think of anything else for the remainder of the day, learned virtually nothing from Azalea's instructive tour of the Trail because all she could see was Marina's smile, her new hair-do, her manicure and her make-up . . . certainly such things were meant to be therapeutic, but really! Marina must be mad as a hatter, it would serve her right if she ran out of puff and Steven ended up having to give her mouth-to-mouth – oh, God! She burst out laughing, and Azalea laughed with her as they emerged from Herman Melville's house.

'You're looking great today yourself, Shivaun. I'm going to have to set my mind to finding you a man for yourself.'

Shivaun winced. 'Oh, no, Azalea. Please don't. I – I'm not over the last one yet.'

'Yeah, well, I kind of guessed that. But it's like falling off a horse, Shivaun, you have to get right back up before you lose your nerve.'

'Yes, I suppose – but Ivor wasn't a horse! He was my lifelong friend, my only lover—'

Azalea stared. 'Your only one? Really? You swear it?'

'Absolutely. I adored him and I – I'm angry with him now, fuming if you want the truth, but I'm still in love with him.'

'Oh, Shivaun! You're in love with a memory, then! A ghost.'

She gazed at the ground. 'Perhaps. But that's the way it is.'

Azalea tossed back her hair, thinking. 'OK. I'll give you until the new year. If you haven't heard from him by January first, then he's history. You can't pine forever you know, waste your life.'

'No. But I am a nurse. I know that healing takes time. You can't force it.'

Azalea grimaced. 'No. I guess not. But you can help it to happen. I'm going to find the right medicine for you, wait and see.'

Azalea meant well, and she appreciated that, but . . . *how* could Ivor have done this, still be doing it to her? Why had he never got in touch, never made the slightest effort, tracked down her address here in America. Alana would have given it to him if only he'd asked? Why had he left no forwarding address of his own, in Australia or wherever he was? Who was he with, what was he doing? Could he possibly be so angry with her that he never wanted to see or speak to her again?

Apparently he could. Incensed, she turned to Azalea. 'All right. If I don't get a Christmas card from Ivor, I – I'll damn well seduce Steven Hunt myself!'

Azalea beamed. 'Right on, Shivaun! Move on! That's how I met Jeff, you know. A friend introduced us after my last guy ditched me. It was gruesome at the time, but it was the best thing that ever happened me.'

Wow. Someone had actually ditched the gorgeous, stunning Azalea? Shivaun was amazed. But in some perverse way, she was heartened too. If Azalea had recovered, ended up with a great guy like Jeff instead – well, maybe there might be a glimmer of light at the end of the tunnel? Maybe?

Oh, Ivor! You bastard! You did steal my KitKat, and you've still got it! But if you won't give it back, then maybe I'll damn well go out and get another one.

Marina was all but purring when Shivaun returned to her later that evening, sitting in state before a roaring fire in the lounge, and the moment they caught each other's eyes a vibe flashed between them, a kind of mutual recognition. Shivaun flushed to the roots of her hair, but stood her ground.

'Good evening, Marina. I trust you had a pleasant afternoon?'

It was none of her business, but – Marina smirked wickedly, and looked not in the least offended.

'Yes, thank you. Indeed I did.'

'H'm. And was Dr Hunt satisfied – with your progress?'

'Very. He said I was really coming on.'

Shivaun's mouth quivered, and then she exploded in laughter. 'Marina Darnoux, you are a disgrace! How *could* you? You're ill, and you said you don't even like the man.'

'No. Not particularly. But he is very handsome. I regard him as an aid to my recovery. Conquest is so very therapeutic.'

'Is it? I wouldn't know.'

Marina pursed her lips, primly. 'Then perhaps you should try it for yourself some time. Meanwhile, why don't you pour yourself a drink, and sit down?'

Shivaun mixed a vodka tonic, and sat. 'Is it my imagination, or did I see a wedding ring on Steven Hunt's left hand?'

Marina nodded. 'Yes. You did. He has a most exquisite wife. His third such, I believe.'

'His *third*? Well – is it any wonder! Where I come from we'd call him a shleeveen, a dirty old man even if he can't be more than – what? Forty?'

'Thirty-eight. A decade younger than myself. But you know, Shivaun, that's one of the few benefits of ageing. The older you get, the freer you get. There was a time when I wouldn't have dreamed of doing what I did today. Like you, I was very earnest, took life seriously. I thought sex always had to mean love. Ideally, I still think it should. But it doesn't have to. It can be whatever you make of it.'

Sipping her drink, Shivaun pondered. She'd never had sex without love, and didn't think she wanted to.

'Is it not – not a bit empty, like that? Soulless?'

Marina smiled. 'No. Not when you're doing it primarily to prove that you can. I regard today as an achievement. It made me feel alive and it made me feel like a woman again. Sex is a tremendous life force – but you must know that, surely?'

'Yes, but . . .' She gazed into her drink, moved closer to the fire. 'You know, Marina, I think one of the reasons Ivor wanted a break from me was so that he could try other women. He said something about not getting into a commitment we didn't fully understand.'

'I see. Well, I have to say I think he was right. It's risky, of course, but risks are worthwhile if there's a point to them. Perhaps you should try some other men, in turn.'

She reached to twirl the hair that was no longer there. 'H'm. That's just what Azalea was saying. But I don't want risks, or flings. I want security.'

Marina looked keenly at her. 'Do you? But Shivaun, there's really no such thing. Anything can happen to anyone at any time, as I know to my cost. Why do you want something so unattainable?'

Was it the vodka, on an empty stomach? Whatever it was, Shivaun stared hard into the fire and then turned directly, blankly, to Marina.

'I want it because – because my birth parents abandoned me, and then my adoptive father was murdered, and my mother died in a fire six weeks later.'

There it suddenly was, out like a live thing into the air between them, so virulent and forceful that Marina recoiled, thrust her hand to her mouth.

'*What?* Oh, my God . . . oh, my poor Shivaun. Why on earth didn't you tell me sooner?'

Bleakly, she chewed her lip. 'Because I'm a grown adult and I'm here to work with you, not whine at you. It's my private life and I try not to bore or burden anyone with it.'

'Bore? Burden? But Shivaun, are you crazy, this is dreadful, nobody should have to keep such a terrible secret! I don't know what I can possibly do to help, but I can certainly listen and would very much like to try to do anything in my power . . . darling girl, come here and sit beside me, tell me all about it. I am absolutely shocked – oh, you poor baby.'

She patted the sofa beside her, so maternally and comfortingly that Shivaun felt the flicker of tears – but then there was a knock on the open door, and Azalea was standing at it.

'Marina – I was just going to let you know before I leave – sorry, am I interrupting something?'

She looked rather anxiously at them both, and Marina looked at Shivaun in turn, gently quizzical.

'It's up to you, dearest, but I wonder whether – whether maybe Azalea should hear this as well? Since we're all living and working in the same house much of the time, and you two girls seem to have become such good friends? What do you think?'

Shivaun took a deep breath, and nodded. 'Yes. I think so, Marina. If Azalea can face it, it probably would be better for her to know.'

Azalea stared. 'Know what?'

Marina sighed sadly, and beckoned Azalea fully into the room, invited her to sit.

'Shivaun has just been telling me the most terrible thing. But we haven't got as far as the details yet. Why don't you start at the beginning, Shivaun, and tell us all about it, at your own pace?'

Yes. Why didn't she, now that she felt she could trust both these women? Everyone, as Marina said, found their own form of therapy. Feeling a huge weight beginning to lift off her shoulders, she sank back into the sofa, curled into the warmth of the fire and began to talk, slowly at first, but then with rising passion, about the church and the blanket and the note, about the knife and the fire, about Jimmy and Viv and Jason Dean.

Chapter Eight

The winding down of St Jude's was a dismal business, and Alana was feeling as if she were being dismantled herself when, one night as she left the hospital, she misjudged the speed of an oncoming car. A hefty Mercedes, it hit her car – Shivaun's – full in the side, and its driver jumped out raving at her.

'Look what you've done, you idiot! This Mercedes is only six months old, look what you've done to it!'

Peering into the headlights, she saw that its fender and front were badly dented, one light was damaged and then – horror – she saw that Shivaun's Mazda was badly damaged too, its door and front panel twisted and buckled. Oh, God! It was a miracle neither driver was injured, but there was certainly going to be pain in somebody's pocket. Shaking a little with shock, she attempted to face down the furious shouting man.

'It's your fault! You were going too fast!'

'I was doing thirty mph! Otherwise we'd both be dead! You're the one who came out onto a main road without looking, you had no right of way!'

No. Legally, she realised she hadn't a leg to stand on. Miserably, she gave the man the insurance details he was demanding, thinking what a total creep he was, not even asking whether she was hurt.

Physically, she wasn't hurt, but she was smarting in spirit as she got back in the Mazda and drove it to the nearest garage for first-aid. When a sympathetic mechanic there asked whether she was all right, offered to make her a cup of tea, it was the last straw, and she burst into tears the moment he vanished into the workshop.

Why was it all going wrong? Why was everything she touched turning to dust? St Jude's was closing down, Christmas was coming up, Ivor Lawlor was gone to Spain, and living in Shivaun's house without Shivaun in it was not at all the fun experience she'd expected. Although she often invited people round for drinks and meals, they rarely seemed to invite her back, and she was feeling lonelier with every passing day. Now she'd trashed Shivaun's car and a Mercedes as well, her insurance premiums were going to rocket . . . meanwhile she had no boyfriend to take her to Christmas parties, she was going to have to go down to Waterford for the festive season and admit that yes, she was still unattached, no, there was still nobody special in her life. Several of her younger siblings were engaged or married by now, and she was beginning to feel distinctly left out, vaguely pitied. On top of all that, Shivaun seemed to be having a wonderful time in America, while not so much as a postcard had arrived from Ivor in Spain. Thinking back to the night she'd managed to get so close to him, only to have it all ruined by her mother's spectacularly ill-timed phone call, she felt absolutely wretched.

When the mechanic came back, wiping his greasy hands on his dungarees, she was still sniffling, and looked up at him with tear-blurred eyes.

'Can you fix it? Will it be all right?'

He grinned cheerily. 'Yeah. Sure I can. Take a few days, though . . . hey, don't cry. It's only a car.'

'Yes,' she agreed, 'but it belongs to a friend. She's going to kill me . . . at least, she would if I told her. Maybe I won't tell her. She's in America. Can you fix it as good as new?'

'Yeah – well, I can fix it so only an expert would know. Come on, cheer up.'

Gratefully, she looked up at him. He sounded nice, and looked nice too, a stocky guy around her own age with big capable shoulders, clear blue eyes and a wide, smiley mouth.

At a moment like this, it was comforting to be smiled at, even if it did simultaneously make her feel a bit weepy and wonky. Or was that just the aftershock of the accident? Whatever it was, she managed to get up rather woozily off the ledge she was sitting on and thank him for his optimistic prognosis. He grinned at her.

'No problem. The car will be right as rain – I dunno about you, though. You're white as a sheet.'

'I – I'll be all right' she murmured. He looked at her, and reflected.

'Hey. Tell you what. I'm off duty in half an hour. If you'd like to hang round till then, I'll buy you a drink. Bet you could use one, huh?'

God, yes, she could. A stiff brandy in a warm chatty pub would be a sight better than going home to eat a solitary dinner, especially if this guy was offering to buy it for her, being so nice to her. He wasn't her type, as such, didn't have Ivor Lawlor's looks or classy style . . . but then Ivor Lawlor had gone to pot anyway, apart from going to Spain; he'd looked like a vagrant the last time she'd seen him, wearing that horrible beard and old clothes. Maybe this mechanic guy would do exactly the reverse, and clean up beautifully?

Touching her hanky to her eyelashes, she batted them a little at him.

'Thank you very much. That would be really nice. I don't mind waiting.'

He grinned again. 'OK. Sit by the heater then, get warm and I'll see you in a little while. The name's Brendan, by the way.'

Pulling herself together, she returned his smile. She was beginning to feel a bit better now.

'Mine's Alana.'

He nodded and left her, went back to the workshop while she rummaged in her bag for her comb and mirror, applied lipstick and blusher to give herself some colour, give herself a chance. Which was more, she thought wryly, than she'd given Ivor with Shivaun – but if he didn't like Spain he might return to Ireland, and at her age a girl had to hedge her bets.

By the time he reached the craftsman's house in Seville dawn had broken over the city and Ivor had pulled on both the sweaters stashed in his rucksack, because it was bloody freezing, so cold his teeth were clattering like castanets. What idiot said Spain was warm? It was icy, bone-crunchingly icy, he wished he'd brought gloves and even that most dreaded of garments, what Cynthia called a 'good warm vest'. Now he knew what his friend Frank had meant, and thought with longing of a spanking hot Irish breakfast, grilled and sizzling. He was absolutely starving.

The craftsman's house was a tall balconied building in a narrow street hung with laundry; every sheet looked stiff as a board and he realised that they actually were frozen – but the sun was coming up, and would presumably thaw everything including himself. Knocking on the thick solid door, he prayed that his new abode would have a scalding hot shower, that the man's wife might even muster a half-dozen sausages. A spare set of woolly socks wouldn't go amiss, either; the cotton ones he'd brought were defeated by Spain already.

The door was opened with apparent difficulty, much muttering from within until finally it creaked back on rusty hinges, and a large, unshaven, irritable-looking man stood before him. Ivor smiled stalwartly and held out his hand.

'Miguel? Miguel Garros? I'm Ivor Lawlor.'

The man stared at him and scratched his ample belly. '*Che?*'

'Ivor? Ivor Lawlor, from Ireland? *Irlanda?*' As he uttered his own name, it rang startlingly hollow in his ears, as if he were suddenly not sure of it himself. But then recognition slowly dawned in Miguel's blackly suspicious eyes.

'Ah. *Si. Si.*' He glanced at a non-existent watch on his wrist and raised a bushy eyebrow, as if to suggest that Ivor was personally in charge of international railway timetables and had a nerve arriving so early in the morning. Ivor thought that Miguel did not appear to be a morning kind of man. In fact he appeared to be a morning grouch.

But then Miguel beckoned him inside, led him through a dark tiled hallway into – oh, thank God! – a kitchen. But there was no sign of life in it, its black pot-bellied heating apparatus was not lit, there didn't even seem to be a kettle. It was only marginally warmer than the street outside. Taking a carton of milk from an ancient fridge, Miguel sloshed some into a glass and plunked it down in front of Ivor, saying something unintelligible. Ivor began to suspect that his few words of phrasebook Spanish were not going to get him very far.

'Uh – your wife – Señora Garros . . . ?'

Miguel cocked an eye at the ceiling as if to convey that his good lady was stashed upstairs, and then placed both hands under his cheek in a way that suggested she might well sleep till noon.

Ivor tried again. 'Er – bedroom? Bathroom? Breakfast?' Oh, please! He'd been rattling around in jolting trains all night, he'd had no money for hot food, he'd had to walk to this house from the station toting a heavy rucksack and taking several wrong turns. He was exhausted.

Miguel sat down at the kitchen table, poured a glass of milk for himself and gulped from it, regarding him in silence for several unnerving minutes. And then, with an air of begrudging resignation, he reached into a basket, drew out a loaf of bread and hacked two slices off it, pushed them across the table to Ivor. As he bit into it, Ivor realised the bread was yesterday's. Oh, for God's sake! The arrangement was that this man would house and feed him, in return for which he would be the man's unpaid apprentice – learning, yes, but working too, doing everything that was asked of him. Suddenly a memory zipped through his mind, so vivid it verged on hallucination, of Sally's perker full of fresh hot coffee every morning in the office – an office he'd hated at the time, and now remembered with yearning affection. At least it had been warm and clean and bright, and at nine sharp a trolley full of fresh Danish pastries came round. He must have been out of his mind to ever leave it.

Miguel was mumbling at him, but he couldn't understand a word. Of course that wasn't Miguel's fault, it was his own but –. Hunger and weariness suddenly drove him to haul out the last of his strength, stand up and speak in crisp firm accountant mode.

'Miguel,' he said loudly, clearly, 'I want to wash –' he made showering and tooth-brushing gestures – 'I want to eat –' he grasped an imaginary knife and fork – 'and then I want to sleep.' He placed his hands under his left cheek, shut his eyes and opened them again. If the guy didn't get this crystal-clear message, he must be thick as a plank.

There was an impasse, rather mutually hostile. And then with an immense sigh Miguel heaved his bulk out of his chair, raised a finger indicating that Ivor should follow him and rolled forward, up two flights of narrow stairs to a door he pushed open with evident reluctance. In the room stood a single iron bed, a wardrobe and nothing else. Then another door, further along the corridor: a tiled chilly bathroom containing a sink and bath that appeared to have been launched round about the same time as the Armada. Miguel leaned up against the wall, drew a clock on it with his forefinger and pointed out ten o'clock.

Ten? It was now five to eight. Ivor understood that he was to be allowed two hours' sleep, and then Miguel made sawing and hammering gestures, indicating that work would begin. Ivor nodded, went back to the bedroom and threw himself face down on the bed, which was so hard he all but bounced off it. In the two seconds before sleep engulfed him, he was aware of a nightmare beginning.

Shivaun never fully understood why she'd done it. All she knew was that she was glad she had. Telling Marina and Azalea her history, her full life story with no punches pulled, was the most healing, rewarding thing she'd ever done; she felt totally drained at the end of it, but she also felt liberated in a way she never expected, as well as comforted by the warm blanket of sympathy they wrapped around her, the concern and care in their faces and voices. Marina said little while she was telling the story, but Azalea asked many questions, drew out long-buried memories and emotions until the full picture emerged, there was nothing at all left to hide or disguise. When she got to the part about Jason Dean, about her feelings for him, she let her anger roll out, admitted all her fear and loathing of the man, the terror that accompanied the prospect of his release, her mad longing to drag him to the cemetery and confront him with what he'd done, her inability to forgive him because he'd never asked for forgiveness.

'No,' Azalea said thoughtfully, 'but he did do prison. That is meant to be a kind of atonement.'

Yes, Shivaun agreed, but that was in a social context, it didn't take account of *her*, of Viv or Jimmy as individual human beings. Why could Jason Dean never have said one word in person, made contact with her, said he was sorry? It would have meant so much.

'Perhaps he isn't sorry,' Azalea replied bluntly. 'Or perhaps he's still on drugs. Some people come out of prison more addicted than they went in.'

Perhaps. Jason Dean, she conceded when Azalea put it to her, might have all kinds of problems, social, psychological, whatever. But his lawyer had claimed at his trial that he came from a 'fine family' – one that should therefore be able to help him, and make some kind of apology to her.

'Maybe they were afraid' Azalea reasoned. 'Maybe they felt too ashamed to ever call or contact you, reckoned you'd spit on their apology or that words would be too totally inadequate.'

Shivaun flushed. 'Dammit, Azalea, whose side are you on here? Theirs or mine?' It was a feeling she'd had ever since the day Jimmy died, that some people cared more about Jason Dean's welfare than they did about Jimmy Reilly's death, and she was stung on the raw.

'Yours, of course,' Azalea replied evenly, 'I'm just playing devil's advocate so we can get as full a picture as possible. This lack of any apology or acknowledgement is clearly eating into you, Shivaun, so I'm trying to figure out reasons why you didn't get one. We'll never know for sure I guess, but we can speculate . . . we might even hit on something plausible that would be a comfort to you. Tell me, what would you do if this guy Dean materialised now here in front of you?'

She was startled by the vision, but didn't have to think very long about it.

'I'd sock him in the face. If I was a man I'd beat the crap out of him. I'd exact full vengeance on my father's behalf, you can be sure of that.'

'Well, there you are. Maybe that's why you've never heard from him or from the Dean family. They might guess that you're so angry they wouldn't even get a word in.'

Shivaun glared. 'Well, they could take their goddamn chances, couldn't they, the same way my dad took his? He intervened in a fight, Azalea, he was trying to save Jason's bloody life!'

'So, it sounds like your dad was a peacable guy. How do you think he'd feel about all this aggression of yours? Would he want you throwing punches on his behalf?'

Well . . . no. If she was being brutally honest, the truth was that Jimmy probably wouldn't. He'd rather see her trying to forgive and forget and get on with her life, the life he'd rescued the day he adopted her. He was a saintly man.

But she was no saint, didn't have his kind of eternal patient goodness. The most she had ever been able to muster was cold iron self-control, enough that she didn't inflict her feelings on all and sundry, tell complete strangers what had happened to her family. Instead she'd bottled everything up, even Alana only knew the bare facts, while Ivor had so often tried without success to make her open up. Much as she loved and trusted him, she'd never once cracked, never sobbed or whined or ranted on about any of it.

Instead she'd ranted on about other things, though, vented her rage in numerous ways, built up a huge head of steam about the health minister and the planning laws and the endless failure of society to tackle this, that or the other problem. Maybe she had gone a bit overboard, at times. But that was still better than having a nervous breakdown, surely? Better than becoming the gibbering puppet of a team of shrinks and therapists, wallowing in self-pity . . . grimly she recalled the stoic silence in which she had listened to those 'experts' who'd tried to counsel her. Under pressure from everyone she had listened to them, but she'd never spoken back, until eventually they gave up frustrated, exasperated.

So why, now, was she pouring her heart out to Marina and Azalea? Why, five years later, nearly six, was she doing this? And why did it feel so right today, so good, so cleansing? Even though some of Azalea's questions needled her, she could see the line of logic behind them, understood why Azalea was deliberately drawing her out. Marina was saying far less, but her silence was absorbing everything like a sponge, soaking up all the hurt and anger until those things no longer belonged to Shivaun Reilly alone, but to all three women sitting round the log fire this winter's night, three thousand miles away from the scene of the crime. For the first time she felt some distance from it, felt she might be starting to distinguish the wood from the trees. It was a positive, healthy feeling, and she mastered her instinctive urge to thank them for listening, because thanks might insult both their generosity and their intelligence.

It took hours to work backwards from the subject of Jason Dean to the subject of her birth parents, and only at that point did Marina become vocal, seeming to take up where Azalea was leaving off.

'So you never found out anything about them? Nothing at all?'

'Nothing, except that they wrapped me up well and wanted a home to be found for me – one of them did anyway, I don't know whether it was him or her, or both.'

Marina considered. 'Well, that sounds as if they were worried about you, wanted the best that could be got. There are even worse forms of abandonment, you know – I've heard of babies being found frozen or starved to death, even taken out of rivers, dustbins . . .'

The way she said it was somehow shocking, even though Shivaun knew of such things herself and had experienced them first-hand; two abandoned babies had been brought to St Jude's in the years she'd worked there, one severely dehydrated and the other suffering from hypothermia. Her heart had bled for them both, and one had died.

'Yes. I know that, Marina. I don't blame my parents, whoever they were, for what they did. I think they did their best, in fact. They even chose my name. I just wish I knew who they were, that's all . . . suppose I have brothers and sisters I don't know, nieces or nephews even? Or suppose there's some medical history in the family . . . ? Or what if –' she could hardly bring herself to say it – 'what if Jason Dean turned out to be my *brother*?'

Marina gasped slightly, but recovered herself. 'Oh, Shivaun, that's very unlikely. How many people live in Dublin?'

'More than a million – but Marina, he's around the same age as me, there can't be more than a year between us.'

Marina thought about it. 'Then I think you should go to the social authorities and ask them to find out his date of birth. Under the circumstances I'm sure they would give you that information.'

That was an idea. A very good idea. It had occurred to her before, but she'd shied away from it, been terrified by the remote possibility; now that it was tangible, she would do it. She'd start working on it tomorrow, face up to it and – almost certainly – have her fears put to rest. After all this time, she would rid herself of the absurd, horrific suspicion that Jason Dean's parents had never contacted her because they were her own parents, had recognised the unusual spelling of the name Shivaun. The unspeakable thought had haunted her for years in the nights, but now with Marina and Azalea around her she could allow herself to hope that daylight, at last, might be dawning. The chance of being related to Jason was so remote that she would risk finding out; as Marina said, some risks were worthwhile, and this one could result in new, enormous peace of mind.

Or it could result in a living, lifelong nightmare. She gazed at Marina, and Marina gazed back, steadily, supportively.

'Do it, Shivaun. Have courage, and do it. Get it out of your head and out of your way. Now, while you're in America, at a safe distance.'

'Yes. You're right, Marina. I will do it. But – but if the worst happens, I will never go back to Ireland. Never! I couldn't live in the same country as – as—'

Marina took her hand, and held it tightly. 'If that happened, darling girl, then we would just have to find a home for you here. Wouldn't we, Azalea?'

Azalea nodded, looking thoughtful in the firelight, her coppery skin reflecting its glow. 'Yes. In a way, Shivaun would have to be adopted all over again, even though she is an adult now . . . but don't worry, Shivaun. Now that we know all about you, we'll look after you.'

She gazed at them both with vastly grateful affection, marvelling at these wonderful people Alana had managed to find for her, shuddering as she contemplated Jason Dean, and his parents, the potentially horrific consequences of prising open Pandora's box. Was knowledge power, or were some things better left unknown? Would Viv and Jimmy always remain her parents, in every true sense, or could biology unleash a force even stronger than their love?

She did not want to start a search for every parental contender nature could provide. But she had to rule out the ones she did not want, would not accept no matter what the evidence might prove. If Jason Dean's parents were her parents, she would refute them, reject their tainted blood and his. She would not, could not forgive.

If Shivaun was not going to spend Christmas with her, Kathy Shreve insisted, then she must spend Thanksgiving instead. Not entirely sure what Thanksgiving entailed exactly, Shivaun set off for Kathy's house with a chocolate cake and small gifts for Kathy's kids, two loud energetic boys called Miles and Kelsey. The moment she arrived they hurled themselves on her, whooping and pummelling, grabbing at their gifts as if the boxes contained gold ingots.

'This is what Thanksgiving's about,' Kathy grinned as she emerged from the kitchen, 'being grateful for vandals like Miles and Kelsey, the privilege of being the hooligans' mother.'

The hooligans, aged six and eight, looked and sounded like a handful as they tore through the house, throwing punches and roaring at each other, ignoring Kathy's pleas for peace. Blond boys in blue dungarees and check shirts, they were cute to look at, but deafening to listen to. Then Kathy's husband strolled into the kitchen, carrying a can of beer and glancing at the two women without much apparent interest. Kathy tweaked at his sleeve.

'Bill, honey, this is Shivaun – Shivaun, meet my husband Bill.'

He raised his can in her direction. 'Hi.'

He didn't sound very enthusiastic, but Shivaun was determined to be, because Kathy's invitation meant a lot to her. 'Hi, Bill. Thanks for inviting me.'

She beamed at him, and he shrugged. 'Oh, well, Kathy's the one who invited you, but – here, have a beer.'

He thrust a Bud into her hand and looked hopefully at the simmering saucepans. 'So, we gonna eat soon, Kath?'

'Sure, Bill. Ten minutes. Send Kelsey in here to do the table, will you?'

He grunted assent as he left the room, but Kelsey did not appear, and eventually Kathy took linen and cutlery from cupboards herself, with an apologetic smile. 'Sorry. Those kids don't listen any more to Bill than they do to me.'

Shivaun took the cutlery from her and started organising the table. 'Here. Let me do that, you've got your food to watch – how many are we, five?'

'No, seven, Bill's parents are here too, they're watching TV in the living room, you'll meet them in a minute – is that beer OK, Shivaun, or would you prefer wine?'

'No, not at all, beer's fine!' She smiled brightly, and Kathy smiled ruefully back. 'Well, if you're sure. We have both. It's just that – that Bill's not the greatest host in the world. I'd bawl him out only he was working late last night, he's still a bit tired.'

'What does he work at?' Something physical, Shivaun guessed, because Bill was a big beefy guy, looked muscular under his jeans and sweatshirt, his ruddy complexion suggested a lot of time spent outdoors.

'He works on one of the whale watch boats. They're not too busy in winter, but there's a lot of maintenance to be done, hulls and engines and stuff . . . sometimes he doesn't get home till seven or eight. But I guess a nurse knows about working long hours, huh?'

Shivaun laughed. 'Not Marina Darnoux's nurse! I used to, in Dublin, but I've got lots more free time here, Marina's always sending me off to go walking or cycling – you know, Kathy, if you ever want time to paint, you should call me, because I could mind the kids for you in the evenings or—'

'Oh, Shivaun, you wouldn't want to mind mine! They're really brats, I've got though more babysitters than hot breakfasts, even their grandparents can't take much of them.'

'H'm.' Shivaun considered. 'Has anyone ever thought of giving them a clip round the ear, if they're that bad?'

She grinned as she said it, but Kathy looked shocked. 'Oh, no, violence isn't the answer. They're only little boys, they don't mean to be bad.'

She looked harassed, her hair curling in the steam rising from the vegetables, and it struck Shivaun that maybe Kathy was one of those mothers who simply found their children overwhelming, couldn't bring herself to lay down the law, insist on a bit of help and respect. There was something sort of *swamped* about her as she rushed about her kitchen, her face flushed and her gestures flustered. From the living room the din was getting louder and louder, it sounded as if the boys were murdering each other, and the tv was at maximum volume. Why didn't Bill or the grandparents do something, take charge? Or was this just normal family life, when beautiful babies grew into monstrous boys?

'Well,' she offered, 'I'd give it a go anyway. I haven't any experience of children, but nurses are bossy by nature! I bet I could put the fear of God into those boys in one hour flat, make them behave like angels.'

Kathy put a steaming tureen down on the table, blew her hair up off her face and looked at Shivaun. 'Yeah, that's what people always think, when they don't have kids themselves. Do you plan to have kids yourself some day, Shivaun?'

Shivaun reflected. She hadn't told Kathy about Ivor, nothing at all about his lost love or the life she'd once hoped to live, because she wanted this one person to take her as she was now, without sympathy or pity or helpful advice. She wanted a clean slate with Kathy Shreve, uncomplicated friendship . . . and besides, she was beginning to suspect that Kathy might have problems of her own. Bill, so far, did not strike her as a helpful or demonstrative kind of guy, he seemed to take it for granted that a kitchen was women's territory. Dinner, tonight, was clearly Kathy's job.

'Who knows? If I ever met a guy who'd make a good father – and what about you, huh? Are two enough for you?'

Kathy frowned, looked slightly evasive. 'Yeah. Two's plenty for me. But Bill's keen to try for another – I've been kinda holding out, if you want the truth. But the pressure's on . . . look, Shivaun, do me a favour and don't say anything more about it tonight, huh? We'll talk about it some other time. I don't want his parents starting in on me.'

There was a kind of appeal in her voice that made Shivaun agree in a tone she hoped was reassuring. 'No, of course I won't. It's none of my business. I'm just keen to see you making more time for painting, that's all. You're so talented – if you have any work on hand, I'd love to buy one of your pieces for Marina for Christmas. If I can afford it! You should be charging a fortune.'

A ghost of a smile whisked across Kathy's features, somehow conspiratorial, but edgy. 'Yeah. I have one or two things – but it's a sore subject too. Bill and his parents think I should be a fulltime mom, they don't like me painting or even working in the gallery, so let's steer clear of that tonight as well, OK? I'll show you the stuff later.'

Shivaun was taken aback by how fearful she sounded, as if she were peddling drugs or contraband. But Bill and his parents should be proud of Kathy, encouraging her! They should be offering to help in here too, not out in the living room waiting to be served – unless his parents were very old, maybe, a bit doddery?

But no. They weren't. When they finally appeared they were only in their late fifties, perfectly fit, still oblivious of the boys who were already fighting over who was getting which piece of the turkey. Jack, Bill's father, was large and ruddy like his son, and his mother Sonia was hefty too, a large lady with a loud voice and clothes to match. By the time everyone sat down around the table the noise was close to unbearable.

Sonia inspected Shivaun and shouted across at her. 'So, do you have Thanksgiving in Ireland? D'you do pumpkins and turkey and all?'

'No, we don't – maybe you'd better explain it properly to me!'

'Well,' Sonia bellowed, 'here in the Ewnited States, we've got plenty to be thankful for. We have one fine prosperous country and we're real proud of it. Jack and I live in North Carolina, but we always come up here to be with our family for Thanksgiving, wouldn't miss it for anything . . . come for Christmas too, and the boys' birthdays, sometimes just for the heck of it. We like to see lots of our little grandchildren.'

At that moment the little grandchildren knocked the gravy boat to the floor, where it smashed and spattered gravy over Shivaun's shoes. Kathy leaped up and ran to get a cloth, stammering apologies while Bill gazed dolefully into his plate.

'Aw hell, now we've got no gravy – Kathy, hon, make another batch, would ya?'

Kathy dashed to do it, and Shivaun gripped her cutlery until her knuckles gleamed, realising for the first time the dogsbody's life her friend seemed to lead. But she knew Kathy didn't want her to say anything, and again she had to wonder – was this all simply part and parcel of married life, of motherhood? Did Jack and Sonia ever invite Bill and Kathy to North Carolina, or was it all one-way traffic? Did those boys behave like this *all* the time? Did Bill really work late in winter, or was that a euphemism for boozing with his buddies?

Whatever the answers, she didn't like the look of the question. Nor did she like the look of Kathy, her heated face and tousled hair, her breathless efforts to please everyone and cope with everything. As she tasted her turkey and made a point of loudly telling Kathy how great it was, Shivaun thought that maybe, this first Thanksgiving in America, she had more to give thanks for than she'd previously realised; if she didn't have Ivor or the life she'd envisaged with him, at least she didn't have this kind of slavery to contend with either.

And, as the conversation progressed in fits and starts, she realised something else. Sonia was telling everyone about a tornado that had ripped half their neighbourhood apart, then Jack interrupted with a gruesome story about some lunatic who'd sprayed a Carolina supermarket with bullets, shot five people dead, and it struck her forcefully that Ireland's problems were not exclusive. Everywhere had its own horrors and hassles, and maybe all you could do was be thankful that they didn't all arrive on any one doorstep at once.

She'd never thought of things that way before, but now that she did, she felt a sudden twinge of affection for Ireland, which for all its faults was no worse than anywhere else, and could at least laugh at itself when everything got too ridiculous. Like Kathy's boys, it was a pretty bad kid, but some day it might grow up to be better.

Ivor knew a mistake when he saw one, and reckoned he'd made a huge one. He'd come to Seville with far more aspiration than preparation, and the result was absolutely appalling. Miguel Garros was the most taciturn, surly man in all of Spain, to judge by the way he grunted and gesticulated, made no verbal attempt to communicate, gave not a damn whether his apprentice settled in or not. Undeniably he was an excellent carpenter, and Ivor was determined to learn from him, but he was also impatient and bad-tempered, dirty and disorganised, a heavy drinker and a serial womaniser; Ivor soon discovered that the '*señora*' who'd been sleeping upstairs on the morning of his arrival was not in fact Miguel's wife, but one of a procession of floozies who never lasted more than a week. Whether the man was divorced, widowed or a bachelor Ivor neither knew nor cared, but he hated the way he was always running into sour-faced half-clad women on the stairs, the way he was left out of every conversation and every meal as well, Miguel apparently taking the view that he could shift for himself. But Miguel was tight-fisted too, Ivor had to stretch every available peseta for food and cook it amidst the ruins of Miguel's own greasy meals, in a sticky smelly kitchen that made his stomach churn. Pampered by Cynthia at home, he was now forced to learn the tedious rudiments of housekeeping, tackle the grim mysteries of laundry and endeavour to stave off frostbite as well, because the house was like an igloo. Since he didn't understand Spanish television there was no diversion at nights, because he hadn't the money for bars or cinemas even if he could have understood the dialogue in either.

His fingers shook with cold as he ploughed his way through the Hemingway novel his friend Frank had given him, and although the book helped him to grasp something of Spain's gritty character it also made him wonder how a dapper bureaucrat like Frank could possibly know a man like Miguel. One day, lonely and desperate, he phoned Frank from a coinbox to ask him, and Frank simply replied that Miguel was known all over Andalucia for the quality of his carpentry, what more did Ivor want?

Ivor almost wanted Cynthia, so awful was life with Miguel, he longed for home and thought he was a fool to have ever left it, would sell his soul for central heating, clean sheets, hot showers. The office, the tennis club, even the car he'd left at home, everything grew daily more alluring in his mind, until he was almost ready to turn around and flee – but he would not go, not under any circumstances, until a letter arrived from Shivaun. Now that she had his address in Seville he had to stay in Seville, and wait – and wait, and wait. How long could it possibly take for her reply to arrive, the reply that would make everything else bearable, irrelevant? If he only had that, he could square up to this wretched sojourn in Spain, surmount the discomforts, live on fresh air, learn to ignore La Macarena which must surely be one of the most depressing neighbourhoods in all of Seville.

Not that Miguel gave him much time to investigate the others, but this one did nothing to encourage further exploration; it seemed to be full of dark depressing churches, shrieking children, roaring vendors and miles of endless washing hung out by clamouring, xenophobic women. Men spat in the streets, vegetables fell off stalls and were squashed into the gutters, the air reeked of fish and at night, when he finally rolled home exhausted from Miguel's workshop, motorbikes screamed up and down underneath his bedroom window. What was more, he was so broke he was going to have to get another job, find extra work that would at least supply pocket money, enable him to buy the odd beer or sandwich in the one decent joint he'd discovered, a bar called El Rinconcillo. But what work, when he didn't speak Spanish, when he slaved for Miguel six days a week, from ten in the morning until eight at night? He was starving and freezing and worn to the bone, his hands were a mass of blisters, every muscle ached and the idea of having to shoulder yet more work made him want to lie down and weep, end the whole thing by blowing his brains out.

But he was learning. He surely was, because Miguel believed in getting his money's worth, not doing anything his apprentice could do for him. The first week was the worst of his life; every morning he trudged to Miguel's workshop through a maze of menacing alleyways, rolled up his sleeves and started hauling the huge sheets of wood which, in due course, would become tables, cabinets, wardrobes and chests of drawers. Mostly mahogany, it was massively heavy, he felt like a pack mule as he shunted and grunted and one day he dropped an entire stack on his foot and was almost blinded with pain.

But Miguel just shrugged, didn't even have a first-aid box for the foot which, when Ivor inspected it that night, was purple and pulped, so swollen he could hardly get his shoe off. Nor could he lift his sweater over his head any night that week, because his shoulders were seized up, his muscles knotted like mooring ropes, he couldn't raise his arms higher than his chest and had to wriggle out of his clothes, almost suicidal for want of a scalding hot bath. Almost homicidal, too; there were moments when he seriously considered throttling Miguel, if only the man's neck was not thick as a bull's.

The second week, Miguel introduced him to the various implements, awls and chisels, hammers and saws, and jerked his thumb at a spare plank to indicate that Ivor could practise on that, imitate him. This boded better than the donkey work, so Ivor watched Miguel eagerly, seized his wood enthusiastically and promptly impaled his finger on a two-inch splinter. Laughing at the dripping blood, Miguel wagged his own callused finger to suggest that a little more care would not go amiss. Ivor yearned for a shotgun.

The third week, he made what he felt was a passable job of planing a cabinet door, got it both smooth and exactly to size. Miguel picked it up, ran his hands over it, stared at it for a moment and then flung it away from him in a rage, as if it were some live thing that had tried to bite him. Furious, Ivor retrieved it and waved it at him, demanding to know what was wrong with it. Miguel pointed to an almost invisible nick in the edge of it, spat on it and roared a phrase with which Ivor was soon to become familiar, one that suggested the Lawlors had long-running difficulties in legalising their marriages. Getting the gist of it, Ivor roared back: yeah, fuck you too pal, you asinine brothel-keeper, may you get the clap and die without drugs. Whereupon Miguel slapped him on the back so hard he nearly shot through the wall, and laughed in contempt.

By Christmas week, Ivor felt as if his body were made of ice-cold, solid steel. The physical pain metamorphosed into numbness, but the emotional pain got worse, he ached for home and for Shivaun, wondered what on earth he was going to do on Christmas day – anything would be better than spending it with Miguel, he'd walk the streets if necessary; if a letter didn't arrive soon he might simply jump in the Guadalquivir. Although there was a phone in Miguel's house Miguel wouldn't let him use it, so he couldn't even phone his friends or his mother, couldn't afford Christmas gifts for her or anyone, unless they'd care for the leg of a table, which he'd tried to turn and Miguel had flung at his head. Christ, he *had* to find some kind of paying work, soon! But after a month his Spanish still wasn't up to taking orders in a bar or restaurant, serving anyone or translating anything, La Macarena wasn't even the kind of neighbourhood where people wanted their gardens tended or their doors painted, windows cleaned – on the contrary, he suspected he might well get beaten up if he unwittingly encroached on any local workman's turf.

Meanwhile, Miguel seemed to be making money. Several lorries inched their way up the narrow alley to the workshop and pieces of finished furniture were loaded into them, heavy elaborate items that Miguel had apparently promised to produce in time for Christmas. Payment was in cash, and Miguel stuffed wads of notes into his filthy pockets – so how come his house was so cold and miserable, his larder so bare, his life so devoid of comfort?

On Christmas eve Miguel threw the keys of the workshop in Ivor's direction, indicating that he should lock up, and then thumbed through a large roll of tattered banknotes, nodding and muttering to himself. Ivor got the impression that he was going out to meet one of his women for a large hearty meal, get very drunk and possibly not come back for a day or two. This impression was reinforced when Miguel slammed a few notes under his nose, the equivalent of about ten pounds, with a look that suggested this was his Christmas bonus, enough to tide him over the festive season. Before Ivor could ram it down his throat, he cackled and turned on his heel, clomped away and vanished into the thronged alleyway.

For one terrible moment Ivor actually thought he might be going to cry. Clearly he'd been abandoned, he was to spend Christmas without one solitary person to speak to, not one friend in all of Seville. His mind was seizing up for lack of mental stimulus, his body was a mere beast of burden, and now he felt as if his heart would splinter. Never in his entire life had he felt so alone, and when he thought of Shivaun it was almost more than he could bear. Tears stung his eyes, and in a burst of self-loathing he picked up one chunk of wood after another, hurled block after block at the workshop wall, his emotions shattering along with the splintering wood.

But he was a grown man, for God's sake! He was a qualified accountant, a trained educated professional, he couldn't just slump down here in a corner and go to pieces! No matter how he felt, he would have to deal with it, pull himself together and get through this nightmare somehow. At the end of it he would have something to show for it, a new career and the new lifestyle that would go with being a carpenter . . . and something told him he definitely had the makings of a very good carpenter.

He must have, because otherwise he'd have left after the first horrendous week – or alternatively Miguel would have thrown him out, because Miguel did not suffer fools gladly. Furthermore, although Miguel had yet to utter one syllable of praise or even encouragement, there were unfinished pieces of furniture here under his very eyes, his hands, to which he had contributed. His input into them was minimal, but it must be acceptable, because otherwise they would not be here, Miguel would have smashed them in a frenzy of disgust. Much as he detested the man, Ivor had to concede that he was a perfectionist, insisted on extremely high standards of workmanship. Nothing was ever nailed or glued into place, screws were always used, the wood was always of the finest quality, if Miguel's hand ever slipped on a joint or decorative cut the piece was always restarted, never repaired or disguised. The furniture was heavy brooding stuff, not to Ivor's taste at all, but it was absolutely top quality, and in due course the techniques he was learning were going to provide the foundation for top-quality output of his own. It was just a question of sticking it out, that was all, of somehow getting through this wretched winter, using it as a springboard . . . when he embarked on his own work the design would change, but the things he was learning would not change, because they were faultless. Miguel was a bastard, but he was a master bastard.

Meanwhile, it was Christmas eve, and Shivaun had not written. If he thought about Shivaun he would go stark raving mad. If he went back to that dismal icy house, he would go certifiably barking mad. If he . . . if he gritted his teeth, swallowed his pride and took the pathetic pittance Miguel had left him, he could go to El Rinconcillo and have a drink. A cheap brandy, that would burn his gullet and warm him up.

El Rinconcillo was a civilised place. He might even stand some chance of meeting someone civilised in it, someone who spoke a smattering of English – oh yes, oh dear God, please, let me meet someone I can talk to. I've scarcely spoken to another human being for a whole month, if I don't do that soon I'll have a nervous breakdown, I have got to have some kind of conversation with somebody.

Gazing with distaste at the money, he fingered it reluctantly, and then picked it up. Human contact, he thought, that's what this is going to buy me: half an hour of beautiful, blessed human contact.

Alana was feeling better, far better than she would have dared to hope or expect only a few weeks ago. Then, she'd been like Shivaun's car, battered and dented, but now the damage was invisible to the naked eye, everything had been magically repaired by Brendan McLaughlin. So much for Ivor's lordly suggestion that she should see a shrink! If anyone needed shrinking it was Ivor himself, because no man in his right mind would dream of chucking a terrific career like his to wander off to Spain without a penny, looking like a vagrant and babbling like an idiot. Carpentry! Ivor Lawlor wouldn't know a chainsaw from a rawlplug, he'd soon be home looking for his Lacoste shirts and Ralph Lauren aftershave.

But it would be too late. He hadn't a hope of getting his job back, after the brusque and sudden nature of his departure, and he hadn't a hope of getting Shivaun back, and now he hadn't a hope of getting her, Alana, back either. Shivaun's occasional cards and calls were full of enthusiasm about America, and her own life, now, was full of Brendan McLaughlin. Brendan wasn't at all the kind of guy she'd ever have expected to take a shine to, but she had – a big shine, because unlike Ivor Lawlor he didn't treat her like a child or a pesky sister, he said she was all woman, a great cook and a 'real beaut'. He took her out and he showed her off, introduced her to all his friends and picked her up in fun, flash cars he borrowed from the garage. One day they'd even gone down to Mondello in a Porsche, torn down the Naas dual carriageway at 100 mph and then spent the afternoon with his car-racing friends, who simply accepted her as if she'd always been part of their gang. Other girlfriends had been at Mondello that day, and for the first time ever she'd felt she was becoming part of a 'crowd', a player instead of an eternal spectator. Racing was Brendan's hobby, his passion in life, but he included her in it, was even talking about taking her over to see some race in England – well, she'd have to pay her own fare, since he wasn't a millionaire, but he did treat her as well as he could afford to. They went to pubs and cinemas and sometimes he picked her up after work in a Mercedes or BMW, which had done wonders for her image and her ego. He was an open, easy, popular guy and she didn't have to work at him at all, he simply lived for the day and took her as she was.

He wanted to take her to bed, too, and already she'd decided that he could, this very weekend. That would kind of cement things, and then she'd be able to invite him down to Waterford over Christmas, show him off to her family not just as a friend but as a definite boyfriend. It would be so great, to have a boyfriend at last! Of course Mother would probably want to know all about his prospects, quiz him about when was he going to open a garage of his own, but Dad would be pleased for her, her brothers and sisters would tease, include him in the ever-expanding Kennedy clan and finally show her a bit of respect. It was a good thing, in retrospect, that they'd never met Ivor Lawlor, because now they'd have nobody to compare Brendan to, nobody would think she was merely settling for him for lack of anyone better. Admittedly, she wasn't exactly in love with Brendan, he didn't have the same shivery effect on her that Ivor had had, but maybe that wasn't entirely a bad thing. It gave her a feeling of control, for a change, she wasn't holding her breath waiting for the phone to ring. But now the funny thing was that it always did ring; Brendan really did seem to be very keen on her. God only knew how or why, after she'd staggered into his garage that night looking like the wreck of the Hesperus, but he did. That was the important thing. This time, she was going to hold on to her man.

Her man! She grinned as she thought of it, rolled the phrase round in her mind. Her man wanted her to have a party, he said, on New Year's eve, in Shivaun's house where there was more room than in his own small flat.

At first she'd hesitated, thinking of Shivaun who probably wouldn't want the kind of rowdy boozy party Brendan wanted. But now she thought what the hell, Shivaun needn't know anything about it – besides, there was every reason to celebrate. She had a great new guy and was having a great time, just as Shivaun was having in America, probably going to masses of parties with all these new people she seemed to have met. Sending her there had been just the ticket, she didn't even seem to be moping over Ivor, never mentioned him at all.

Yes. A New Year party was definitely on the cards. A little shopping spree, too, for something hot to wear. Brendan wouldn't want any little black dress, he'd want to see her in something sparkly and festive, you could go the whole hog at this time of year. Maybe he'd even dress up a bit himself, knock her new colleagues dead when she invited them from St Peter's – she might as well invite them, since he said he wanted to invite all his friends she'd better produce a few of her own. Food too, of course, and music and plenty to drink . . . he had a friend who was a barman, could probably rustle up some kegs and bubbly. Shivaun had only had about twenty people at her little farewell party, but this would be a real shindig, it would launch Alana-and-Brendan as a couple.

Humming to herself, she began to think out the guest list, and look forward to a very happy new year.

Steeling herself, Shivaun sat down and wrote her letter of enquiry to the Department of Justice in Dublin, explaining her very private reason for wanting to know the date of birth of one Jason Dean, recently released murderer of Jimmy Reilly. Then, anxious to despatch it out of her sight, she threw it in with her bundle of Christmas cards to friends in Ireland, and went to put the whole lot in Azalea's out-tray, which was emptied and mailed every evening.

But as she approached Azalea's office she heard voices, the first raised voices she had ever heard at Chederlay. It sounded as if Azalea was having some kind of row with Marina, and snatches of it drifted out to her.

'– totally disastrous, we don't even know for sure –'

'– we never will, but the point is –'

'– it's too risky –'

'– could be the only –'

She stopped at the door just as they caught sight of her and fell silent. 'Sorry! Is this a bad time? I just wanted to post – mail—'

They both shook their heads so vehemently she realised it was a bad time, and turned away, whereupon they both called out to her.

'No, Shivaun, come on in! We were only having a chat!'

She grinned sceptically. 'A chat, huh? It sounded to me like you were at each other's throats. Isn't this supposed to be the season of goodwill?'

Marina smiled nonchalantly. 'Pay no attention. I was merely trying to remind Azalea who's boss around here – in vain, it seems.'

Azalea smiled in turn and sighed exaggeratedly. 'It's a bummer working for a tyrant, huh, Shivaun? Why don't you take Marina away with you, make her do some yoga or something, get her out of my face?'

Marina snorted, but Shivaun saw that she wasn't affronted; after ten years Azalea knew Marina well enough to say such things and get away with them. But Marina was looking ruffled and exasperated.

'All right, I will. Come on, Marina, chill out, some yoga will calm you down.'

Unexpectedly, Marina resisted. 'No. I'm not in the damn mood for yoga. I'm going to go to Dorothy and speak to her about the Christmas menu – we're having Japanese sushi delivered from Boston, by the way, I don't believe in this traditional nonsense – and then I have some work to do.'

Firmly, with a look that put an end to the conversation, she left the room, and Shivaun turned quizzically to Azalea.

'What was all that about?'

'Oh, nothing . . . she can just be so damn stubborn sometimes, up on her high horse, it's the French in her. She thinks she's the Duchess of Rheims.'

Shivaun laughed. There was something aristocratic about Marina, she could imagine her in another era, giving orders for everybody to be guillotined.

'Did she upset you?'

Azalea shook her head. 'No. She just annoyed me, that's all. I don't like to be opposed any more than she does!'

'About what? Or is it none of my business?'

Azalea looked at her frankly. 'Well, let's say it doesn't concern you for the moment – oh, hell, I've had enough of this office for one day. Have you time to come for a walk? I need to take this stuff to the mail anyway.'

'Sure. I'll get a jacket.'

Muffled against the biting cold, they set off, the long way

into Gloucester around the headland, and Shivaun shivered. 'Boy, it gets cold here!'

'Yeah – well, it'll get a lot colder in January. It'll be starting to snow soon up in the Berkshires, on Mount Greylock . . . I'm thinking of taking a week off to go skiing, maybe at Mount Tom or Wachusett. You ever been skiing, Shivaun?'

'No – oh my God Azalea, *look*, quick!'

'What? Where?'

Shivaun pointed and jabbed, and Azalea followed her line of vision out to sea, just in time to see the huge thrash of a whale's tail, a crash of spray and a shooting spume of water.

'Oh, wow! You hardly ever see them at this time of year – isn't that magnificent?'

Shivaun was ecstatic, her face flaming with cold and excitement.

'Jesus, it's fabulous! I've never seen one before – oh, wow! This is brilliant! Come on, run, if we go up higher we might see it again!'

They ran to the highest point, and were just in time to see the whale surface again, like an island erupting from under the water, throwing up a massive wave before it plunged back down to the depths. Panting, Shivaun stood riveted.

'Oh, beautiful! Sensational!'

Azalea had seen many whales before, but she was infected by Shivaun's enthusiasm, struck by the vibrancy in her face and voice. In the sinking sun she stood tinged with flaming light, her eyes sparkling and her skin glowing, as if a match had suddenly been touched to her. Lightly, Azalea turned to her and touched her sleeve.

'You're getting over him, aren't you?'

Shivaun spun round. 'What?'

'Ivor. You're starting to enjoy things without him.'

Shivaun stood arrested, thinking about it with her hands plunged in her pockets, her hair blazing in the sunset.

'I'm facing reality, Azalea. That's all. I've got much stronger since I came here – strong enough to face the fact that Ivor hasn't got in touch, because he doesn't want to. He doesn't want me. It's over.'

They walked on, and Azalea looked at her candidly, curiously. 'You're sure of that, now? Absolutely sure?'

'Yes! No! I mean – I am sure, in my head. It's only in my heart that – that it still hurts! Hurts so much, sometimes, because he was my best friend all my life, I thought I could trust him, I miss his friendship, I miss his love and his laugh, I can't believe he's done this and – and I don't know where he is, how he is! If I only knew he was all right, that there's no other reason for him to lie low, at least then I wouldn't have this worrying niggling feeling, I could set my mind to letting go and moving on. It – it's the *mystery* of it that's so painful. He's just completely vanished without trace. The Ivor I knew would never do that.'

Azalea mulled it over. 'Then find him! Lay this damn ghost! Get his phone number, surely his family must have it, call him and say hi, have you been run over by a truck or what? If he hasn't, then you'll know where you stand, that it is over. Hard as that might be to accept, at least it will leave you free to live the rest of your life. You're young, you have a lot of life in front of you.'

Yes. Azalea was right. Shivaun knew she'd made progress, wasn't wasting every day pining to death – but she still couldn't rid herself of the belief that it had all been a horrible misunderstanding, a breakdown in communication that had driven her and Ivor apart at a time when she'd been stressed and tense, maybe not making very much sense even to herself. Ivor had always been so good to her, she could afford the loss of face that one brief call would cost . . . but could she bear it if he said no, you're not mistaken, I haven't got in touch because I don't want to, get out of my life and stay out of it?

She wasn't sure that she could bear it. But she could see that she had to do it. His mother, Cynthia, was a cold fish, but she'd certainly have his phone number or address, and anything was better than living in limbo, not knowing. Christmas would be an excuse to call . . . even as her mind ran back over all the ones they had spent together, she felt him pulling at her, heard his voice and smelled his skin, his warm eyes and his wide smile began to chip away at the anger in which she'd insulated herself from everything that ran even deeper, everything that had made him so special. Her heart and her mind were completely at odds, fighting each other like tigers, but beyond that there lay something fundamental, some gut instinct that told her something was wrong, something more than hot hurting dignity was holding them apart.

Even now, on the days when she was furious with him, she couldn't entirely blame him, because she'd been the one who walked away, refused to travel with him for love of a job and a hospital which no longer even existed. Alana must have told him she was in America, so if he hadn't written it must be because he was equally furious with her – but, whatever the outcome, she was going to have to risk finding out. Only then, if he still rejected her, stuck to his guns and refused all hope of a reconciliation, could she finally accept that their lifelong love was dead, and that the new life she was trying to build now was real, was permanent.

As she walked on, thinking, Azalea was talking about Christmas and its impending delights. 'We do it real well here in Gloucester, Shivaun, you're going to love it – there are parades, sleigh rides, ice sculptures, hayrides, carols, the works! The town is all lit up and there are holly fairs, crafts fairs, Marina puts candles in all the windows at Chederlay . . . with Ivor or without him, you'll have a great time, you'll see.'

She smiled and put an affectionate arm around Shivaun, and Shivaun hugged her back. 'Azalea, you're wonderful. Did you know that? You and Marina both, you couldn't be a better friend if you were my own sister and Marina reminds me all the time of my mum. I'm incredibly lucky and grateful that I have you both. I feel like I've known you all my life.'

Azalea nodded, and coloured a little. 'Yeah, well, we've got very fond of you, too – you're a hell of an improvement on Marina's last nurse! You fit in much better and the house is much happier since you came.'

Surprised and touched, Shivaun looked at her questioningly. 'Is it, Azalea? D'you really think so?'

'Yes. I do. We both do. No matter what might have happened to you in Ireland, you never whine or mope, you always have a smile for everyone and you've worked wonders for Marina with all your yoga and music and whatnot.'

Shivaun laughed. 'H'mm. I think maybe it's Steven Hunt who's worked wonders for her!'

'Yeah . . . well, she'd had her wicked eye on Steven for ages, but it was only after you came that she took the bull by the horns. It's only a fling, obviously, but the point is that she felt strong enough to do it. You've restored her confidence.'

Shivaun was bemused. She'd never have thought Marina was the kind of woman whose confidence needed restoring. But everyone's must, at times, even the indomitable Marina whose illness had come as such a shock to her, a reminder that nobody was invincible. That was the great thing about nursing; it demonstrated over and again that anything, good or bad, could happen to anyone at any time, and that people had powers within themselves they'd never known they possessed. Where there was life, there was always hope. She would phone Cynthia Lawlor first thing in the morning.

El Rinconcillo, just like any Irish bar on Christmas eve, was crammed. Ivor fought his way to the counter, ordered a brandy and looked around him while he waited for it, trying to spot anyone else who might be alone. But nobody appeared to be, so he took his drink and made his way to the edge of a group of people around his own age, all laughing and shrieking in Spanish. They were noisy, but they were young enough that one or two of them might speak a few words of English, if he took the initiative and attached himself to them.

At first they didn't even notice him, paid no attention while he emptied two dishes of tapas in rapid succession, thanking his stars for the free snacks. Then, just as his mouth was full, there was a sudden lull in their conversation, and he plunged into it spluttering.

'Hi. My name is Ivor. Does anyone speak English?'

They blinked at him, looking more bemused than interested, and then a dark stocky girl smiled at him with merry, friendly eyes.

'Yes, I speak, a little. My name is Pilar. Also my friend here, Luis, he speak. You are English? You are a tourist?'

The girl looked a little sceptical, as well she might; not many tourists were likely to make their way to La Macarena on Christmas eve.

'No. I'm Irish. I work here.'

'You work? *Here?*'

'Yes. With Miguel Garros, the carpenter.'

'Ah!' Pilar translated for everyone, and they all laughed, seemed to be much amused. Ivor grinned at them.

'Why? Is that funny? Do you know Miguel Garros?'

Pilar laughed again. 'Oh yes. We know. Everyone know Miguel.'

Ivor wondered exactly what they knew. Did they know that Miguel was a mean, irritable, cheapskate bully? Maybe they did – or maybe he'd better watch his step. Luis, a tall thin guy drinking beer, was squinting at him suspiciously.

'You are his assistant? You are carpenter also?'

'Yes – well, I'm learning to be. Miguel is my tutor. What do you do?'

He worked in a bank, Luis said; Pilar ran a new cybercafé nearby, their other three friends were all teachers. Ivor wondered whether it was his imagination, or whether he detected a tremor of disdain amongst them; they were all white-collar workers and he, now, was blue-collar. A labourer, in filthy dungarees with dirt under his fingernails. At best, they seemed indifferent to him.

But then Pilar shifted a little in his direction, revealing a strong aquiline profile, several studs and rings in her left ear. 'How you like Miguel?'

Cautiously, Ivor shrugged. 'He's OK. I'll probably get to know him better when I learn more Spanish.'

And by the way, he wanted to shout, I'm doing this by choice you know! I used to be an accountant! But he didn't say it, because he wasn't one any more. This was his life now, he was going to become a fully fledged carpenter if it killed him. Which, at the rate things were going, it very well might. He wondered whether his starvation was actually showing in his face, because Pilar was studying him with a kind of pity.

'Miguel very hard man. He pay you good?'

She giggled, and he shrugged again. 'Not good, no. But he's teaching me, and I live in his house.'

The others had lost interest now, gone back to their chat in Spanish, and she turned around on her bar stool, so that he could see her full on. She was pretty, he thought, especially her smile which was the first one directed at him in longer than he could remember. But when she spoke again, she frowned.

'Miguel not pay anyone. My father is butcher, he wait many weeks for Miguel to pay him.'

Oh? Interested, Ivor leaned towards her, wondering whether it was because her father was a butcher that she was bothering with him, wondering also whether Miguel was known for not paying people.

'Really? How many weeks?'

Her face crinkled in amusement. 'Oh, many many! Ten, twelve, five – how you say, fiveteen? My father very angry. Everyone always angry when Miguel no pay. But some day, he always pay. He not very – how you say? – not very good businessman.'

No. Apart from his carpentry, Miguel was a good-for-nothing. Ivor was astonished by what he heard himself saying next, the completely unexpected loyalty in it.

'No, well, not everyone can be good at business. He's good at the work he does with his hands, though. Really good. That's why I'm sticking with him.'

Pilar looked at him in surprise, and he noticed that her glass was empty. Could he possibly afford . . . ? He fingered the change in his pocket, and decided with regret that no, he couldn't. It was very humiliating. But there it was. He was a long way now from the bar in the tennis club, where he'd bought rounds of drinks without even thinking about it, for people who'd probably recoil in horror if they could see him here, with his career down the tubes and welts on his hands.

'So, you are learning? You will be carpenter?'

'Yes,' he said firmly, 'I will be. Tell me more about Miguel. And about yourself.'

Cheerfully she told him, and he learned without surprise that Miguel was notorious in La Macarena as a womaniser, a boozer, a chronic debtor to all and sundry. All of which might even be funny, have a certain amusing romance if only Miguel had any charm, if he made up for it by joking or apologising or made the slightest effort to endear himself to anyone. But he didn't, Pilar said, he was gruff and indifferent, could get quite aggressive with people who tried to make him pay his bills. Ivor should watch out, not get on the wrong side of his boss if he could help it.

Well, he thought, Miguel is a big lunk, but I'm fairly well-built myself, I can take care of . . . Jesus, surely that's not why Miguel is starving me? So I won't have the strength to – oh, get a grip, your imagination is running wild. Things surely won't come to that. This lady Pilar is exaggerating. She's nice, though – God, is it good to talk to her, or what! If I had the money I'd buy us both another drink and stay here all day, get to know her better. Shame about the rest of them, but she's really friendly.

Even as he thought about it, felt warmed by the sound of her voice and the openness of her smile, she slid to her feet and groped for her jacket.

'I have to go now.'

Oh, no! Oh, damn, was this because he couldn't offer her another drink? But he'd just explained – she must understand – oh, hell. It was so long since he'd had a conversation with anyone, he felt as if she were almost stealing something from him, taking away some cherished possession.

'Do you have to?'

'Yes. I must go back to work. Cybercafé very busy today. But if you want to e-mail anyone, you come with me and I let you do it for free, OK?'

Briefly he seized at the chance, until he remembered that Shivaun was in America now, had some new online address if she had one at all. As for his former friends, those he might want to talk to wouldn't be at their offices today, everyone would be out Christmas-partying.

Sadly, he looked at Pilar. 'No. Thanks, but that's OK. I have to go now myself anyway.'

She looked at him in turn, apparently thinking, and then without warning she called the barman, exchanged some rapid chat with him in Spanish. Then, to Ivor's puzzlement, she patted his shoulder, her near-black eyes sympathetic and somehow conspiratorial.

'No. You stay here. I tell barman to bring you another drink and some food.'

Open-mouthed, he was taken so unawares he didn't know what to say. By the time he figured out a speech of thanks and reluctant protest, she had slipped the barman a note, said adios to her friends and gone.

Chapter Nine

As Shivaun picked up the phone she thought of Cynthia Lawlor with a mixture of apprehension and puzzlement. For some reason she'd never understood, Ivor's mother had never been as friendly to her as her parents had been to him. Still, it couldn't be much fun for her now with her only child so far away, so she steeled herself to sound chirpy. It would be well worth the effort to get Ivor's number, talk to him and—

'Hello?'

'Hello, Mrs Lawlor?' Cynthia had never invited first-name familiarity.

'Yes, can I help you?'

'Mrs Lawlor, it's me, Shivaun! I'm calling from America.'

'Oh. Yes. Shivaun. How are you?'

'I'm great thanks, and how about you? Have you your Christmas tree up and Santa on the radio?'

As little kids she and Ivor had always listened to Santa's radio programme on Christmas eve, it had been a family joke for years. But if Cynthia remembered it, she gave no indication.

'Actually no, I haven't, I was just about to leave the house, I'm going to friends in Wicklow for Christmas.'

Cynthia's tone conveyed that she was looking at her watch as she spoke, not pleased to be delayed. Not thrilled, either, to hear from her son's former girlfriend.

'Oh, well, I hope you'll enjoy it there, there might even be snow on the hills, it's beautiful here, all frosty and twinkly—'

'How nice. But I am in a bit of a hurry – if you're looking for Ivor, Shivaun, I'm afraid he isn't here and won't be. He's not coming home for Christmas.'

Not coming home from where? It was mortifying to have to ask, but there was nothing for it.

'No, I didn't expect him to be there, Mrs Lawlor, but I just wondered – I – I wanted to wish him a happy Christmas, only I don't have his phone number, I wondered whether you might—?'

There was a pause. And then Cynthia's voice seemed to ice over like a pond.

'Shivaun, if Ivor didn't give you his number of his own accord, then I'm really not sure whether it would be right for me to. He was terribly upset, as I'm sure you know, when you broke off your engagement to him.'

'But – I – we – oh, Mrs Lawlor, that's what I want to talk to him about! I'd really be grateful if you'd give me his number, or even his address.'

Another silence, in which Shivaun could somehow envisage Cynthia examining her nail polish, deliberating.

'But Shivaun, as I said, it's not up to me to do that. Ivor has gone to Spain, left his job and been terribly traumatised by the way you treated him, after he'd always been so good to you.'

Too good, Cynthia's voice suggested; far too good to you, and look at the thanks he gets for it. But Shivaun wasn't listening to the accusation, her mind was too busy latching onto the word 'Spain'. *Spain?* But Alana had said Australia—!

'Mrs Lawlor, I'm terribly sorry about what happened, I know Ivor must have been as upset as I was myself. We – we had an awful misunderstanding, we were both—'

'Both to blame? I really don't think it's right to say that, Shivaun, my son always treated you extremely well and then you threw him over, out of a clear blue sky.'

'D – did he say that?'

'More or less. I gather that your work mattered more to you than he did.'

'Oh, God – look, Mrs Lawlor, I can't go into it all with you now, but it's not as simple as that. That's why I want to talk to him.'

'Yes. Well. Whether he wants to talk to you is another matter. Frankly I can't blame him if he doesn't. At any rate, I think he should have the choice. If you'd care to give me your number, I'll pass it on to him when next I speak with him, and he can decide for himself. I'm afraid that's the best I can do for you.'

Shivaun felt a huge surge of disappointment. It had never entered her head that Cynthia would be hostile; instead she had fully expected to get the number and was all keyed up to ring Ivor immediately.

'But—'

Cynthia sighed audibly. 'Shivaun, I will give it to him and then he can do whatever he chooses with it. I have a pen here beside me – and as I said, I am in somewhat of a hurry.'

There was no option. In a rush, she gabbled it out, and was relieved to hear Cynthia repeating the digits back to her, apparently at least writing them down correctly.

'All right, I've got that. Ivor already phoned me earlier today, so it'll probably be New Year before he calls again, but I'll give it to him then.'

Shivaun felt like shouting at her, making her promise, but that would sound undignified to the point of pathetic.

'Then I'll look forward to hearing from him – thank you very much, Mrs Lawlor, and best wishes for a lovely Christmas.'

'The same to you, Shivaun. Goodbye.'

With a click she was gone, leaving Shivaun staring at the phone. For a moment she was flummoxed, and then she felt the pinprick of tears. Had she really deserved as frosty a reception as all that? How could Cynthia possibly know what had really happened between herself and Ivor, the nuances of it all, the undercurrents? Clenching her fists, she felt deeply undermined, as if some power had passed from her grasp to Cynthia's. All she could do now was pray that Ivor would get the number, and want it, hurl himself on the nearest phone in – in *Spain*? What the hell was he doing in Spain?

Cynthia had given her no chance to ask, not given her an inch. But surely Ivor had not painted her as the villain of the piece, told his mother that she'd ditched him when *he* was the one who'd wanted a separation . . . ? In a million years she couldn't imagine him doing that, in fact she couldn't imagine him telling Cynthia very much at all, he was not the type to go crying to mummy when things went wrong, or divulge private information.

Nor could she imagine what was happening, that chilly day, three thousand miles away in Ireland. She did not know that Cynthia Lawlor blamed her for Ivor's departure to Spain, for giving up the excellent job he'd only just got after years of study, for leaving the home that was now so empty without him. She did not know that Cynthia had turned against her years ago, when she was only twelve, the day she came running in tears to the front door, howling that she'd been adopted. Cynthia did not feel that an adopted girlfriend boded at all well for the Lawlor pedigree, she felt that Ivor's children would have unknown grandparents of extremely dubious status, and that marrying Shivaun Reilly presented considerable risks in such circumstances. But Cynthia worshipped her son, and for his sake she had said nothing, biding her time for years until, finally and happily, the relationship had broken up of its own accord. Now, she did not intend to facilitate any reconciliation. On the contrary, it was her dearest wish that Ivor would get whatever he wanted out of Spain, come home and settle down with – with someone ladylike, an accountant like himself perhaps, not someone who went on protest marches, got herself arrested and her name in the papers.

With Shivaun Reilly out of the way, the path to such perfection was considerably clearer, and Cynthia was damned if she was going to strew any impediments in it. Ivor was going through a funny patch at the moment, but it was only a patch; if she played along with it this carpentry business wouldn't last even as long as Shivaun had lasted, he would simply work it out of his system and come home to resume his proper career.

That was all he would resume. Cynthia's conscience was clear as glass as she picked up the page with Shivaun's American number on it, tore it neatly into little squares and dropped it in the bin.

On Christmas morning Ivor rolled over, as he rolled over so many mornings on the cusp between sleeping and waking, to gather Shivaun into his arms. It took him a chill blank moment to realise that he was holding nothing in them only a lumpen pillow, and he sat up with an oath. Christmas Day, for fuck's sake, and still nothing! No love, no hugs or kisses, no sex, no Shivaun. His emptiness was as cold as his fury, and for the first time he wondered – could it possibly be the carpentry that was the cause of all this? He'd never have believed it of Shivaun, but was she thinking the same thing those people in El Rinconcillo had been thinking, that he was only a workman now, poor and struggling, unable to provide any of the comforts he had once promised her?

He'd thought she'd be delighted to hear he'd had the courage to do it, to break away from a cushy unfulfilling life to embrace something much harder but more rewarding; she'd said she didn't want him turning into a 'real accountant'. But women were notoriously odd about these things, and Shivaun had been behaving oddly to begin with – because of Jason goddamn Dean, no doubt, but the end result was still the same. She wasn't here and he was irrationally, totally livid with her. Jumping out of bed, he took a half-cold bath in the even colder bathroom, dressed in everything available and went down to the ghastly kitchen, where he rustled up a meagre breakfast and a sheet of paper.

'Shivaun,' he wrote on it, 'this is last-chance saloon. If you don't write immediately, then that's the end. I'll take it you never want to hear from me again. Got that? Crystal clear? Good. Ivor.'

Without giving himself time to think, he slugged back his coffee, tore his room asunder searching for a stamp and envelope, went out and threw the missive in a postbox. There. That was putting it up to her fair and square, that would settle— With a suddenly sinking feeling he stared at the postbox and realised that yes, that would certainly settle things between them, once and for all.

Well, so be it! He had his pride after all, in fact it was about the only thing left to him, he wasn't going to beg like a dog. What, as a matter of fact, was he going to do in Seville, on this horribly lonely morning?

Shoving his hands in his pockets, he set off in no particular direction, gazing at the deserted streets which might or might not liven up later on. He knew Spain started its day late, but he didn't know what it did on Christmas day, whether everyone would remain closeted at home in the bosom of their families or whether there might be some kind of craic somewhere . . . but even if there was, he had barely tuppence to his name, couldn't afford to join in anything that wasn't free. All he could do was walk, hang out like a vagrant, give thanks that at least it wasn't raining even if it was bloody freezing. It was quiet too, quieter than he'd yet known La Macarena to be, and as he trudged on the silence began to settle into his bones. This, he thought, is a make-or-break day: not only because of that last-ditch letter to Shivaun, but because if I can get through this I can get through anything.

Eventually, after a long aimless walk down Espiritu Santo and Calle Gerona, his footsteps led him to the edge of the neighbourhood, where he heard a bell tolling and saw, at last, some signs of life. A few people, mostly elderly women in shawls and men in baggy suits, were trickling into the church of Santa Catalina, evidently to attend mass. Although he'd been brought up Catholic, it was a full year since Ivor had last attended mass, on the same day for the same reason these people were now going. Should he join them? The church would be warm, but he didn't want to be a hypocrite . . . sometimes he believed in a god, sometimes he didn't. That kind of lukewarm faith, he felt, didn't really deserve refuge or sanctuary.

To go into the church just to get out of the cold would be a cheap, pitiful thing to do. Yet something stirred in him, something from some long-forgotten schoolday probably, a voice intoning low calm words about the wretched of the earth, the sinners and the disbelievers, everyone being welcome in the house of God. Did that include him? He never prayed, he wasn't at all sure he believed a word of any of it – as he stood wondering, conscious of his tatty jeans and greasy sweater, a passing woman smiled at him, and muttered something.

Happy Christmas. He didn't know the phrase in Spanish, but he knew that was what she was saying to him, a total stranger. Without further thought, he followed her into the church, found a pew at the back and knelt down, smelling the incense that jolted him sharply back to his childhood. For no reason he could name, he found himself thinking of his father.

'Our Father, who art in heaven . . .' As the mass began he thought of Shivaun's father as well, and wondered why, if there was a God, He or She or It allowed good men to die. Why were there murders, massacres, mayhem all over the world, all the time, probably even today, why was it all such a mystery? His mathematical mind couldn't account for any of it, he knew his only hope at this moment was simply to accept, to permit himself to believe in something better even if there was nothing better. Feeling a fool, he murmured a prayer for Jimmy and for his own father, for Viv and for Cynthia, the only survivor of their generation.

And then a prayer for Shivaun, because whatever she was doing today or whatever she felt about him, he still loved her. He loved her with absolute devotion, with the purest certainty; as he thought of her his whole body went still, and he felt the most extraordinary sense of calm.

Afterwards, when the mass was over, that sense of calm remained with him. But it focused him too, took him by an invisible hand and led him with his mind almost suspended back to Miguel's house, where he found the keys of the workshop, went round to it and let himself in. Then, taking off his jacket, he turned on the lights and the paltry heater, rolled up his sleeves and began to search.

Miguel, he knew, would kill him if he chose an expensive piece of mahogany or beech. It would have to be something cheap and inconspicuous. As he dug through the piles of wood his body began to warm up, his sense of purpose clarified, and by the time he hauled out two large abandoned chunks of pine he was working almost on autopilot, driven by the vision of what he was about to create. Lugging the pine across the workshop to the trestle bench, he unearthed an array of tools and got to work.

Hours passed, but time stood still, he was not aware of morning sliding into afternoon, or evening falling or night darkening as he worked on and on in the consuming silence, broken only by the intermittent sound of the tools, the one thing Miguel always maintained in peak condition, smooth and steady in his hand. Twice the saw slipped, he was vaguely conscious of pain, but he kept on, and on, until the shape began to emerge and he stood back, mesmerised, to look at it.

When he did, two things struck him. The first was that he must be lightheaded, hallucinating with hunger and exhaustion, to have done such a crazy, unaccountable thing. The second was that he had achieved his goal, he had created a thing of beauty at last; even if the wood was worthless the workmanship was fine, and sure, and lasting. He had made, on this day of memorable loneliness and arguable insanity, a crib.

Standing back, he kicked it, and it rocked without so much as a squeak, because its rockers were curved and perfect, the balance was purely mathematical, the weight was distributed exactly on the centre of gravity. The only thing it lacked was the child to go in it, the child that he and Shivaun would one day create.

With that thought locked in his mind, he lifted it up over his head, carried it to the far end of the workshop and wedged it behind a heap of debris, where it would remain hidden from

Miguel's sight for as long as he could keep it there. Some day Miguel would find it, explode with rage at the insolence of it, and that would be fine, he would take all the abuse that would be hurled at him unless it was physical, in which case he and Miguel would come to blows. At this moment Ivor didn't care in the least, if broken bones resulted they would be worthwhile, because whatever he might have to apologise for in his life, he would not apologise for this.

Then, almost faint with hunger, every muscle throbbing triumphantly, he laughed a laugh that sounded manic even to his own ear, shut down the workshop and returned to the dark empty hovel that passed for home.

Alana thought it was the best Christmas of her life. The minute she arrived in her family home in Waterford she sensed the difference in the atmosphere, the way everyone was paying attention to her, asking teasing but curious questions about this new boyfriend of hers, remarking on how well she looked and the smile he seemed to have put on her face. But where was he, when were they going to get to meet him?

'He's visiting his own parents first,' she said, 'but then he'll be coming here – and everyone's to be nice to him, OK?'

They promised they would be nice, not tease him the way they teased every other would-be new member of the family, and she felt they meant it, because they so much wanted her to have a boyfriend at last. Maybe even a fiancé, if everything went well . . . of course it was early days yet, but now that she was sleeping with Brendan, the next logical step was to get engaged. Not for the world would she breathe a word to anyone, not even her sisters when they pestered her to know, that sleeping with Brendan had not quite lived up to expectation so far. He was, if the truth be known – which it never would be – a bit of a wham-bam-thank-you-ma'am kind of lover, with a not very romantic habit of falling asleep immediately after making love. He snored, too. But they'd only slept together three times so far, which left plenty of time for improving things, and besides sex wasn't everything. Any woman of twenty-seven with her head screwed on knew that other things mattered far more in the long run, and Brendan had the raw materials of a grand husband. He drank a bit, and swore a lot, but he worked hard, he was fun to be with and when he made the effort he looked really good. Naturally he wouldn't be wearing his overalls when he arrived on Christmas afternoon, he'd be in the nifty new Chinos and navy jacket she'd bought him.

In turn, she dressed up herself on Christmas morning, went to church wishing he was there beside her, and then stayed as far away from her mother's kitchen as possible while lunch was cooking. She didn't want him to find her in an apron smelling of brussels sprouts when he arrived. Instead she volunteered to supervise her siblings' numerous children, because it would be good for him to see her in a maternal role, coping sweetly but firmly with the riotous hordes, looking capable and in command.

Because of its size, the Kennedy clan limited its Christmas presents to one each, but she was touched to find that her parents had got Brendan a present, an illustrated encyclopaedia of cars, and that the kids had clubbed together to buy him a Metallica CD. Metallica was his favourite group, he didn't share Ivor's enthusiasm or her own for Mary Coughlan, he liked his music red-blooded and loud. And it had to be loud, she conceded, for him to hear it above the din of his workshop with all those revving engines. When she heard the rev of his own car arriving – well, whichever one he had borrowed from the garage – she flew to the door, and was thrilled to see him getting out of a shiny, nearly-new Jaguar. Wouldn't that wow her mum!

'Hi! Come on in!'

She ran to him and he scooped her into a huge, hearty hug, beaming from ear to ear.

'Hi! Hey, you look great! Happy Christmas!'

He kissed her in full view of everyone, and she led him in to meet them all. 'Mum – Dad – everyone – this is my boyfriend Brendan McLaughlin, Brendan, this is my brother Cormac, my sister Sorcha—'

There were so many of them she was afraid he might be intimidated, but not a bit of it; he shook hands with all the men, let himself be kissed by all the women and threw mock punches at all the boy children while patting the girls on the head.

'God, there must be at least two soccer teams here! Did Santa come to all of you?'

Yes, they whooped, he did, come and see our presents! Pulling and tugging at him, they led him to the Christmas tree in the living room and in no time he was sitting on the floor draped in toys and infants, while Alana's father reached for the drinks on the sideboard.

'What'll you have, Brendan?'

'A Jemmy'd be great' he replied, and Alana smiled; anyone would need a whiskey to cope with so many rowdy children.

'Now kids,' she said sternly, 'there are twelve of you but there's only one Brendan, so go easy on him, OK?'

She didn't want him to feel overpowered. But he seemed perfectly at ease, casually finding a niche in the family as if it had always been there for him, exclaiming with delight over his CD and insisting that it be played immediately. Her parents both winced when it was, but she turned to them and to her adult siblings with a beseeching smile.

'Oh, just a few tracks – he's driven such a long way?'

For her sake they agreed to the pumping music, and she felt blissful when one of her sisters nudged her in the ribs.

'He's good fun, Alana. Good-looking, too.'

Yes. She thought he was beautiful, with his sparky blue eyes and thick curly hair, wearing his new clothes and looking his best. Far from putting a foot wrong, he seemed to be making a great impression on everyone. Which, devoutly, was what she wished him to do.

Her mother's attempts to ask him a few pertinent questions got swallowed up in the din of the children, but he redeemed himself by eating a full meal even though he'd already eaten with his own family, and then telling Mrs Kennedy she was an even better cook than her daughter. Flattered, Mrs Kennedy smiled at Alana.

'Well, I must say, your young lad is very nice, and you seem to have found the way to his heart!'

'Yes, Mum,' she whispered back, 'I think I have.'

At that moment Brendan caught her eye, and winked at her in a way that said yes, I like your family, this is great craic. Thrilled, she winked back, and blew him a kiss, and her father pressed another Jemmy into his mercifully well-scrubbed hand.

Shivaun kicked off her Christmas morning with a long walk round the headland down to the beach, getting her mind in gear for the rest of the day. There were only two options at Christmas, she thought; one was nostalgia for home, for Viv and Jimmy and Ivor, the other was to make the most of this first Christmas in America and enjoy the colour all around her. Although Gloucester was a mixed community with many races and religions, everyone seemed to have got caught up in the festive atmosphere, the whole place was crackling with holly and log fires and a fine layer of bluey-white frost. Marina, with help from everyone, had put up a huge tree dressed in gold, decked the house in leaves, branches and acorns, and at noon several of her friends were expected for drinks. Azalea had the day off, but Shivaun was invited to visit her later this evening, 'when mad Max and his insufferable brats finally drive you over the top'.

Shivaun thought it would be fun to have Marina's niece and two nephews around today, as well as her brother Max; after all Christmas was about families. For one piercing moment she thought of Ivor, so acutely it took her breath away, but then she reminded herself that he hadn't even sent her a Christmas card, and pushed him down to the bottom of her heart. If he did ring her from Spain, she'd want a bloody good explanation for that. Quickening her pace, she hastened back to the house, which flickered a welcome in the mist; Marina had lit dozens of white candles that made it look magical.

Outside, several cars were parked on the flagstones, and

inside it was already surprisingly warm and noisy, filling up with far more of Marina's friends than she'd expected. As she shook the frost off her shoes in the hall, Marina came sweeping out in a vivid gown of rose-red silk and gathered her up into a perfumed embrace.

'Darling girl, happy Christmas!'

Laughing, she kissed her back, suddenly happy and relieved to be here in this beautiful, cheerful house. If it wasn't home, it was as close to home as could be got, and her cards from home stood along with Marina's own on the mantelpiece, as if she were part of the loose, vague family.

'Oh, Marina, you look so well! But you can't cope with all these people by yourself, let me get changed and give you a hand—'

'That'd be great. It's chaos without Dorothy, but she's left everything ready in the kitchen and Max is playing barman. If you wouldn't mind just passing round a few snacks—?'

'Sure. I'll put on my French maid's outfit!'

She ran up the stairs to her room, but when she got there she stopped dead, confronted by an enormous gold-wrapped box on the bed with a card on top, simply inscribed 'Enjoy! Marina.' Opening it, she gasped as she unfolded layers of silvery tissue and drew out a stunning dress of sorrel-coloured silk. Hand-made by a top American designer, it was one she'd eyed lustfully the day she went shopping with Marina in Boston, and she could believe neither the beauty nor the generosity of it.

'Oh, my God!' Breathlessly, she held it up to her, flirted with it in the cheval mirror and then stripped to her underwear, threw it over her head in a flurry of sheer delight. Instantly, even before she found the accessories to go with it, it transformed her, gave her a surge of high-voltage confidence that made her laugh aloud. Some of Marina's friends downstairs, she knew, were high-profile people, celebrities in their various fields, but in a dress like this she could tackle the Archangel Gabriel should he materialise looking for a pretzel. It was a short, sleek dress with long sleeves and a low square neckline; by the time she'd put on some make-up, found her one pair of stilettos and brushed out her new hairstyle, she felt like a million dollars. If Ivor could see her in this, he would burst into flames – suddenly she felt a razor-sharp stab of lust for him, wanted to seize him and fling him on the bed and reclaim his body by force, possess every inch of it and . . . damn him! Damn, damn, *damn*!

Breathing hard, clenching her fists, she caught sight of her flushed face in the miror and realised that yes, he was right; she had taken him for granted, and she was furious with herself. She'd let those bawling babies and that doomed hospital and every other stupid thing gain the upper hand, distract her from the gorgeous man who adored her. Like a slap across the face, it struck her that she had let Jason Dean win, let him win the battle for her emotions without even trying.

Glaring at her reflection, she shouted at it: you fool! You prize idiot, you threw Ivor Lawlor *away*! No wonder he doesn't want you back! You'll never see him again and it serves you right, he's probably wrapped around some Spanish *señorita* at this minute because you were such a pig-headed pain in the arse!

For one horrifically vivid moment, she had a vision of Ivor doing battle with two people, pushing away a menacing Jason Dean with one hand, pulling some Spanish lady to him with the other, and she didn't know whether to laugh or cry, all she knew was that Marina's dress was having an electrifying effect on her, she felt like some completely other person in it.

Right, then. She would be some other person in it. Stabbing Viv's best gold earrings into her ears, she completed her new look with a slash of scarlet lipstick and ran out of the room, slamming the door behind her. Racing down the stairs, she located Marina amidst the throng in the lounge, stalked up to her, grasped her and kissed her on both cheeks. Then she marched out to the kitchen, grabbed a platter of canapés and returned to the lounge, her eye roving over the crowd until it located an apparently unattached man standing by the fireplace. Without the least idea who he was, she went up to him, proffered the platter and beamed hugely.

'Hi. I'm Shivaun. And who are you?'

⋆ ⋆ ⋆

'Well,' Max Darnoux drawled several hours later, 'that was quite a party, Marina. And that nurse of yours was the life and soul of it. Why didn't you tell me she was such a siren?'

Marina frowned. Even though Shivaun was out in the kitchen, and the sound system was pulsing out Aretha Franklin, she didn't want his words to carry.

'Don't get any ideas, Max. Shivaun is a good kid. Far too good for an old lech like you.'

Max was over fifty, with a paunch and a round bald head like a football, but he grinned complacently at his sister. 'Jesus, Marina, she didn't look like a kid to me. Didn't act like one either. She flirted with every man in the room, she even squashed Steven Hunt flat on his face!'

Marina laughed despite herself. Steven, not recognising Shivaun, had made a beeline for her, whereupon Shivaun had looked him archly up and down, peeled his hand off her hip and swivelled him in Marina's direction with a remark to the effect that his Christmas present was waiting for him over there. Steven's jaw had all but clanged off the floor, and Marina thought he'd got exactly what he deserved. It was just lucky for everyone his wife hadn't been within earshot.

'Yes, well, Steven's well able to take care of himself. But Shivaun – Shivaun doesn't need any hassle, Max. She's had a rough time.'

'Hah! I wish she'd give me one! Will she be joining us for dinner?'

'Yes, of course. You just behave yourself, and get those kids of yours to do the same. In fact they can help to serve dinner, it's mitzo soup and sushi – I hope that's Californian enough for you?'

He put down his cigar and patted her knee affectionately. 'Well, I hardly expected you to serve turkey or anything predictable, dearest. Let me find the kids and light a cracker under them.'

Amiably, he trundled off, and Marina sat back by the fire, reflecting. Shivaun's behaviour had certainly been rather startling, as had her dazzling appearance; she hadn't expected the new dress to have quite such a radical effect. But, all things considered, it was a positive effect. Yesterday, after phoning Ireland, Shivaun had looked like someone emerging from a car wreck, devastated that Ivor's mother would not give her his phone number. Today, she looked ready to swop Ivor for any other man on the planet, to get on with her life and – and that was the whole point, really, about it. Shivaun was up and down like a yo-yo, an emotional minefield whether she knew it or not. Christmas was a dodgy time of year for people as fragile as her, they steeled themselves to get through it and then, afterwards, some of them shattered. Marina had become very fond of Shivaun, and she did not want her to shatter. What Shivaun needs now, she thought, is something new to latch on to in the New Year, some fresh blood to divert her from this wretched Ivor in Spain, or wherever he is. Maybe Azalea has the right idea after all. It is a risk, but . . . should I let her take it? What might be gained, what might be lost? I don't want her hurt, but she might be cured . . . if she were my daughter, what would I do?

Stroking her dogs, she sat thinking about it, vaguely conscious of Max carrying plates into the dining room, Shivaun bringing cutlery, the three children arguing over something – for heaven's sake, could they not give anyone a moment's peace, even on a day when they were knee-deep in gifts and goodies!

'What's going on?' she called irritably, and they came running to her, hurling accusations at each other, demanding justice and retribution at the tops of their voices. And then, abruptly, Shivaun was standing amongst them in her shimmering dress, brandishing a serving fork like an avenging angel.

'Cut it out! Go and set the table and leave your aunt alone, she's had a stroke, she doesn't need three spoilt brats wearing her out!'

They gaped at her, and fled. Marina looked at Shivaun in astonishment, and then laughed. 'Well done! You don't even know them, but you sorted them out. I've wanted to for years, but Max thinks the sun shines out of their butts. They play him off like a tennis ball against their mother.'

Shivaun could hear them now complaining to him, and found her taste for children suddenly waning. They were older than Kathy Shreve's kids, but equally unappealing; clearly parenting wasn't all about kissy-coo and fluffy little bundles.

'I'd recommend,' she said on reflection, 'that Max buy himself a cricket bat and use it liberally on all three of them. They've been sulking and pouting all day.'

Marina grinned. 'That's the thanks you get for drowning them in consumer goods. Unfortunately, Americans don't play cricket. D'you think a baseball bat would work?'

'It would if I got my hands on it! I don't mean to criticise your niece or nephews, but—'

Max came back into the room, looking harassed. 'Marina, George says he doesn't like sushi, and Eleanor doesn't want mitzo soup, could we give them something else?'

Marina glanced at Shivaun and nodded. 'Yes. We could give them the name of that charity that sends food to starving children in Africa.'

Max stared at her, and Shivaun laughed outright. Marina sounded like a woman definitely on the mend.

Miguel did not return home until several days after Christmas, by which time Ivor was surviving on a daily loaf of bread, a dwindling block of cheese and whatever fruit and vegetables he could cadge cheap when the markets were closing. But by then he knew that he could survive, knew he had come through a rock-bottom experience which had toughened and tempered him; after nearly a week in complete isolation he was learning to handle solitude, and what was more he had finished his crib, honed it, waxed it and stashed it safely back in its corner. Bemused as he was by it, he was immensely proud of it too, and did not want Miguel charging at it like a bull at a red rag. But eventually, inevitably, Miguel did find it, and Ivor winced as he dragged it out from under its camouflage looking as if he'd discovered a cache of contraband.

'*Que—?*' he yelped, yanking it into full view so roughly that Ivor raced to protect it, as fiercely as if it contained a live baby. 'Miguel, go easy, I made that, it's only—'

Miguel stood panting, holding the thing aloft in his meaty fists, his eyes blackening first in amazement and then in wonder. For what felt like a quivering eternity he was silent, and then a hail of words shot at Ivor like arrows.

'Yeah, yeah, I made it, calm down, I only used a bit of pine, get a grip.'

Miguel stood transfixed. Then, dropping the crib, he stabbed Ivor's chest with his forefinger and shouted some question at him; Ivor caught the word 'papa' and understood. Miguel thought he'd got some local girl pregnant.

'No! No baby! No trouble!' Frantically he gestured to make himself understood, until finally Miguel stood back, shook his head, scratched it and gazed at the crib again.

'*Por que?*'

'Because—' Ivor groped to explain, but he couldn't. His Spanish wasn't up to explaining something he didn't understand himself. For a moment, there was a mystified impasse. And then Miguel gave the crib a shove, set it rocking and ran his hand along its contours.

'*Bueno. Muy bueno.*'

Ivor nearly fainted. 'Good? You think it's good?'

Miguel bellowed laughing. '*Si! Muy bueno!*' And he started yattering in Spanish at such a rate Ivor had no idea what he was saying, but was very relieved. He'd fully expected Miguel to hurl the thing at the wall and him after it. Instead there didn't even seem to be any mention of reducing his rations to zero until the wood was paid for. After another baffled pause, Miguel merely screwed his finger to his temple to indicate he thought Ivor was barmy, clapped him resoundingly on the back and sent him back to work.

After that the atmosphere between them thawed to a bearable degree. But it was early in January, one stunningly cold day, before a light finally shone at the end of the tunnel in which Ivor felt he was living. Trundling down to the kitchen in his vest one morning, Miguel picked up the post and began to riffle through it, without much apparent interest. Ivor guessed that it was mostly bills, and sure enough Miguel threw several unopened envelopes away with a contemptuous snort.

But then he came to a franked, official-looking envelope bearing a logo that looked, Ivor thought, as if it might be the Spanish government's equivalent of the Irish government's harp. Envelopes bearing harps almost invariably contained bad news, and Ivor grinned gleefully.

'Uh oh. Not the rates or the Minister for Misery, I hope, trying to prise a peseta out of your padlocked pockets?'

Miguel ripped the envelope open with both suspicion and caution, as if it might explode, gazed at the single page it contained and gasped. Then he read the page again, threw back his shoulders and bellowed like a wounded elephant. For a moment Ivor was actually alarmed, thought he might be going to have a heart attack as he collapsed onto a chair, his forehead popping with sweat.

'Jesus, Miguel, what is it?' In spite of himself he felt a brief flash of pity, but curiosity got the upper hand as Miguel held the paper out to him, groaning and blessing himself.

'Madonna. Oh, Madonna.'

Ivor took the page, and at first all he could make out was a long line of zeros that seemed to extend into infinity. Then, concentrating, he deciphered it: it was a tax estimate from the Department of Revenue, for a huge sum of money that stretched back, apparently, several years. A wide grin spread across his face, and then he burst out laughing.

'Hah! They've gotcha! You're up to your neck in hot chocolate!

Wringing his hands, rocking back and forth, Miguel looked on the verge of tears, all his machismo melting into an anguished puddle. Ivor felt a sense of déja-vu, and then it came back to him, the pitiful clients in his company office, caught in a swamp of deceit and bureaucracy and panic. Slowly, thoughtfully, he sucked his lower lip.

'H'mm. This looks like pretty bad news to me, Miguel.'

Miguel got the drift, and looked up at him with eyes sorrowful as a spaniel's, beseeching and somehow defeated. Ivor guessed that this must be the resounding last salvo in a long battle, that the authorities had finally nailed their quarry after many skirmishes. The words made no sense to him, but the figures spoke for themselves. Leaning against the wall, he surveyed Miguel without betraying compassion.

'So where are you going to start? Where's your paperwork? Do you have any receipts, dockets, invoices you can set off against this?'

'*Que?*'

'Receipts, Miguel, exit visas from prison! Where-are-your-papers?'

He enunciated slowly, but it was useless. Miguel sat slumped in despair. They both gazed at the bottom line of the page, which was underlined in red, and Ivor began to think quickly, exultantly. But it was too complicated, they needed an interpreter. Where—?

'Hang on' he said suddenly, threw on his jacket and ran out into the street. Where was the cybercafé? He'd seen it somewhere in the maze of alleys, the only one in La Macarena, but – he set off at a run, and it took him some time to find it, but eventually he was standing before a surprised Pilar, panting.

'Pilar – it's kind of an emergency – Miguel has a problem – we need an interpreter, could you possibly come?'

Reluctantly, she got an assistant to take over her work, and hurried out with him full of questions. 'What is it? Is he ill?'

Ivor roared with laughter. 'Sick as a dog! Follow me!'

When they got back to the house Miguel was knocking back a tumbler of brandy, and Ivor seized him by the shoulders.

'Idiot! Put that down and pay attention! This is Pilar –' he realised he didn't even know her second name – 'and she and I are going to help you, but only if you co-operate.'

When Pilar greeted Miguel he saw that the pair did in fact

know each other, were on nodding terms at least. Rapidly she translated what Ivor had said, and Miguel gazed at him in wonder, asked her how he could possibly help. Ivor drew breath.

'Tell him that I'm a qualified accountant, and that I can get him at least halfway out of this mess on two conditions: one, if he can produce some documents' – he outlined everything Miguel would need – 'and two, if he agrees to pay me for my work. I want a chunk of money now, in cash, and I want a hundred pesetas for every thousand I save him.'

Ten per cent was lower than what he would have charged in Dublin, but he wanted to make sure Miguel accepted, because he was heartily sick and tired of starvation. But Miguel looked dubious, began to babble at Pilar.

'What's he saying?'

'He says you can't be an accountant, he doesn't believe you, you are a carpenter and – and a liar.'

Ivor didn't know whether to be flattered or insulted. 'God, I'll brain him. Tell him I *am* an accountant, specialised in taxation, he can phone my former employers if he wants a ruddy reference.'

Ivor knew Miguel couldn't phone them, because he spoke no English, and he knew they wouldn't give any references because of his swift departure. He also knew Miguel was torn between trusting him and throwing himself on the mercy of some expensive Spanish accountant. Well, your choice pal, he thought, I wouldn't call your choices unlimited here.

The conversation began to get more heated as Miguel stalled for time and Pilar tried to persuade him. Nonchalantly, Ivor stood back, folded his arms and waited. If Pilar convinced Miguel, he would take a roll of notes from him immediately and treat her to the second breakfast Spaniards ate mid-morning, a magnificent *desayuno* with lots of *suizos*. He could still taste the life-saving meal she had bought him.

Eventually Miguel whimpered, sighed and threw up his hands in surrender. She grinned hugely.

'He says yes, OK. He will give you two hundred thousand pesetas now and then you will start work tonight – there is a date on this tax bill, it must be paid by the end of February.'

Seven weeks. Ivor thought the Spaniards were generous. He could easily untangle this knot by then – not without some pain to Miguel, but a lot less than might otherwise be incurred.

'Tell him I want four hundred thousand now.'

Pilar raised an eyebrow, laughed and broke it to Miguel. Ivor scarcely needed her to translate his response.

'He says you are the son of a – a night lady!'

Ivor thought of Cynthia, and exploded laughing. 'Fine. Tell him he's the son of a night lady's dog, and he's to pay up now, and I'll save him a hundred times that amount. Oh, and I want a bonus for working it all out in euros.'

Miguel winced again, glared at Ivor, spat on the palm of his hand and then, with a look of mixed cynicism and new respect, shook Ivor's. There was a moment's silence before he went to a drawer, pulled out some money and peeled off notes as if they were his own skin. Throwing them on the kitchen table, he turned on his heel and went upstairs with a final mumble. Pilar turned to Ivor.

'He says he will get dressed and you are to go on to the workshop, get started on the bookcase for Señor Ramirez.'

'Tough. I'm not going to work this morning. I'm taking you out to *desayuno* to thank you. You've been fantastic.'

'Oh – but I must get back to the cybercafé.'

She looked resolute, and they frowned at each other. But Ivor was very grateful to her. 'Lunch, then? At El Rinconcillo? My turn?'

She considered, and smiled. 'Yes. All right. That is very nice. Two o'clock.'

It was agreed, and she went on her way, leaving Ivor with a heady sense of victory. With a little money to his name at last, and more to come, he could now start to see something of Seville, take buses and get around, start living a semi-normal life. But, humiliating and searing as it had been, he was in no hurry to forget his taste of abject poverty. In its way, it had been worth its weight in gold; he knew now how the other half lived, and that he could if necessary live with them.

'So, d'you want to come with us or what?'

It was snowing in Massachusetts, not on Cape Ann but up in the mountains, and Azalea was mad keen to go skiing while the powder was perfect. She was a keen and experienced skier, but if Shivaun came along she could join the other rookies, their group would include ten or twelve people of varying ability. Shivaun, perched on the edge of Azalea's desk, swung her legs and considered.

'I'd love to. But Marina didn't seem entirely convinced when I mentioned it to her.'

In fact Shivaun was baffled by Marina's response, which was yes, she could have the week off if she wanted it, but was she sure about skiing? It was a dangerous sport and, she said, she didn't want her nurse breaking a leg. One person walking on a stick was bad enough, two would look ridiculous.

'But you don't even need your stick for short walks any more, Marina! I wouldn't ask you if I didn't think you could manage without me – am I wrong about that? If you don't feel up to it, just say so, maybe you're not as confident as you look?'

Sounding uncertain, Marina said that she was well able to manage now. It was just that – well, if a dozen people were going someone was sure to sustain some kind of injury, and she didn't want it to be Shivaun. Shivaun couldn't make out whether she was genuinely concerned, or secretly afraid of being left alone with only Dorothy and Joe to help her. But she was able to bathe and dress by herself these days, albeit slowly; Shivaun's role had become more therapeutic.

In fact it looked likely that Marina would be fully recovered by late spring or early summer, she wouldn't need nursing until Shivaun's contract expired in the fall. Neither of them was too sure how she felt about that.

Azalea leaned her elbows on her desk, fiddled with her

long braid and then tossed it back with an air of resolution.

'Let me talk to Marina. It's you she's worried about, not herself.'

'But she might be right. I'd be damn all use to her hobbling round on crutches.'

'You won't. We'll keep you on the nursery slopes. We're not talking Mount Everest here.'

'No . . . but Azalea, there's no point in my going unless Marina is happy about it. I wouldn't enjoy it either, I'd be worried about her.'

'Oh, what a pair of fusspots! You can call her every day and check up on her, come back if she needs you. Wachusett is less than an hour away.'

'Then maybe I should just join you during the daytime, sleep here at nights.'

Azalea looked impatient. 'But then you'd miss all the fun, the après-ski! We stay in a couple of big cabins, make fondues and get drunk, have a great time – you'll meet lots of new people too. One of the guys is Irish.'

Shivaun perked up. Much as she was enjoying America, it would be good to hear a voice from home. 'Is he? Who is he?'

'Oh . . . just a guy. You'll see. If you come with us.'

She laughed. 'You're not by any chance trying to fix me up, are you?'

Azalea grinned. 'Why, do you want fixing up? Is Ivor history at last?'

No. Ivor wasn't. But it was mid-January now, and he had still not responded to Shivaun's effort to contact him. She'd phoned Cynthia again, to be curtly assured that yes, Ivor had been given her number, was Shivaun suggesting he hadn't? After that she called Alana, twice, but there was no answer. Shivaun was still mystified why Alana should have told her that Ivor was in Australia instead of Spain, but supposed that it must have been some mistake, maybe hearsay pub gossip from someone who scarcely knew him. Anyway, what matter, the point remained his silence. Resounding silence. She wasn't going to make a fool of herself by getting Interpol on his case.

She hadn't heard from Ireland either, about Jason Dean. Never since her teens had she ever wanted to know who her real parents were, because her love and her loyalty lay with Viv and Jimmy, but she longed to know for sure that she was not in any way connected with that vile, repugnant man. Somehow she was keeping a lid on the fear, but it haunted her. Abruptly, she looked frankly at Azalea.

'Is this Irish guy nice?'

'Yeah. Cute as a button. When you get to know him. He's a bit – bit shy.'

'What's he doing in America?'

'Working, like everyone else! He's been here for years. But he can tell you his own life story. Some people from the commune are coming too, and Jeff even though he skis like a chimp on Ecstasy . . . is there anyone you'd like to bring?'

It occurred to Shivaun that she'd like to bring Kathy Shreve, who'd been looking tired and deflated lately. Nonsensically, Kathy had refused to accept more than token payment for the painting that had been Shivaun's Christmas gift to Marina, so here was a chance to present her with a *fait accompli* she couldn't refuse; with all her expenses taken care of by Marina, Shivaun could afford to treat Kathy to the short holiday. In winter, Bill would surely have time to mind the boys and give his wife a break.

'I'll ask Kathy, if Marina lets me go.'

Azalea dug the end of her pen into her desk. 'Marina will. Leave her to me.'

'All right. You know her better than I do. Get round her if you can.'

'Trust me.'

Shivaun jumped down off Azalea's desk and went back to work, but didn't raise the subject with Marina, who in any event was now much preoccupied with the house she was designing for clients in Utah.

'I need to visit the site soon, Shivaun. D'you think I'm

up to going out there? Obviously you'd have to come with me—'

'Sure! I'd love to see another state. And your house. Maybe in another few weeks, if Steven says it's OK. But Marina, no cheating, OK? I don't want you talking him into letting you go and then when you get there you find it's all too much.'

Marina grimaced. 'No, I won't do that. The last thing I need is to collapse into my clients' arms. Americans are so preoccupied with looking young and fit, I don't want word going round that Marina Darnoux is looking like her own granny! But I look a hell of a lot better than I did a few months ago – what do you think?'

She preened a bit, touched her jewelled hand to her hair, and Shivaun grinned. 'You'd give Demi Moore a run for her money.'

'Darling girl, I wouldn't be caught in the same room with Demi Moore. You're supposed to say I look like someone classy, Sophia Loren or maybe Caroline of Monaco. I'm only eight years older than her, you know.'

'Yes, and you're a good bit younger than Sophia Loren! I'm sure you'll bring Utah to its knees when you get there. You've already brought Steven Hunt to his.'

'Mmm. That was fun, for sure. Sadly, Steven is more show than substance. When I'm fully recovered I'll be aiming a little higher.'

'Will you? Would you like to get married again, Marina?'

'No. Not married. Been there, got the T-shirt. But . . . you know . . . life is more fun with a man in it, Shivaun. I'm open to the possibility of finding one.'

She looked candidly at her, and Shivaun thought how feisty Americans were in this respect, when they fell down they seemed to be able to pick themselves up again. You had to admire their positive, bounce-back attitude. She smiled to herself, and Marina raised a quizzical eyebrow.

'You think that's funny? You reckon that at forty-eight I've got two chances, slim and zero?'

'No, not at all! I was just thinking that you're quite likely to find someone. Your work must bring you into contact with lots of men.'

'Yes. It does. I'm sorry the same can't be said for yours. If you decide to continue with private nursing you should pick some gorgeous guy next time. If you met one, would you be open to dating him?'

Shivaun knew that logically she should say yes, sure, why not? At twenty-four I can't lie down and die, spend the rest of my days in mourning for Ivor Lawlor. But – oh, hell, how long does it take to get over the love of your life?

'I – might. Eventually. It would depend . . . it's years since your divorce, Marina, but it's not even six months since mine, if you want to call it that.'

Marina looked at her, rather sharply. 'No, actually, I'm not sure that I do want to call it that. You hadn't set up house with Ivor, had you? You hadn't lived together as a couple, blended into a unit, lived and worked under the same roof, you didn't have to decide who was getting custody of the dog . . . I'm not trying to trivialise or belittle your last relationship, but at your age you have a lot of advantages. Just try to pick someone a little more reliable next time!'

'But that's exactly what I thought Ivor was. That's the bit I can't understand.'

'Then try harder. Figure out where you went wrong and don't make the same mistakes next time. I hope there will be a next time, because it would make me very happy to see you happy.'

Shivaun was touched, and patted Marina's hand. 'You're so sweet, I'm nearly sorry you're getting better! I love working here with you, I could stay forever.'

Thoughtfully, Marina gazed at her. 'Sometimes I think it would be great if you could stay. But that's a selfish thought. Even if I had children of my own I'd rather see them spreading their wings and making their own way in the world. But America seems to suit you – I must start asking my friends and clients whether they have any sons I could fix you up with. Some nice man here in Massachusetts would be ideal, then we could still be friends and visit each other – unless you're mad keen to go back to Ireland?'

Marina looked doubtful, and Shivaun felt doubtful. 'No . . . oo . . . not at the moment, anyway. When I think how hard I worked there, for so little reward at the end of the day . . . it was so damp and grey too, I much prefer this climate where you can tell one season from another. Plus, Boston is so clean and attractive, and out here a woman can walk round without getting mugged or murdered – I can even walk through the woods to Azalea's house after dark, feeling quite safe. By the way, did I tell you that she's got some Irish friend? Some man, I think she's as bad as you, trying to fix me up!'

She was surprised when Marina stiffened. 'I hope she's trying to do no such thing. I told her not to interfere.'

'What? But you just said – I thought you—'

Abruptly Marina stopped exercising, straightened up and frowned at her. 'What I say and what Azalea says are not quite the same thing. I know she means well, but – look, Shivaun, would you do me a favour?'

Shivaun sat back on her heels, bemused. 'Sure. What?'

'Would you – oh, look, I know you're a grown adult and I'm not your mother. But there's a bit more to some of Azalea's friends than meets the eye. I'd be glad if you'd let me know if you meet any of them, including this Irish man. She hasn't introduced you to him, has she?'

'No, not yet – it was only a passing remark – oh, Marina! What's the matter? D'you know this guy? Is there something wrong with him?'

Slowly, Marina shook her head. 'No . . . nothing, that I know of. It's just that – that you're new to America and in some weird way I feel kind of responsible for you. This is a much bigger society, you could put Ireland in its back pocket.'

'Well, yes, I realise that! But I like the diversity. Azalea is Native American, Joe is black, Gloucester is full of Italian and Portuguese families, there are all kinds of oddball religions I'd never even heard of . . . it's fun. What are you trying to tell me, that there's some deep sinister mystery underneath it all?'

Reluctantly, Marina smiled. 'No. Mostly, what you see is what you get. Maybe I'm just being an over-protective mother hen. I apologise if I am, or if I sound negative.'

Shivaun began to wonder whether Marina might be merely tired, hugged her briefly but affectionately. 'No, you don't. You're the most positive person I ever met, besides my mother. I think you're great and I think maybe it's time you took a nap! Doctor's orders, you know.'

Marina huffed. 'Hah. A fat lot Steven Hunt would know about anything.'

'Still, he's got you this far. If you want to go to Utah, then do as you're told.'

Marina stood up, but then pursed her lips primly. 'Perhaps a little dose of your own advice would do you no harm, Nurse Reilly.'

On that enigmatic note she went upstairs, and left Shivaun to ponder it.

The next day Shivaun cycled over to Kathy Shreve's house during her lunch break, enjoying the cold clear air and the salt tang of the ocean. The house was three or four miles distant, near Annisquam beach, and when she reached it she was glad to see no sign of Bill's car or the boys' bikes. If Kathy was home she would be alone, they could have a girl chat. Dropping her bike on the grass, she went up to the front door and knocked before walking in; very few doors in this little community were ever locked.

'Hey, Kathy, you here—?' As Shivaun looked around she saw that the house was in chaos, with laundry strewn everywhere, books and papers on the floor, boots and jackets left where their owners had dropped them. Kathy must be painting somewhere.

Sure enough she appeared with a paintbrush gripped between her teeth, and Shivaun was struck by how frazzled she looked, her curls tangled and her normally plump face looking drawn, harassed.

'Is this a bad time? Sorry, I should've called—'

But Kathy looked genuinely glad to see her, dropping the brush and wiping her hands on her trousers as she swept debris off the sofa and pulled out its cushions.

'No, my tummy was starting to rumble anyway, let's have some coffee and a snack, sorry about the mess.'

'D'you want a hand with it?'

Kathy looked surprised, and grateful. 'Would you? It's got a bit out of hand, I don't know where the morning went – here, if you'd just fill this pillowcase with all the stuff you can fit in it, I'll throw it in the washing machine – thanks! What brings you over?'

Shivaun took the pillowcase, and explained as she stuffed clothes into it, filling a second one while Kathy made coffee out in the kitchen.

'I came to ask you whether you'd like to go skiing. Azalea is organising a group to go to somewhere called Wachusett, I think it's near Princeton—'

'Yeah, I know it.' Kathy didn't sound exactly bursting with enthusiasm.

'Well, I'm not even sure if I can go myself, it depends whether Marina is in favour and she's being iffy about it for some reason, but if she does agree then I thought maybe you'd like to come along too?'

There was a silence from the kitchen, a ponderous pause before Kathy returned to the living room carrying a tray.

'I would love to go. Absolutely love it.'

Shivaun was delighted. 'Great! Then let's—'

Kathy put down the coffee things with an air of finality, and sat down even more emphatically. 'But I can't. I just can't go, Shivaun.'

'But – but Kathy, let me explain. You wouldn't take half enough money for that painting I bought, so this trip is my treat to make up for it. It's only for a week, surely you could work something out with Bill about looking after the boys, or get a friend to help? What about your neighbours?'

Kathy poured the coffee, and stared into it. 'It's not that, Shivaun.'

She looked so blank that Shivaun was baffled. 'Then what is it?'

'It – it's that – look, if I tell you, promise you won't tell Azalea or Marina or anyone?'

'No, of course I won't – tell them what? What's wrong?'

Kathy pushed back her hair, put down her coffee and looked out the window. 'It's that my – my marriage is falling apart. Collapsing like a punctured balloon.'

Although she was not a big fan of Bill Shreve, Shivaun was both astonished and horrified. 'Oh, Kathy! Oh, Jesus – since when? What's happened?'

'Nothing has happened. I just can't go on with it any longer, that's all. I – I feel like I'm being slowly strangled.'

'By what? By – by all this?' Shivaun waved a hand round the room to encompass the mess. 'But it's only housework, everybody gets a bit behind sometimes, why don't you make the boys do their share?'

Kathy's pretty face crumpled, she looked smothered in a kind of despair.

'No. That's only a symptom. It goes way deeper than that. It's Bill's *attitude*. He thinks I should be cleaning and cooking all day, he hates my painting and the boys are catching the vibes . . . Kelsey threw all those darts at that canvas last night, look at it.'

Shivaun looked, and sure enough a canvas standing against the wall was peppered with darts, torn and ruined.

'My God. Kelsey did *that*?'

'Yes. Bill laughed, thought it was hilariously funny. You know, Bill's laugh was one of the things that attracted me to him . . . I used to think it was so carefree and seductive. Now, I think I must have been out of my mind. He couldn't be more different to the man I thought I was marrying.'

Despite the central heating that Americans kept at tropical

temperature, Shivaun shivered. Marina's husband had apparently turned out so different too, and Ivor . . . only a fool would hope any longer to hear from Ivor Lawlor. Sadly, she leaned forward to Kathy.

'Did you love him, once? Did you absolutely adore him?'

'Oh, yes. We were only teenagers, he worked on the boats and I thought that was so romantic, so free-spirited . . . in summer we used to make out down on the beach, swim to the islands, have so much fun together, nothing seemed to matter . . . now, he wants a daughter and I don't want to have any more kids at all, because the two I've got are turning out just like him.'

Shivaun was silent, thinking. 'Does he say he still loves you?'

'Oh yes. He says he does. And then he mocks me and hinders me and goes off drinking, never helps with anything or disciplines those boys, if I say anything he tells me I'm turning into a nag. So sometimes now we hardly speak for days on end. It's like being in prison, solitary confinement. If I didn't earn money at the gallery he wouldn't even let me work there on weekends, but it's a lifesaver, at least I meet civilised adults there – only how am I going to go on here? If it wasn't for the boys I'd leave him . . . but they are my sons.'

'H'mm. They're his sons too.'

'Yeah. Chips off his block. If I could even get them away from him they might improve – but where would we go, all three of us? Not that he'd let them go.'

Kathy's normally bright, bouncy features looked tight and drawn, and Shivaun felt a wave of compassion for her. She must have been so happy when the boys were born, so thrilled with them and proud of her achievement; now they had become a source of frustration and anxiety. Shivaun could guess what the answer to her next question would be, but Kathy looked so trapped she had to ask it.

'Would you go without them?'

'What? Abandon them? Shivaun, are you crazy? I'm their mother, I love them in spite of everything, because I know it's only Bill's influence that's making them into monsters. They'd only get worse if I deserted them, and besides they're way too young, they need their mom.'

Shivaun couldn't argue with that. 'But if you stay, you'll never be able to paint properly . . . I can't understand why Bill doesn't encourage you, because if he let you get on with it you could earn a lot of money. Wouldn't that make him happy?'

Kathy took up a shirt and began to twist its sleeves into knots. 'Shivaun, that's exactly what he's afraid of. Bill is an old-fashioned, traditional kind of guy and so are all his buddies. They'd give him hell if they thought his wife was earning more than he does, and he'd give me hell. My role is to keep house and shut up about art, which is a medium that frightens him because he knows nothing about it.'

Shivaun sighed. She wished she could help Kathy, but it was hard to know what to say. Relationships seemed to be such delicate, volatile things.

Still, getting back to her original purpose, a break might help Kathy to stand back and think clearly. It might do Bill no harm either, or the boys.

'Look. You're not a prisoner, Kathy, or a slave. I think you should tell Bill you're going skiing for a week and that's all about it. It won't cost you anything, all you need is to find a babysitter if Bill won't mind the boys himself . . . there must be someone who'd do it, after all the boys are at school most of the day. But if you can't find someone, then down tools and come anyway. Bill will just have to cope as best he can.'

Kathy hesitated, but Shivaun didn't give her time to raise objections.

'Come on! Say you will? It'll do you a world of good.'

'But . . . you said you weren't even sure you were going yourself, it depends on Marina—'

'Yes, well, Azalea is working on Marina, I'm sure she'll get round her. Not that I really need her approval, I'm entitled to a week off, I'd just rather have it because I'm so fond of her. If she says yes, will you say yes too?'

Kathy looked at her, and she was pleased to see a glimmer

of hope in her face. 'Yes. OK. If you go, I go. God, Shivaun, you can't imagine how much a week off would mean to me. I really need to sit down and think about this whole mess – think on my own, without those boys bawling and their father on my case. Thanks for asking me. You're a real pal.'

Shivaun stood up, went to her and embraced her supportively. 'Oh, Kathy. I'm so sorry to hear what you've told me. It sounds as if things can only get better. Let's both try to get to Wachusett, and talk more about it when we get there. You might see some new perspectives from that distance.'

Also standing up, Kathy looked at her curiously. 'Have you ever been through anything like this, Shivaun? You sound as if you understand, you're not telling me to get a grip or offering any magic solutions . . .'

What was it Marina had said, about her 'looking divorced'? Shivaun laughed wryly. 'No – well, I've never been married or had kids. But I was once involved with a man who – who didn't turn out quite the way I expected. Maybe nobody ever really does. All I know is that everyone seems to be changing all the time, and the best anyone can do is try to shape the changes in a way they can work with.'

Kathy tugged at her hair, looking ambivalent and sad. 'Maybe. I wish things weren't changing, wish I could still love Bill . . . but how can you love someone who won't let you *be*? I was so young when we married – if I'd known I was painting myself into a corner, I'd never have done it.'

At that moment there was a whoop outside, and the two boys came charging in, roaring at each other as they threw their jackets on the floor and dived for the fridge. Shivaun said hello to them, but neither one answered, and she looked at them without enthusiasm, wondering whether she had been crazy to have ever wanted anything like this. What on earth must life be like now for Brona Mulcahy, the sixteen-year-old mother of Buster who, like Miles and Kelsey, had seemed such a good idea at the time?

Chapter Ten

It was a very belated party, because to her chagrin Alana had been put on a night roster that meant working New Year's eve, and she didn't get back on day duty until the middle of January. Brendan was very put out about their thwarted plans, so she resolved to make the party extra special when it finally happened. Driving to the supermarket, she spent far more than she could afford on food and wine, then she went to the hairdresser, got her highlights done and carried on to the boutique where her new dress was awaiting collection. It was reduced in the January sales, but it still cost over a hundred pounds, and the expense of the whole event began to nibble at her mind. To banish the guilt she poured herself a stiff drink when she got home – but only one, because there was a mountain of preparation to be done, cleaning and cooking, plates and glasses, cutlery to be borrowed because Shivaun's supplies didn't run to the size of the party. The guest list had somehow got bigger and bigger, until now there were over ninety people on it, and Alana grinned to herself when she thought of them all crowding in. Shivaun would have a fit if she knew, her idea of a party was twenty at most, but this was going to be a real shindig.

Brendan had said he would come at six to help with the preparations, but by the time he arrived at eight everything was done, and Alana was putting on her make-up, thinking how much handier it would be if Brendan simply moved into the house. It was high time they started living together, she was fed up being here by herself and besides, she and Brendan were a couple now, they might even get engaged sometime around Easter. Should she tell Shivaun, if and when Brendan moved in? On balance she thought no, there wasn't really any need to say anything yet, because if for any reason Shivaun objected it would only cause hassle. Much simpler to simply let Shivaun meet Brendan whenever she came home from America; by then he'd be firmly ensconsed and Shivaun would see what a great guy he was. Hearing him let himself in with the key that had once been Ivor's, she called down to him from the bathroom.

'Hi! I'm up here!'

'Hi! I've brought the music, and Shay is bringing a few kegs from the pub, he says he can probably get whiskey too – c'mon down, let's see the glamour girl!'

When she came downstairs she was glad she'd spent so much on the dress after all, because Brendan whistled when he saw her poured into its red satin contours. 'Wow! You look great!'

As he kissed her cheek there was a knock at the door, and his friend Shay stood outside with a laden pushcart from the pub where he worked.

'Hey Bren, here we are, give us a hand, there are more kegs in the van.'

Alana wasn't quite sure on what basis Shay had got so much drink – wholesale she presumed, but who was paying for it? Nobody had specified exactly, but after all she'd already spent today she assumed it must be Brendan's contribution. He couldn't expect her to pay for everything as well as providing the venue. Deciding to say nothing, she stood back while the kegs were wheeled in, pumps were set up and a full case of whiskey was trimphantly produced.

'Great stuff! That'll keep us going for a while!' Looking delighted, Brendan grabbed a couple of snacks off a plate and passed it to Shay. Alana frowned, wondering where his good clothes were and when he was going to change into them. Both he and Shay were in their everyday denims, and after all Brendan was the *host*, she'd look silly in her red satin if he didn't rise to the standard it set. Pointedly, she glanced at her watch.

'Brendan, love, people will be arriving soon, the bathroom's free now if you want to freshen up and get into your glad rags.'

He clapped his hand to his forehead. 'Glad rags! I knew I'd forgotten something. Oh, hell, Alana, it's an awful long drive back to the flat – tell you what, I'll put on the gear I left here last weekend, how's that?'

'But you only left an ordinary shirt and trousers, I didn't take them to the cleaners—'

'Oh, well, they'll have to do. I'll have a shave as well, don't worry, everything'll be fine.'

Kissing her with a wide smile, he ran upstairs, and she struggled to hide her disappointment from Shay, who was munching from the buffet already, leaving an empty plate in the middle of it. He winked at her, and said something muffled by a mouthful of food.

'Sorry, Shay?'

'I said this is great, Alana, you're a smashing cook.' He started into a second plate, and she decided she might as well put on some music. Brendan had brought dozens of CDs, but when she went through them all she could find was heavy metal, so she put on one of Shivaun's CDs instead, U2's *Joshua Tree*. When Brendan reappeared, looking presentable but hardly glamorous, he laughed, and took it off.

'God, that'd put years on you! This is supposed to be party time, Alana, let's get in the mood!'

She didn't recognise the disc he put on next, but it nearly lifted the roof off, and he beamed. 'That's better! Now, let's have a drink – and why don't we leave the hall door on the latch, then we won't have to open it every time someone arrives.'

She'd envisaged standing in the hall with Brendan at her side, greeting each guest, but evidently that wasn't what he had in mind at all.

'You mean, just let everyone walk in? But we could get gatecrashers, people off the street—'

He ruffled her hair, kissed her cheek and handed her a brimming glass.

'Here, my little fusspot, drink this and chill out. Everything will be grand if you just relax.'

With a sudden surge of mixed deflation and desperation, she took the glass and knocked back half its contents, feeling the whiskey kick like a mule.

'OK. I'm relaxed. Let's enjoy ourselves.'

He waved his glass at her and grinned. 'Yeah, let's – hey, is that Tommy O'Neill's car I hear?'

He knew all his friends' cars by the sound of their engines, and sure enough Tommy came in a moment later, with two other guys and two giggling girls, none of whom Alana recognised. She went up and introduced herself and the girls giggled again. 'Hi. We're Dee and Evanna. Do we pour our own or what?'

Before she could answer there was the roar of another car pulling up outside, and five more of Brendan's friends came in, evidently in high spirits, laughing and waving scarves; they'd been to a football match and their team had won. Feeling outnumbered, Alana began to wish some of her own friends would arrive, but as yet there was no sign of any of the people she'd invited from St Peter's. But Brendan was doing his bit, handing round food while Shay installed himself behind the pumps and started pulling pints. Too late, Alana realised she should have put some plastic or something on the floor, to protect it from the drips that were already forming a small pool on the boards. Oh, well, it was old wood and it was varnished, with any luck it wouldn't stain.

Brendan was right. If she was going to fuss she wouldn't enjoy the night, and he'd sense her tension, the whole thing would be a disaster. Taking her empty glass over to Shay behind his makeshift bar, she handed it to him and he refilled it with practised speed. Sipping from it, she drifted back to Brendan's side, to find him immersed in conversation with his friends about the football match. Knowing nothing about football, she stood listening in silence, smiling, vaguely attaching herself to him so everyone would know who she was. She had met one or two of these people before, but couldn't remember anything much about them, so maybe they needed a reminder to put her in context too. It felt good when one of the men eyed her up and down, winked at her and raised his glass in admiring salute. But she was aware of other people arriving, a lot of them now, pouring into the room around her, and was torn between the need to greet them and the need to stay beside Brendan; if she left his side she felt he might be swallowed up and she wouldn't see him again for God knew how long.

The chat about the football seemed to go on forever, until gradually it was overpowered by the din of other voices, getting so loud that it was becoming impossible to speak without shouting. Seizing a brief interlude, she plucked at Brendan's sleeve and he turned to her questioningly.

'Everything OK? Enjoying yourself?'

'Yes, but – let's just go say hello to the others? My friends from work might be here now and I'd like you to meet them.'

She couldn't tell whether they were or not, because the room was now crammed, overflowing into the kitchen and hall, and someone had put on music so thunderous it drowned out individual voices. Brendan nodded agreeably.

'Sure. I'll be with you in a sec. I just want a quick word with Gavin about his new Cosworth . . . tell you what, why don't you find your pals and bring them over here.'

There didn't seem to be any hope of shifting him from where he was, so she left his side reluctantly and began to make her way through the throng, which was starting to sway as the party gathered rapid momentum. Getting through it was clearly going to take time and determination, but she gave it her best shot, smiling at everyone, stopping to shout hello, let them know she was Alana Kennedy, this was her party and Brendan's – but it was like shouting over the roar of a departing jet! Her throat began to rasp and ache, her eyes filled with stinging smoke, and with mounting dismay she saw someone stub out a cigarette amidst the food, another one being scrunched underfoot into the timber floor. She'd put out dozens of ashtrays, but nobody seemed to be using them . . . with relief she spotted her friend Niamh, a staff nurse from St Peter's, pinned up against the far wall, and waved at her, tried to make her way through the mob. But someone jolted into her, lurched unsteadily and spilled a trickle of Guinness down the back of her dress. As it soaked into the satin she didn't know whether to protest or laugh it off, although if she were honest she felt more like crying.

Her brand-new dress, a hundred and twenty quid's worth, and she'd barely got an hour out of it . . . all she could do was try to fight her way to the bathroom upstairs and try to wash the stain out without making the damage any worse.

When she reached the hall it was full of total strangers and she had to pick her way through them, no longer eager to introduce herself now that her outfit was dark and sticky with beer. But as she jostled through a hand suddenly touched her right on the wet patch, and she turned around to see, with horror, Dr Jonathan Kilroy from St Peter's. Jonathan was dapper and handsome, a bit of a glamour boy well on his way to becoming a consultant, the kind of man she suspected normally went to dinner parties, not bunfights like this was turning out to be. Mortified, she flushed to the ears and gave him the most elegant smile she could muster in the circumstances.

'Hello, Jonathan! Glad you could make it!'

Not looking exactly thrilled himself, Jonathan took a handkerchief from his breast pocket, dried his hand on it and attempted to introduce the woman with him, a cool slim blonde who was still wearing her coat. But even though he shouted his words were inaudible, and Alana's offer to take the woman's coat got lost in the noise; as they were carried apart on the surging wave of humanity Alana got the feeling it probably didn't matter, because the couple would be leaving as soon as they decently could. This party, she realised with dawning dismay, was going to do her reputation far more harm than good, jammed as it was with swearing, swilling hooligans.

By the time she managed to reach the bathroom upstairs, nearly twenty minutes later, the wet part of her dress had turned cold and rigid and she knew it was ruined. But by then she needed to fix her hair and make-up anyway, because the former was askew and the latter was melting, so she joined the queue which sounded disgruntled; some woman in blue sequins angrily informed her the bathroom door had been locked for ages and nobody could get in. Deciding not to think about it, but cheat instead, Alana slithered away as discreetly as she could, towards Shivaun's bedroom which had an en-suite bathroom nobody knew about.

The sight that greeted her, when her eyes adjusted to the dark of the bedroom, literally took her voice away. She couldn't make out faces, and probably wouldn't have known them anyway, but there were bodies in the bed – not just on it but in it, undulating like ectoplasm in the dark. For a long moment she stood transfixed, until she heard herself emit a high-pitched squeak, and then she snapped. Throwing herself at the moving shape, she thumped it and roared at it.

'Hey! Cut that out, get out, what the hell do you think you're doing? This is my house, you—'

A man's head emerged from under the duvet, and two eyes surveyed her with considerable hostility.

'Yeah, well, you should've locked the bedrooms if you didn't want anyone in them, shouldn't you? So why don't you take a hike?'

Aghast, she groped for a reply, but no words would come. With a rush of panic she thought of Brendan, wondered whether he could deal with this, if he could be found and dragged up here, if she could even shout loud enough to tell him what was happening. This had been Shivaun's parents' bedroom, Shivaun would go ape if she ever heard what – oh, *God*! Feeling the whole night spinning out of control, Alana backed away and tried to get back down the stairs, search for Brendan – but there were throngs of people clogging the stairs now, all trying in vain to get to the other bathroom whose door was apparently still locked. Some of them looked furious, as if they'd waited all night for a bargain in the sales only to discover it had been sold; others were just waiting and drinking stoically, jogged by people trying to climb over them, dripping their drinks on the walls and carpet. Meanwhile, the music was at such a level that the whole house was vibrating, when Alana put her hand on the banister it shuddered under her touch. Below her, she could see numerous people smoking in the hall, and began to wonder with mounting terror what on earth would happen if anything caught fire. There was no way a drunken, deafened horde like this could get safely out.

Brendan, she thought frantically, *do* something! Where the hell are you, this is insane, there are far more than ninety people here, more like two hundred, it's not a party, it's a riot!

It took her another twenty minutes to get back to the room she had left him in, where the blasting music made her head feel like a cave filled by a freak tide, overwhelming and terrifying her. As she tried to jostle her way through the sweating sea of bodies several people swore at her, and she sensed a mob mentality taking hold.

She couldn't see Brendan, but she could see some other guy lurching at her with his hand over his mouth; just as he reached the hall in his hopeless attempt to get out, he threw up violently and a dozen people jumped back screaming. Alana froze, stood rooted for several seconds, and then burst into tears. *How* could Brendan have invited all these awful people, and left her alone amongst them? The house was like a battlefield, if it didn't burn down it was certainly going to be wrecked at the very least, she'd have to not only hose the whole place down but repaint and redecorate it . . . Sobbing, she put one hand over her ears and the other to her face, shuddering with sheer anguish and, in the midst of all these roaring milling people, an agonising sense of loneliness. Nobody even seemed to notice that she was crying, or if they did they probably thought she was drunk, just one more drunk amongst so many – what on earth was she going to *do*?

Eventually, still weeping, she thought of Shay. He was stationed near the door, if he hadn't abandoned his role of barman by now and simply left everyone to help themselves. He was the only person she could think of who might not have been drinking much himself, if she could reach him she could try to get him to—

'*Alana!*'

Someone bellowed her name, into her ear so loudly she yelped, and spun round to confront the outraged, furious face of Fintan Daly. Whether he had accepted her invitation to attend the party, or come in from next door to protest, she didn't know, but she was dizzily relieved to see him.

'Fintan! – oh, thank God, I can't find Brendan, I need help—'

He grabbed her by the arm, digging his fingers into her flesh like chisels, and dragged her with superhuman strength out through the hall, wrenching her behind him so fast her feet scarcely touched the ground, and abruptly she found herself deposited on the grass out on the front lawn, panting and gasping. But her relief evaporated when she saw the look on his face, so livid she began to cry again.

'F-Fintan, I'm sorry, I didn't mean, I didn't know – oh, please, Fintan, do something! Get them all out! Get rid of them, I can't cope with—'

Fintan was a tall muscular man famed for his fine physique, but at this moment she found him menacing, thought she'd never before seen anyone look so incandescently angry. When he spoke, his words bounced off her like bullets.

'What kind of little fool are you? Do you realise this is a death trap, apart from blowing the entire street into orbit? I've just called the police! And they said someone else had called them already, they're on their way – I tell you, Alana, when they get here you'd better have a bloody good explanation for this – this carnage! I've been searching for you and none of these people even knew who you were, half of them seem to be—'

He spluttered to a stop as a blue light came flashing up and a police car braked outside the house, two uniformed cops came striding up to him and Alana, looking astonished as they confronted the scene. One of them shone a torch into her face and Fintan's.

'Who's the owner?' he demanded without preamble, and Alana quailed.

'I – I am,' she stuttered, 'I mean, I live here, the owner is away—'

The cop peered at her, and she knew he was assessing her condition.

'Is this your party? Are you responsible for it?'

'Yes,' she admitted in a whisper, 'but I didn't invite all these people, only about half, my boyfriend—'

'Who's your boyfriend?' the cop barked, 'and where is he?'

'He – he's in there somewhere—'

'What's his name?'

Suddenly the full import of the situation hit Alana. There was going to be trouble over this. Even more trouble than she'd imagined. But she had no choice, she had to answer.

'His – his name is Brendan McLaughlin – but it's not his fault—'

Even as she said it she was torn, didn't want to incriminate Brendan even though she knew it was his fault, these were his friends and this bedlam was his doing.

'Right' said the cop, and turned away from her, headed into the house with his colleague. Seconds later the music slammed to a stop, and then she heard shouting, a crash of glass, thundering footsteps as people began to run out of the house. Fintan watched them grimly, looking not at all surprised when several of them dashed past him, leaping over the garden wall in their haste to disperse.

'Drugs' he said curtly, confirming what Alana suspected. But cold and shock were hitting Alana so hard now she couldn't speak, simply stood shuddering and sobbing silently. Glacially, Fintan looked at her.

'I never knew you were such a prize idiot.'

She'd never known either, but now she thought it was true.

'Does Shivaun know about this – this event?'

Dumbly, she shook her head and made a gulping, strangled sound. Looking disgusted beyond words, Fintan pulled off his sweater and flung it at her.

'Here. Cover yourself up, you don't want the police thinking you're a tart on top of everything else. You're in enough trouble already.'

A tart? She was wounded to the bone. And she was certainly in trouble. She and Brendan both. Pulling the sweater around her she sank down on the frozen grass, leaving her so-called guests to stampede around her as she abandoned herself to engulfing grief, humiliation and despair. She knew her relationship with Brendan was not going to survive this appalling disaster, and she didn't think she could survive it either.

Muffled in a wool sweater and warm trousers, Shivaun hummed to herself as she toted her rucksack downstairs. It was a sunny, silvery day edged with frost, and she was fired up for the drive to Wachusett where, amidst the pristine pines and mountains, she would learn to ski and maybe make new friends into the bargain. Finally, guardedly, Marina had given her blessing to the trip, and Shivaun turned towards the library to say goodbye to her.

But before she could reach it Marina came out of it, enveloped in layers of amber and graphite fabric topped off with a furry headband that made Shivaun smile; bejewelled and wearing full warpaint as ever, Marina looked like a cross between Mata Hari and Davy Crockett.

'Darling child, let me look at you.' Not knowing what there was to look at, Shivaun twirled ironically in the way she had twirled as a child for Viv. But after close inspection Marina nodded, satisfied.

'Good. Warm clothes, boots . . . you do have a hat and thermal gloves somewhere, I presume?'

Shivaun grinned at her affectionately. 'Yes, I have, and a couple of thermal vests, in case you're wondering.'

'Well, somebody has to look after you! When I think of the

things I wore when I was young – I'd have gone skiing in a bikini if that was the fashion. Pride feels no pain, at your age.'

'Oh, I've never been a slave to fashion. Too expensive, too time-consuming.'

'And too ephemeral! It's style a woman wants, Shivaun, not fashion. A style of her own, that's all.'

'Well, you've certainly found yours! Come here and give me a hug, Marina, tell me again that this trip is really OK with you.'

Marina drew her to her and hugged her, more tightly than Shivaun expected. 'Yes. It is OK with me. Only promise me you'll be careful.'

'I promise. I'll call you every day and I won't break any more bones than can be helped.'

'No, but – but it's not just your bones I'm talking about. I want you to really look after yourself.'

Shivaun eyed her quizzically. 'Marina, you're so enigmatic! I wish you'd tell me what exactly is bugging you.'

'Nothing is bugging me, as you put it. I just don't want you drinking too much with Azalea's oddball friends, that's all, or doing anything silly.'

'Then don't worry. I think there's a limit to how much drinking and skiing anyone can do simultaneously. I'm going to learn this sport and have fun and see a bit of scenery, that's all.'

'Very well, then. Off you go, and enjoy yourself.'

Shivaun kissed her cheek and took up her bag. 'I will. And you look after yourself too, make sure you do your exercises twice a day and Dorothy makes you plenty of low-salt meals . . . You have the phone number, haven't you, in case you need me for anything?'

'Yes. But I won't call you except in an emergency. Steven will be dropping by, I'm sure he'll take good care of me.'

They both laughed, and Shivaun went out to the little red car feeling full of high spirits. What a beautiful day, so crisp and sparkling! Throwing her bag in the back, she got in, started it up and waved to Marina.

'Go on back inside! It's cold out here!'

But Marina stood waving on the steps until she was out of sight, making Shivaun feel cocooned in her warmth and care as she drove off to Kathy's house, hoping that Bill Shreve would kiss his wife goodbye with as much fondness. But when she arrived Kathy was already out on the porch waiting for her, alone, and ran to the car as soon as she saw it.

'OK, let's go while the going's good!'

She jumped in and Shivaun turned to look at her. Kathy looked well, her skin was glowing in the cold and her dark eyes were bright, but—

'Where's Bill? And the boys?'

'He's taken them to some shipyard to see a trawler being built. C'mon, Shivaun, hit the gas!'

Kathy sounded like a convict on the run, Shivaun thought, trying not to laugh. 'OK, but calm down, we're only going on a little trip.'

'It's not a little trip to me. It's paradise. This light is just brilliant for painting – Madge Kosovitz is going to look after the boys at her house in the afternoons, her son is in Kelsey's class, and Bill will pick them up in the evenings. I've left a stack of food in the freezer. He growled about it, but he agreed in the end.'

'And why wouldn't he? You're not asking him for the Hope diamond, are you? I'm sure they'll all pig out on pizza and ice-cream and have a great time.'

'Yeah, maybe – anyway, I said I'll call home every night just in case. Now, tell me more about this trip. Who exactly is going?'

Kathy settled comfortably back in her seat, with the eager look of a child about to be read a story, and Shivaun tried to recall everyone Azalea had mentioned.

'Well, apart from Azalea and Jeff, there are four people from their commune, that guy Denis who sells real estate, Karl who I've never met, I think he works in some kind of factory, then there's a couple called Dale and Amy, she's an actress but I don't know what he does. And there are four others – this Irish guy Patrick who lives in Lowell, plus Ellen who has a little boutique in Boston, and two more whose names I can't remember, but I think they're married to each other.'

'No kids?'

'No, not that I know of.'

'Bliss.' Kathy beamed, rummaged in her bag and dug out some chocolate. 'Here. Let's start enjoying ourselves right now.'

'Right! But you know, Kathy . . . I've been enjoying America ever since I got here. Everyone's been so friendly, and look at this scenery, it's so gorgeous, the driving is so easy, and now I'm going skiing!'

Shivaun munched her chocolate with relish, but Kathy was curious.

'You're weird, Shivaun. If I was as far away from home as you are I'd be so homesick . . . don't you ever miss Ireland?'

Shivaun considered. 'Yes. Sometimes I get these little pangs, kind of like hunger pangs, something sort of grabs my stomach and it hurts until I think of the reality, which isn't a bit like the tourist brochures. Dublin isn't, anyway. It's a dirty expensive city and it's got kind of hard in recent years, there's a – a lot of crime. I do miss the hospital I used to work in, and my friends, but right now America suits me very well. I needed a change of scene.'

'H'mm. Well, I guess I can relate to that. Apart from my honeymoon in New York and a couple of visits to Bill's folks in North Carolina, this is my first vacation since I got married.'

'Really? Well then, we'd better make sure you enjoy it!'

'Don't worry,' Kathy replied with a new note of grim determination Shivaun had not heard before, 'I intend to. I will paint and ski and make the most of every blessed minute, and I can't thank you enough for pushing me into it.'

'Hah! I hope you'll still feel that way when they're putting the pin in your leg and your arm in a sling!'

'Actually, that's unlikely, because I've skied before. I used to go to the Berkshires with my parents when I was a little girl. I used to do lots of things, before I met my boy Bill.'

Abruptly, Shivaun felt a huge slam of nostalgia. Yes, she

thought, I used to do lots of things when I was a little girl, too. I used to go places with Viv and Jimmy, on picnics and to concerts and forests and beaches, I used to swim at Red Rock with Ivor and we had this tree house my dad made us, it felt like it was always summer and we thought the sun would never stop shining . . . only then I grew up, and it did stop. It went down and it took everyone with it, every single person I ever loved or might have loved. All I've got left is Viv's books and earrings and a faded old piece of paper with my name spelled wrong on it. And a house I don't even live in any more.

That's why I hardly ever feel homesick. There's nothing left to go back to. I can only go forward.

The two log cabins were nestled at the foot of Mount Wachusett, and when everyone had arrived Azalea lost no time in assigning everyone to their berths; a natural organiser, she stood up in the midst of the group and read from a list, ticking it off as she went.

'OK, couples in this cabin, that's you Dale and Amy, Leigh and Rachel, Jeff and myself – everyone else is in the other on the left, Shivaun, Kathy, Denis, Patrick, Karl, Ellen, there are three bedrooms with two beds apiece and you can shack up any way you like! Now guys, I want volunteers to light fires and cook supper tonight, we'll take turns after that . . .'

Only half listening, Shivaun stood by the window with her arms folded around her, gazing out dreamily through the pine-spiked snowdrifts to the horizon where a huge fireball sun was igniting the glass-green sky with glowing streaks of scarlet light, trailing out to pink and orange and mauve . . . evening was still falling early, at this time of year, but a stunning star was rising above the tops of the pines, gleaming brilliant and pure. There was a stillness and clarity in the view that fixed her to it, and she was unaware of being spoken to until someone touched her shoulder, and she jumped.

'Oh! Sorry, I was dreaming.'

It was Jeff, looking amused. 'You Irish sure do dream deep dreams. Come and meet your compatriot, and the others.'

Agreeably she let him lead her back into the midst of things; the cabin was strewn with luggage, rugs and knockabout furniture, a vast pile of logs in front of an even bigger fireplace, and a mezzanine ran overhead where, she supposed, the bedrooms were. Somebody was uncorking bottles of wine and somebody else was kneeling by the fireplace, looking mystified, while Kathy was already stretched lengthways across an armchair yawning luxuriantly. Jeff indicated everyone in turn.

'That's Karl opening the wine . . . you know Denis . . . this is Leigh and this is Rachel . . . that's Dale playing boy scout . . . and here's Patrick Nulty, the pride of old Ireland.'

Everyone variously smiled and waved to her from where they were, except Patrick who came up and shook her hand rather formally.

'Hello, Shivaun, nice to meet you.'

Whatever she had been expecting, Patrick was not it. Most of the group were in their twenties but he looked older, well into his thirties, and there was nothing Irish in either his appearance or his accent. Tall and tanned, he wore navy cords with a sharp green sweater, his hard callused hand belying the neatness of his dress. Under thick dark hair that might have been Greek or Italian, he had a high wide forehead, a nose that looked as if it might once have been broken, full firm lips and two very clear, serious green eyes. If Jeff hadn't said otherwise, she might have taken him for the ski instructor.

'Hello, Patrick. So you're the man from—?'

'From Lowell,' he said in pure American tones. 'I have a landscaping business over there.'

Ah! Now she remembered; Joe Santana had mentioned this man, said Marina got her garden done – but of course he must only do it in spring and summer, that was why she hadn't met him before. That must be, also, how Azalea came to know him. His handshake was firm, but she thought she sensed a degree of reserve in him, he was not the kind of Patrick you could call Pat or Paddy.

'My father worked at something related,' she said, 'he was a tree surgeon.'

The moment she said it she regretted it. The last thing she wanted was for anyone to start asking her about Jimmy. But Azalea looked up, and came to her rescue.

'Shivaun is Marina's nurse, Patrick.'

'Oh yes,' he said, still formal, 'I hope she's making good progress?'

Shivaun said Marina was, and Patrick said he was glad to hear it, and there, to her surprise, the conversation foundered without any reference to Ireland or 'home' at all. Patrick turned to accept a glass of wine from Jeff, passed it politely to her and then got into some discussion with Karl about black runs.

Well, Shivaun thought taken aback, that's put me in my box. That man is more American than any American I've yet met, and not nearly as friendly as most of the ones I have met. I don't think we're going to be singing Boulavogue round the old turf fire here tonight. He wasn't exactly rude but he doesn't win first prize for charm either.

Somewhat miffed, she turned away from him and went to talk to Azalea. 'D'you want me to chop wood or feed the huskies or anything? I'm available for all outdoor tasks.'

Azalea grinned ruefully. 'Well, I see you two didn't exactly fall into each other's arms! But Patrick is a bit shy, Shivaun – he'll thaw when you get to know him.'

'H'm. *If* I get to know him. Meanwhile, I wouldn't mind making the acquaintance of a hot shower and some food – what's the game plan for tonight?'

'The plan is that Leigh and Rachel are cooking and we're all going to eat in this cabin. Meanwhile, why don't you take your stuff to your own and get settled in? What d'you think of this place, anyway?'

'I think it's great, you're a genius! The trees and mountains are so beautiful, the cabins are huge and warm and everyone is so relaxed . . .'

'Yeah. I've been here lots of times, with various people, but everyone always loves it. I hope you will too.'

'I know I will,' Shivaun replied firmly, 'all your other friends seem really nice.'

After a few lessons and trial runs Shivaun discovered that she loved skiing, was filled with vigorous delight in the challenge of it, the speed with which she rushed through the crystalline air with a glowing sense of achievement. A couple of falls left her black and blue, but she didn't care, was too busy enjoying the sport in the day and the fun in the evenings, which started with hot chocolate in a mountain café when dusk was falling and everyone gathered to compare notes. To her surprise Kathy hardly painted at all; after a few brief sessions in the early mornings she virtually packed it in and began, instead, to attempt ever more daring ski runs, impressing everyone as her rusty skills came back with grace and flair. Soon she vanished up to the highest slopes, where only Azalea and Patrick could keep up with her, and Shivaun rarely saw her before dark fell.

'But what about your painting?' Shivaun asked her, and she grinned airily. 'Oh, the hell with it, I'll worry about it later.'

Shivaun found herself feeling the same way. Up on the mountain, fighting to master this new activity, she simply hadn't time to worry about Ivor or Jason Dean or any of the things that had consumed her in Ireland. Instead she seized each day, each sparkling slope, and made the most of the freedom, the intense concentration, the incredibly energising air. This, she thought, is great, I love it! It clears your mind and powers your body, the adrenalin is like a drug, I could stay out here forever . . . I have no idea where I'll go or what I'll do when Marina is better, but I don't think I can go back to suburban Dublin after this, the lifestyle here is much more – more *me*. I could just ski off into the blue and never come back.

After hot showers and various activities in the evenings, everyone congregated for dinner in one or other of the cabins, making a lot of noise between all twelve of them. Gradually Shivaun got to know them, and took a particular shine to Denis when she was paired off to cook with him. Fair-haired and good-humoured, Denis was a much better cook than she was, and made her laugh with tales of houses he had sold, the nutty reasons people had for selling them and the even sillier reasons people had for buying them.

'It's a great job for a snoopy person like me,' he said, 'you find out all sorts of things about all kinds of people . . . do you have a house in Ireland, Shivaun, or did you just rent or what?'

'I have a house,' she admitted, 'but I didn't buy it, I inherited.'

'Oh?'

'Oh, yes! It's a long story, but I'd really rather not talk about it, what you see now is what you get. Why don't you tell me about *you*?'

She liked him and she was genuinely interested; as they worked together in the steaming kitchen she even realised with a sudden flicker of astonishment that she found him attractive, was drawn to his easy warmth. But – but I can't be, she thought, Ivor would kill me! And then, as if someone had thrown a bucket of ice over her, she remembered that Ivor was gone. Gone for good, leaving her free for the first time in her adult life to look at another man, to admire his physique and—

'I'm from Kansas originally,' Denis said, 'but it wasn't big enough for me.'

'Big enough?' She was surprised. 'But I thought Kansas was huge.'

'It is,' he said, 'geographically. I just didn't find it spiritually big enough. The east coast is more congenial for gay guys.'

Oh! She laughed at her own innocence. 'Are you gay? I didn't know! Azalea should have told me.'

His eyes widened as he handed her a dish to put in the oven. 'Why? Does it matter?'

No, it didn't matter, but it was a good thing she knew now, or she might have— Can this really be happening, she thought in amazement, can I actually be noticing men as *men*? And getting it wrong first time, too! God, I'm really out of touch with this stuff, I'll make a right fool of myself if I don't cop myself on here.

'Of course it doesn't matter,' she spluttered, 'but at least that explains why you're sharing a room with Ellen.'

'Yeah,' he grinned, 'I'm harmless.'

Suddenly she thought of Patrick, who had been so cool to her, and wondered.

'Is anyone else gay?' she asked him, 'or only you?'

'Only me, as far as I know!'

'Would you be able to tell, if anyone else was?'

Chopping celery, he considered, but not for long. 'Yeah. I can nearly always tell. But I don't get any vibes here. Shame. I wouldn't mind meeting someone.'

Denis looked about twenty-eight or thirty, and she was intrigued. 'Did you ever have anyone? A relationship, I mean?'

He nodded and wiped his hands on his apron. 'Yeah. Sure. But it broke up more than a year ago. I'm ready to move on.'

'Are you? How long did it take you to get over it?'

He pulled off his apron and went to wash his hands. 'How long is a piece of string? You don't wake up one morning and say hey, that's it, I'm fine now. You just gradually . . . evolve . . . come on, let's leave this stuff to cook and go join the others.'

The others were gathered in the main room round the fire, chatting and playing Scrabble in little groups; Shivaun looked round for Kathy but saw that she was engrossed in conversation with Azalea, so she stuck with Denis and he poured her a glass of wine, continued to talk to her with frank curiosity.

'Tell me about this house of yours in Ireland. Did you live in it all by yourself or what?'

'No, I shared with a friend. She's still in it.'

'So will you be going back? How long do you plan to stay in America?'

'I don't know,' she mused. 'It depends – but I—'

She was grateful when Rachel and Karl drifted over and the talk widened out to include them, until eventually dinner was ready and everyone sat down around the big oak table, starving after their day's skiing, passing hot dishes round enthusiastically.

At first there was much discussion of black runs and moguls and poor Jeff who'd crashed into a tree, and Shivaun was enjoying the laughing camaraderie until she heard Patrick say that Jeff was useless and should take up embroidery.

'Oh, don't be so mean!' Jeff was looking crestfallen, Patrick was looking smug and she didn't like his patronising tone. From the other end of the table, Patrick turned slowly round to look at her.

'I beg your pardon?'

'I said,' she shouted back down to him, 'leave Jeff alone! At least he's not a show-off like you!'

Everyone laughed, and she realised they thought the same thing, that Patrick was a bit too pleased with his own prowess. He skied very well, but had no patience with the learners, left them immediately every morning for the top slopes without offering any help to anyone.

He frowned, and gazed down the table at her. 'Well, I'm terribly sorry if I've offended you, but I wasn't actually talking to you.'

His visible sarcasm stiffened the atmosphere, and everyone turned to her as if watching a tennis match. She had no idea what had made her butt in, but still she felt a heated dislike of Patrick.

'You were talking loud enough to be heard,' she retorted, 'which makes a change for someone who's hardly talked to anyone since he got here.'

As she said it she realised she specifically meant he hadn't talked to *her*, and she was insulted by such coldness from a compatriot, and that was why she'd leaped to Jeff's defence. There was a taut silence, and then Azalea laughed.

'Oh, chill out, Shivaun, Jeff can take care of himself! But –' she turned to Patrick – 'she's got a point, you have been a bit moody, so lighten up, huh?'

Everyone now focused on him, and he looked furious, but faced them defiantly. 'What would you like me to do, sing "Waltzing Matilda"?'

They all laughed, and the moment passed, but for the rest

of the meal Shivaun was acutely conscious of Patrick ignoring her, deliberately keeping his back turned from her end of the table. When she cooled down she wondered whether she'd gone too far, after all Patrick had been part of this annual jaunt for years whereas she was a newcomer, but . . . still. There was something about the man she definitely did not like. Later, when they were out in the kitchen stacking dishes, Denis grinned in much amusement, and squeezed her hand.

'So someone finally socked it to Patrick! Hallelujah! I've been wanting to do that myself every year!'

Oh? She was heartened, and curious. 'Have you? Why?'

'Because he's a smug bastard – you know he's rich as Croesus, absolutely loaded?'

'No – is he?'

'Oh, yeah, makes a fortune out of his landscaping, does every celebrity garden for miles around, struts his stuff like a peacock. But he's never really fitted in anywhere, either with the rich crowd or with ours. Azalea is the only one who really likes him, but don't ask me why. Maybe she knows him a bit better than the rest of us, because he does Marina Darnoux's garden so she sees him more than we do. But once a year is enough for me.'

Shivaun thought it would be enough for her, too. Patrick Nulty was a handsome man, a fine athlete and evidently successful entrepreneur, but there was a repellent coldness about him. Despite Denis's assertion that he was probably straight, she wondered whether he liked women very much.

'Is he married?'

'No, never even brings a girlfriend, but I really don't think he's gay. He's just a loner. I'm sure his money is a babe magnet, but so far it doesn't seem to have bought him love. Not that anyone would know if it did, because he never talks about his personal life. He's one Irishman who doesn't have the gift of the gab.'

'But . . . he doesn't sound Irish at all. How long has he lived here?'

'Too long! I don't know what brought him to America, but

he's been part of this skiing group for eight or nine years at least – I think he came here when he was pretty young, he had an uncle in Massachusetts or something, but if you want to know any more than that you'll have to ask Azalea.'

'Or she could ask me,' said a voice in the doorway, 'if it was any of her business.'

They spun round, and there stood Patrick, holding a glass of wine and surveying them calmly. Horrified, Shivaun wondered how much he had overheard, and knew Denis was wondering too – but if the man had been eavesdropping, then it served him right.

Nonchalantly, Patrick looked at Denis. 'If you wouldn't mind, Denis, I just came in to have a word with Shivaun?'

Recovering rapidly, Denis stood his ground and looked at him in turn.

'Certainly – if she wants to have one with you?' He eyed Shivaun enquiringly, and she hesitated before nodding. Undoubtedly Patrick had come to tick her off for being rude to him in front of everyone – but if he had then now was her chance to tell him he'd had it coming.

'Yes, OK, why don't you bring out the coffee, Denis, and I'll be with you in a moment?'

Without saying a word, Denis made his feelings plain, took the coffee pot and marched out. When he'd gone Patrick stood in silence for several seconds, pondering his wine and, apparently, his words.

'So. Um. Azalea sent me in.'

He grimaced, and Shivaun waited coolly. 'Did she?'

'Yes. Er – she thinks you're annoyed that I didn't make much of you just because you're Irish.'

Shivaun raised an eyebrow. 'Being Irish has nothing to do with it. I just thought you were unfriendly when we met, and have been distant ever since.'

'Then you must be paranoid. I've hardly seen you since, except in the evenings amongst a dozen other people.'

Shivaun supposed that was true. If she was honest, being Irish *had* something to do with it. She'd felt entitled to more than a mere hello. And then silence. And now he was calling her paranoid. He had a bloody nerve.

'So what exactly did you want to say to me?' She folded her arms and leaned against the kitchen wall, waiting for what she supposed might be a grudging apology.

'I wanted to say that I don't make friends easily. I have a reputation for being cold, which I understand but dispute, because I do make friends with some people when I get to know them well enough. Azalea is one such friend. That's why I'm here – because I respect her wish that there be no more scenes such as the one we had tonight.'

What? Shivaun had to fight down the surprise she felt rising in her face, the astonished thought that he might actually be expecting *her* to apologise to *him*.

'Well,' she said at length, 'Jeff is Azalea's boyfriend and I think you were nasty to him. I like Jeff a lot, because he's been so kind and warm to me, but provided you don't do it again I see no reason for another scene.'

She drew herself up to her full height for this speech, and was astonished when Patrick laughed a short, gruff laugh.

'So that's my cards well marked for me, huh? No more trouble provided I behave myself?'

'Yes,' she said curtly, 'that's about it. You can ignore me if you wish, but I won't let you insult anyone who's been good to me.'

For a moment Patrick stared hard at her; then he sipped his wine and chewed it round his mouth, contemplatively.

'Look, lady. Let's get something straight here. This is your first visit to Wachusett, yes?'

'Yes. What's your point?'

'My point is that I know Jeff and Azalea far better than you do. I've been coming here to ski with them for years and that long acquaintance gives me the right to kid Jeff about something we've both found funny from the start, namely the fact that he can't ski for toffee. He knows it and he has a sense of humour about it, so there's no need for you to gallop in on your white horse. In fact I'd invite you to butt right out only Azalea seems to think I should humour you.'

'*Humour* me?'

'Yes. It's a pain but I told her I'd do it, since she's one of the few friends Denis doesn't think I've got.'

Oh, no. He had overheard everything Denis had said. Guilt made her defensive.

'It's a wonder you have any, since you listen in on people's private conversations.'

He looked provoked, even angry. 'You weren't exactly whispering – I was simply waiting to get a word in whenever our gay pal stopped talking. Too bad he is gay, huh?'

He raised a sardonic eyebrow and Shivaun recoiled, with a suddenly appalling sensation that this repugnant man could see right under her skin.

'Excuse me,' she said stonily, 'but if you've finished your speech I think I'll go and join him now.'

Gathering up the coffee things on a tray, she stalked out, but by the time she reached the living room where someone was strumming a guitar, her legs were shaking. Well, she thought, I've been skiing all day, is it any wonder?

Shivaun longed to talk to Kathy in their room that night, but Kathy fell asleep in mid-sentence, burbling something about 'no kidzzz' that left Shivaun amused and mystified. Next day it proved equally impossible to talk to Azalea, who went skiing at first light with Kathy and Patrick, and Shivaun sighed; it looked like girl-talk was going to have to wait until they got home.

Home! If only she knew where home was. For now she supposed it was Chederlay, and she would always have a roof over her head in Dublin, but she felt her soul was a vagrant, her spirit was rootless. The emotional challenge of getting through Christmas and New Year had left her so drained she thought she might fall apart if she thought any further about the future, and so she drew on her physical resources instead, filling every minute with fresh air and flying snow, pushing every muscle to its limits until she was conscious of little else. In the evenings she savoured the feeling of being part of a group, took refuge in the fun and friendship, the music that Dale played on his guitar; apart from Patrick who remained aloof, everyone was in tune and in harmony.

On their last night together they made a fondue and drank a lot of wine, and Shivaun let herself go with the flow, laughing as Denis described his 'gruesome' childhood in Kansas and Amy wickedly recounted her life with a father who had got through five wives and toted his family through ten states. This led to a long discussion of childhood, and Shivaun was fascinated by the diversity of it, the resourceful ways some of them had survived it.

Her own had been stable by comparison, far more secure than some of these rambling tales. But still she hoped nobody would ask her about it, because she didn't want to talk about Ivor, who had been such an essential part of it. Patrick, she noticed, wasn't saying much either, until Ellen turned to him wanting to know the difference between growing up in Ireland and in America.

'Well,' he said reluctantly, wryly, 'we didn't have McDonalds or the Simpsons! I grew up on a remote farm in the Irish midlands, way out in the middle of nowhere, without even a phone or a television. But we had other interests. There was a huge black lake where we went swimming and fishing, there were fields full of animals, I remember making a pet of an orphan lamb and feeding it from a baby's bottle, riding a donkey in the firm belief that it was a stallion . . . I can still feel the freshness of the mornings, the dew on the grass . . . at night we lit turf fires that smelled more memorable than anything Dior or Rabanne ever manufactured.'

This was a lengthy contribution from Patrick, and everyone nodded at the romance of it. Except Shivaun, who was suddenly roused.

'When was that?' she asked. 'Twenty or thirty years ago?'

Yes, he agreed looking affronted, obviously it was a long time ago.

'And when were you last back in Ireland?'

He frowned vaguely. 'I haven't been back since I left. Too busy.'

'Well,' she said, 'you should go back and see it now. Maybe the midlands haven't changed out of all recognition, but the whole place has changed radically. In body and even more in spirit.'

'How so?' Karl wanted to know. 'What's it like now?'

'It's a shambles,' she said candidly. 'Ever since the bishop of Galway ran off to South America, there's been one scandal after another—'

'A Catholic bishop? Why'd he run off?'

'Because the media discovered he had a mistress and teen-aged son, living here in America. Then a whole lot of priests were exposed and jailed for child abuse, the banks were caught fiddling the tax system, the former prime minister was disgraced – he'd already been accused of running guns for the IRA – a bunch of millionaires were found shipping all their money off to the Cayman Islands . . . a girl who'd been raped by her father died giving birth . . . women started being murdered all over the country, all the cities filled up with drugs—'

She didn't realise how heated she'd got until Ellen interrupted in amazement. 'Wow! This sounds more like Sicily! I always thought Ireland was a cute little—'

'Well it isn't,' she said bluntly, 'it's a mess and a rip-off and it's full of liars and criminals—'

Ellen was agog. 'But isn't it a really ancient civilisation?'

Shivaun laughed drily. 'Civilisation? Every kid in the country wears a Nike baseball cap! The girls want to be Jennifer Aniston and the boys want to marry her! Woe betide the parent who doesn't produce the Japanese software for Christmas! The Old Head of Kinsale, one of the most beautiful moors in the country, has been turned into a golf course complete with shopping facilities! Old people lie on hospital trolleys for days!'

As she gathered momentum all of Shivaun's smothered fury erupted volcanically, she could see the knife slicing into Jimmy's chest, feel the flames engulfing Viv's body, hear Jason Dean's lawyer saying what a fine young man he was.

'Ireland isn't full of pixies and rainbows! It's full of thieves, thugs, fraudsters and gangsters, crime, incest—'

Gazing at her aghast, Patrick suddenly exploded in turn. 'That's a lot of rubbish! Ireland is a beautiful country and—'

'And you left it years ago, you know nothing about it! If you don't believe me, go back and see it for yourself!'

There was a crackling silence, in which she realised she'd cleared the decks, everyone was waiting for the next salvo in a discussion that had turned into a blazing row between herself and Patrick. Incandescent, she stared at him.

'Why don't you, huh? Why don't you go back, if it's so wonderful, and see it?'

Everyone looked at him, expecting him to shout back. But when he spoke his tone was very low.

'Maybe I will. Maybe I will, one day.'

'Huh! Is that the best you can say? Why have you stayed here for so long, never gone to visit your lambs and your fields?'

Why hadn't he? Why was he sitting here three thousand miles away spouting romantic claptrap about a place he'd long abandoned? She waited for his response, and was infuriated when it came in the same restrained tone.

'You seem a little excitable, Shivaun. I don't know why, but I do think you're exaggerating.'

'*Exaggerating?* For what reason? Don't you think I'd love to be able to say my country is beautiful, wonderful, a great place to live? Do you think I like admitting that my house has been burgled twice, my car has been stolen and vandalised, I've been mugged four times?'

These were the only attacks she was prepared to talk about, the common ones that were part of Irish daily life; even now she would not disclose the real, much deeper trauma. But it was enough to send shock waves round the table – even the Bronx, Dale said astonished, wasn't as bad as Ireland sounded.

'But what Shivaun forgets' Patrick murmured, 'is that every country has its ups and downs. Ireland does have an ancient history, but it's only been independent for about eighty years, had a long hard struggle for freedom and—'

Shivaun winced. 'Oh, don't start the Mother Machree sob stuff. It's got cobwebs on. The reality today is that Ireland's a dump, in the literal sense that people use it as a garbage tip, carpet it in litter and feck their old fridges into the rivers. It's a cesspit of dirt and lies and deliberate—'

'Shivaun,' Denis said wryly, 'were you by any chance turned down for a job with the Irish tourist board?'

Everyone cackled, and she laughed herself, feeling better for having spoken her mind. The explosive atmosphere was defused, but Patrick sat silent and unsmiling, gazing at her.

'With friends like you,' he drawled at length, 'what country needs enemies?'

'Oh, knock it off,' she retorted, 'and buy yourself a plane ticket back to the old sod next summer, if you can see it for the burger joints and the chewing gum.'

They glared at each other, and Azalea sighed. 'Well,' she said, 'isn't it nice to see the Irish getting along together so well. Remind me to book next year's vacation in Hawaii.'

Driving back to Gloucester, Shivaun felt unsettled and edgy, and was glad to leave the talking to Kathy who babbled endlessly on about what a wonderful time she'd had. Pleased, Shivaun smiled at her.

'I'm really happy to hear that. Is it hard for you to go home, now?'

Kathy licked her wind-chapped lips and hesitated before answering.

'Shivaun, I – I'm not going home.'

Swerving with surprise, she had to fight to keep control of the car.

'What? But – but we're on our way home! Where else can you go?'

'Azalea says I can go to her commune. She's going to let me live in it for free until I start selling paintings for decent money, which she thinks I can. I'm going to tell Bill tonight and move in tomorrow.'

Shivaun was stunned. 'But what about the boys? Kathy, this is so sudden, have you thought—'

'Yes. I've been thinking all week, and talking to Azalea. The commune is a child-free zone, she says, nobody who lives in it is allowed to have kids. But it's only a twenty-minute walk from my house, quicker by bike, so what I plan to do is divide my time between the two. I'll sleep in the commune at nights and paint there in the mornings, then in the afternoons I'll go home to the boys. I'll be there when they get in from school and I'll cook their evening meal. Bill's too if he wants, I'll even do a bit of housework. But then, when the boys are in bed, I'll leave.'

'But what if Bill – or the boys—?'

'Don't like it? Tough. It's the best I can do, Shivaun. I'll still see them every day. I just won't belong to them any more, body and soul, round the clock. For the moment Azalea only has a small room available, but it'll do, I'll have my own space and the bit of money I earn in the gallery. That'll be enough until – well, Azalea reckons some of Marina's clients might start buying my work if Marina talks it up. D'you think she will?'

'I – well, yes, I do. She loves your work. And she knows how it feels when a marriage breaks up, I think she'll be very supportive . . . but God Kathy, this is a bombshell! I had no idea you were hatching all this with Azalea.'

'It just came about by itself really, when we got talking. It wasn't planned, it just seemed to fall into place, but I'm determined to do it.'

Shivaun glanced at her. 'Are you? Then I hope you'll succeed. But don't you feel a bit sad? After all, you and Bill were in love once, you—'

'We've run out of road. Our only hope is to build a new stretch. If he accepts this blueprint then we can stay friends, which I want us to be for the boys. I don't mind if he finds himself another woman, although I don't want another man. I just want to paint in peace.'

'But you hardly painted at all at Wachusett.'

'I know. I needed to stand back and get things in perspective. I can't wait to get started again now, though – you know how it is, Shivaun, when you have a passion for something. Sometimes you need to let go of it for a little while to make sure you can't live without it.'

'Well, I—'

'You know! You've let go of Ireland, but I can see you really care about it. You should've seen your face last night, you were so fired up – you'll go back to it some day, and do great things there.'

She snorted with laughter. 'Go back? And do – what? Kathy, you're raving!'

But Kathy sat back unperturbed, with an aura of quiet certainty. 'You will. I can see it in you.'

'Then you need to visit Jeff the optician! Your rose-tinted specs are too strong!'

'Shivaun, trust me. Painters have an inner eye. I can see these things. Some day – soon, in a year or two – I'm going to be painting flat out, and you're going to be president of Ireland, or prime minister or whatever they have over there.'

Shivaun laughed aloud, and continued to laugh the rest of the way back to Kathy's house, where she dropped her off with all the optimism she could muster for the coming confrontation. Bill might agree to Kathy's plan, in the end, but she didn't think he was going to be any pushover. Musing on the speed of Kathy's decision, she turned the car and headed back to Chederlay, where the dogs came bounding out to greet her with Marina in their wake.

'Hi! I'm back, intact, how are you, let me see you!'

Marina looked very well, reaching out to embrace Shivaun and lead her into the house which, in the chill gathering dusk, was warm and welcoming.

'Darling child! Dorothy has lit a fire, come and sit down, have a drink, I'm dying to hear all about it.'

Shivaun put her arm around her waist and they went up the steps together, each delighted to see the other. In the library Marina sat back with a pot of camomile tea and looked expectant.

'So how was it?'

'It was fantastic,' Shivaun enthused. 'I loved the mountains and the trees, the air was all crunchy and I not only stayed upright on skis, I went halfway up the mountain and did some quite long runs – I think I have a natural talent, I may ski for my country in the next Olympics.'

If I knew where it was, she thought with a pang, if I knew which team I belong to. Marina smiled and fingered her earrings.

'And Azalea's friends? Did you like them?'

Shivaun nodded vigorously. 'They were terrific. We had a ball, I got really pally with Denis – the only one I didn't like was your gardener, Patrick Nulty.'

Marina raised a curious eyebrow. 'Oh?'

'Oh, Marina, he was awful! Cold, distant, I had two rows with him – why didn't you tell me he's such a pain?'

'Because I didn't want to prejudice you. I've always found him distant myself, but Azalea seems to see something in him that I never have. I – well, to be honest I've often wondered what exactly brought him to America. But as you say, he's not the chatty type. He is very attractive, though, and wealthy – I'm sure he'd faint if he heard you call him my gardener! He sees himself as a landscaping consultant. Most women of your age swoon over him.'

'Well then they must be idiots, or gluttons for punishment. I'd say life with Patrick Nulty would be a one-way street. He has a head on him the size of that thing at Epcot.'

'Hah! I thought you might gravitate to him, on account of his being Irish.'

'No way. Being Irish and good-looking doesn't do it for me – anyway, he didn't seem Irish at all. He painted a rosy picture of Ireland right enough, but it was real brochure stuff. He's been away so long he seemed far more American to me. He was dressed to kill and he sounded like a Kennedy. Give me Denis Turner any day – did you know by the way that Denis is gay?'

'Yes. I hope you didn't find out the hard way?'

Marina eyed her, and Shivaun paused. 'No – but – before I found out, I must admit I did feel a – a little attracted to him. Just for a moment.'

Marina considered. 'That sounds like good news to me. It's a pity he's not available, because he's a nice man, but at least you felt some response. Could it be that you're beginning to get over Ivor?'

'Oh Marina, I *have* to get over him! Where's the use in moping, or pretending? Missing him will never get me anywhere.'

'No, but that doesn't usually stop people from doing it. You speak very rationally from the head, Shivaun, but sometimes I wonder what's going on in your heart.'

Sometimes I wonder myself, Shivaun thought. But whatever it is, I can't talk about it. You're a lovely lady and a wonderful friend to me, but – I can't. You've been ill and you don't need me to worry about.

'I hope you did your yoga and exercises every day?'

'Yes. If you insist on changing the subject, I did. My behaviour was exemplary. And Steven says I should be able to go to Utah next month. I've booked plane tickets for us both.'

'Oh, great! That reminds me – if your clients are looking for any artwork for their new house, Kathy Shreve is in the market for commissions. She's leaving her husband and going to live in Azalea's commune.'

'Is she? My goodness! That's very sudden – what about her children?'

'She'll spend evenings with them, if Bill can be persuaded to play ball. I feel kind of responsible! It was the trip to Wachusett that seemed to decide her.'

'H'm. I hope you didn't say anything to influence her?'

'No, nothing. I didn't even know she was planning it, she only told me in the car on the way home.'

'Good. I know you're fond of her, but friends should never interfere in each other's marital affairs. Dissolving a marriage is a very painful and personal business.'

'Yes . . . Marina, how long did it take you to get over yours?'

Sipping her tea, Marina reflected. 'About two years. A year to grieve and a year to restructure. I never thought I'd do it, but I did.'

'And do you ever regret – leaving?'

'Yes. Sometimes, even now, I do. I gained a lot, but I gave up a lot too. A divorce is never cut and dried, and you only start getting over it when you accept that, when you feel that on balance you've won more than you've lost. If it's any comfort to you, I'm sure there will be many moments when your Ivor will regret his decision, and wish you were still together.'

Wistfully, Shivaun looked at her. 'Do you?'

Emphatically, Marina put down her cup. 'Yes. Absolutely. Decisions have consequences . . . long-running consequences, sometimes. Nobody is fully adult or mature until they can face that fact and accept responsibility for their actions.'

'No,' Shivaun mused, thinking of Jason Dean, 'I think not. I hope not.'

'Trust me. Meanwhile, Shivaun, speaking of responsibility . . . I didn't want to throw it at you the moment you came home, but – a letter has arrived for you. From Ireland.'

'Oh!' Instantly, Shivaun caught the weight in Marina's tone, and knew what it must be. 'Where is it?'

'I left it upstairs by your bed. I thought you'd rather read it in private.'

'Yes – thank you – Marina, will you excuse me?'

In a blur of urgency she ran out of the room, up the stairs and into her bedroom, where a long cream envelope with a franked postmark stood propped on the dressing table. For a moment the room rocked, before she seized it and tore it open, praying for the strength to cope with its contents, gasping for breath and for courage.

'Dear Madam, Further to your enquiry of December 19 . . .'

Oh God, where was it, where *was* it?

'August 14 1974.'

The words whirled like leaves in a storm. August 14, 1974.

For five or six seconds her mind stalled, wouldn't do the simple maths, and then the truth hit her like a hurricane. Her own birthday, the day she'd been found in the church porch, was April 27. She had been born nearly four months before Jason Dean. There was no way he could be her brother.

Time stood still as she clutched the letter, as faint with elation as if a doctor had told her a tumour was benign. At last, after this eternity of fear, she had rid herself of a demon that had terrorised her night after night after night. She would never know who her natural parents or siblings might be, but now she knew who they weren't. She had untied one of the knots, freed herself of one of the ropes that bound her to the man who had killed Jimmy Reilly, killed her dad and propelled her mother Vivienne to her death.

Shuddering, she sank down on her bed, panting, feeling purged of poison. Her sense of liberation was engulfing, and yet Marina's words swirled through it; she knew she would never be fully liberated until Jason Dean recognised and accepted the consequences of what he had done that night so long ago. Recognised, and regretted, and wished with all his heart that he could undo. He never could undo, but the means of resolution lay within his power, only he could utter the single word that would give her peace. *Sorry. I am profoundly sorry for what I did, and for all that followed. I am truly sorry.*

But was he sorry? And even if he was, would he ever have the courage to say it? If he had not, how could she ever find out what he thought, how he felt? Was Jimmy's death a source of pain and shame to him, did it haunt and shape his life? Or was it shelved in his mind, exonerated, just a youthful escapade that had gone wrong, been put right by the social workers? Did he hold his head high today, did he even laugh at Jimmy Reilly's crazy heroism? Did he know Jimmy's widow was dead, or that Jimmy had a daughter who still grieved, still suffered, still held the pain like a gleaming crystal in her hands?

I carry that pain to this day, she thought, and I *have* to *know*! I cannot forgive a man who does not ask for forgiveness, and I cannot live without forgiving. That knife is embedded in my heart, and it will remain there until the man who plunged it in pulls it out. I would give anything to get free of it, anything on God's earth – but life is so much more easily stolen than restored. Jason Dean is out of prison, but I, despite this liberating letter, am still his captive. How long is my sentence, will *he* ever let *me* go free? How would he feel, if *I* killed *his* father?

How does a man feel, when he has killed? How does he feel, five years later, ten, twenty? If only I knew that . . . if only I knew.

Chapter Eleven

It was early February, and then it was the middle of February, and finally it was, Ivor recognised, hopeless. Thinking he was only loosening his moorings, he had cut himself completely adrift. Shivaun had rejected him, his friends had forgotten him with callous speed, even his mother now held herself aloof. Once, in desperation, he phoned Alana, but got no answer. Like Shivaun she was apparently busy elsewhere, and the hollowly ringing phone seemed to mock him, to reinforce his sense of isolation.

Well, he reminded himself with an effort at logic, you wanted out and now you are out. You're an apprentice carpenter in the south of Spain and nobody gives a damn whether you sink or swim. You may as well get out and see something of the place, do something with your freedom.

It was a very odd feeling, not at all as exhilarating as he'd hoped or expected, and yet there was a curious impetus in it too, a sense of both gain and loss that reminded him of something he'd once read about manic depression: apparently it was possible to feel euphoric and melancholy almost simultaneously. As the days lengthened and brightened he felt the former, but when night set in it seemed to penetrate right through to his soul, he ached for Shivaun and then got furious with her, if he drank any of Miguel's cheap wine he got furious with himself too, felt as if a length of twisted wire were caught in his gut.

When Miguel's fudged taxes were finally returned, as optimistically as was possible without receipts to back up the man's plea for clemency, Ivor mercilessly demanded full payment regardless of the outcome, and set off to explore Seville praying that the rest of it would be an improvement on La Macarena. The weather was still bone-crunching, but sometimes now there was a tantalising glimpse of light and warmth, and he sensed that the worst winter of his life was nearly over. But even as he thawed physically he felt frozen spiritually, which was infuriating, because after all had he not got what he wanted?

Yes. In many respects, he had. Above and beyond all else, he had learned carpentry, discovered a real passion for it, absorbed much of Miguel's mitigating talent, precision and patience. His muscles still throbbed from dawn to dusk, the workshop was still arctic, but he felt infinitely fitter, and more fulfilled, than he ever had in his centrally-heated days as an accountant. Miguel continued to treat him like a dog, but at least they understood each other, there was no stifling politeness or palaver, he always knew exactly where he stood. Refreshingly, Miguel was one boss who actually respected candour.

'You and I,' Miguel said to him one day after a heated row, 'we hate each other, yes?'

'Yes,' Ivor agreed emphatically, pleased that his Spanish was now up to understanding most insults, 'we do.' And there they left it, neither of them in the least offended. Why Miguel hated him he neither knew nor cared; it seemed to be just chemistry, or else Miguel systematically resented any apprentice who might one day challenge, even rival him. Ivor made up his mind to not only rival but outshine the bastard completely, and dreamed with mounting ardour of the day he would have his own workshop and his own apprentices. And, he thought gleefully, at least I'll be able to run my own financial affairs, I won't have to pay some opportunist brat like me to do it – hah!

Not that he had made more than pocket money out of Miguel's fiscal muddle; but it was a lifesaver, it enabled him to confront Seville with his head held high, to pay for the petty things that salvaged his dignity – a hot drink, a bus fare, a ticket into a basketball game that everyone else in Seville was attending. He had little interest in basketball, and had not known that Seville was so mad about it, but it interested him to attend the game as a cultural event, infinitely preferable to the bullfights that Miguel was always raving about. Slowly, very gradually, he began to get a feel for his adopted city, to read the newspaper headlines and understand them, to exchange greetings in shops and cafés without feeling conspicuously foreign. Sometimes he had tapas at El Rinconcillo with Pilar, who assured him that he still sounded extremely foreign, but she helped him when she was in the mood and his linguistic limits began to stretch.

One evening they sat at a table in the corner, sipping hot chocolate laced with brandy, talking about a hideous sculpture that Ivor had seen in a park. When he got stuck for words she supplied them, and they muddled along half in Spanish, half in English.

'It was vile,' he said, 'so stiff, so pompous, as if the guy did it just because he could or because someone paid him to. I never want to make anything like that in wood.'

'So what do you want to make? Will people not pay you to make furniture, just because you can?'

'Yes,' he conceded, 'I hope they will. But I'll only make what feels right. I want every piece to live and breathe, to serve a purpose – not just to sit there looking smug and virtuoso.'

'Oh, Ivor! You are a closet romantic!'

'There's nothing closet about it. That's just the way I feel. I gave up an entire life in Ireland so I could do what I really want to do. I'm not going to compromise it and end up right back where I started.'

Pilar looked unimpressed. 'You gave up being an accountant. Big deal. Many people change their minds, change their careers. All you sacrificed was money and comfort.'

He was stung. 'That's not true. Not true at all. I gave up far more than that.'

She looked at him curiously, sceptically. 'Such as? What did you give up?'

He hesitated, but then decided he might as well tell her. He wanted to talk to someone about it, and women were good at this stuff.

'I gave up a girl. A woman. A woman I loved very much.'

Again she surveyed him sceptically, in his threadbare sweater and scruffy jeans, as if wondering what woman would want him. Pilar, he had discovered, was a pragmatic girl and rather traditional too, she believed that relationships involved entire families, that people married for security and social position; he knew that the concept of love would cut no ice with her. Still, she must have some views on the subject, surely?

'Why did you give her up? Why not bring her here to Spain with you, if you loved her so much?'

'Because she wouldn't come. She was too busy with – with the things she loved.'

'What did she love?'

'She loved her work as a nurse, she loved all the social causes she was always fighting for, she – she—'

To his horror and mortification, Ivor suddenly faltered, felt tears trembling at the back of his eyes as Shivaun's face came forcibly to his mind. He had wept many tears over Shivaun in private, but to do it in public was as startling as it was unthinkable. Looking faintly horrified, Pilar waited until he mastered his voice.

'She was wonderful. One in a million. Sorry, I didn't mean to get emotional.'

Angrily he brushed his face with his hand, and took a swig of his drink, embarrassment making him defiant.

'Haven't you ever been in love? Huh?'

'No,' she said thoughtfully, 'I haven't.'

'Well, if it ever happens to you, run a mile! It's like a fatal illness, it hurts like hell and there's no known cure.'

She raised a thick, dark eyebrow. 'So I've heard. Maybe that's why I've avoided it. And tell me, Ivor, how old were you when it happened to you?'

Even as he opened his mouth to reply he knew he was going to sound a fool, but then maybe he was a fool.

'I was – five!'

They both exploded laughing, and Ivor felt a light-headed rush of something; Christ, a laugh, at last! A slightly hysterical laugh admittedly, halfway to a sob, but it felt powerfully good, so good that he could hardly stop, sat grinning like an idiot. 'Oh, dammit, Pilar, there's no point trying to explain. It was just one of those things. Logic and love are completely incompatible.'

She was still spluttering. 'Yes, but – really! Five! And now you are – what, twenty-five?'

'Twenty-six.'

'And there has never been any other woman?'

'No. Well, we both flirted a bit in our teens, but neither of us ever clicked with anyone else. We just seemed born for each other.'

Still grinning, she thought about it. 'So what are you going to do now?'

In a cold clear flash it came to him exactly what he was going to do. 'I'm going to get on with my life. Find someone else and forget her.'

Pilar peered at him. 'Can you do that? Simply forget?'

He nodded vehemently. 'You can do anything you make up your mind to do. Come on, let's finish our drinks and go dancing.'

In a gulp he slugged his drink back and stood up, waiting for her. Sceptically, she drained her glass and they left El Rinconcillo together, heading for the Plaza del Alfalfa where the nightlife would be just starting to rev up. Ivor liked Pilar, but he wasn't attracted to her; she was too calm and sensible for what he had in mind. What he had in mind, quite abruptly and vividly, was a bimbo. Some pretty, easy little bimbo, followed by another bimbo, a whole series of them, all the sexual variety he should have tasted years ago. Well, better late than never. At a street kiosk he stopped to blatantly buy a large packet of condoms, and grinned triumphantly.

Pilar thought his grin was quite manic, but she grinned back, and they elbowed their way into the cruising crowd.

* * *

Shivaun could not for the life of her understand where Alana had got to. Five times running she phoned her house in Dublin, and got no further than leaving voicemails which were never returned. What the hell was going on? Finally she got up at five one Saturday morning; it would be eleven in Dublin and at that time on Saturdays Alana was normally just awake – unless she was on night duty, or had gone down to Waterford?

But at last the phone was answered. Not by Alana, but by a cheery-sounding man. Taken aback, Shivaun asked who he was, and he said he was Jim, the painter.

'Painter? What painter? What are you painting?'

Why, the whole house, he replied nonchalantly, he was under orders to do every room except the main bedroom, which apparently belonged to the absent owner.

'*I'm* the owner,' Shivaun informed him, 'and I don't know anything about this. Would you mind getting Alana for me?'

But she's not here, Jim said, she doesn't live here, she's only the caretaker.

'What? But she *does* live there!'

No, Jim insisted, she didn't. He'd been working on the house all week and it was definitely unoccupied. He'd only met Alana Kennedy once, to choose the colours and get his instructions, and she'd told him to leave his bill on the kitchen table when he was finished. He'd leave a message too, if Shivaun liked, to say she'd called?

Shivaun was bewildered. But this Jim seemed to be her only hope. 'Yes, leave an urgent mesage then please, tell her to call me immediately – why are you painting the house, anyway? I didn't want anything done to it.'

There was a silence, in which Jim seemed to be deliberating. When he spoke, she heard caution in his voice. He was just refreshing the décor, he said, Ms Kennedy wanted everything to be in tip-top shape.

'But—' Oh, hell, she couldn't deal with this from such a distance! Repeating her request and her number, she hung up and went down to the kitchen to make some coffee, pondering the oddness of it until it hit her – there must have been some damage. Something had happened to the house. There was no other reason why Alana would re-decorate it, without even consulting her.

All day she waited for the phone to ring, and by the time Alana called back that evening she was ready to kill her.

'Jesus Christ, Alana, what in hell's going on over there? I haven't heard from you for ages and now I get a painter who says you don't live there any more! What *is* this?'

Sounding distant, Alana replied that the painter had got it wrong, that she'd just been away for a few days, out of the way while the house was done up. 'But don't worry, it's finished now and it looks lovely.'

'Alana, I want the truth. What happened to it?'

'Nothing . . . I just thought it would be a nice surprise for when you come home. You'd already done your own bedroom so I got Jim to do the other rooms in the same style. You'll love it.'

'But why didn't you *ask* me?'

'Oh, Shivaun, stop fussing. I'm paying for it myself, it's a present to you for letting me stay here.'

Oh. Was she being churlish, was Alana telling the truth? Maybe she'd better stop looking a gift horse in the mouth . . . but she thought of her parents' décor, and felt a wrench. This was a decision Alana had had no business to make.

'And another thing – Ivor's mother tells me he's in Spain. Why did you say he'd gone to Australia?'

There was only the briefest pause before Alana answered chirpily. 'Did I? Well, I only heard some gossip down in the pub, it must have got mixed up. Anyway, what does it matter? You haven't heard from him wherever he is. have you?'

It was a question, but Shivaun thought it sounded more like a statement. 'No, you're right, I haven't. Have *you*?'

'Me? Why would I?'

'I just wondered whether – there'd been any news of him, that's all.'

'No. Nothing. He seems to have vanished completely.'

There was a finality in her tone, and Shivaun recognised

the futility of pursuing the subject. Ivor had, unarguably, vanished.

'Well, look, keep in better touch from now on, OK? Don't do anything else to the house, and make sure to send on any post.'

Alana said she would, and talked briefly about other things before saying she'd better not run up a big bill. Hanging up, Shivan was left with the faintly puzzled sensation of being excluded from some invisible picture. Why that should be she couldn't exactly say, but it was unsettling and it persisted.

It was a short winter by New England standards, and Azalea lamented the lack of snow for another skiing trip. But Marina was pleased; the one thing she missed about California, she said, was the sun. Spring couldn't arrive soon enough for her.

Gradually there were hints of it. The forest filled up with snowdrops and then Chederlay's lawns put forth thousands of mauve and yellow crocuses, the handiwork of Patrick Nulty it seemed. 'Don't be fooled,' Azalea crisply advised Shivaun, 'we often get cold snaps right up to Easter. But doesn't the garden look good, for March?' It did look good, as did Kathy Shreve who'd produced three new paintings since moving into Azalea's commune. She sold one of them in the gallery she worked for, infuriating her newly-estranged husband and 'majorly', as she said, impressing her sons. Shivaun was thrilled for her, and for Marina who was in good shape too. Counting the days to her trip to Utah, she all but turned cartwheels when it came.

'C'mon Shivaun, shake a leg, our plane's at noon! I've got work to go to!'

Off they flew, and Shivuan found Marina's excitement infectious, glued her nose to the plane's windows like a child as they crossed the American continent, watching the verdant land of the east turn to the chrome yellow of the west, losing its neat, orderly look to dusty, infinite prairies. Marina's clients lived outside a small city called Ogden, and when they landed at Salt Lake City they hired a car to drive to it. As Steven

Hunt still hadn't given Marina permission to drive, Shivaun found herself playing chauffeur, setting off on the unfamiliar roads with a keen sense of adventure.

'This is fun! I don't know the first thing about Utah, never expected to see it – have you been here before, Marina?'

'Only once, I came last year to inspect the site. The soil here is different, it affects how you plan the foundations . . . I must say I enjoy the challenge of diverse terrain.'

'Have you designed houses in every state?'

'Not all. But I've done everything from a Manhattan loft to an adobe house in New Mexico, worked with sand, rock, swamp – I even did a house in Alaska once, boy did it need insulation. There were a lot of problems with timber contracting and expanding, too. But we worked our way around it.'

'We?'

'Yes, there's a lot of consultation with engineers and builders, it's always best to use locals because they know the climate and the soil. You'd be amazed how much I've learned about American geology.'

'You must have travelled a lot, before your stroke?'

'Endlessly. Apart from commissions, there were lots of conferences too, I visited Europe and South America, Australia, parts of the Middle East and Far East . . .'

'Wow! I've only ever been to Portugal, and once or twice with my parents on sun packages to Spain. I think my mother would have liked to venture further, but Dad always got itchy when he was away, was really happiest in Ireland.'

'Didn't your mom ever travel without him?'

'Yes, but only before she married him. She hitched around France and went with some girlfriends to Greece. When I got into my teens she was always telling me to travel as soon and as much as I could, she gave me a backpack for my eighteenth birthday.'

'And did you use it?'

'A bit. I went hostelling round Ireland with Ivor and then we went to Portugal. But we always seemed to be either studying or broke. Then when we were able to afford Italy, we split up before we got to it.'

'Oh, Italy is gorgeous! The Renaissance architecture is mindblowing. Don't miss it – you must go!'

Well, Shivaun thought, I might at that. Now that I've started to see a bit of the world I'm starting to see what I've been missing. But better late than never. There's nothing to stop me any more.

Chatting, they drove on, enjoying each other's company as much as the blue sky and the open road, the dry white air and the raw unfolding scenery that held a harsh, uncompromising allure. Some of the parched ridged stone, Shivaun thought, looked superbly indifferent to centuries of human assault and endeavour, invincibly enduring.

When they reached Ogden they checked into a hotel, but Marina barely glanced at it, visibly simmering to see her site as she changed into an unprecedented shirt, trousers and suede jacket.

'God, it's so good to be getting back to work! C'mon Shivaun, hurry up, it's still forty minutes' drive out to the site.'

Out they drove, and Shivaun looked askance when, just before arriving, Marina threw her walking stick on the floor behind her seat.

'Won't you need that?'

'Whether I do or not, I won't use it. I'll walk this site and—'

'I'm not letting you up any ladders!'

'Oh, don't start playing Nurse Reilly. I'll do what I have to do.'

Shivaun was about to argue when she realised that, psychologically, it would do Marina more good to be given free rein. Unless she actually caught her heading up on the roof, she would say nothing.

But the house, when they drove up to it, didn't have any roof. It was just a bunch of spikes and pillars projecting from the ground. Marina beamed.

'Here we are! Come and meet my clients, Shivaun, come see the plans!'

She all but leaped out of the car and was engulfed by a huge florid man in Western gear that almost made Shivaun laugh aloud; he was actually wearing cowboy boots and a Stetson. So was his wife, a tall chunky brunette talking further away with the driver of a JCB, who turned and waved as she recognised Marina.

'Now, Shivaun, this is Dexter and this is Cassie – Cassie, Dexter, this is Shivaun, my personal assistant.'

Oh, really? Stifling a grin at her sudden change of job description, Shivaun shook hands with them both, and they all went to admire the pile of rubble that had been started off the faxed plans. The only thing Shivaun could see for sure was that it was going to be a big house, and was fascinated when shown the plans, unable to imagine how they connected with this mess. Marina looked skywards, as if watching the house rise majestically in front of her.

'Oh yes, I think we were right about the elevation . . . you'll have light all day in your kitchen and workroom . . . Dexter, where's the foreman?'

The foreman appeared in a hard hat, the driver of the JCB came to join them, and as Marina huddled into discussion Shivaun saw a new 'boss', one who didn't need help with anything. Yet she must be the old Marina too, the strong assured woman who, for fifteen years, had run her own life her own way. Not without cost, not without sacrifice, but here was the reward, as she took charge and seemed to look, suddenly, years younger. Before Shivaun knew what was happening she had climbed down into a pit, waist-deep, and was scooping up handfuls of wet cement, kneading it to check its texture with almost sensual pleasure. Next she picked up a heavy length of steel cable and flexed it in her bare hands, testing its strength; Shivaun suppressed a wince while Marina nodded, satisfied.

But Marina's bad arm stood up to the challenge, for long enough to impress her clients at any rate, although she asked Shivaun to take some notes after that and grimaced furtively, unable to write them herself. Shivaun mouthed at her to take it easy, but Marina was off the leash, grinning like a kid with a new box of Knex. On she ploughed, kicking and punching at various structures, measuring distances, assessing substances with the aid of various, mysterious implements that Shivaun was summoned to haul from the trunk of the car. They weighed a ton, but Marina was oblivious, and nearly five hours elapsed before the lowering, flaming sun reminded anyone that evening was gathering. It took ages to pack everything away, and then Dexter invited them all back to his 'place in the city' for drinks; Shivaun was relieved when Marina briskly declined, citing a dinner engagement in Ogden.

'What dinner?' she hissed at her as she started the car, 'with whom?'

'With you,' Marina groaned from between gritted teeth, collapsing into her seat as she was driven away, 'if I make it beyond a hot bath. I'm whacked.' But she still managed an airy wave to her clients, with a wide smile that fooled everyone except Shivaun.

'You overdid it,' she accused, 'Steven Hunt will kill you.'

'Steven' Marina pointed out, 'is in Massachusetts, and to the best of my knowledge he doesn't have coast-to-coast vision. Don't you dare tell him.'

Laughing reluctantly, Shivaun drove her back to Ogden, where even a hot bath and a muscle massage failed to alleviate the pain Marina now felt in her arm. 'Go to bed,' Shivaun commanded, 'and I'll order room service for you.'

'All right,' Marina conceded, exhausted. But then she added defiantly, 'So long as you order me a big cold glass of champagne with my dinner. I think I deserve it, don't you?'

Shivaun heartily agreed that she did.

Next day Marina went back to the site again, but this time she wanted to talk with the engineer, electrician, carpenter and plumber. 'You may as well take the car' she told Shivaun, 'and do a bit of sightseeing. Come back for me at around five.'

'And what if you collapse before then?'

'I won't,' Marina replied a touch irritably, 'I never felt better in my life. Beat it.'

Shivaun frowned. Marina was at the danger-point where recovering invalids were determined to prove they really were better. She wanted to stay with her, and a heated argument ensued, but in the end Marina prevailed by shamelessly pulling rank.

'My orders . . . I'll take all responsibility. Off you go.'

Left with no choice, Shivaun delivered her to Cassie and Dexter, issued a final warning and drove uneasily away to no particular destination. It didn't matter where she went, the entire state of Utah was new to her, and after a few miles she veered off the main road onto a smaller one that wound out through rough dusty terrain, resolving to enjoy the sense of adventure. There was nothing further she could do about Marina before evening; meanwhile her day was full of vast space and promise, she felt the pull of a foreign land.

The map indicated villages here and there, but when she came to them they were just ramshackle strips along the edge of the road, a few houses, shops and petrol stations that barely punctuated the canyon of sky; its blueness was like a glass wall all around her. The car radio was on, but after a while she turned it off, and savoured the intense, penetrating silence. What a huge quantity of nothingness! She'd furrowed into little pockets of it in Ireland, waiting for hours for the one car that might pick her up in Mayo or Kerry, but this was infinitely lonelier, the heat and quiet were so deep and dense it was like driving on Mars. Emptying her head of every thought, she let the road take her where it would, out across a plain where even the birds and animals were still and human life evaporated. So this was America, as it must have looked to the first European who ever penetrated its depths.

For no reason a vision of Viv came to her, and she smiled; today she was travelling for Viv, exploring as Viv had always wanted to do, and urged her daughter to. Today there was nothing in the way, time was a blank page, it didn't matter what she put on it. Nothing at all would be good; this silent void was complete in itself.

For nearly three hours she drove in total solitude, over the Wyoming border without registering anything other than slightly cooling, fresher air and beautiful, natural columns of stone rising out of the flatness . . . it looked exactly like the Westerns on a cinema screen, only without the wagon train or flying arrows. What a gift, she thought; today is a gift of absolute peace.

No wonder people came out here to start new lives. You could start from scratch, from zero, in a place like this. You could travel far and you could travel light, if you were driven out West, or running away from anything . . . was I running away, when I left Ireland?

Yes. I guess I was. But I can't run forever, the world is circular, sooner or later you're bound to – what was it Viv used to say? – meet yourself coming back. Can I face up to myself, then, when I – oh, *God*!

A needle of horror pierced her as she registered a flashing red light, urgently signalling that the car was nearly out of petrol. Jesus, here at the end of the world, a zillion miles from anywhere! She couldn't remember the last time she'd seen a station, only knew that it was a long time ago. A *long* time.

No use in going back, then. She'd have to go forward. Pulling in, she opened a map and consulted it, but it was meaningless. She had no idea where she was, the next marked town might be ten miles away, or a hundred. Afraid to switch off the engine in case it refused to start again, she let the car idle a moment and then, clenching down on a bite of fear, she drove off into the suddenly monumental infinity.

Marina was furious. 'I was worried sick! We all were! What the hell kept you – seven o'clock, and everyone drumming their fingers since five! We couldn't even go to Dexter's place in case you showed up, I was about to call the police!'

'Sorry,' Shivaun muttered guiltily, 'my apologies, Marina, to you and to everyone.'

'But where *were* you?'

Shivaun's face lit up, her hair flamed against the last streak of scarlet sun. 'I was out! Out in the wilderness and out of petrol!'

Marina gaped in horror. 'Gas? You let the car run dry in the middle of Utah?'

'Uh, no – I think it was Wyoming, actually.'

Marina stared. And then, decisively, she turned to her clients, who had stoically kept her company for two hours after her ride failed to show up. 'Thank you both very much. Shivaun and I are extremely sorry for having taken up so much of your time. We'll be off now.'

They were gracious, said it didn't matter, the important thing was that Shivaun was safe. And that the house was going so well, they were delighted with it.

'Yes,' Marina replied grimly, 'I'll be in touch next week.' Frostily, she marched to the car, and despite her guilt Shivaun stifled a giggle; Marina certainly didn't seem to need her stick right now, unless maybe to belt her over the head with it. They drove away, and for several minutes Marina remained speechless, almost snorting at the indignity of having been left high and dry by her nurse. Then she exploded.

'So – you drove off to nowhere with an empty tank? What kind of stupidity is that? Have you any *idea* the things that can happen to a woman alone at the side of these roads, miles from anywhere?'

'Yes,' Shivaun conceded contritely, 'but the tank was full when I started out. I just lost track of time and distance . . . oh, Marina, I've had the most wonderful day!'

'Is that so? Well, I'm glad one of us has. Mine went fine until I realised I'd been abandoned by my idiot nurse.'

'Yes – I feel awful about that. I'd have been in time, the next town was only twelve miles away actually, but I had to hitch to it, Rick's truck didn't show up for nearly an hour and then I had to hitch back with the can of petrol—'

Marina looked faint. 'You *hitched*? *Alone*? And – and who's *Rick*?'

'He's a truck driver. The one going the other way was called Spencer. They were both so sweet—'

'Is that a fact?' Marina's tone and face were glacial.

'Yes, honestly! I know I was lucky, they might have been rapists or murderers, but somehow . . . I don't know, I just felt nothing could go wrong today, it was all so beautiful, and the last part was such fun, it felt like a real adventure to be out there trusting to luck, in Wyoming of all places, on my own.'

'But Shivaun, for heaven's sake, weren't you frightened?'

Shivaun thought she detected a softening note, and smiled. 'Yes, for a few seconds I was terrified. But then I said to myself, hey, there's nothing you can do about it, only use your wits and hope for the best. As it turned out, there was nothing to be scared of at all. Fear would only have made things worse, if I'd let it win I'd be sitting there yet, well and truly stuck.'

'Well . . . all I can say is, don't ever do such a thing again.'

'No. But I'm glad it happened. I was in a fix and I faced up to it. It was what you Americans would call a very *pawsitive* experience.'

She mimicked a drawl, and suddenly they were both laughing. When they got back to their hotel they ordered a vodka gimlet apiece, and Shivaun knocked hers back with a light-headed feeling of liberation. In its various ways, this trip had been a turning point for both Marina and herself.

Women, Ivor realised mutinously, were not turning out to be quite the piece of cake he'd anticipated. Pilar said that was because he'd had no practice at them, all he'd ever had was a relationship on a plate. This time, if he wanted one, he'd have to work at it.

He didn't want one, as such. All he wanted was someone to fool around with, nothing to do with love or commitment – just sex, which men could notoriously enjoy without involvement. So how come he wasn't enjoying it?'

The night he went dancing with Pilar he met a girl – or 'pulled a bird' as his pals in Dublin would put it – in a club wryly called the Cathedral. Everything was going fine, she was rosy and voluptuous and he was snogging with her in a dark corner, when suddenly she drew away from him looking prim and stern and said she'd have to be getting home now, to her mama and papa. Ivor reckoned the girl was at least twenty, and wasn't impressed.

But it turned out that the girl was a carbon copy of Pilar, a good Catholic from a respectable family, and that she lived at home with her parents. Parents hadn't come into Ivor's picture at all, and so this was when he discovered the bane of Spain, the virgin maiden who vanished like Cinderella back to her home and her duties. What a pain, he thought, what a drag. Viv Reilly was never one of those mamas, she practically pushed her daughter into bed with me!

Next, a few days later in a market, he met a small but merry creature called Paola, who like himself was out shopping for vegetables. They went for coffee and got acquainted, and Ivor eagerly accepted her invitation to visit her apartment for dinner the following night. Surely, if she lived in an apartment, there wouldn't be any mamas or papas in it? It turned out that there were not, but something even worse lurked in store: three shrieking, giggling flatmates who all sat down to eat with them, and never left their side thereafter. Apart from making no progress with Paola whatsoever, Ivor also floundered in the rapids of conversation, and suspected that some of the shrieking giggles were at his expense. That was the end of Paola.

Daunted, but determined, he then visited Pilar's cybercafé, to send an e-mail to one of the colleagues who no longer bothered to return them. But he didn't care, his ulterior motive was to chat up the first single woman he could spot, and Pilar helpfully pointed out one who she knew lived alone. This blue-eyed, thoughtful-looking lady was a dental receptionist, she said, and her name was Josita. Her boss didn't let her use the office computer for personal communiqués, and that was why she came here.

Dutifully sympathetic, Ivor said that was a shame, his boss was a mean sod too, and would Josita care to have a drink with him that night? Josita said she'd love to, what about going to Cunini? Taken aback, because Cunini was an oyster and champagne bar far beyond his means, Ivor recoiled slightly and suggested a more modest tapas bar instead. Josita surveyed him coldly, gathered up a handbag which he belatedly noticed bore a designer logo, and said that now she thought about it, she was busy tonight actually. Exit Josita.

Christ! Could Seville not yield one single, good-natured, outgoing woman? Pilar had to give him a pep talk at this point, to remind him that OK, he might not be able to match Bill Gates for money, nor El Cordobes for drama or King Juan Carlos for status, but he was after all a nice guy, decent and hardworking and blessed with a sense of humour. He was young and fit and he'd surely find someone if he persevered. Ivor was on the point of praying to the Madonna that he would, because a twenty-six-year-old man could not go without sex for very much longer. In some desperation, he chatted up the daughter of one of Miguel's customers one day, a sweet shy young lady who dimpled and returned his smiles. She was picking up the commissioned piece of furniture, she said, because her parents were away on holiday and – seizing this information, Ivor promptly wangled an invitation to visit her home. When he got there, she produced an album of bullfight photographs, and her sweet face flared with sickening ardour; she was a huge fan and explained the 'sport' in such gory detail that Ivor's visit ended prematurely in the bathroom.

But at last, one day in early April, he struck lucky. Carla was a museum curator, he met her when visiting the Museo de Bellas Artes and she explained to him how the monastery's cloister had been remodelled by Seville's famed architect, Leonardo de Figueroa, in 1724. Ah, thought Ivor, a woman of culture and sensibility. Good figure, too. I wonder whether she has any parents, or flatmates, or bullfight pictures?

It emerged that she had not. All she had was two small rooms and a kitchen, but they were in the historic old district of Santa

Cruz, overlooking a house once occupied by Murillo. Perhaps Ivor would care to see them?

Bingo! He turned up with a bottle of wine and a romantic single rose, to find Carla's glasses exchanged for contact lenses and her sombre work outfit replaced by a tight, if overly-shiny, short dress. They ate lightly, drank sparingly, talked vivaciously and everything went swimmingly – until they reached the bedroom. Ivor could by no means claim to be an experienced lover, he'd only ever slept with Shivaun, but he did know a dead duck when he saw one. Carla undressed in camera, slid coyly between the sheets and simply lay there, like an empty vessel waiting to be filled. Ivor gave the challenge his best shot, did everything in his power to ignite some passion in the woman, but it was like trying to ignite an iceberg. Worse, she was aware of her inhibition, pleaded that she couldn't help it and burst piteously into tears, sobbing that it was 'always the same'. Gallantly he soothed and comforted her, but yearned to smack her over the head. This lamentable episode added absolutely nothing to his self-confidence, and although he was pretty sure it was not his fault he departed with a dismal feeling of failure.

'I'm giving up,' he told Pilar, 'I'm joining the Benedictines.'

She had to concede at this stage that he did seem to be – um – rather unlucky. But soon it would be Easter, there would be lots of young tourists in town, what about a nice tall healthy American or one of those game-for-anything English girls?

Well, maybe . . . a one-night stand would, he supposed, be better than nothing. Except then there was the question of suitable premises. He couldn't take anyone back to Miguel's place, a horror from which any woman would run screaming except the kind Miguel himself brought back. He certainly didn't want one of those, not unless he planned to shoot himself afterwards. But tourists stayed in hostels (communal dormitories, no use), or in hotels which, as far as he knew, did not encourage nocturnal visitors. God! How could such a simple thing turn into such a nightmare?

Frustration made him impatient, and when Miguel approached him rather conspiratorially one day, offering him a fraternal cigarette, he was not in the mood to play games. 'You know I don't smoke,' he retorted shortly, 'and I know you must want something. What is it?'

It was . . . er, well, it was the crib. One of Miguel's customers had come looking to him for just such a crib, on rockers, with latticed sides. His wife was pregnant and it was to be a surprise for her. But he, Miguel, had never made such an item, was not interested in such fiddly work. He did not think he could duplicate the one Ivor had made, the one the customer had spotted and set his heart on. So – would Ivor be willing to sell the original, or make another? They could get a good price and— wrenched to the heart, Ivor thought of Shivaun, and of his pathetic efforts to kindle any kind of sex life since. His carpentry had attained both refinement and lustre, but his masculinity felt severely undermined. All he could see ahead of him was loneliness, the kind of life that ended up exactly like Miguel's.

'Sell it' he said curtly, so wretchedly that even Miguel looked at him disconcerted. 'Give the man what he wants.'

When the man came to collect the crib, Ivor contrived to be absent, and when Miguel handed over the money later – minus a few pesetas, undoubtedly – it never even struck him that he had sold his first-ever piece of furniture. All he saw was the space in the workshop where the crib had been, and all he felt was the void that it left. Clearly Miguel believed he could make another crib, but for what? He could never make another Shivaun.

That night he went out and got smashed, and succeeded in seducing a lovely Australian girl called Justine.

One morning when the sun had heat in it, Marina sat out working on the wooden deck, designing another house in Connecticut while Shivaun talked about Sinclair Lewis, whose books had shed a lot of light for her on the way America worked.

Of course the man was nearly fifty years dead, but some things didn't change and some were, apparently, universal. Out of nowhere, a cold shadow suddenly fell between the two women and the rays of the sun.

'Good morning, ladies.'

They looked up, and there stood Patrick Nulty. Their chat interrupted, they greeted him and he accepted an offer of coffee, sitting down with them in muddy boots, a waxed green jacket and a peaked tweed cap. He had come, he said, to check out the spring planting and inform Marina that her beloved cherry tree would have to go; its roots were spreading dangerously.

'Oh, no – surely you can save it, Patrick? It's so beautiful, just coming into blossom?'

No, said Patrick firmly, those roots were a menace. Unless Marina wanted the foundations of her house threatened, he proposed to set about it this very day with a chainsaw. The logs could be used for firewood.

'It never should have been planted so near the house in the first place.'

Sighing, Marina supposed that it shouldn't, while Shivaun noted Patrick's detachment. Not much emotion there, she thought, he sounds so adamant and ruthless. It used to break Jimmy's heart when he had to cut down a tree, but this guy might as well be a dentist pulling a tooth.

'Couldn't you transplant it somewhere else?' she asked him, and he grinned at her indulgently. 'I'd have thought a tree surgeon's daughter would know better.'

Oh. So he remembered what little she'd told him about herself? She said nothing more, letting Marina entertain him until, to her chagrin, Azalea called Marina indoors to a phone call. Crossing his legs, he sat back in his chair and regarded her coolly.

'So, how's the Irish ambassador this morning?'

Reluctantly, she grinned. 'She's fine thank you.'

'H'm. Shouldn't she be back home where she belongs, setting Ireland to rights?'

Stung, she looked at him. 'But according to you Ireland is perfect already, there's nothing to fix.'

They gazed at each other. Then he peered at her. 'Do you ever miss it, at all?'

'Occasionally. What about you? Or have you forgotten everything about it, after such a lengthy absence?'

He shifted on his seat, and looked out over the lawn. 'I miss the taste of Barry's tea. And Tayto crisps. And Galtee sausages.'

She laughed outright. Such things hallmarked him immediately as a countryman, one who hadn't been back for a long time. 'Is that all? Food?'

'No. Don't be naive. It's not the food, it's the associations. A packet of Tayto crisps was my big treat on Saturdays, if I'd been good all week . . . my mother used to drink Barry's tea and fry Galtee sausages for us kids, they remind me of her and of our kitchen. I can still taste them and I can see it, with her bustling round in her blue apron.'

'Oh? And is she still there? Still alive?'

'No' he said abruptly, and fell silent. After a few moments she felt impelled to close the yawning gap. 'I'd have thought it would be the Guinness you'd miss.'

'I don't drink stout any more. It's not the same here. Besides, it's fattening.'

'So it is. You're a weight watcher, then?'

'I watch whatever I have to watch.' For a moment he fell silent again, and then he stood up. 'Marina doesn't appear to be coming back. I may as well get started on the cherry tree. Want to watch?'

His tone was slightly mocking and she was about to refuse when she thought of Jimmy, who'd so often had to do this job himself. She had seen him plant many things, but she had never seen him cut down a tree; it was dangerous for little girls, he'd said when she was small, and then later he'd told her 'it would only upset you.' Well, now she was an adult, it was a small reality to face up to. 'All right,' she said, deliberately brisk, 'somebody had better supervise you. I'm sure Marina doesn't want the branches coming through her windows.'

It satisfied her that this caught him off guard, the way his mouth briefly opened before he checked himself. 'You forget' he retorted, 'that I've been Marina's landscaping consultant a lot longer than you've been her nurse. I know exactly what I'm doing.'

'Landscaping consultant? In Ireland they're still mostly called gardeners.'

Not deigning to reply, he set off, to his jeep round the front where he threw his jacket into the back and exchanged it for a buzz saw, a pair of gauntlets, an eye shield and a roll of extension cable.

'Here. Go plug this in for me.'

Huh? No please, no would-you-mind? Ignorant lout, she thought as she went inside to do it, and came back out to find him gazing at the tree, assessing the geometry of its relationship to the house. Then, without further ado, he seized the saw and made a first incision on the near side. Involuntarily she winced, and he looked up at her laconically.

'Sad, isn't it?'

'Tragic' she retorted, 'that you're not able to save it.'

But the saw drowned out her words, and the flying splinters forced her to move back until, with a rending groan, the trunk toppled forwards. She felt her heart breaking with the wood, but Patrick straightened up and merely nodded. 'There we go. You can't make an omelette without breaking eggs. If you'd like to make yourself useful, Nurse Reilly, you can get the hand saw and start cutting off the smaller branches. I suppose Marina will want some carpenter to make them up into pencil holders or something.'

'Possibly she will. We're not all as callous as you seem to be.'

He pulled up his eye shield and regarded her with a look like frozen malachite. 'You don't know the first thing about me.'

'No,' she agreed, 'I don't. You're not exactly the chatty type, are you?'

He wasn't. But—! It was suddenly maddening to be so dismissed, so misunderstood, and as he looked at her bending over the branches, touching them tenderly, he felt a dangerous surge of something. For nearly twenty years he had mastered these reckless flashes, survived every provocation, and he was aghast when, out of today's blue sky, he heard himself snap like a twig.

'I'm not chatty at all,' he retorted, 'but it's not for lack of anything to say.'

'Really? So what would you have to say, if America were a free country and you had the power of free speech?'

Her arch tone stung like something shot from a catapult. 'I'd say' he riposted, 'that you're no open book yourself. You're on the run . . . from who or what I don't know, but you've got the cut of a refugee about you.'

She lifted her head and met his gaze, eyed him keenly. 'Is that so? Well, Mr Nulty, perhaps it takes one to know one?'

They stared at each other. And then, abruptly, she marched off to get the saw, leaving him looking as if she'd turned the hose full blast on him.

Justine Adams was a tall, pliant redhead with a passion for sport and she aroused two strong emotions in Ivor: one was vast relief that he'd finally found a bed partner, and the other was delight that he'd found a tennis partner. Justine threw herself into both activities with brio, matching his physical strength with some very sneaky stratagems, making him work for every point he scored. He was entranced by the way she threw a ball in the air and poised for a split second before hitting it; he loved the way her hair whipped round her face as she swung forwards, the way it curled and stuck to the nape of her neck when she'd worked up a sweat. At twenty-two she was as sleek and fit as a racehorse, full of energy and a bouncy lightness that was very appealing. What he saw in Justine was exactly what he got, a blithe uncomplicated girl with a bright smile and sunny disposition, fleet of foot and light of heart. After his harsh chill exile her skin felt warm as sun-baked cedar, her brown eyes glowed golden, and from the moment he met her Ivor was nailed to Justine's rangy, lycra-skimmed side, thinking of only one thing – sex, sex and more sex. Justine supplied it unquestioningly, unstintingly, and Ivor could not get enough of it, felt as if he'd been rescued at the very last moment from a sinking ship. Justine was warm and supple and, in his deliriously relieved opinion, the most delicious woman in all of Spain, arguably all of Europe.

Working as a waitress in a big busy restaurant didn't faze her at all, her only complaint was the smokers she had to put up with for the sake of the tips, and hey, it was only a short-term job. Just transient, Ivor enquired, not a 'career'? No way, she asserted, careers didn't interest her, although she'd probably end up working at something-or-other eventually, back home in Adelaide. Before getting on that hamster wheel she was 'doing Europe' and had decided to settle in Seville for a while; it was a buzzy city and she wanted to learn Spanish, might become an interpreter some hopefully distant day. She wasn't in any hurry to start, but at least interpreting was varied and sociable – nothing could be more boring than sitting in the same office shuffling the same pointless old paperwork every day for forty years, could it? Ivor heartily agreed that it couldn't, and warmed to Justine for her simple, unstressed airiness. She was vivacious and casual and here, he thought, was one woman who wouldn't rate her work higher than she rated him.

It was a pleasure to discover that she rated him quite highly, candidly complimenting him on his 'great bod' and infinite reserves of sexual energy (he didn't tell her how long he'd been storing them up). She kissed him with eager, luscious lips, she stroked his skin with a featherlight touch, and she enthusiastically endorsed his courage when he told her of his aborted climb up Dublin's corporate ladder.

'Good for you! Life's too short! So when do I get to see some of your carpentry?'

He took her to see the workshop, in which she delighted, and then he snuck her into Miguel's house to see the horror of what passed for home. 'Oh, my!' she gasped shuddering, 'this is truly Chillsville!' That was exactly the word for it; even now in May a ray of sunlight had yet to penetrate the gloom, and Ivor felt somewhat heroic when she wondered how on earth he had weathered the winter there. Her own abode, a small but bright studio on the Calle San Luis nearby, barely accommodated the two of them, but Ivor felt snug as a bug in it as his nocturnal visits became more or less a fixture. But he felt uneasy that he couldn't chip in to food or electricity bills, now that his one-off fee from Miguel was running out.

'Why not sell a bit of your work?' Justine suggested. 'Put an ad up in shop windows or something?'

This inspired Ivor to ask Miguel whether he could make some pieces on his own time, if Miguel would defer payment for the wood until they were sold? Grudgingly, Miguel agreed that Ivor could give it a try, provided he confined his activities to Sundays or early mornings, didn't get in the way of daily business. Instantly Ivor placed a free ad in a local freesheet: 'carpenter available' and waited for the commissions to roll in. The ones that did were humbling, mostly requests for shelves from women living alone, a dog kennel in one instance, but they yielded enough that he could contribute, and salve his dignity. After all he'd only been at it six months, and a man had to start somewhere. The municipal masterpieces could wait. Meanwhile, after a hectically sexual start, he began to get to know Justine, and to feel comfortable with her almost to the point of happiness.

It wasn't a profound happiness, because Justine was not a profound girl, but it was fun and it was reviving, combined with the warming sun it put him in a cheerful, mellow frame of mind, and he could hardly believe the upturn in events. The first time he slept with Justine he didn't even have to brace himself against comparisons with Shivaun, because there wasn't time, his body sprinted way ahead of his mind, and thereafter he made a resolution. He was going to enjoy Justine, and live each day as it came, looking neither forwards nor backwards. There was considerable freedom in this attitude, which Justine shared, and it worked very well. Often they laughed over nothing, and talked about less, with their arms around each other as they wandered through the streets at dusk, partaking in the *paseo* like old hands. Once or twice they dropped into a shop called Antiguedades Angel Luis Friazza, which sold over-the-top Spanish furniture, and Justine hooted. 'Boy, is this stuff fussy or what! I bet you can make much nicer!'

It was the first encouraging thing anyone had ever said to him, apart from Miguel's brief admiration of the crib, and he looked at Justine with genuine gratitude. Her idea of furniture was something to sit on and something to eat off, but she was so positive, so generous and optimistic. He was really beginning to like her, he realised, a lot. She was generous with everything, her time and her laughter and her lithe, beckoning body, and even after the toughest day's work she always shrugged it off, saying she was way too young to be tired. For the first time in six months, Ivor found his own muscles aching less, and his sense of resilient youth resurging like molten lava.

The next time Patrick's dark green jeep drew up at Chederlay, Shivaun was packing Marina and Kathy Shreve into her little red convertible, and merely returned his wave. But he jumped out of his jeep and called to her before she had time to start the engine.

'Girls' day out, huh? New hats all round?'

'I' replied Marina briskly, 'am going to visit my specialist actually. Kathy is coming into Boston with us because she needs some equipment for her work. Nobody has any frivolous plans at all. Good morning to you, Patrick.'

With a regal wave she dismissed him, and Shivaun grinned as she drove off, wondering whether Marina had deliberately scheduled her medical appointment so that Patrick would be left to work on his own at Chederlay. Dorothy was on a day off, and apart from Azalea the house was empty. Marina made no secret of the distance she preferred to maintain from the man, although she never explained it beyond her vague curiosity as to what had originally brought Patrick to America. Interested in everyone and everything, it provoked her that she had never found out, and she said she found him 'taciturn'.

In Boston they dropped Kathy off at an art supply shop; since leaving Bill she had no car of her own, and was grateful for the ride.

'A pleasure' Marina purred, 'to help a woman who does so much to help herself. I'm sure by this time next year you'll be driving a Lexus, Kathy.'

Kathy nodded and beamed, exuding new confidence as she disappeared into the shop. Shivaun drove Marina on to the specialist's consulting rooms at the hospital, where she was left to read endless magazines while tests were conducted. After nearly two hours, Marina reappeared, looking annoyed and accompanied by the specialist.

'Nurse Reilly?' he asked, frowning over his bifocals. Fiftyish, formal and firm, Dr George Lawson was a noted neurologist, to whom Steven Hunt referred many patients and even, on occasion, deferred.

Shivaun jumped up. 'Yes?'

'A word, please, about our patient.' He indicated that she should step into his office, but Marina waved an impatient hand. 'Oh, for God's sake George, I'm not a child, just say whatever it is you have to say. Shivaun will tell me anyway.'

Dr Lawson sighed and plunged his hands into the pockets of his white coat. 'Very well then, let's all be clear here. Marina is moving far too fast, Nurse Reilly, and now she tells me she even plans to visit Europe in the summer. I've told her that this is out of the question, and it's your job to make sure she does no such thing. I'm horrified to hear she's already been on a working trip to Utah. You're her nurse and you should know the dangers of travel, how stressful it is.'

Shivaun nodded. 'Yes. I do know. But getting back to work is cheering Marina up, doing her good—'

'Please allow me to judge how much good. My verdict is that she can work at home at her desk, make the occasional short trip, nothing further than New York at most. If she ventures beyond that, for more than a day, I will not be responsible for the consequences. You will.'

Marina snorted. 'Oh, really, George, don't be such a colossal bore! You hardly expect Shivaun to tie me to my chair, when I feel perfectly—'

Ignoring her, the specialist continued to address Shivaun. 'It's up to you to restrain her. Need I say more, or do I make myself understood?'

Ruefully, Shivaun nodded. 'Yes. You do. I'll try to put the brakes on her.'

'Pah!' Marina swept her linen wrap around her and headed for the door. 'What a pair of fusspots! Come along, Shivaun, I want to call into Downtown Crossing and pick up those books I ordered. Goodbye, George.'

Out she marched, and Shivaun barely had time to whisper to the doctor that she would call him later for a chat.

'Make sure you do,' he said, 'Marina still needs a lot more care than she realises. Or admits.'

Sorry to hear it in one way, Shivaun was delighted in another.

Marina fidgeted and protested all the way home, insisting that her new European clients lived in the Cotswolds and where on earth could be more restful than that?

'Chederlay' Shivaun said firmly.

'Oh, don't you start! You'll come to the Cotswolds with me, we'll have a great time, nip into London at night for a bit of fun.'

'Right. And then you'll be stretchered home in an air ambulance. Sorry, Marina, but England's going to have to wait.'

'Huh. Well, if you're going to side with George, then I'll get Steven to work on him. He'll let me go, you'll see.'

Pouting, Marina examined her nails sulkily, and Shivaun laughed, thinking that she looked like a thwarted child.

'Face the facts, Marina. You're grounded.'

'Is that so, Nurse Reilly? Then you're – you're fired!'

Shivaun laughed aloud, and grinned at her. 'Oh, stop whinging. You'll get wrinkles, you know, if you scowl like that. Tell you what. I'll let you have a gin and tonic when we get home.'

Marina looked at her, hopefully. 'And a cigarette?'

'No! Your smoking days are over and you may as well face that too.'

'Huh. Well, I must say, you're a great one to be telling people to face things.'

'Hey? What's that supposed to mean?'

For a moment Marina was silent, considering. But then she ploughed on. 'You're delighted about this, aren't you? Delighted that George thinks I still need nursing? It means you can stay on here and not have to decide yet where to go next, whether to go back to Ireland or not.'

Shivaun hesitated only fractionally before deciding to be honest. 'Yes. I'm sorry for your sake. But I do admit I'm in no hurry to leave you, Marina. I – I'm very fond of you, you know.'

Unexpectedly, almost shyly, Marina laid her palm lightly on Shivaun's arm. 'Yes. I do know. And I'm very fond of you, too. For all my money and staff and ritzy pals, I sometimes think that you and Azalea are my best friends. There aren't many people who care about me the way you do.'

Surprised more by the gesture than the words, Shivaun turned to smile warmly at her. 'Of course we care. You – you're like our surrogate mum!'

Marina gazed down at the floor of the car. 'Yes, well, Azalea has her own mom, or mum as you say, and she has Jeff. But you . . . if I'd ever had a daughter, I'd have liked one like you. I think we understand each other, Shivaun, don't we?'

'Yes,' she agreed, 'we do. Neither of us has a family, but at least now we have each other. You remind me so much of Viv . . . if I ever have kids, Marina, you'll have to be their godmother!'

Marina smiled wryly, but Shivaun saw she was both touched

and pleased. 'If you ever have kids, Shivaun, I'll be their *grand*mother, and you'll be bringing them here to Chederlay to spend every summer with me.'

Shivaun swung the car into the drive, and beamed. 'Right. That's a deal. Massachusetts every summer, to visit Granny Marina.'

'*Mémé* Marina,' Marina corrected her loftily, '*Mémé*. I am French after all, it sounds more appropriate, darling, don't you think?'

Azalea was in her office, looking rather smug Shivaun thought when she went into it.

'We're having drinks in the library, fancy one before you leave?'

'Sure. Be right with you.'

She was winding up the last of the work on her desk, and Shivaun peered curiously at her.

'You look like the cat that swallowed the canary. What have you been up to?'

'Oh, nothing much.'

'Such as?'

'Oh . . . just paperwork. Bills, salary cheques, faxes, dinner arrangements for tonight.'

'Dinner? Is Marina going out? Or are you?'

Looking up, Azalea smiled airily. 'No. You are.'

Shivaun blinked. 'I am? But I – what do you mean?'

'I mean . . . Patrick is taking you out. To Rockport I believe, he knows a nice little restaurant there and I told him you'd love it.'

'I – what? Azalea, what are you talking about!?'

Sweeping up her papers and clicking off her computer, Azalea laughed, wickedly. 'Well, after you left this morning, he did a lot of work around the garden and then we had a late lunch together. He asked so many questions about you that in the end I said why didn't he just ask you them all himself. So then he said, why not, were you busy tonight and did I think you'd accept if he asked you out to dinner? I said you were free as a bird and you'd love to—'

'Azalea! You didn't! He – he didn't!'

'Jeez, Shivaun, stop gabbling! It's only a casual supper.'

'But – but Patrick Nulty detests me, and I detest him!'

'Yeah – well, he did mention your quite unreasonable coolness to him, but I assured him he was entirely imagining it. I told him you're just shy and that if he wanted to get to know you better, you'd really enjoy having a chat with him. That was when he mentioned this restaurant in Rockport. They do terrific oysters and crayfish, I said you love crayfish—'

Shivaun was aghast. 'You – you witch! You've set me up!'

Lazily, Azalea nodded. 'Yeah. I guess I have. You may as well get dolled up and wear those nice shoes of yours, because the restaurant has a little dance floor, live music . . . Jeff sometimes takes me there when I'm good. Now, what did you say about a drink?'

She waltzed off towards the library, and Shivaun marched after her, fuming.

'Marina! Wait till you hear what Azalea has done! You won't believe it!'

Marina was sitting in state, with Jiffy on one side of her chair and Daffy on the other, and as was her custom when Dorothy was absent, she indicated that the girls should help themselves from the drinks cabinet.

'Plenty of lime for me please, Shivaun – now, what are you so steamed up about? What has Azalea done?'

Shivaun seized the gin and poured liberally. 'She's set me up on a *date*! With Patrick Bloody Nulty! Tonight! In Rockport!'

Azalea laughed as she flopped into an armchair with the drink Shivaun frostily held out to her, and raised her glass as she crossed her long legs. 'Cheers. Here's to Mother Ireland. I just thought it was time you two compatriots buried the hatchet, that's all.'

But Marina frowned. 'Azalea, you know Shivaun doesn't – doesn't care for Patrick. You really had no business to do this.'

'Oh, chill out, Marina. He was just asking me a lot of questions about her, that's all. Since I didn't know the answers to half of them, I thought she may as well answer for herself.'

'What questions? What did he want to know?'

Marina sounded cross and, Shivaun suddenly realised, protective. But Azalea was unrepentant. 'He wanted to know how she got her job here and what part of Ireland she was from and whether she was going back to Ireland and—'

'And' said Marina slowly, 'all the information he never discloses about himself. I think he had a nerve. And frankly Azalea, so had you. It's not up to you to make arrangements for Shivaun without even consulting her – Shivaun, you don't have to go if you don't want to. You can call him and cancel.'

'But then,' Azalea persisted, 'he'll simply ask her to arrange it for another night. She can't say she's busy for the next six months, can she? Besides, he's gone dashing off to Lowell to change and get ready, the restaurant is booked for eight o'clock – she may as well go and get it over with!'

Marina drew breath to argue, and Shivaun saw that she was getting irate. Exactly what stroke victims were not supposed to get. Clenching her glass in her hand, she forced herself to calm down. 'Oh, never mind, Marina, since it's apparently all organised I may as well just do it. Who knows? Maybe it'll even be a nice restaurant.'

'It is' Azalea asserted forcefully. 'At the very worst, you'll have a delicious dinner and a casual chat about the price of Irish potatoes. I'm not exactly sending you out to the guillotine here.'

Shooting her a daggers look that Marina didn't see, Shivaun sighed and leaned up against the drinks cabinet. 'No. It's no big deal.'

Looking unconvinced, Marina sipped her gin and tonic. 'Well, it's up to Shivaun of course. It's no secret that Patrick Nulty is not my favourite person, but I know you like him, Azalea, and I don't suppose she'll come to any harm with him. I just wish – wish we all knew a bit more about him, that's all.'

'Well,' Azalea reasoned, 'maybe we will, if Shivaun finds

anything out. He might tell her more tonight than he's ever told us in all the years he's been working for you. Shivaun might prise him open like an oyster.'

'H'mm. Well, that would certainly be interesting. Oh, very well then, let her go – if you're sure you feel like it, Shivaun?'

Marina's face was anxious, and so Shivaun waved a nonchalant hand. 'Yeah. Let's not dramatise the guy. There's probably nothing much to find out! We'll all have a laugh about it over coffee in the morning. Now, what'll I wear – T-shirt or sweatshirt? Jeans or jeans?'

'Oh no,' Azalea interjected adamantly, 'not to this restaurant. Not for dancing.'

'Azalea,' Shivaun retorted, 'I may be having dinner with him, much to my surprise, but don't hold your breath to see me dancing with him. I'd rather dance with Muammar Ghadaffi, thanks very much.'

Thinking it might be wiser to take her own car and have the freedom of it if things went wrong, Shivaun made Azalea call Patrick to tell him she'd meet him at the restaurant, and chose some presentable but not fussy clothes to wear; it was warm enough now for a simple summer dress and sandals. Before leaving, she went to kiss Marina.

'You'll probably be in bed before I get back. Sleep well, and don't worry.'

'H'm. I may or may not worry, or sleep well, or be in bed when you get back. That's a nice perfume you're wearing, what is it?'

'Oh, it's just the same one I always wear, nothing special! Ivor gave it to me last summer. But it's nearly all gone now. Anyway, I'm taking the mobile so you can call me if you need me – call me whether you do or not, then I can pretend there's a crisis if I want to get away!'

'OK. I will. Good idea. I'll call you around ten.'

'Great. See you later then, or in the morning.'

As Shivaun departed it struck her that Marina herself would now have to dine alone tonight, and she felt a pang. Dammit, why couldn't Azalea fix Marina up with some man, if she had to go into the dating-fixing business! But Marina, for all her beauty and style and charm, was probably the kind of woman who scared men . . . and her age was against her, in this youth-mad environment. Feeling suddenly sorry for her, and protective as if roles were reversed, Shivaun kissed her again, and went off to meet Patrick Nulty.

Chapter Twelve

'I'll have a baby Caesar,' Shivaun decided, 'and the crayfish please.'

The waiter jotted and smiled at her and she looked at him bemused, as if he might be able to explain what on earth she was doing here with this man. Granted, Patrick looked well, clean and fresh in Chinos and a pale linen jacket, somehow younger than he did in his hefty working clothes. But honestly—! It all felt too bizarre for words.

'I'll have the oysters,' he said amiably, 'and then a steak, medium rare with green vegetables – crispy, no potatoes.'

The waiter swished away and she wanted to shout after him – no, don't leave me here alone with him, we loathe each other, this is going to be a disaster! But the waiter vanished inexorably, and Patrick smiled sociably.

'So, d'you like American food, Shivaun?'

She was glad he'd picked something positive to start out with. 'Yes, I love it, especially the seafood, the way nobody has to save up for a month to afford it . . . I saw a kid on the beach the other day eating crab claws straight out of a carton, just the way nature intended. The pizzas are great too, and the ice-cream, Marina fattened me up on that when I arrived.'

He surveyed her with a wry grin, and she was as surprised as a child with a new doll; hey, it could smile if you pushed its buttons!

'Well, Marina didn't make a very good job of it. You can't weigh more than what, a hundred pounds?'

'Hah! A hundred and twenty-six! I've been living the life of – well, the life of Reilly since I came here!'

She laughed as it struck her and he laughed too, his face relaxing so that he looked different in the candlelight, quite normal and cheerful.

'Uh-huh. And what have you been doing exactly?'

She sat back and thought about it, vaguely noting the other diners around her, the nets and marine décor, the three musicians playing gently at the far end of the room. 'I've been earning a ridiculous amount of money for work I love. I've been cycling and reading Sinclair Lewis, skiing, visiting Utah, making friends . . . I've been having an absolutely wonderful time.'

He raised an interrogatory eyebrow. 'Better than you were having at home, huh?'

'Yes. Way better. This is a gorgeous part of the world and everyone has been so friendly – well, I wouldn't be too nuts about Steven Hunt, but everyone else, Marina mothers me and Azalea's practically like a sister—'

The waiter arrived with their starters and he waited until the dishes were distributed before leaning forward, with a slightly confidential air, to murmur at her.

'Did you know that Steven Hunt's eldest daughter is epileptic? He has an older brother in a wheelchair too, the guy got caught in some ambush in Viet Nam when he was a kid . . . I often see them at baseball or football games, Steven gets him out and around as much as he can.'

'God, really? No, I didn't know that. It – it kind of puts him in a different light.'

'Yeah. Steven's an asshole in many ways, but the more you know about someone, the more it helps to understand him, how he got to where he is . . . tell me, Shivaun, how did you get to where you are?'

In a flash she was fencing, on guard. She still didn't know what had piqued his curiosity, but her life story was none of his business.

'Where I am? Well, where exactly is that, in your opinion?'

He didn't immediately reply; instead he filled her glass and his own, lifted an oyster aloft and swallowed it thoughtfully, gracefully. She was glad to see he was not the kind of Irishman who suspected anything in a shell, or demanded potatoes or Guinness to go with it. Either Patrick Nulty had been expensively educated, she thought, or America had put manners on him. He had the comfortable aura of someone who ate out a lot, probably entertained clients in even ritzier restaurants than this one. Was his polish innate, she wondered, or acquired? Her own ease was entirely due to Viv, who'd insisted she be taken to restaurants from the age of sixteen . . . and then later Ivor had taken her to some nice ones, too. For one startling second, her mind flew to Ivor, his fine features sharply contrasting with the broader, more rugged ones before her. Despite tonight's impeccable manicure, shave and preppie clothing, Patrick still somehow had the texture of a man who worked outdoors, his skin was tanned and his hands were robust.

'You're on the ocean floor. Scuba diving, struggling up to the surface from some deep scary dive . . . something frightened you, way down there on the ocean bed, and now you're kicking back up to the light and air before it grabs you by the ankles and pulls you back down.'

Even as his unexpected words washed over her she could hear the swish of ocean currents, feel the swirl and the tug . . . but she could see the sun glinting overhead too, the rising breaking bubbles that told her she was nearing safety. With resolute nonchalance, she sipped some Perrier.

'Well. What a colourful imagination you have. Tonight I'm an underwater diver. The other day I was a refugee on the run. It wouldn't be possible that I'm just in America to have some fun, no? Footloose and fancy-free, seeing the world, that kind of thing?'

He impaled a cluster of snow peas on his fork and considered, twirling them in mid-air.

'No. I don't think so. You strike me as the kind of girl who likes to be – um – grounded. Earthed. Not blowing in the wind, rolling along like a tumbleweed.'

She reflected in turn. 'H'mm. OK. You could be right about that. But then at your age I guess you must be a bit of an expert on all kinds of girl.'

Grinning, she determined to make light of his unsettlingly accurate perception, and turn the conversation round on him. It appeared to work, and he smiled with a rueful shrug.

'I guess I must, at thirty-six.'

'Mmm. That's a fair old age. How old were you when you came to America?'

'Eighteen.'

'What – is that all? But then you've spent most of your life here . . . you're American, really.'

'Yes. In many ways. But not all. The childhood years are very formative.'

Yes. She knew they were. 'You said you grew up in the midlands? On a farm? In the darkest Ireland of – what – the mid-sixties?'

'Yes. It's funny to think now that it was the time of the Stones and the Beatles, that the rest of the western world was heading into flower power and mass telecommunication . . . our little world consisted only of what we could see and touch around us, the fields and animals, the sky and the earth, Brennan's bread, Cadbury's chocolate, confession on Saturdays and mass on Sundays. Rain. Hurleys. Fights in the school yard. Darned socks that rubbed your heels raw. Mrs O'Hagan's navy wool hat, she wore it like a warrior's helmet for donkey's years . . . may be wearing it yet for all I know.'

His voice trailed off, his gaze was wandering away, and she wondered whether she was the first Irish person he had spoken to for a long time.

'But Patrick, Shannon airport is only six hours away. If you wonder what Ireland's like today, why don't you go back and find out?'

For a moment he said nothing. Then his gaze returned to her, his eyes dark as jasper. But his voice lightened, he laughed rather metallically. 'Or why don't you tell me what it's like, that'd be cheaper!'

Cheaper? But he had lots of money, a plane ticket wouldn't cost him a thought! Bemused, Shivaun tried to think back to Ireland, realising as she did so that it had receded in her mind, felt a long way off.

'I told you when we went skiing what it's like now. Prosperous, corrupt, full of burger joints and chewing gum. Like a tacky little American colony really, or British – the shopping streets and malls are full of Nike, HMV, McDonald's, Marks and Spencer, Boots . . .'

'*Boots?*' He seemed amazed. 'Boots The Chemists?'

'Yes! Every British brand Ireland ever wanted. My mother told me that when she was young it was everyone's dream to be able to get Mars bars and Opal Fruits, to shop in Habitat or Mothercare . . . well, the dream came true.'

He looked perplexed out of all proportion to the issue. 'But, Shivaun – d'you mean just Dublin, or everywhere?'

'I suppose I mean mostly Dublin. But Limerick and Cork aren't far behind, even Galway. Ireland just can't get enough stuff from Curry's and Next, Laura Ashley and Virgin, every British brand in creation. It's funny really – when my dad was a kid there was a slogan, "Burn everything British except their coal."'

'Yes,' he murmured looking dazed, 'I remember it. My father used to say it too.'

'Well, he was wasting his breath! It's shop-till-you-drop time in Ireland now. Not that I've anything against shopping. I just wish . . . wish there wasn't so much crime as well. The place is awash on drugs and nobody believes a word the government says about anything any more, there've been so many scandals. I wasn't exaggerating, you know, that night in the ski cabin.'

'No,' he said, looking closely at her, 'perhaps you weren't. You were so vehement . . . why was that?'

For a fleeting moment she almost told him, was tempted to pour out the whole story about Jimmy and Viv and Jason Dean. But she still scarcely knew Patrick Nulty, was still reserving judgement on whether she even liked him. She wasn't going to get personal.

'I was angry' she said finally. 'My hospital had been closed down. I'd worked there for years and I loved it, we all did, it was a landmark in the community and it was small enough that we could give the patients personal, individual attention. Then the stupid bloody minister decided it would be more economic to merge it with some massive hypermarket hospital out in some faceless suburb. It made me feel like Ireland has no time for individual human beings any more, everything's all about economics and cutting corners. The big hospitals are already flooded, patients lie in corridors for days on trolleys . . . as a nurse I felt there was something radically wrong. And now, the irony is that I earn twice as much for nursing one woman in comfort as I did for working twice as hard back home. Nurses are underpaid and undervalued in Ireland, they have to go on strike even to get a decent living wage.'

She heard her voice rising, and checked it abruptly. 'So. That's why I got mad that first night we spoke.' Her face felt flushed, and she became aware that he was scrutinising it intently.

'I see. So that's why you came over here. I guess I was wrong.'

'Wrong? Were you? Why did you think I came?'

He sat back and drank some wine, fiddled with the unfinished steak on his plate.

'I thought maybe there was a man in the picture. Male ego I guess. You looked to me like a woman with a broken heart under her belt.'

She was both surprised and pleased to find that she could laugh. 'Well. Yes. That was another factor. I'd broken up with a man I adored. We'd been together since we were toddlers.'

'Toddlers.' He repeated the word and seemed to dwell on it. 'But surely toddlers can't—?'

'Oh, they can. They're very strong-willed. Ivor Lawlor and I knew we'd been born for each other. But then last year things suddenly . . . changed. We broke up. Or maybe we just grew up. We—'

The phone in her pocket vibrated soundlessly, and she realised it must be Marina calling, ten o'clock already? Mobiles weren't permitted in the restaurant, so she excused herself and went outside, smiled as Marina's fretful voice punctuated the starry, velvety night air.

'No, it's OK, don't worry! We're just talking, nobody has punched anybody yet. He isn't even wearing what Alana would call his broody Gabriel Byrne face tonight. Go to sleep and I'll see you tomorrow.'

Clicking off, she returned to Patrick, and as she neared their table she saw that he was lost in thought, looking a little broody after all, leaning his chin on his hands and staring at the low-key musicians without appearing to hear a note they were playing. The plates still sat on the table around him, as if the waiters had either forgotten their corner or discreetly decided to leave it alone.

It also dawned on her, as she went to sit down and Patrick rose briefly, politely, that she still hadn't learned very much about him, not nearly as much as he now knew about her.

'So, where were we? On your farm in the Irish midlands?'

'No, we were—'

'So tell me, why did you leave it?'

He didn't answer. Instead there was a long silence, in which he seemed to be reminiscing, or deliberating, or both.

'Patrick?' She waved her hand in front of his face. 'Earth calling . . . are you receiving me?'

He snapped alert, and smiled. 'Sorry. I was miles away.'

'Yes, well, that's not very flattering! You're the one who asked me out, remember? Why did you, anyway? I thought you didn't like me at all.'

Again he hesitated, but then apparently decided to return her candour.

'No. I didn't like you at all, at first. You didn't like me either, did you?'

'No. I could've killed Azalea for arranging this.'

'H'mm. Well, perhaps I should have invited you myself, directly. But Azalea likes us both. I thought I might stand a better chance doing it through her. And it seems I was right.'

'Yes. But why did you do it?'

'I did it because . . . because you intrigued me. Caught my attention.'

'How so?'

'You said – when I said you looked like a refugee, the day we were chopping up the cherry tree, you said I looked like one too.'

'No,' she corrected, 'I said maybe it takes one to know one. Was I right? Are you running away from something, or someone?'

He put his hand behind his ear and brushed back a lock of hair, rubbed his cheek with his forefinger. 'I . . . oh, God, Shivaun. What made you think that?'

'I don't really know. It was just a sudden flash of – something or other. Call it feminine intuition if you like. Anyway, I hit some kind of nerve, didn't I?'

He lowered both his tone and his eyes, studied the pattern on the tablecloth and traced it with his fork. 'Yes. Maybe you did. Maybe, after eighteen years, I . . .'

His sentence hung in the air unfinished, and she had no idea what suddenly enabled her to complete it. All she knew was the certainty of someone tuning into a wavelength, picking up some distant, crackling signal.

'You should move on? Is that what you were going to say? It's time to pick up and run off again, because Shivaun Reilly has—'

Something else hit her. 'Patrick, you don't hang out in Irish bars or clubs, do you? You don't socialise with Irish people?'

He looked defiant, but she thought she caught something evasive in him too.

'No. I don't. Too busy.'

'Right. And you've been too busy to go back to Ireland for eighteen years. But you're not too busy to go skiing. Or to have dinner here with me tonight. Azalea says you're shy, but

Denis says you're a loner. He doesn't like you, and Marina's not sure about you either, after all the time you've worked for her. Patrick, what is going on here? Who or what are you running *from*?'

No answer. Evading her gaze, he looked around as if for the waiter, but none was in sight, and the colour began to rise in his face. Rise hectically, she thought – and yet he had invited her here of his own volition, almost as if . . . what? He must have known she would be curious, ask questions, if he didn't welcome them he must at least have expected them.

'Patrick, you don't have to answer me. I apologise if I'm treading off limits here, if there's been a – a divorce or bereavement or something. But Jesus, you're not running away from anything worse, are you? Not from the – the police or anything? You can't be, not after eighteen years here, you're an established businessman – Patrick, answer me! This is *unnerving*!'

Dropping his fork with a clang, he sat bolt upright and faced her full on, with something between anger and – she couldn't make out what.

'Don't be ridiculous! I am an established businessman, as you say, respected if not universally popular, and I assure you that the police are not looking for me!'

She was engulfed with relief. 'But then who is? You're not the only one who can detect a refugee, I can too – so who *are* you running from?'

As swiftly as it had risen, his anger seemed to subside, and he sank back in his chair looking stricken. When he spoke he was almost inaudible.

'Myself. I'm running away from myself, Shivaun. That's all. Only me.'

She was completely nonplussed. For several moments they sat facing each other until the waiter, sensing a hiatus, came to clear the table and sociably propose dessert. But neither of them wanted anything.

'Just coffee, please.'

Even after it was poured the silence continued; he seemed

lost in thought and she was trying to put some shape on hers. Eventually, she was able to articulate calmly.

'If you're running away from yourself, Patrick, I think maybe you'll run a long way. For a long time.'

She spoke quietly, and he nodded. 'Yes. I already have. But not far enough or long enough.'

'I see. Do you want to tell me why?'

She sensed that he did. Something under his skin seemed to be almost visibly struggling to get out, she could see that he was doing battle with himself. His next remark left her dumbfounded.

'So, tell me more about yourself. And this Ivor guy. And your family.'

'But – but we're talking about *you*! I can't just switch off like that!'

'Off me? Sure you can. I'm not worth the time of day. Would you like a brandy or something, Baileys maybe?'

She was so shocked, she would have said yes if she didn't have the car, was sorry now she hadn't taken a taxi. 'No, I can't – thank you anyway.'

Briefly, lightly, his hand touched hers. 'Look, I'm sorry if I upset you. It's all ancient history.'

What was it Viv used to say? That ancient history was the root of all evil? That only the winners got to tell their side of it? That it took ten generations to clear the skeletons out of family closets? The room was very warm, and she felt faintly dizzy.

'Whatever you say. Let's forget it, then.'

'Sure. Are you OK? You look a little pale.'

'I'm fine.'

'All right. Then let me get the bill, and take you outside. A breath of air will freshen you up. Pity we didn't get to do any dancing.'

Other couples were dancing now, and she thought that if the conversation hadn't taken the turn it had she would have liked to join them. She hadn't danced anywhere, with anyone, for ages. For a sickening moment she thought with absolute longing of Ivor – and then, slowly and deliberately, she sat up straight, took a deep breath and smiled at Patrick.

'Actually, I'd love to dance.'

Taken aback, he frowned at her. 'Would you? Really?'

'Yes, really. Why don't you wait here and keep our table while I just go splash my face?'

She smiled brightly, and waltzed off to what the Americans so aptly called the restroom. There she doused herself in cold water, fixed her make-up, took another deep breath and confronted herself in the mirror.

You're crazy. This guy is trouble. You don't want to dance with him.

Yes. I do. I'm twenty-five years old and I want to dance, if not with Ivor goddamn Lawlor then with Patrick goddamn Nulty. He's on the run but so am I, and I think maybe we're both very tired of running. Let's dance instead.

Let's!

Virtually overnight, it seemed, Seville had turned from a fridge into a furnace. Ivor lay on Justine's narrow bed, sweltering in only his boxer shorts, wondering at the quantity of thrashing humanity such a small bed could contain. Not that anyone in their right mind could have sex *in* a bed, in this heat; they simply collapsed onto it and the floor was soon strewn with tangled, sweaty sheets. Even after midnight the heat was massive, a thick stifling blanket that forced them to throw the window wide open, whereupon the sound of two shrieking housewives and several screaming motorbikes drilled up from the street below. After six months, Ivor still marvelled at what an incredibly *noisy* country Spain was.

From somewhere further down the street he could hear men shouting, visualise them waving their glasses of beer and wine as they argued, amidst hearty insults, the pros and cons of the protest march that had taken place earlier on the Plaza Nueva. Spain was always yammering and protesting, in the apparent belief that a march a day helped you work, rest and play, and today's placards had voiced the city's furious opposition to the proposed raising of municipal charges. Wondering whether Justine might be hit by a rent increase if the levies were ratified, Ivor ran a thoughtful finger down the side of her gleaming body. She was lying on her back, leaning on his chest, idly browsing a magazine and chewing an apple; the romantic afterglow of sex never occupied her attention for more than five minutes.

'Hey, Jus. What do you make of that march today?'

'Huh?'

'The protest march. About the levies . . . d'you think they'll get through?'

She turned a page of her magazine and took another juicy bite of her apple. 'Jeez, who cares? What's it got to do with me?'

'Oh, not a lot, I suppose. I just hope your landlord doesn't put your rent up. They're all such gangster profiteers.'

'Oh well, if he does I guess I'll just have to move. I was kinda thinking about moving anyway.'

Was she? It was the first he'd heard of it. But maybe it wouldn't be a bad idea; he could move out of Miguel's hovel and they could get a bigger place together.

'Were you? To where?'

'Anywhere cooler! It's summer, it's time to be by the sea. I might go down to Malaga or Nerja. There'll be plenty of tourists now, plenty of jobs.'

What? But – where did he fit into this? Somewhat disconcerted, he kissed her shoulder, ran his tongue over the salty shiny skin. 'Oh? Well, I hear Nerja's worth seeing. It's a bit far from Miguel's workshop, though! I'd have to commute at weekends or something.'

She flicked another page. 'Yeah. Well. Whatever. If you want to stay with Miguel, I guess you'll have to figure something out. Alternatively, you could chuck Miguel and come down with me. Your Spanish is pretty OK now, you'd get work in a bar or whatever.'

His Spanish was passable, and he knew he would get work; that wasn't what threw him at all. What threw him was her apparent indifference to whether he moved with her or not, the casual way she could consider leaving him behind. Admittedly, they'd only been lovers for a couple of months, and 'love' didn't actually come into the picture at all; they were more like friends whose bodies happened to fit very nicely together. Their current loose arrangement was ideal – after all, he'd been effectively married since he was five! – and he certainly didn't want anything tighter, anything clingy or stifling. Still . . . it wasn't very flattering to feel as disposable as a bus ticket.

'Would you like me to go with you?' He stroked her neck as he said it, and she took his finger over her shoulder, kissed its tip with her juice-sticky lips, but did not turn around to look at him.

'Yeah. That'd be nice. But, I mean, I wouldn't want you to leave Miguel if you think you still have something more to learn from him.'

No. He didn't think he had. One way or another, it was nearly time to cut loose, make some decision about what to do next. The obvious thing, of course, was to return to Ireland and set up shop as a carpenter, see whether he could hack it on his own. But where in Ireland? Suburban Dublin held no appeal any more, nor did life with Cynthia . . . some coastal or rural village would be good, maybe, somewhere with a bit of character and atmosphere. But once he settled on somewhere, he'd have to start making money immediately if he was to survive. Meanwhile, it was heading into high summer here in Europe, Spain was teeming with backpackers and the streets were crammed with young, hot, noisy life – the kind of life he wanted, suddenly, to sample, throbbing with music, ablaze with flowers, overflowing out into the streets and down to the sunny, surging beaches. Nobody seemed to take life too seriously in Spain during the summer, already everything was shifting into a fun, festive mood.

Oh, feck Ireland. It could wait.

'No,' he said, 'I don't think I have much more to learn from Miguel. He'll probably be thrilled to be shot of me. I could go down to the coast with you.'

'Great,' she replied, 'you'll look cute in a bartender's apron. Especially if you don't wear anything else.'

He laughed and tugged her hair, and she turned over at last, let her magazine slide to the floor as she took him in her arms with a firm, intent grip. Again, for the second time in an hour! Briefly and bizarrely, Ivor thought of the new petrol station just open a few kilometres down the road; bright and shiny, it was a twenty-four-hour station, its pumps on the go round the clock. Clearly Justine was a girl who approved of such services.

But then, frowning, she lifted her head and looked round in the direction of the window.

'God – what *is* that racket? Sounds like they're never going to shut up down there. I know it's hot, but let me just close the window a bit. These damn Spaniards could talk for Olympic medals.'

She got up and went to close it, and as he surveyed her taut athletic body Ivor suddenly and unwillingly thought of Shivaun. Shivaun would not only have joined in the commotion, she'd probably have been out there on the Plaza Nueva today, waving her protest placard and getting arrested, shouting that the proposed levies were a bloody disgrace.

'There,' Justine smiled, 'that's better. God knows what the hell they're making such a fuss about. Hey, Ivor, about the coast, that reminds me, I must get a new bikini.'

'There you are,' Azalea smirked complacently, 'I told you so.'

Shivaun couldn't deny it. Azalea had been sure she'd get on with Patrick Nulty once the ice was broken, and now it was broken. She still wasn't sure what lay underneath, apart from some mysteriously muddy waters, but at least he seemed to have some kind of depth. Now that the spring planting was blooming he wasn't around Chederlay as much as before, apart from the occasional check-up, but once having extended the hand of friendship he did not withdraw it. Since their first dinner together, when she had so unexpectedly danced with him and revelled in the sheer physical pleasure of it, they had casually gone on several other excursions. One Sunday a client invited him to go sailing on the Charles river, and he asked her along 'for the craic'; another evening they went to a beach barbecue with Azalea, Jeff and Kathy, and Shivaun discovered what fun a clambake was. Then one day when she mentioned a trip into Boston, he arranged to meet her there for coffee. While they were having it he offered to take her sightseeing, not around the Boston she already knew, but out to its seedier, rowdier areas.

'Why?' she asked, surprised.

'Just so you'll know,' he replied, 'that America has them too, they're not exclusive to Ireland.'

She thought about it, but then she thought about Jason Dean, and turned down the invitation. The past had receded so much in her mind lately, like a neap tide that had wreaked havoc, the last thing she wanted was any reminders that might bring it flooding back. Not now, she thought, not when I've got so much better, can hold it at bay for long stretches even if I can never turn it around entirely.

When Marina asked her about her dinner with Patrick, wanted to know what they had talked about, she laughed lightly and said they had talked about Boots and Padraig Pearse.

'What?'

'Boots is a chain of British pharmacy stores,' she explained, 'and Padraig Pearse was the leader of the Irish rebellion in 1916. He was executed. I was telling Patrick how Pearse effectively died for an Ireland which today is full of British shops. Died with his Boots on, you might say.'

She grinned, and Marina frowned, said it sounded like a very curious conversation to her. But of course Shivaun must discuss whatever she liked with the men she dated. Emphatically, Shivaun asserted that she was not 'dating' Patrick Nulty.

Primly, Marina pursed her lips. 'What are you doing, then?'

'I'm hanging out a bit with him, that's all, the same as I hang out with Kathy and Denis and the others.'

'I see.' Saying no more, Marina picked up a Lalique candy dish, admired its prisms in the sunlight and blew some non-existent dust off it. Shivaun wanted to throttle her.

'Usually,' Azalea contributed helpfully, 'it's after the third date in America that things get physical. I just mention it in case you were wondering about the etiquette.'

'Azalea,' Shivaun retorted exasperated, 'I am not dating Patrick. I am not going out with him, I am not *seeing* him, he is not my vision of joy. We are not an item and I have not the faintest intention of "getting physical" as you so romantically put it.'

'Uh-huh.' Azalea nodded sagely, and Shivaun wanted to throttle her too.

It was something of a relief when Patrick neither phoned nor dropped in for about ten days after that, and when he did eventually suggest a pizza one night she turned him down because she was babysitting Kathy's boys; Bill was away at a football match and Kathy wanted to attend the opening of an art exhibition in Concord. With Marina's blessing Shivaun had even loaned Kathy the little red car, and she had biked over to the boys with a kind of grim enthusiasm. But when she got there they behaved like savages, and she began to see the difference between having babies and actually raising children. What a nightmare! You'd want to be well able for this, she thought as Kelsey wrestled her for the tv zapper and Miles waved a breadknife, before you'd embark on it. I still want kids of my own, but I'll think it through before I do it. And then only do it with a man who – 'Miles, give me that knife, *now*!' – who knows what he's getting into. Phew!

Meanwhile, the weather got hotter, and she made Marina start swimming in the pool every day, building up laps, muscles and strength. She swam in it herself too, as did Azalea, Joe and even the stately Dorothy; Marina liked everyone to enjoy it and the atmosphere around the house became summery, beachy, there were sandy footprints in the hall and shells propped on windowsills. Shivaun thought of the horrible St Peter's hospital, in whose vast system she would now be a cog if she'd stayed in Dublin, and beamed. Good old Alana had done her a huge favour . . . not that she heard much from Alana any more, which was odd, but she decided to work on the principle that no news was good news. If there were any problems with the house, if the plumbing was leaking or the slates were loose, she no longer cared. Alana was the caretaker, let her take care of it. It was too sunny to worry, she was enjoying life too much.

'What about the fourth of July?' Azalea asked Marina one morning. 'Are we doing the usual?' Marina replied that yes, they certainly were, she wanted everyone to know that she was back to her old self now – well, almost – and the flag was to fly high.

'We fly it every year, out on the lawn,' Azalea explained to Shivaun, 'and have a big party. Casual, you know, shorts and swimsuits, but big. Marina invites everyone. Even Patrick, although he rarely comes. I'd say he might come this year, though.'

'Really' Shivaun replied archly. 'Well, if there's going to be a big crowd, one more or less will hardly make any difference.'

But the fourth of July, as things turned out, was destined to make all the difference.

Shivaun had never tasted the cocktail called a Boston Tea Party, and the moment she did she knew it was a mistake. It contained rum, vodka, gin, Tia Maria and Grand Marnier, mixed with coke and some bittersweet potion, and it was absolutely delicious.

'Yum,' she said in the kitchen where she stood watching Dorothy mix huge pitchers of it, 'this is fantastic.'

'Yes, everyone loves it. But take my advice and don't drink it on an empty stomach. It's a powerful brew.'

Well, there wasn't any reason to drink it on an empty stomach, because a vat of chilli con carne was bubbling on the stove and the caterers were already filling Marina's marquee out on the lawn with trays of iced shellfish, snacks and savouries of all descriptions, and a white-toqued chef was setting up the griddle on which he would sear hamburgers, steaks and goodies galore. It was a Saturday afternoon party, and since Shivaun had had muffins for breakfast she didn't bother with lunch; there would be lots to eat for the rest of the day.

But then there was an accident. Joe Santana slipped on the wet deck of the pool, tore an ankle ligament and turned ashen with pain. Shivaun knew it was a ligament as soon as Marina called her to come examine the damage, felt the puffiness already rising over the distended joint.

'Sorry, Joe,' she said sympathetically, 'but this is a hospital job. You need strapping up, maybe a cast, and they're going to have to put you on crutches.'

'You're sure it's not broken?' Joe groaned, wincing.

'No, I'm sure it isn't, but they'll have to X-ray it just in case . . . actually, ligaments can be worse! The good news is that you'll probably be off work for a while – come on, let's get you into the car and I'll drive you to the hospital.'

Feebly, Joe protested that maybe Steven Hunt could take care of it when he arrived for the party. But Shivaun was adamant: hospital. Finally he was hauled, with help from Azalea and Dorothy, into the larger more comfortable car, and Shivaun drove him off for attention in Boston. But every town along the way was celebrating the fourth of July, as well as the city itself; several routes were diverted, streets were crowded, and it took an hour and a half to reach the hospital. There it took another hour or more for Joe to be patched up, and the return journey took as long again. By the time Joe was delivered to his home and Shivaun got back to Chederlay it was nearly four o'clock, the party was in full flight and breakfast was a very distant memory.

Shivaun heard her tummy rumbling and realised she'd better eat something, made her way towards the smoking griddle where the chef was handing out plates of food.

'Hey, Irish! How are you! C'mon, join the party!'

It was Karl Schwartz, who'd been on the skiing trip to Mount Wachusett, waving a glass in one hand and a hot dog in the other. Grinning, he kissed her with a mustardy mouth.

'What, no drink? Are you Irish or aren't you? Here, have mine, I'll go get another.' Before Shivaun could answer he thrust his full glass into her hand and wandered back to the bar, weaving rather unsteadily. Again she started off towards the food, and again she was waylaid, this time by Leigh and Rachel, whom she also remembered from the ski trip.

'Hi there! You're late! Where've you been?'

'At the hospital – Joe had an accident—' They were all concern when they heard this, and demanded details, pinning her to the spot. It was so warm she felt her T-shirt sticking to her back, and after a few minutes she raised the glass in desperation, and took a cooling sip. Wow, wonderful.

By the time she finally succeeded in acquiring a plateful of food Karl's glass was empty and she was grinning hugely. God, that Boshton Tea Party was terrific shtuff.

'You seem to be enjoying yourself' a voice murmured in her ear, and she turned to find Patrick, looking fit and tanned in cuffed shorts and a Lacoste aertex.

'Yesh – I mean yes,' she burbled, 'I am. Are you?'

'Uh-huh. Er, tell me, how many drinks have you had?'

She gazed down speculatively into her empty glass. 'Only one,' she answered truthfully, 'how about getting me another?'

He looked doubtful, but eventually did as he was asked and returned with a glass that appeared to contain more ice than anything else. She held it up and squinted into it. 'Well,' she giggled, 'that looks harmlesh.' In no time it too was empty, and she was laughing at its speedy despatch.

'Shivaun,' he said firmly, 'I really think you should sit down and eat something. Something solid and sustaining.'

'Yep,' she beamed, 'I think sho too. Where did I put my plate?'

Wide-eyed, she looked around for it, but it had vanished. Putting a commanding hand on her shoulder, Patrick instructed her to wait where she was and not move, he would go and get her something. For a few moments she stood obediently waiting, but then she saw him standing in the line for hot food, which was now lengthy, and shrugged. It was going to take him ages, she may as well go and socialise in the meantime – hey, look at that flag, all starry and stripy in the sunshine! 'High as a flag on the fourth of July,' she sang to herself, 'the corn is as high as an elephant's eye . . .' Kicking off her shoes, she sauntered amiably across the grass to Leigh and Rachel. And it all went downhill from there.

The sun was going down, and Shivaun had the distant feeling of going down with it as she sank onto the warm soft sand. How it had got to be evening she wasn't sure; it seemed like only minutes since she had been partying up on the lawn at Chederlay, dancing barefoot, laughing with everyone, having a wonderful time. But then Patrick, as she fuzzily remembered, had taken her into the kitchen and started plying her with coffee . . . when she'd baulked at the second cup, or maybe the third, he had taken her by the arm and led her out, down here to the beach, saying something about brisk walks and sea breezes. But it wasn't very breezy, only the tiniest tickle caressed her face and arms as she sat down in the dunes and he sat beside her, and they gazed in silent unison out to the gleaming, purpling horizon. Music still drifted down from the house, but it was remote, and the beach itself was quiet.

Was she still drunk? She supposed she was, and didn't care. Marina was surrounded by friends, safe and sound, while she felt her mind emptying, wandering away to nowhere in particular. Patrick offered her the sweater that was knotted round his shoulders, and she shook her head, feeling the accumulated warmth of the day, a lazy relaxing glow. For some time they simply sat there, idly pondering their separate thoughts, until eventually he turned to her with a quizzical smile.

'You OK?'

'Mmm. Fine.'

'Want to talk about it?'

'About what?'

'About it. Whatever it is. The monster at the bottom of the sea . . . it wasn't only a broken romance that chased you out of Ireland, was it?'

She sighed, and scooped up a handful of sand, let the

grains fall slowly through her fingers. Would it matter, change anything, if she told him? It could hardly make things any worse, and talking to people seemed to help over here, in a way the counsellors never had in Ireland. Patrick was looking at her with genuine interest and concern, and her defences were down; she felt warmth in his body, some sense of comfort and refuge that reminded her of Ivor. It was a long time since she'd felt that shelter, that strength.

'No. It wasn't only that.'

'So . . . what was it, then?'

His voice was low and slow as he moved closer to her, taking her hand, drawing her to him. He had never touched her like this before, but she didn't resist, feeling pliant and drifting as she leaned into his shoulder, going with the flow of some unexpectedly awakening sensation.

'It was a murder.'

He gasped and stiffened, she felt an electric jolt shoot through him. But 'murder' was a shocking word, to anyone.

'Well, the judge called it manslaughter. But whatever you call it, it amounts to the same thing. My father is dead so the word makes no difference to him.'

'Your – father – was murdered?' The words lurched out of him, staccato, she could feel him turning pale even without looking at him.

'Yes. By a youth called Jason Dean. Jason stabbed him with a six-inch blade, through the heart.'

Sitting up, Patrick gripped her to him, and said nothing for a long time, staring out to sea over her shoulder.

'But – but *why*?'

'Because . . . are you sure you want to hear this? It's kind of a long story, my mother comes into it as well.'

As she thought of Viv Shivaun felt a sudden terrible ache, and had to fight to keep her voice steady. But Patrick insisted he wanted to hear it all, everything.

'All right. If you're sure.'

Composing herself, she began at the beginning, and told him everything. The church porch, her unknown parents, Viv and Jimmy, their deaths, Jason's trial, her break with Ivor, Jason who was now out of prison and, presumably, back in the bosom of his family. Or maybe starting one of his own, while she still grieved for hers. It took a long time, and night was falling by the time she got to the end of it, and Patrick was still sitting with her, not interrupting once, his arm around her. She realised it had been tightening around her all the time she had been talking, almost fiercely, with a kind of protectiveness in it. When she finished he sat rigid, and she turned to look into his face. It was taut and tense, etched with . . . what? Not sympathy, but something else, some foreign emotion she couldn't fathom.

'Oh, Shivaun,' he breathed at length, 'oh, my God.'

She drew a circle in the sand with her forefinger, looked out on the blackening sea. 'Yes, well, you did ask. Now you know.'

'Yes.' His voice was barely a scratch on the night. 'Now I know.'

They sat together, not moving or speaking, not looking at each other. His arm remained around her, but the contact was broken, as if his mind had moved away from her. Why? To where? Unlike Marina and Azalea, he did not ask questions, offer sympathy or involve himself in any aspect of the story. He simply sat, his eyes empty, his breathing slow and deep. Expecting some word of comfort, or perhaps even some challenge on the details, she was mystified by his silence, his hollow aura.

'Patrick?'

At length, he turned to her, looked into her eyes. 'Yes?'

'What's wrong? Have I upset you?' She could see that she had, and was reminded of their first night together, when he had talked about 'running away from himself'. More than ever she was convinced she recognised something in him, a look of loss. In some shape or form, she felt certain, he shared her sorrow, had experienced something close to what she had experienced herself.

'Yes,' he admitted candidly, 'you have.'

She bit her lip. 'I'm sorry.'

With sudden vehemence, he whirled around and gripped

her hard, so hard his fingers dug into her collarbone. '*No!* You are not to be sorry! *You* are not to be!'

Stunned, almost frightened by the harshness in him, she recoiled. 'But I—'

'No! You have nothing to do with it! It is not your fault!'

She couldn't make out what he meant, could only see agitation in him, something that was not her fault, because it was coming from somewhere else. Abruptly she felt her head clearing, felt sober, and cold.

'Patrick, I – I don't know what you're talking about. Of course none of it is my fault, except maybe the part about Ivor, and I'm not even sure how much of that. I know it's a painful story, but you did want to hear it.'

His breathing had become rapid and she saw that his left hand was clenching, every bone in him was tight, almost defensive. Abruptly, he plunged his other hand into his pocket and pulled out a packet of cigarettes, thrust it under her nose. Baffled, she shook her head.

'I don't smoke. I didn't think you did either.'

He shook a cigarette loose and lit it, took a long pull. 'I don't usually. But I used to. I still carry them in case of emergency.'

He took another deep pull, and the ash glowed scarlet. She was intrigued.

'Is this an emergency?'

No answer. Instead he sat smoking, immobile, gazing down the beach to where some teenagers were having a distant barbecue, their laughter carrying over the water. Then he exhaled, crushed the half-smoked cigarette into the sand and extinguished it.

'Sorry' he said, and she heard the newly quiet note in his voice. 'Maybe I over-reacted.'

'But – but why?'

He stood up and reached his hand down to her, pulled her to her feet. 'Why? Because . . . because it is, as you say, a long story. Too long for a lady who's shivering, and needs to be taken home. Come on.'

She realised that she was shivering, and did not object when he took off his sweater, allowed him to pull it over her head and even push her arms into its sleeves. It warmed her a little, as did his hand when he took hers again, but by the time they got back to Chederlay she felt chilled to the bone.

So, Ivor thought, this is freedom. This is what I wanted and this is what I've got. Sunny Spain, burning with colour, oranges I can reach up and pluck from the trees, the bloody bellow of summer bullfights. Life is so Latin here, not just the food and the language but the rhythm too, the attitude, the pace. I needed to travel, and I'm very glad I did. This is what life's like when you live it hand-to-mouth under blue skies, cheap and easy, with a girl who doesn't give a damn from one day to the next. It's not often that people get exactly what they want.

Finding work in Nerja turned out to be a snip. Justine got waitressing shifts in a tapas bar by no greater effort than strolling in to offer her services, and Ivor was about to offer his in the restaurant next door when a series of hammering noises caught his attention. Just around the corner, he found a team of toiling workmen, repairing a small hotel which they told him had suffered fire damage. Ivor promptly found the foreman, mentioned the renowned name of Miguel Garros and was taken on as a carpenter. Miguel's name carried weight all the way down to the coast, and Ivor had to laugh; Miguel had barely blinked when informed that his apprentice was leaving, merely grunted and waved adios with a chisel. And yet, although they had never become friends, Ivor felt some small tugging emotion. He had learned a great deal from Miguel, he respected his dogged craftsmanship and in some strange way he felt sorry for the lonely man, whose fierce independence left him so isolated, cost him so much in terms of human comfort. Furthermore, it was unsettling to discover his own instant, complete disposability.

Miguel accepted his resignation with shrugged indifference, made no attempt to argue or detain him, didn't even say whether he intended to take on a new apprentice or what his plans were. Ivor doubted that he had any, because Miguel was a man who simply lived for the day. Now, he was free to do the same himself. In a way, he thought, I've become rather like Miguel. No worries. No ties. *Mañana* will take care of itself.

And so he hitched to Nerja with Justine, they found their jobs within hours of arrival and then scouted round for somewhere to live. All the sunny apartments overlooking the beach were taken, apart from being too expensive, so they asked around and eventually found a couple of rooms on the top floor of someone's holiday house, which was rented out for the summer and would be shut up for the winter.

'That's OK,' Justine chirped airily, 'we won't want to stay beyond October anyway.' What they would do then, where they would go, was left unsettled, because they could think about that when they came to it, couldn't they? Ivor supposed that they could. Tossing their backpacks on the floor of their new abode, they grabbed their swimsuits and ran straight down to the beach. It was full of tourists around their own age, and after a long warm swim Ivor stretched out in the sun with a book, while Justine got chatting to a German couple on nearby beach mats. Uninhibited and sociable, she was a popular girl, and Ivor's only role in things for the rest of that day was the occasional rubbing of sunblock into her shoulders and back. She had bought a new bikini, in vivid lime with a pink motif, and seemed to want nothing else whatever out of life. God, he thought as he looked at her laughing with the Germans, she is such an easy girl. She is so incredibly *easy*.

Their new flat had no kitchen, but that didn't matter, because they could eat out, couldn't they? Ivor thought maybe just a kettle would be good, but she waved a dismissive hand and said he could pick up a coffee in any old café. There wasn't any fridge so cold drinks were out of the question too, but that didn't bother her either, they'd just run down to the nearby shop for them. Ivor felt as if he were living in a shelter for the homeless, some very flimsy temporary structure, but for the moment that suited him fine. Apart from what he had learned from Miguel, plus a handful of abiding memories of cold and semi-starvation, he travelled light from Seville, left it without regret. The only friend he had made there was Pilar, and he sent her a card from Nerja, but she did not reply to it. He was confirmed in his impression that Pilar was the kind of pragmatist who got on with life, shed no tears over any spilt milk, and that for all their shouting and screaming the Spaniards were not emotional people. This, he thought, is a harsh arid country, and I couldn't live in it permanently. But it's exactly what I needed.

At work he got talking with his new colleagues, and discovered that one of them was a Basque separatist, an ardent ETA supporter who entirely favoured the terrorists' intention of returning to violent tactics. Appalled, he went out that night with Justine to eat, and told her about his militant workmate.

She nodded, and helped herself to another slice of pizza, not very interested. He persisted. 'But Jus, the guy is all in favour of guns and bombs, killing anyone who gets in ETA's way! He sounded like he might even be *in* ETA . . . I'm working with an aspiring murderer.'

She pushed a strand of hair out of her freckled face and bit into the pizza, looking around the restaurant as if scanning for other newcomers, and then frowned. 'Ivor, why don't you stay out of local politics, huh? It's none of your business, you'll only make enemies if you get involved.'

'I'm not involved,' he retorted, 'I'm concerned! ETA have killed and maimed a lot of innocent people. I can't just stand there and say nothing about something I find deeply disturbing, as well as morally offensive.'

She sighed and poured some wine. 'Sure you can. You're not going to be here very long. What's the point?'

'You're *missing* the point' he replied sharply. 'Don't you care about this kind of thing, give a damn about kids maybe getting shot or babies blown up?'

She gazed at him. 'Yeah, well, there are a lot of places with a lot of problems. I can't solve the entire world's and neither can you, so what's the point of banging on about it? You're a foreigner, nothing you say is going to make a whit of difference.'

'No, of course it isn't, but I still have to say it! That's one of the reasons I left my job in Dublin, because I didn't want to spend the rest of my life pretending to agree with things I didn't agree with, saying yes when I meant no – Justine, you can't seriously mean to tell me you don't give a damn about freedom of speech.'

'Look,' she snapped, 'we have the freedom of it in Australia. That's good enough for me. I can't waste my time worrying about Spain or anywhere else, they'll just have to sort themselves out.'

What? Was she really so callous? Or did she genuinely not care? Either way, he was alienated, and thought with absurd annoyance of the pretty picture she presented in her new bikini. She was so sunny, so lovely . . . on the beach. On the outside. Mutinously, he dropped the subject but did not raise another, leaving her to find alternatives. At first she did, and chattered brightly, but by the time they finished their meal they were reduced to resentful silence.

Later, wandering back to their new abode, she seemed to change tack. Putting her arm around him, she entwined her fingers in his, and murmured warm, wine-scented words into his ear. But he was unmoved by her touch, her velvety breath on his cheek, and when they got home did not react even to her instantly naked body. It had, he thought, the sleek cold sheen of marble, and for all its allure it was only a body. After his lengthy celibacy he had thought a body was all he wanted, any woman's would do, but tonight he was suddenly, acutely aware that it was only a shell, and that Justine's rang hollow.

Feeling hollow himself, he tried restlessly to sleep. But it was what Spain called 'a white night', full of dust and whispering demons. Lying on his back, staring into it, he strangely thought of Miguel with his troops of transient women, feeling no longer free but adrift.

Chapter Thirteen

Shivaun slept deeply but awoke early, feeling gruesome. Apart from a thundering hangover, she was filled with a sense of conflict, a warm memory of Patrick's arm around her, a cold memory of Jason Dean, and an urgent impulse to escape from both. Getting up too fast, she was knocked almost off her feet by a wave of dizziness, and had to grope for her robe, pick her way downstairs to drink some juice. In the kitchen, Dorothy took one look at her and tactfully suggested a swim.

The pool was cold in the dawn air and she dived into it, forced herself to do twenty laps with her head underwater. When she finally surfaced she found Marina standing on the deck, watching her.

'Morning' she mumbled.

'Good morning' Marina replied crisply. 'Or is it?'

Shivaun pulled herself out of the pool and huddled into the towel that Marina held out to her. 'No,' she admitted, 'not very. Not yet.'

'Hmm.' With somehow maternal vigour, Marina wrapped the towel around her and rubbed her hair with one end of it, as if she were a child lifted from its bath.

'Sorry,' she muttered. 'I may as well confess straight off that your nurse is as sick as a parrot. I have a hangover from hell.'

Marina eyed her. 'Yes. One generally does after drinking an entire jug of cocktails. Or was it two? Anyway, I gather it wasn't entirely your fault. Why don't you take some aspirin and then you can tell me about your trip to the beach with Mr Nulty.'

Oh. How did she know about that? She must have eyes in the back of her head, Shivaun thought as she went to find some aspirin, and came back to flop down beside her. Marina was looking her most regally imposing this morning, fully made up and draped in some vivid yellow garment, bracelets jangling in a way that tweaked Shivaun's teeth on edge.

'He just took me for a walk to sober me up. But then we . . . kind of . . . got talking.'

Keenly, Marina looked at her. 'Oh? About what?'

'About me. About my parents. About Jason Dean killing my dad, and my mother dying because Ireland couldn't rise to one lousy fire engine.'

'I see. And what did he make of that?'

'I – I don't exactly know. I probably wouldn't have told him if I hadn't been drunk, and now I'm not sure whether I should have. It seemed to upset him.'

'Well, it's an upsetting story.'

'Yes, but . . . it was more than that, in itself. He went very quiet and distant, almost as if he were . . . I don't know, hearing some kind of echo or something. I got the impression I was opening up some old wound in him, that he might have been through something similar himself.'

Marina gazed into the pool, reflecting. 'Well, very few people go through as much as you have. But there always has been some mystery about Patrick. I would dearly love to know what drove him out of Ireland, and why he's never been back. But, Shivaun, I'd advise you not to delve too deep, not unless you're prepared for whatever you might find. It could be something we're all better off not knowing.'

Yes. There was that possibility. But Shivaun felt as if she had lifted the lid of some tantalising box, only to have it slammed shut. *What* was in it? Why did she feel such a pull to it? Or was it a – the thought hit her like a whip – was it a pull to Patrick she felt? To the man himself? How had she gone from disliking him to allowing him to embrace her, to telling him the things she hadn't even told Kathy Shreve?

God, she thought with sudden panic, what is going on here?

For several minutes she sat staring down into the dripping water at her feet, clutching her towel around her, feeling numb. Completely numb, apart from the two spots on her collarbone that Patrick had gripped, so fiercely that she could feel his fingers yet, imprinted on her skin. She was almost afraid to look down, in case she should see his fingerprints. Yet she had not resisted, had not flailed free of him; on the contrary, she had felt a kind of fascination, been aware of both some faint fear and some beckoning closeness.

Abruptly, Marina stood up and looked around her. 'It's a beautiful day, Shivaun. I think I'll do my exercises here and now, outdoors, and then after breakfast we'll go for a walk somewhere. Have you been to Sturbridge yet?'

No, Shivaun said absently, she hadn't.

'Then we'll go there. It's quite historic and absorbing. Since Joe is crocked, you can drive us . . . in fact I may need you to do some of the things he usually does, you're going to be busy for the next few weeks.'

Nodding, Shivaun realised that Marina was trying to divert her, and intended to keep her busy. Intended to keep her away from Patrick, for however long it might be possible.

Several weeks passed, weeks in which Shivaun was consumed with curiosity, had to fight constantly against invasive thoughts of Patrick. But Marina became a slavedriver, assumed an unprecedented bossiness and demanded all kinds of new services, new attention. Shivaun was run off her feet with tasks and errands that had precious little to do with nursing, leaving her with no time to see or speak to Patrick if he should show up, which he did not. One day a truck drew up with his company logo on it, and her heart almost stalled, she turned to it as if to a magnet; but one of his employees got out and said he'd been sent to spray the bug-infected roses. Crushed, she felt as if he'd been sent to spray her, disinfect and cleanse her of whatever contagion she had contracted.

That evening, she went up to her room after dinner and took out the photo of Ivor she kept tucked in a drawer, holding it at arm's length, thinking. It was a couple of years old, creased and starting to fade, but his boyish face touched some tender spot in her, the way she might have touched a scar to see if it was healing. He was standing on a tennis court, holding his racquet over his shoulder looking happily victorious, and she flinched; who was he playing with now, who was his partner? As she held it she could hear his voice, smell his skin, taste his mouth, the memories catching fire until suddenly she flung it away from her as if her fingers were burning.

I loved you so much, she thought. I loved you so much. You were my man, and I adored you. And then you left me. I thought you'd come back but you didn't, you left me alone . . . I don't want to be alone, Ivor. You've always known that being alone is the one thing I cannot bear. If only you'd ever written, ever got in touch or showed that you still cared . . . but it's been nearly a year now, and I can't go on alone. Not forever.

The summer reached its zenith, hot and arid, and still Patrick did not come. July was turning into August when, one restless evening, Shivaun saw Kathy Shreve cycling up to Chederlay, waving; she was going into Rockport, she shouted, would Shivaun like to come with her? In a flash Shivaun was running out to the garage, yanking her bike out of it, telling Kathy that Marina had been driving her nuts fussing over trivia all day and she'd love to get away. Jumping on, she pedalled off down the dusty drive, exploding with pent-up energy.

At first Kathy talked about her work, which was blossoming since she'd left Bill, and her boys who'd settled into acceptance of the fact that their mother only spent afternoons with them.

'It helps that I've sold so many paintings. I can buy them

things out of my own money now, they see the relation between me getting what I want and them getting what they want. They'd never dream of using my canvases for target practice any more.'

Shivaun was glad to hear it. And how was Kathy enjoying life at the commune?

'It's great! There's so much creativity there, everyone's so interesting, we discuss all kinds of things . . . actually, Shivaun, that's why I wanted to see you. Azalea and I were gossiping last night and – and she told me something. Something you're not supposed to hear, only I think she wanted you to hear it, and that's why she told me.'

Intrigued, Shivaun asked her what it was. Kathy pulled on the brakes and stopped her bike, threw it on a grassy ledge overlooking the sea and sat down beside it. Shivaun did likewise.

'Well, the thing is – Patrick Nulty has been looking for you.'

Shivaun was astonished. She hadn't heard a word from him since the fourth of July, was full of churning speculation as to why that might be.

'But – he hasn't! He hasn't phoned or been to Chederlay for ages.'

Kathy nodded emphatically. 'Yes. He has. He called twice and asked to speak to you. But Azalea told him you were busy, and didn't give you the message either time.'

'What? But why not?'

'Because Marina told her not to. Issued strict orders, apparently, that the two of you were to be kept apart. Azalea was told to field any calls he might make, and Dorothy was told that if he arrived in person he was to be kept out of the house and told you weren't in it.'

Shivaun gasped. 'Kathy, you can't be serious.'

'Yes. I am. You know, as do we all, how dictatorial Marina can be! There's a line even Azalea is afraid to cross. This was a definite order and she didn't dare defy it.'

Reeling, Shivaun took a moment to take the information

in. Whatever enigma lay behind Patrick, Marina must be far more deeply concerned about it than she had realised. This was – was the kind of thing a parent might do, to keep her daughter away from an unsuitable man! And now she was reacting like a daughter, because her instinct was to find the nearest phone and call Patrick immediately.

'Damn, why didn't I bring the mobile with me!'

Kathy sucked her lower lip. 'Maybe it's just as well you didn't. You'd better give it a bit of thought first. Knowing Marina, I'd say she has her reasons, and she'll be mad as hell if you go against her.'

'Yes . . . so that's what happened. I thought I'd driven him away with my tale of woe. But it wasn't that at all.'

'No – what tale of woe?'

'Oh, Kathy. Maybe I should have told you in the first place. But I didn't want to blather on to everyone. I'll tell you some other time, because I don't want to be late getting back tonight. Marina has been watching me like a hawk lately.'

'Yeah. A hawk defending its young, by the look of it. What's this all about? Are you involved with Patrick, in a way nobody told me about?'

'No. I'm not.'

'Then . . . could you be? Marina must think the potential is there.'

Shivaun pulled a blade of grass, and groaned. 'Yes. That's the problem, Kathy. I think the potential is there too. He scares me in some way I can't define, but he attracts me too. And I think he feels exactly the same way about me.'

In her room that night, Shivaun hesitated only momentarily. Then she called enquiries and got Patrick's number in Lowell. His home wasn't listed, but a voicemail clicked on in his office. Speaking softly, she left a message: he was not to call her back, but to meet her instead on Sunday at Park Street church in Boston, at one o'clock.

Marina was having lunch with friends in Boston on Sunday,

and in the interim she prayed that nothing would go wrong, did not even tell Azalea what she was planning because, if Marina found out, she did not want Azalea implicated. Once or twice a glance flashed between them, and she thought that Azalea suspected, had got some feedback from Kathy. But neither of them said a word.

On Sunday, she drove Marina into the city, told a bare-faced lie about spending the afternoon visiting Harvard, and promised to come back for her at five. Marina frowned, rather grimly.

'Yes, well, in Utah five o'clock turned out to mean seven. Don't be late this time.'

'I won't' Shivaun promised tersely, and sped away. Parking the car, she walked the half-mile to the church, breathing fast, thinking urgently, fully conscious of having made a dangerous decision. But then she saw Patrick, standing waiting under the soaring spire with his hands in his pockets, and knew there was no going back.

As she approached him his shadowed, sombre face emerged into the sun, lighting up in a way she had never seen before, and he held out both hands to her.

'Shivaun! It's been so long – I thought you mustn't want to see me.'

'No,' she replied, steadying her voice, 'it was Marina who didn't want me to see you. She blocked your calls. I only found out the other night.'

'She – but – why would Marina do that?'

She looked him full in the face. 'She did it because – because she thinks you're trouble.'

Expecting him to take issue, to protest, she felt a frisson when he didn't. Instead he stood holding her hands, considering her words.

'Yes,' he said at length, 'I have to tell you she may well be right. I also have to tell you that I have been able to think of absolutely nothing but you since last I saw you. You have invaded my mind and my soul and I can't get you out of either one.'

She stood back, almost jumped back as if he had lobbed

a live grenade at her. But then she stood her ground, feeling flooded with defiance. Defiance and desire, the smouldering gunpowder of igniting sensations about to burst into flames. I'm playing with fire, she thought with certainty, and I'm going to get burnt.

She seized his hands. 'Patrick, is it far to Lowell?'

He looked like a man about to leap off a cliff. 'No. Half an hour.'

'Then let's go there. I want to see where you live, and find out who you really are.'

The sun was beating down, torching Ivor's naked back as he bent over a stack of wood, sawing it into lengths with savage satisfaction. It was the hottest day of the entire summer, and a Sunday at that, everyone else had poured down to the beach in the dripping heat. But Justine was amongst them, and he didn't want to be with her; he wanted to be on his own, Why, he didn't know. All he knew was that he felt like a caged animal, had to get away, and the deserted work site was the only refuge he could think of. Tomorrow, his colleagues would be baffled to see how he had spent his day off.

The physical graft was gruelling, but he kept at it, on and on and on, head down, eyes blinded with sweat, letting the sun sear him like a steak on a skillet. After so much outdoor work he was hardened to it, his skin had the colour and texture of leather, he could keep going for hours. Was determined to keep going till he dropped.

Miguel, he thought, you toughened me up. No wonder you weren't interested in me when I arrived in Seville, I was so soft, fresh out of my suit and tie. I was twenty-six, but I was just a boy. Well, the boy's gone now. I've grown up. I know who I am, and who I'm not.

I'm not a corporate accountant, that's for sure. I'll never sit at a desk again. Now that I've got muscles I'll flex them every day for the rest of my life, I'll use every bone and every sinew, never let my body lose the tone and strength it's gained. I'll work like a Trojan, in all weathers till all hours, and I will make something beautiful. I will be fully alive, fully fit, the owner of my own life.

Today I'm just a labourer, but even that's so liberating! Nobody expects me to wear Armani or attend those pointless meetings that used to go round in circles. I'll never have to join a golf club or buy an identikit house in one of Dublin's deathly suburbs, get flattened under a mountain of debt trying to maintain an image or a lifestyle. I'll never have to marry a woman I love with less passion than I love carpentry. And Christ, I *do* love it!

But I don't love Justine Adams. Nor does she love me. That's OK, we never told each other any lies. We just wanted sex, and the sex was great as long as there was friendship in it. But now the friendship's gone out of it, and the respect, and my heart. It's time to cut loose.

I could find another woman if I wanted one. The beach is sizzling with them, natives and foreigners, blondes and brunettes, it's like choosing fruit off a supermarket shelf, any flavour you like. But supermarket produce doesn't interest me now any more than Justine does. I don't want exotica flown in from abroad, bright wrappers or chemical sprays, hothouse forcing out of season. I want something fresh, native and earthy . . . something organic. Someone.

Shivaun was organic. She was bloody difficult, too. That gorgeous little girl grew up into a troubled, starving soul, and there were times when she drained me dry. She needed so much care, so much input and affection. Justine doesn't need me. She'll have a new man by the time I finish telling her we're through. She won't look at me the way Shivaun did, that day on Portmarnock beach. There'll be no pain this time, no heartbreak at all. Jesus, I felt like an axe murderer, that day!

But at least I felt something. I truly did. That's why I've run out of road with Justine – because I feel nothing. I feel the same way with her I used to feel at work in that office in Dublin, indifferent, detached, only in it for the goodies and gratification. It was just a learning curve, and now it's time to move on. I can have tremendous quality of life as a carpenter, doing something so absorbing, so challenging, but then my partner's going to have to be absorbing and challenging too, and unless I want to pay the price Miguel pays for his devotion to work, I'll have to find a partner. Just as I had to lose the one I had, because although Shivaun was the right woman we were in the wrong place at the wrong time. I'll never regret striking out on my own or coming to Spain or even that fierce, freezing winter with Miguel, but I'll always bitterly regret losing Shivaun.

Where is she? How is she? Who is she – no. God, no! That's one reality I can't face up to. If I live to be a hundred I will never, ever be able to think of her with another man, bear the thought of – *no*! If I ever saw her with anyone, saw him kiss or touch her, I'd knock his block off, leave the bastard for dead. Shivaun Reilly was my girl and in my heart she always will be mine.

But then, how can I ever love anyone else? How can *she*? She can't. She's still under my skin and – it's just not possible. She can't have found anyone else. I want her to be happy, but not at that price. *Not with another man!*

She'd understand that. It's selfish and possessive but she'd understand. Unlike Justine she understands things, and people. That's what made her such a bloody good nurse, so interested in her damn patients . . . even if we'd stayed together I'd always have had to share her with them, with her work. Until I became a carpenter I had no idea how totally absorbing work can be . . . but now I know. And now I need a partner who knows.

Fucking *hell*! You were always there for your patients, Shivaun Reilly, for your hospital and your politics and your causes, so why aren't you here now for me? How come I'm last on your list of priorities? If we'd had kids, I'd have come even lower. Wouldn't I? Huh? There'd always have been a Kilo Finnegan in the way, or a Buster Mulcahy or a Stan or a Somebody. And now in my life there'll always be a piece of pine or a length of oak, a crib to be carved or a church to be panelled . . . my career is *my* baby now, you're no longer the only one with commitments. So there.

Just so long as you haven't made any commitments in

America. If I ever hear that you have, I'l go over there and I'll kill him. I swear I will kill the bastard stone dead, whoever he is.

Standing up, Ivor suddenly snapped out of his reverie and lifted his face to the brutal sun, feeling sick as it hit him like a blowtorch. Normally he could take it, take the ache and fatigue too, but today . . . what's wrong with me, he wondered aloud, what is wrong with me today?

Shivaun saw only brief snapshots of Lowell as Patrick's car sped through it, but she was reminded of parts of Dublin; it looked tough and gritty, with ugly concrete buildings and plastic bags flapping from the overhead wires. Why, she asked Patrick, had he picked Lowell to live in?

'I got involved in it,' he said simply, 'and I'm still involved.'

In what, exactly?

'Oh – stuff. Youth clubs, sports . . . there are a lot of kids here who need a hand.'

She mused on that, but didn't pursue it. Lowell seemed beside the point right now, everything did; her body was revved up like a jet engine and all she could think of was Patrick beside her, the solid bulk of his body, the sharp cut of his profile, his eyes dark as jasper. He hardly spoke at all, looking intently ahead of him until at last they reached the outskirts and he slewed the car up in front of a white, shuttered clapboard house surrounded by high thick shrubs. Without a word he cut the engine, yanked the keys from the ignition and jumped out, stood waiting for her.

She got out, slammed the door and ran to his side, her heart thundering, her body gunning for action. When he opened the door she found herself standing immediately in the living room, staring at the stairs that rose out of it. Without preamble, he turned to her.

'You're sure about this?'

She had a flash of Ivor. 'Yes,' she said, 'I'm sure.'

He grabbed her wrist and led her roughly up the stairs, all

but pushed her into a shady, darkened bedroom and had ripped off his shirt by the time her eyes adjusted to it. Gazing at his body, she felt a surge of pure physical delight; years of working outdoors had honed every muscle, even under his thick chest hair she could see hard chestnut surfaces, sinews like ropes. In one movement she grasped the hem of her dress and pulled it up over her head, was reaching for her underwear when he beat her to it.

'God' he gasped, and she realised he was as tense, as primed as she, had the hungry drive of someone who, like herself, had not had sex for a very long time. Too long, she thought with sudden fury, and grasped the buckle on his belt. In unison, they hit the bed with a violent slam.

Yes, she thought as he gripped her, go for it! His lips felt like lighted matches on her skin, his weight was crushing and she knew he was going to have welts on his back where her nails were digging into him, but she was unleashed, beyond caring, determined to do maximum damage. Already soaked in sweat, he enclosed her in one arm, reached for the inside of her thigh with the other and drove his tongue into her mouth, flooding it with the taste of salt as his eyes clenched shut. His bones were so hard, his weight so heavy that she clenched her own in pain, and simultaneously their bodies dissolved, fell over the cliff together. He entered her at speed and force and every nerve in her torched, exulted and exploded.

Was it hours, or days or only minutes? She had no idea, felt whipped away to some other dimension, suspended outside her own body and engulfed in his. There was a force, a ferocity in him that was primal, an urgency that would have been terrifying had she not shared it – but she did share it, fought to keep pace and was hurled aloft on a tidal wave of joy.

Afterwards, neither of them could speak, lay panting amidst the wreckage of scattered pillows and saturated sheets, silenced and astonished. His hand held hers so tightly she thought her fingers would snap, but he said nothing, not one tender word. She felt as if she'd been hit by a truck, could feel the bruises purpling all over her body. With a smile of the sheerest satisfaction, she kissed his cheek, nuzzled her face against the dark bristles on his chin. He was the kind of guy, she thought, who needed to shave twice a day.

Groaning, he opened his eyes and looked into hers. Looked astonished, whether at her energy or his own she couldn't tell.

'So' he said at length, unromantically.

'So' she repeated, and laughed aloud. 'So now! So there!'

For the first time since she had met him, he laughed too. Laughed loudly, his eyes crinkling at the edges as he ran a hand through her hair, and propped himself up on one elbow.

'Christ almighty. You're dynamite.'

Another first: she thought his American accent was slipping, there was some trace of Irish in it. Little as she knew him, she had hit some mark in him, some hidden target.

Twirling a finger through a curl behind his ear, she lay back and pondered it.

'Cavan, I'd say, or Monaghan.'

He blinked. 'What?'

'Maybe Leitrim, at a push, or Roscommon. You're definitely from one of those four counties.'

With a sigh, he rolled over onto his back, dropped her hand and lay gazing at the ceiling.

'Do we have to go into that now?'

'Well . . . no, not now. But if we're going to do this again, it would be nice to know something more about you.'

No answer, only an intent scan of the ceiling. And then something seemed to shift in him, click into gear. He turned his face to her and looked at her sidelong.

'Are we? Do you want to do this again?'

She certainly couldn't accuse him of being Byronic, of making flowery empty speeches. But she ran her hand down his chest, revelling in the roughness, the muscular masculinity of it. Unlike Ivor he was not fine-boned, there was something meaty and hard-packed about his body. Still drenched in salty sweat, it held her in thrall.

'Yes,' she said candidly, 'I do. D'you?'

He steepled his hands to his face, pushing the tips of his

fingers into his forehead, thinking and frowning. It was not very flattering. But then he sat up and pulled her to him, onto him, so that they were facing each other.

'Shivaun' he said, and stopped. She was incensed.

'*What?* What *is* it, Patrick? You know all about me, I know nothing about you. Why? What's holding you back?'

'Shivaun' he said again. 'You don't want to know.'

'I do' she replied fiercely, and thumped his chest in frustration. 'I do! I can't start sleeping with an enigma!'

'You've already started' he said bleakly, but then his tone softened, there was new warmth in him as he put his arm around her and drew her close. 'Oh, God . . . what have you done to me? What have I done to you? I knew this was going to happen, the moment I met you I knew . . . after all these years. All these empty pointless years – and then, there you were.'

She was bewildered. 'What empty pointless years? You're surely not telling me you – you haven't slept with anyone for *years*?'

He sighed, and flinched. 'No. I'm not telling you that. What I am telling you is that this is the first time it's ever meant anything. The first time I've ever felt anything more than – than lust.'

'But – but you haven't said a word! No whispers, no murmurs, no endearments . . . it felt like plain, good old-fashioned lust to me.'

That was what she'd felt herself. Sudden, searing desire, coupled with some kind of lethal attraction, a form of hypnosis. She felt it still; but she did not feel love, not one shred of anything she'd ever felt for Ivor. There was nothing *to* love, only a tantalising enigma.

Drily, he laughed. 'Yes, well, lust certainly played its part. But it's more than that . . . you've ensnared me. You may not love me, and I don't ask you to pretend that you do, but you love life. You love Ireland. You were so passionate that night in the ski chalet, hammering away at it like a demon, but I could see that something had gone wrong, got turned inside out. I wanted so badly to turn it right way round again . . .

wanted to make you happy. I knew you had the potential for happiness, and I'd never done that for anyone before.'

She was incredulous. 'Hadn't you? Ever? Not even in the smallest way, for anyone?'

'No. Not in any lasting way. I do not make people happy, Shivaun. I cause them pain and misery and I'm telling you now for a fact that Marina is absolutely right about me. I'm bad news. If you have any sense you'll get the hell out of here and never come back, pretend that today never happened.'

Stricken, she bit her lip. 'But Patrick, you've made me happy today.'

Pulling her to him, he breathed into her hair. 'Have I?'

'Yes. You've given me huge pleasure and made me feel like – like myself again! It's a year since I last saw Ivor Lawlor, but I still felt somehow in his grip, under his spell, until today. Now I've broken free, had sex with you, moved forward – you carried me forward, and made me feel wonderful! I want to feel wonderful again, with you, but we can't do that unless . . . unless you're honest with me.'

He kissed the nape of her neck, with a tenderness that felt like a new bud in spring, breaking through the frozen earth.

'Shivaun, I'm trying to be honest with you. As far as I can be, without making you hate me.'

'Hate you? But why would I do that?'

'You would, if . . . oh, God, Shivaun, I have no right to you! I want you and I'm falling in love with you but I – I can't do it to you! I wanted so much to see you but I was glad when you didn't return my calls, glad you could resist me when I couldn't resist you. I've resisted all my life and now you, of all the women on this earth, are the one woman I can't resist! This is – this is some kind of punishment from God!'

To her horror his voice cracked, for a terrible moment she thought he was going to weep. He buried his face in his hands, breathing huskily, until with visible effort he composed himself.

'I – Shivaun, I need to think about this. I let things get out of hand today and I've confused you, confused us both—'

She certainly was confused. And then in one bound she was leaping out of the bed, shrieking.

'Jesus! Marina! What time is it?'

He glanced at the bedside clock. 'Ten to six.'

'Oh no, oh *fuck*! She's going to sack me this time for sure, kill me – get *up*, quick, here, get dressed and take me back to Boston!'

She flung his clothes at him, and it was his turn to be confused. 'But you – we—?'

'Will have to talk later! Patrick, she's my sponsor, I can only stay in America as long as I'm working for her, if she blows a fuse I could be deported, or an illegal! Come *on*!'

Wildly she threw on her clothes and raced out, down the stairs, leaving him to run after her with his face full of anguish, pain that squeezed his heart as she leaped into the car with the sun firing her face, and waited levitating for him to join her.

He got into the car, and managed to drive it, but could not speak.

No, Marina's hosts said coldly, she was not here. She had waited an hour and then taken a taxi home. Shivaun knew from their faces that she was in big trouble, and drove away in a panic, racing to Chederlay, battling to calm herself.

If it was only a job, she told herself, I wouldn't care. I'd be sorry, but I'd accept the consequences, leave with grace if I was thrown out. But it isn't only a job. It's Marina. Marina Darnoux who is still not fully well and relies on me, trusts me . . . loves me, I think. Since the day I first set foot in her house I have had nothing but kindness and goodness from her, she's treated me like a daughter and made up in so many ways for the loss of Viv. She's helped me to recover every bit as much as I've helped her, I cherish her friendship and I will be devastated if I lose it . . . but I've risked it, endangered it. Endangered it for a man I hardly know.

She could still feel Patrick, taste him and smell him on her skin, but she couldn't see his face, Marina's was engraved on her mind instead. Marina who *was* the boss, when the chips were down, could be so intimidating that even Azalea, as Kathy said, didn't dare defy her. And now she had been abandoned, left in the lurch for Patrick Nulty above all, defied with a vengeance.

Shivaun shot the car into its space in the garage, jumped out and flew into the house amidst a whirl of barking dogs.

'Marina! Oh Christ, I'm so sorry!'

Marina sat rigid in the library, with her back to the window, looking stony. Looking, Shivaun thought, absolutely livid.

'Well?'

Her glare hit Shivaun like a hurley, smack between the eyes. Gasping, she strove for composure, for words. 'I got delayed – I – didn't realise the time—'

Marina surveyed her, fingering the pendant on her neck, twirling it several times between thumb and forefinger.

'You were with Patrick Nulty.'

No. Oh, *no*! For one split second Shivaun thought of lying, denying. But she couldn't.

'I – yes. I was. How did you know?'

'By looking at you. It's written all over you.'

Every plane of Marina's face seemed to have sharpened, heightened, her cheekbones had been been tightened as if with a wrench. Shivaun quailed, sat gingerly down on the edge of the chair opposite her.

'I slept with him' she breathed.

'Yes. I can see that.'

Shivaun followed her gaze, looked down and saw that her dress was on back to front. Hysterically she fought to stifle laughter, and was aghast to find it swirling with tears.

'You did everything to keep me away from him, didn't you?'

'Yes. I did. Every single thing it was in my power to do, with Azalea fighting me all the way. It was she who invited him to that party in July, not me. After that, I gave orders that she was not to interfere again. Not to tell you if he tried to contact you. Evidently she has let me down, just as you have yourself.'

From deep within her Shivaun had a memory of Viv, angry with her over some childhood misdemeanour which, at the time, had felt colossally serious. Expecting to be chastised or punished, she had instead been reduced to tears by Viv's 'utter disappointment' in her. She felt worthless then, and she felt worthless now.

'But Marina, I – I'm a grown woman!'

'Quite so. I merely felt it was my duty, *in loco parentis*, to try to shield you from the great unhappiness that Patrick Nulty will cause you.'

Shivaun drew a deep breath. 'Marina, look. Two things. One is that Azalea obeyed you, has no idea where I was today. The other is that Patrick – Patrick didn't make me unhappy at all. On the contrary.'

As if electrified Marina drew herself up, imperious, her eyes flashing.

'But he will! He will crucify you, if you let him ensnare you!'

Ensnare. The very word Patrick had used. He was ensnared, he said, but . . . was she?

'How do you know? Huh? After all you're the one who's sleeping with a married man! Yet keeping it all under perfect control!'

She heard the pitch of her own voice, knew she had gone too far, broken whatever fragile boundary was left between them. This was not a showdown between boss and employee, this was a major row between two very angry, emotionally charged women. Marina looked as if Shivaun had thrown a grenade at her.

'Yes. I am sleeping with Steven Hunt, and I am keeping it under control. I don't give a damn about his wife, who has her own agenda, but he has an epileptic daughter. Other children, too. Responsibilities. It is my duty to see that nothing gets out of control. Have you any idea what that is costing me? Have you any *idea*?'

Marina's tone was glacial, but it made Shivaun flush with shame.

'No' she admitted. 'I thought you – you didn't care.'

'Did you? Well, let me tell you, Shivaun, there's only one kind of woman who can sleep with a man without caring, and that's a professional. A prostitute. I am not a prostitute.'

There was a quivering silence, in which both of them edged very near to tears.

'Oh, Marina,' she whispered, 'I am sorry. I am so sorry.'

Reaching forward, she touched Marina's hand, but got no response. Not even a reply, until Marina had mastered the feelings she had never revealed before.

'Yes. Well, it was my choice, and now the consequences are also mine. As they will be yours, if you choose a man who has the power to make you suffer. Steven has that power over me, and all I can do is try to manage it, contain it. At my age I'm unlikely to find anyone better – but at least at my age I'm also mature and experienced enough to handle it. You, on the other hand, are young enough to find someone much better, and young enough to get very badly hurt. You've been hurt already, Shivaun, and I do not want Patrick Nulty to do you any more harm. There are other men of your age out there, and I want you to find one. I want you to be happy.'

But – but that, again, was exactly what Patrick had said. She began to feel as if she were hearing echoes, fighting in her head.

'What are you saying, Marina? That you're forbidding me to see Patrick again?'

'Yes, I would forbid it, if I could! That man is poison!'

'But you have no proof!'

'I know it! I've always known it! The only reason I let you go to that restaurant with him that night is that you didn't want to – if I'd made a scene about it, you might have defied me, been seduced by the lure of forbidden fruit. And now, despite all my efforts, you have been seduced!'

'Yes,' she said slowly, 'I have. He made me happy, he revived me from the coma that Ivor Lawlor left me in. Now I'm free of Ivor and I'm very happy about that.'

Marina's gaze seemed to bore right through her. 'Are you? Are you really? Are you sure, Shivaun?'

'Yes! That's why I did it! I don't love Patrick, I just—'

'You just what? Thought you'd grab a quick fix? Well, you can tell me it's none of my business if you like, Shivaun, but I'd never have put you down as a hit-and-run type of girl. I'd have thought you were like me in that respect actually, that you'd be incapable of sleeping with a man for whom you felt nothing.'

Trembling, Shivaun caught the rawness in Marina's words, understood how much they were hurting her. Physically vulnerable as she was, she had always disguised the slightest sign of emotional vulnerability. Steven Hunt, she thought with aching rage, is a goddamn bastard.

And yet – and yet Marina is still with him. Whatever draws her to him has to be the same thing that drew me to Patrick today. Something inevitable. I found out nothing about him, except that he has the sex drive of a bull and causes, according to himself, pain and misery to people. But if Marina can handle Steven, I can handle Patrick. I know she thinks I'm too young and inexperienced, but I'm not. I've already survived Ivor Lawlor.

Getting to her feet, she went to Marina and embraced her, let a kiss drop on her hair along with a tear.

'Marina, I love you dearly and think of you as my other mother. I know I've behaved unforgivably today, on every count, and you're absolutely right to be furious with me. I am also deeply touched, more deeply than I can tell you, by your care and concern for me. I don't sleep with men who mean nothing to me, and I apologise with all my heart for letting you fool me into thinking you did. I should have known better. From now on I'll be watching out for you in the same way you're watching out for me – if, that is, you still want me.'

Marina grimaced, twisted her head away to hide, Shivaun thought, the wet sheen in her eyes. But she reached up her hand to where Shivaun's lay on her shoulder, and took it.

'Yes. Of course I still want you. You're like a daughter to me.'

'Then I'll try to be a good one.'

'Does that – does that mean you won't see Patrick again?'

Shivaun winced, and braced herself. 'No, Marina. It doesn't mean that. I know he's not what you want, you're trying to protect me from him and save me from myself. But that's the terrible thing about daughters – they don't listen to their mothers and never take good advice about getting involved with the wrong men. I have to see Patrick again.'

Marina closed her eyes, and sighed. 'Well, at least I tried. I never met Vivienne Reilly, but if I did I know I could look her in the eye and say I tried.'

'Yes. You did, and I love you for it. I'll try too, if I can't be good, as Viv used to say, at least to be careful.'

Marina drew her to her, and hugged her.

But already Shivaun had been careless. Beyond a quick calculation that she was unlikely to get pregnant, she had taken no contraceptive precautions. Somehow Patrick struck her as the kind of man unlikely to fall headlong into the tender trap, and in retrospect she was surprised that he hadn't mentioned it. It seemed too soon in their tentative relationship to go on the pill, but she'd better mention it and see what he thought. Since last year her feelings about children had changed, she'd seen the reality of them in Kathy's sons and Marina's brother's kids, and was no longer sure she wanted any as soon as she'd once thought. Certainly she didn't want any with Patrick Nulty, who'd cut down Marina's cherry tree with such cold swift ruthlessness, and besides her attention was diverted elsewhere now, she sensed that maybe she had other things to do first, some more immediate destiny. She had no idea what it might be, but she knew for sure that the prospect of early motherhood was receding. I'm awake now, she thought with a rush of adrenalin, I'm young and alive and I have other things to do.

Warned off calling her on Marina's phone, Patrick had given her his mobile number and taken hers, but she hesitated, gave serious thought to Marina's reservations and to his own. He was what the Irish called 'a hard man' and she could see, with clarity, that he would never mellow into a devoted partner or comfortable companion. At thirty-six his character was set and formed, it would be idiotic to think that she could ever change him.

But here and now, today, what good he was doing her! Her body glowed from the release of his, she couldn't wait to savour its warmth, its solidity again. Finally she threw caution to the wind, and called him.

'Saturday?'

'Yes.' He sounded thrilled to hear her. 'Can you stay overnight?'

She could, she said, and she would. Her body seemed to have developed a will of its own, was propelling her inexorably. God, Ivor was a long time ago! Not that one man could be compared with another, because everyone was unique, but she was delighted she'd grasped this new bull by the horns.

On Saturday she drove to Lowell in the early evening, noticing more about it this time, sensing the weariness in its pockets of poverty and yet some faint tinge of hope, as if it knew that things could be better and was struggling to do its best. When she parked outside Patrick's house she sat looking at it for a moment, thinking that it was decent but far from the luxury she knew he could afford.

He did not emerge to greet her, but when he brought her inside he kissed her ardently, and she was touched to see flowers in a vase on the table, as if specially for her. Everything else was in a bachelor's state of disarray, books, newspapers and CDs, miles of cable connecting the phone to a computer and a fax. It could hardly be more different to the lush, effete homes of society gardeners she'd sometimes seen in magazines.

He opened some wine and poured her a glass. 'I had a look around Lowell,' she said, 'it's kind of industrial, huh?! I thought landscapers were supposed to live in leafy luxury.'

'Perhaps they are,' he said, 'if they feel they deserve it.'

'Don't you feel you deserve it?'

'No. I don't.'

She would have pursued it if she had not been distracted by the wine and the flowers, the signals they were sending her and the desire that was already rising in her. She hoped he wasn't planning to cook dinner, because it would be burned to a cinder. Suddenly the question of contraception loomed urgently, and she raised it.

'We don't need to do anything,' he said quietly. 'I've had a vasectomy.'

Really?! But – her mind spun back to St Jude's, the fathers swearing never again, that four children were enough, or five or six. Even with substantial families under their belts, they'd had to undergo counselling and justify their case. For a single, healthy, childless man of thirty-six, vasectomy would be virtually out of the question, unless he could prove some serious genetic disorder or carried hereditary disease.

'Have you? I'm amazed you found a doctor to do it, if you have no children and there's nothing wrong with you.'

'Shivaun,' he said, 'in America you can get anything you want. All you need is money. It buys everything.'

'But – don't you want children? Ever?'

He stared down into his glass, implacably sustaining a lengthy silence.

'I think' he said finally, 'it's more a question of them not wanting me.'

Oh, Jesus! Alarms went off in her head like gunfire.

'What? What do you mean? You – oh, God, Patrick, you've never – you're not—' She could hardly go on, but forced herself to. 'You're not one of those sexually twisted guys, are you, who was abused by the Christian Brothers and ended up abusing children himself?'

She sat immobilised, and her relief was enormous when he shook his head.

'No. Nothing like that. It's nothing to do with sex, I've never touched a child in that way. I work with them, in the youth clubs I'm involved in, any of their parents will tell you that I'm absolutely trustworthy.'

'But then – what did you mean?'

He looked away, but not before she saw the conflict in his face.

'I simply mean that I wouldn't make a good father.'

'Why not?'

'It isn't meant to be. That's all. Other people have kids and I try to help the ones who get off to a bad start, or need extra attention, facilities, whatever. I grew up in a poor family myself, I know what a football or an outing or a sports kit can mean, never mind luxuries like swimming pools, or holidays or ski trips.'

'I see. Well, I'm sorry if I insulted you, but I had to ask.'

He didn't seem offended. On the contrary. 'Of course you did. You were quite right. I'm sorry if I scared you.'

He had scared her, and it took her a few minutes to recover. Drinking her wine, she accepted a second glass. He looked reasonable, and sounded convincing, but she thought he was not a man who would ever enrich a woman's life or heart. It was a pity, because he was certainly good at enlivening a woman's body, engaging her mind. She didn't know what to make of him.

Getting up, he put on some music, a soothing Ronan Hardiman instrumental that calmed her, eased the mood.

'I see you're up to date on Irish music.'

'Yes. I keep up with the culture as much as I can. The Internet makes Ireland accessible. I can even read the newspapers, within minutes of publication.'

'Then you must know that most of what I said that night at the ski chalet was justified. Ireland's gone to pot.'

He smiled wryly. 'OK. I'll admit that some things have. Money has not been the solution to every problem. But it depends what you're looking for, how you look at it when you find it. At least the problems are out in the open now, it's not the grim silent place I grew up in.'

'No! Everyone bleats on about everything now, chat-show fodder round the clock.'

He didn't seem to want to discuss it further. 'Mmm . . . Shivaun, can I ask you something?'

'What?'

'Do you still want to go to bed with me?'

Yes. Although they'd got off to a shaky start, she had only to look at him to know that she did. His body was beckoning like a beacon in the night ocean. Putting down her glass, she was suddenly glad he'd said no more about children or about Ireland, let go of everything that might have put her off. She didn't want to talk or even think any more.

'Yes . . . but you're fully clothed . . .'

In the event they didn't even make it to the bedroom, nor undress, they were lying on the living room floor and he was grasping her in a grip like a vice, drilling into her as if down to Australia, clenching his teeth until his face was contorted, reminding her of the way the babies used to grimace at St Jude's, as if in either ecstasy or agony. She hoped it was the former, but his face was beyond reading.

Much later, when it was dark and getting cold, he swept her into his arms and carried her upstairs, undressed her and rolled her into the blissfully warm bed. When he was naked he stretched beside her and they lay quietly together for a while, drifting into the night until he suddenly tautened again, began to explore her body with his mouth and fingers, stroking and probing with new finesse, more control than before. She held off in turn, waited until she was arched with desire, and then flew at him like an arrow from a bow.

It delighted her to make him cry out, to see him sweat and reach for her until they were fused, locked in unison, he was captive in her arms. Dazed, they collapsed into each other, and she shuddered in ecstasy.

It's a drug, she thought, and we're getting addicted.

Ivor was perplexed, and irritated. Justine was making a fuss over nothing, sobbing like a child, as if they were engaged or even married. But they were only ships in the night, that had sailed temporarily together! He hated having made her cry, but he couldn't understand how or why he had.

'Come on, Jus, it's not the end of the world! It's only the end of a fling. I'm sure you'll have plenty more.'

She raised her sodden face and looked at him with a mixture of anger and appeal. 'I don't want plenty more! I want you!'

He leaned against the wall and spread his hands as if searching for sanity.

'You don't! We're chalk and cheese! You want someone who'll give you an easy comfortable life, fun, a good time . . . I'm an itinerant carpenter for God's sake, I've no money and no interest in the things that interest you.'

As he said it he wondered what exactly *did* interest Justine. He'd never known her voluntarily to do any of the things that now interested him, visit an art gallery or even read a book, watch a documentary or talk about anything of substance. As far as he was concerned they'd simply amused each other, and now the party was over.

Sitting on the futon that doubled as bed and sofa, she hiccuped and rubbed her eyes with her fists. They were swollen, her hair was a fuzzy ball of fluff, and he felt vaguely sorry for her.

'It doesn't matter about money,' she said, 'you'll earn that when you start your business.'

'But that'll be in Ireland – Justine, you're Australian, you're a sun-and-fun girl! Ireland is wet and tiny, you'd hate it. You wouldn't last six months.'

'I would' she said stubbornly.

He was exasperated. 'You would *not.* You'd hate both it and me, for taking you there. I intend to incarcerate myself in some small remote village, when I eventually get back. But first I'm going off on my own, and you are not coming with me.'

She stiffened, interrogated him with her teary eyes. 'Where are you going?'

'Off. Just off, to see a bit more of the world, or Europe at any rate. I'm going to hitch up through Spain and France, probably England too, wend my way very slowly home. It'll be October when I get there, chilly I dare say, especially for anyone who won't even have a roof over their head. You really don't want to know about it.'

Suddenly, she threw him a look like a knife. 'Have you someone else there? Is that it? Are you in love with some Irish woman?'

He drew furious breath to protest, and the words that emerged from his mouth astonished him.

'Yes. I am in love with an Irish woman. She's in America.'

He could see this was beyond her, as it was beyond him. His chances of ever retrieving Shivaun Reilly were a snowball's in hell.

'Ivor,' Justine sniffled, 'why did you never tell me?'

'Because it had nothing to do with you! I don't even know whether it has anything to do with *me*! I haven't seen her for a year, nor heard a word, she may well be in love with someone else herself by now.'

His heart tightened as he said it, contracted as if he'd been punched. Resolutely he wrenched his mind back to Justine.

'Look. We split up. She was an old flame, and we'd burned ourselves out. I don't know how or why the ashes are still smouldering. But I do know I was honest with you, never said anything about love or one misleading word of any kind.'

'Still. You slept with me when you loved her.'

'Yes. I did. And you enjoyed it. We both did, up to a point. But now the point has been reached.'

'Well,' she said, suffused with fresh pain and rage, 'I hope she makes you miserable for the rest of your life. I hope she stays in America and you never see her again and you pine to *death*.'

He knew she was upset, there was no point in striking back. 'Well, if she does wreck my life, that's my problem. But I don't want you to wreck yours. Not over me, Jus! I want you to find—'

'Don't worry,' she shouted, 'I will! I'll find someone much better than you! Which wouldn't be bloody difficult!'

There was a barb in that, one that made him catch his breath. If she meant someone richer or suaver or otherwise better suited to her than himself, well – fine. But he wondered whether she meant better in bed.

Christ! How could he have been any better, when he didn't love her? Bodies were only instruments, a means to an end; after the physical end, there had to be a spiritual beginning. Otherwise you ran out of steam, were left with a handful of dust. In fact, now that he thought about it, you really needed both body and soul from the start, if you were to get anywhere. Now that he'd experimented sexually, he knew that he no longer needed to. There would be no more Justines, he would *not* become a replica of Miguel Garros.

'In that case,' he suggested coldly, 'consider yourself free to do so. I'll be leaving at the end of the week.'

She burst into renewed tears, and he swore to himself. Women! They'd drive you mad. The one he loved didn't want him, and the one he didn't love now, apparently, did want him. Was that only because she could no longer have him? Nothing would surprise him, where these crazy creatures were concerned.

But at least Shivaun . . . even when their sex life had been dimmed and doused, by external forces, she'd never made him feel less than a man. Never once, because she loved him and knew he loved her.

Love had always mattered more to them than sex, was a far deeper bond. That was what sustained him now, the thought that she was surely unable to sleep with anyone she didn't love, or enjoy it if by any remote chance she was. He couldn't imagine it in a thousand years. Women got so – so emotionally *ensnared*, entangled with men. They just didn't work the same way men did.

But then, if she was sleeping with anyone else, she must love him. She wouldn't be able to do it otherwise.

Snatching up his jacket, ignoring the wailing Justine, he went out to get massively, roaring drunk.

Chapter Fourteen

Darting into Azalea's office while Marina was not about, Shivaun handed her friend a bottle of champagne and a small packet containing a silver bracelet studded with turquoise. Bemused, Azalea opened it.

'What's this for?'

'For being you. For sticking your neck out for me.'

Conspiratorially, Azalea smiled. 'So things are up and running at last, huh, with Mr Nulty? I always knew you two were made for each other.'

'Yes – I know I fought it, but I can't deny it. We just can't get enough of each other.'

'H'mm. And d'you know each other, now? Are you friends, or just lovers?'

Shivaun considered. 'Well, we're certainly lovers! And maybe . . . becoming friends. I hope so anyway, although you'd get more chat out of a rock. He's uphill but he – he's fascinating. Marina says he's poison, but he's a tonic for me, hasn't done anything to frighten the horses! I don't know why she's so set against him.'

'Oh, Marina thinks she's clairvoyant. Vivid imagination. I suppose you need one to design visionary houses, but sometimes it runs away with her. I've known Patrick for years and he's never stepped remotely out of line, the only thing he ever needed was a good woman to warm him up.'

'Well, he's certainly warming me! He's not cold at all when you get to know him.'

'Are you getting to know him?'

Was she? 'Yes. I think so. Slowly. Up to a point.'

'What's his house like?'

'Haven't you ever been in it?'

'No. Patrick's never been the party-throwing type. Like most bachelors I guess.'

'Well, it's nothing out of the ordinary, very low-key, but he probably doesn't spend much time in it. He can't be accused of flamboyance, that's for sure! It's just a white frame house a mile or so outside Lowell. If Marina starts grilling you, you won't have much to tell her, because he seems to lead a quiet respectable life.'

'Yes, well, fond as I am of Marina, I've learned when to take evasive action. She forgets that her authority doesn't extend into everyone's private life.'

'No – but still, Azalea, I don't want you getting into trouble on my account. You've done enough.'

'Yeah – I've fixed you up, anyhow! What happens next is up to the two of you. Have you thought about what to do, Shivaun, when your contract expires?'

'I'm thinking about it night and day. All I know for sure is that I want to stay in Massachusetts. There's damn all chance of finding another job as great as this one, but I'll take anything that keeps me within range of Patrick, of you and Marina and all the friends I've made.'

'Then why don't you register with a few nursing agencies in Boston and work on getting yourself a green card? If you're sure you don't want to go back to Dublin's fair city?'

Shivaun shuddered. 'No way. I'm totally sure of that. Dublin's too like Lowell, Azalea. Downbeat. Except that Lowell seems to know it, whereas Dublin's so busy preening and admiring itself it hasn't time to look itself in the eye. The Celtic tiger just purrs away – meanwhile the roads are crap, public transport is crap, the beaches and parks are full of litter, dog dirt, jetskis, rapists . . . on Sunday mornings the city centre's full of vomit, if a kid leaves a bike in a front garden it's stolen in five minutes—'

Azalea groaned. 'Oh God, here she goes again – Shivaun, lay off!'

'But it's my city! I hate what's happening to it, I want it to be livable like Boston or Gloucester or any of these civilised places! If I ever went back to Dublin I'd shake it till its teeth rattled.'

'Would you? Well, maybe you're just not cut out for city life. Anyway, you can't shake it from three thousand miles away, can you? You've copped out.'

'Huh?'

'I said you've copped out. Left, hightailed, vamoosed.'

She was stung, as much by the truth of it as by Azalea's sardonic grin. 'I'd had enough. I wanted out. What d'you expect me to do, stay and stew?'

'I dunno. Stand your ground, maybe?'

'I did stand it, for five years after Dad was murdered. Wasting my time.'

'Shivaun, to mix a metaphor, a battle's never over till the fat lady sings. My people – the Indians now so correctly known as Native Americans – never quit. Never ran away. They fought with every breath in their bodies.'

'Right. And what did they get? Ripped off and shunted onto reservations.'

'True. But at least they tried. Stayed and tried. Fought, and never lost their pride. They can tell their grandchildren they did their best, they kept their honour and their dignity. That counts for a lot, you know, when you look yourself in a mirror of a morning.'

Mutinously, Shivaun was forced to agree. 'So what are you saying here, huh? That I should go back to Ireland and carry on where I left off? Azalea, my mother got arrested for trying to save a Georgian building, for Chrissake! I got arrested for opposing a toxic dump! If Ivor hadn't intervened and somehow talked me free, I'd have a prison record! Can you imagine being *accused* of caring about your country? Ireland's like that fast-food chain, Chock Full O'Nuts!'

'Then one more shouldn't make much difference. But you might make some difference.'

'Yeah. I might. If I went back. But right now I'm a lot more interested in staying here and enjoying the charms of Mr Patrick Nulty, to whom you so thoughtfully introduced me.'

Azalea laughed. 'OK, I did. I thought you'd be good for each other. But d'you think it might get serious, Shivaun? Like, as in permanent? Marriage? Could you live in Lowell?'

Shivaun paused, considered. 'Nooo . . . I couldn't live in Lowell. But as for serious – you know, Azalea, I thought Ivor had cured me of all that. But now I don't know. I just don't know. All I can tell you for sure is that I'm spending next weekend with Patrick, and looking forward to it. Looking forward a *lot.* I just hope Marina doesn't throw any spanners in the works.'

'I don't think she will. She's so much better now, she doesn't need you as much as before . . . but Shivaun, that's just the point. Some day soon, you're going to have to decide what to do with the rest of your life. Marina adores you, but – in a way, you've rehabilitated each other. She's got to stand on her own two feet now, soon, and so do you.'

Yes. Shivaun knew that she had to, and knew that she could. If only she knew in which direction to turn. Back to Ireland, away from all these wonderful friends, without Patrick whose life was here in Massachusetts? Or stay here, with the nagging feeling of having left unfinished business at home, that Azalea was now accusing her of evading? Did 'home' mean the house she grew up in, Viv and Jimmy's house, or did it mean Chederlay and Marina, the bonds she had forged in America? Both were dear to her, she didn't think she could bear to sever either one; but neither could she hold on to both.

Ivor didn't feel he was leaving Justine so much as sliding off her; there was nothing to get a grip on, nothing to hold him as he fell away like a mountaineer from a glassy surface. Besides, the repairs to the hotel were finished, autumn was starting and he had no desire to linger in a beach resort out of season. Nerja was a nice little town, but after reading Aidan Higgins's book *Balcony On Europe* he knew that it was no longer the charmer it had once been. Tourism was tainting the entire southern coast of Spain and soon Nerja would resemble Mijas, where sombreroed donkeys waited in hobbled chain-gangs for the camera-clicking coachloads, or Marbella with its flash vulgar yachts and Arab gin palaces.

Not that I've anything against money, he thought, but I never want to be a slave to either the lack of it or a surfeit of it. I simply want it to enable me, free me to do the things that are more interesting than the making of it. Meanwhile, I haven't tuppence to my name, I'm going to have to hitch north. What about Granada, first? Let's see if this Alhambra Palace is all it's cracked up to be. Then Córdoba, Madrid, Zaragoza, Barcelona? Maybe Andorra? That'll take me up into France, where there'll be grape-harvesting if no carpentry is to be found. After that I can wend my way up into Brittany, cross the Channel from there to Plymouth. If the truth be told I'm not in any hurry to go home. But it is time to go.

Yet he felt a wrench as he kissed Justine's angry, averted face.

'Come on, Jus. Cheer up. We had fun, didn't we?'

'Yeah,' she muttered sullenly, 'and we could have had a lot more.'

But he knew they could not. The season was turning, the Costa del Sol was cooling and soon it would be hibernating, shuttered, reclaimed by those who were born and belonged here. Soon Justine would move on herself, to a new man or a new country, maybe back to Australia. Some day he would like to see Australia, India too, China, Asia, so much more of the world. But not now. First, he thought, I have to set up a life which, later, will allow me to travel again. Thus far I'm only a journeyman, but if I can turn the chrysalis into a craftsman, I can do it. I can trade the things I would have had – cars, houses, brands, logos, status – for freedom. I'm going home, but I'm never going to be the same person again. Andalucia was my watershed.

Does Shivaun like America, I wonder? I can't say I liked Andalucia. It's so bright and yet so bleak, loud, harsh, confrontational. You know where you stand here – ice in winter, fire in summer, sharp spires and bloody bullfights – but Ireland casts a long shadow. I miss its shadows, its subtleties. But Andalucia shook me up, widened my perspective, taught me so much even if I forged no lasting ties. Has Shivaun made friends, across the Atlantic? Has she settled down there, rooted and blossomed?

Or has she had enough? Home is where the heart is, and hers was always in Ireland. Always so bloody *in* it, even when she was wrestling it like a prizefighter. It fought right back, but still I'm amazed she left. I never knew her to quit before. She never would have, if St Jude's hadn't been closed down and Jason Dean hadn't been released. I never could get her to talk about him, but he did something to her. She should have joined some kind of victim support group, if only she'd been a joiner, or a groupie. She was a victim, though, in the end. He drove her out. Which leaves the little bastard in the driving seat . . . Jesus, I'd pulp him if I ever got my hands on him.

They're tough hands now, you know, Jason. I've put on a hell of a lot of muscle. Do you ever wonder whether there might be a pair of hands out there somewhere, waiting for you? Do you ever open your front door and feel fear, look around before you dare step out? You'd be well advised to look around, *amigo*, for the rest of your life. You'll never know the time nor the place.

I'm going to Granada now, hitching home; it'll take weeks, but I'll be back. And maybe some day Shivaun will be too. Maybe some day you'll be carted into hospital after some drug deal goes wrong and you'll look up and her name tag will swim before your eyes: Nurse Reilly.

Or your kid will be in an incubator and she'll be there, holding its life in her hands: Nurse Reilly.

Maybe. Or maybe not. You'll never know, will you?

* * *

Once she had made her views clear, Marina said not another word about Patrick, asked not another question, and Shivaun got the provocative impression that she was biding her time until, inevitably, it all went wrong. Then she would sail in with support and sympathy, picking up the pieces while silently whooping 'I told you so!' in that gleeful, maddening way mothers had.

But it was not going wrong. Far from it. As summer waned the relationship waxed, gradually extending beyond the purely physical until Shivaun discovered that Patrick was much more than a mere shelter from the storm that had once raged in her life. Unlike Steven Hunt, who still bedevilled Marina, he was not arrogant; in fact there was an endearing modesty in him, he never bragged about his successful business, previous women or anything he achieved with the needy youngsters who sometimes hung around his house, smoking and bouncing basketballs. Sometimes Shivaun heard him talking to them, words drifted in from the garden where they hung out, and she thought he was quite skilled with them, resourceful but never patronising. Whether his resources included money she wasn't sure, but she got the feeling it was sometimes quietly given, and even stood a chance of not being abused. The lads seemed to trust him, and sense that he trusted them.

If these kids can trust him, she thought – deprived kids, or abused – then surely I can? He's kind to them and he's more than kind to me, he's generous, even lavish, he'd spend a fortune on me if I'd let him. Not that he's a man for the big romantic gesture, but he won't let me split restaurant bills, that day I saw so many things I wanted to buy in Filene's sale I had to stop him from buying them all for me. And when I stay overnight he always makes breakfast, never expects me to do anything he can do himself. Maybe he still doesn't talk very much and I still don't know everything about him, but we're drawing closer, I can feel it in every look and every gesture. God, the way he looks at me sometimes! It's almost unnerving, that hungry look of his, so full of longing. But what can he be longing for? We're established now, we're together, we have a lot more than either of us had before. I must ask him what it is that's bugging him.

But the days and weeks went by, and she did not ask, because he had a way of seeming to sense when she was bubbling with questions, and putting his finger to her lips.

'Don't, Shivaun. The sea is calm now, so let's not rock the boat, h'mm?'

'But—'

'But curiosity killed the cat! Come on, relax. Be happy.'

'I am happy.'

'Well, then. Give me a smile, and a kiss?'

She gave him many smiles and many kisses, and he returned them ardently, drawing her to him in a way that seemed to say he was unable to believe his luck, that he cherished every moment with her.

'After all this time,' he murmured into her hair one night, 'after all this time.'

'After all this time, what?'

'I've found you. I've found somebody to love.'

She sat up and wriggled free of him. '*Love?* Oh, Patrick . . . I know you said you were falling in love with me, but I didn't think you actually had.'

He pulled her back to him. 'Yes. I have. I've fallen. I have no right to do it, but it's done. I love you.'

She waited for him to ask whether she loved him, and wondered what she would say. She was on the brink of it, she knew, holding back only with an enormous effort of will, because there were still so many shadowy corners, empty spaces in his previous life, that had yet to be filled in. She knew now that he was from Monaghan, that he had a widowed father still living there, two married sisters, one in Glasgow and one in Kerry. His mother had died of cancer. His former school, which he'd left at sixteen, was now a golf club. His favourite song was 'The Fields Of Athenry'. His favourite food was steak. He liked the colours blue and green. His first kiss had been to a girl called Aileen, when she was twelve and he was fourteen, round behind the oak tree in Delaney's field. He'd come to America just before his eighteenth birthday, to live with an uncle who was a keen gardener and got him interested in it. His birthday was on August 20.

She knew all these things, and yet she did not fully know him. Therefore she could not fully love him, not wholly. If only he would tell her everything, she might be able to give him everything, abandon her heart to him. It grieved and frustrated her that he would not, when he gave her so much else. So much happiness.

And now, even love?

'But if you loved me, you'd tell me—'

He shut his eyes, clenched them in the way he had, whether to keep her out or keep himself in she could not tell.

'Shivaun –' he paused to kiss her – 'will you tell *me* something?'

She lay back on her pillow and looked down at his upturned face in the darkness. 'Yes,' she said candidly, 'I will if I can. I have nothing to hide.'

Ignoring the innuendo, he took her hand and drew a deep breath. 'This – this other guy. Ivor. Do you still think of him?'

She nodded. 'Yes. Sometimes I do.'

He winced, and she knew it was not what he wanted to hear. But it was true – and it was rare, too. She had succeeded in getting away from Ivor, as from so much else.

'And – and do you still love him?'

Sighing, she thought about it. 'Patrick, we were lovers for a long time, and best friends all our lives. I think when you've been that close to someone, for so long, you always love them a little bit afterwards. Maybe forever. But you tuck it away, it's in the past. It's over and done with.'

'Is it?'

'Yes. It is.'

'But, Shivaun . . . do you think anything can be over and done with? Really in the past?'

'Yes! It can, Patrick. It has to be, otherwise none of us would have any today or tomorrow. We'd be prisoners, we'd have no future.'

He rubbed his hand and forearm across his eyes, and was silent, lying on his back in the dark.

'And – and this other guy, who made you so unhappy in a different way? Jason Dean? Do you ever think of him?'

Again she nodded, and stiffened. 'Oh yes. I think of him.'

'Do you? What do you think?'

'I think he – I – I hate him! I'm trying to get past him too, but he's different. Ivor made me happy, whereas Jason Dean killed my father, my mother died as a result and my life has never been the same since. I'm trying to mend it, and have largely succeeded now, but it'll never be the same again. If I ever marry, my parents will never be there at my wedding, my children will never have grandparents, Jimmy and Viv will never see them or get to do any of the other things they would have loved to do . . . I can try to forget, but I can never forgive.'

He gripped her hand. 'Can't you, Shivaun? Ever?'

'No. Never.'

The word hung in the night between them, ghostly as the moon, glowing pale and phosphorescent. It was a long time before Patrick spoke again, still holding her hand, looking up at her.

'But then . . . you'll always be Jason's prisoner. You'll never be free of him – oh, God, Shivaun, can't you try? Can't you try that little bit harder?'

'I am trying, as hard as I can, but – Patrick, do you think he ever thinks of me? Thinks of Jimmy, or has any idea what he did to the rest of us?'

'Yes.' Turning on his side, he embraced her, and held her fiercely. 'You're not the only captive, Shivaun. Jimmy's death and its repercussions will always haunt Jason, maybe in ways he doesn't even know about yet. Ways that may only hit him when his own father dies, or his own child is born . . . he'll pay, believe me. He'll pay all his life.'

'Do you think so?'

'Yes. I do. But I don't want you to keep on paying. He's not worth it, Shivaun! Besides, he was very young, you say, when he did what he did. High on some drug, not thinking, not aware . . . he could be rehabilitated now for all you know, a different person. A decent person, trying to make something of his life, make up for yesterday and reach for tomorrow.'

'If he wanted to make up for it, he could have started by apologising for it. That would have meant so much, you know, if only he'd ever said sorry. One little word. But he never did say it.'

'Perhaps he felt it would be inadequate. A kind of insult, in proportion to the crime.'

'Yes. Perhaps. That's what Azalea thinks. But I think it was just cowardice. Take his knife away, and all you've got left is a pathetic little coward.'

'Oh, Shivaun . . . let go. Please try to let go. You must try. *Please?*'

There was something almost desperate in his tone, and for his sake she attempted to soften her own. How, when they had started out talking about love, had they come round to this? For several seconds she lay wondering, and then, lightening her touch, she brushed Patrick's face with her finger. It was wet with tears.

Aghast, she clutched him to her. 'Oh, my God – Patrick – what is it? What's wrong?'

He tried to speak, but a sob tore from his throat, and he buried his face in her shoulder.

'Shivaun, I love you! I love you, and I don't want Jason to have you! I want us to have a future, not a past!'

His voice rasped on her shoulder, and something in him tore at her heart. Something that told her she must lose Jason Dean, or she would lose Patrick Nulty. She could have yesterday, or she could have tomorrow, but she could not have both.

Marina was doing almost everything for herself now, and the doctors were agreed that she could soon go to her clients in the

Cotswolds, albeit not unaccompanied. Shivaun must go with her, or if her contract had expired by then, Azalea should go. Thinking about it, Shivaun decided to talk to Marina, who was not looking as happy as she should be. One grey stormy afternoon, she went up to the studio where Marina was working, sitting at her easel sketching with Rachmaninov thundering loudly around her.

'Hi.'

'Hi. Come on in.'

Marina didn't look annoyed to be interrupted, and Shivaun was encouraged.

'I just came up to have a word about – well, you know, my contract's nearly up, and you're nearly good as new.'

Marina chewed the end of her pencil and looked out the window to where some seagulls were squawking and spiralling.

'Yes. Isn't God good. I am, as you Irish say, fit as a fiddler.'

Shivaun thought she detected irony in her tone, and something else.

'But?'

'But – oh, dammit, Shivaun, dammit to hell!' Hurling her pencil at the window, she thumped her fist on her sketchpad, jumped off her chair and marched to the window. Throwing it wide open, she inhaled several lungfuls of gusty salt air, and slammed it shut again.

'Bad hair day, huh? Sketches not good?'

'No. It's not that.' Marina looked truly frazzled, and Shivaun was slightly alarmed. Tantrums were not good for blood pressure. Going to her, she put her arm around Marina's shoulder and steered her to the daybed, sat her down quivering amidst the books and throws and majestic mess.

'What is it? Not – not my imminent departure, surely?'

Marina grimaced, and raised her face. 'Well, yes, if you must know, it is partly that. I'm going to miss you terribly.'

Shivaun sat down beside her. 'Yes. I know, and I'll be very sorry to go. But Marina, I'm not going very far. The agency in Boston has two job offers already, one in Concord and the other in Martha's Vineyard, all I need is references from you and I can choose either one. We'll be able to see each other all the time.'

With rare self-deprecation, Marina shrugged. 'Oh, you won't want to come visit an old hag like me.'

'What? Marina, get a grip! You know I love you and that we'll always be friends, very close friends I hope . . . what's wrong with you? Unless I get turned down for a green card, I'll be here every other evening, driving you nuts!'

'Oh, you'll get your green card. I'll see to that. But you'll be with Patrick. I can see it already, you're getting closer to him every day . . . I hoped it would burn itself out, but it hasn't, has it?'

'No. It hasn't. He says he's – he's in love with me.'

Sure that Marina would expostulate, tell her she was a fool if she was in love with him, she was amazed when, instead, Marina clutched her hand, and looked at her with tears in her eyes.

'Well, Shivaun, if he is, then he's getting a gem, and maybe it is for the best. Maybe you should take whatever chance of happiness life offers you.'

At first Shivaun was bewildered, knowing that Marina felt as she did about Patrick. But then she looked at her again, saw the anguish in her eyes, and the penny dropped.

'It's Steven, isn't it? He's making you unhappy?'

Gazing down at the floor, Marina nodded almost imperceptibly. 'Yes. I won't go into detail, or lose my dignity if I can help it, but you're right, Shivaun. It is Steven. I feel – apart from anything else, I feel such a fool, at my age.'

'Oh, would you Americans ever give over, you have age on the brain! As if the capacity for love or pain snapped off on your thirtieth birthday! As if – Jesus, Marina, you know what I went through with Ivor, and that I must understand how you feel! Now, spit it out – what exactly has Steven done, or not done?'

But Marina shook her head, and gathered her cashmere folds around her. 'No. I won't demean myself by prattling like a schoolgirl. I do appreciate your sympathy, but let's leave it at that. Let's just say that I have to break away from him, if only I can find the courage.'

'I'll find you the courage. I'm not letting him make you unhappy. You're my friend and – and my patient! Tell Steven he's endangering your health!'

Wryly, Marina summoned a smile. 'Yes. It's ironic, because he helped me back to health, but he's certainly not doing me any good now.'

'Then – let's see. How about those Cotswolds? Would now be a good time for you to go, get away from him?'

Marina plucked at her drapes. 'Yes. It would be a very good time for me to go, and I'd like you to come with me. But would it be a good time for you? I don't want to come between you and Patrick, if things really are—'

Shivaun smiled. 'Yes. Things are. He's warm and kind and he – I think he really cares about me. But I care about you. So Patrick can wait. I reckon he'll still be here when I get back.'

'Yes, well, if he says he loves you, then he'd better be. Maybe I should arrange a small dinner and—'

'And grill him? Oh, Marina! I know you don't like him, but I'd be thrilled if you ever did get to like him. He isn't nearly as black as he's painted, you know, I think maybe Azalea was right about him being just shy.'

Keenly, Marina inspected her face. 'Do you? Have you got to know him well enough to judge?'

'I've got to know him much better, and I like what I've found so far. But let's not talk about him now. Let's call your clients in the Cotswolds and tell them that Madam Herself is coming over in person at last, with her humble assistant.'

Looking cheered, Marina patted Shivaun's hand, and got to her feet.

'Yes. Very well. Let's do that. Let's see whether a trip to England can get Steven bloody Hunt out of my head for a week, and Patrick out of yours for half an hour. Not that I hold out much hope any more, but it's worth a try.'

Shivaun grinned. 'Yeah, well, you can give it your best shot,

Marina. Your last shot. But if it doesn't work, I'm bringing him here to dinner when we get back, OK? And you're going to play Mom and be nice to him, OK?'

'OK. Now scram. I'm too busy a woman for any more of this romantic rubbish.'

Pleased to see her mood improved, Shivaun left her, and a few moments later Rachmaninov gave way to Queen.

Pressure of other business meant that Marina could not leave for England until early October, and Shivaun was delighted to be in Massachusetts for another glorious fall as the trees began to ignite and flame gold, copper and bronze, the sky a deep solid blue above the burning canopy. Nearly every day she walked around the coast or though the woods, where the local artists were out in abundance, eagerly painting while the light lasted. Sometimes Kathy Shreve was amongst them, and she stopped to watch.

'What in hell is that?' she asked one day, peering into an oily mass of scarlet ridges.

'It's the pride and joy of Citibank,' Kathy grinned, 'they've commissioned a landscape for their new lobby.'

'Wow!'

'Yeah, wow – and wait till you hear what else. Kelsey has asked for a set of oils for his birthday. He wants to try painting too – can you imagine, my son the roaring monster? Apparently he's caught the bug. Bill's furious, says he must be gay and it's all my fault.'

They both laughed, and Shivaun sat down cross-legged amidst the crunchy leaves.

'So there's hope, huh?'

'For my kid? Yeah. I think there might be. You just never know how they'll turn out.'

No. Apparently you didn't. Not that she'd ever find out, Shivaun mused, if she stayed with Patrick who'd had a vasectomy. No kids for her, no 'grandchildren' for Marina. Not unless . . . was Patrick too old to adopt, or averse to the idea?

Why did he feel he wouldn't make a good father, when he was so good with the kids from the youth clubs? Could he maybe be persuaded, some day, if . . . ? As she thought about it it dawned on her that she would love to adopt a child, when the time was right. Not now, but whenever she could give it all that Viv and Jimmy had given her. It would honour their memory, be a living memorial to them. It would be great.

'Kathy – did you always want kids?'

'H'mm . . . not always. On and off. I thought I did until I had them! Then I found them such hard going, I kind of went off them for a while. But now I'm enjoying them again. I guess moods and relationships are living things, they change according to circumstance, or whether the moon is in Pisces or there's an east wind blowing or whatever. Nothing's fixed in stone.'

Shivaun was cheered to think it wasn't. If Kathy's feelings had changed, Patrick's might too. Of course she was putting the cart before the horse, because their relationship was not yet on a permanent basis, no commitments had been made – but she wondered whether they might be sought, soon, because Patrick had seemed agitated lately. When he heard about her trip to England with Marina, he'd gone very quiet, even when reassured that it was only for a week.

'Yes,' he'd said, 'but a week can be a long time in politics.'

She'd laughed and said it was hardly enough time to organise a revolution, was it, one lousy week? No, he admitted, but what if she got a taste for life back on the other side of the ocean?

'I won't have time' she asserted. 'Marina has a full schedule, not just work but a major assault on Harrods too, and friends in London to visit. Besides, England isn't Ireland, is it?'

No, he conceded, it certainly wasn't. It was a very different country. Personally, he didn't care much for it.

Surprised, she asked whether he'd ever been in it, and if so where, exactly? Sounding nettled, he'd then had to admit that he'd never been there, but he 'didn't like the sound of it'.

'You' she retorted crisply, 'are talking cobblers. And I am very much looking forward to England.'

Now, thinking about it, she wondered whether he had a

possessive streak in him, didn't want her to travel without him. Well, he'd better watch it if he had, because she was going, and that was that.

Looking up at Kathy, she smiled. Kathy was all in favour of the trip, said she'd never been to England but would adore to go.

'Hey Kath – what would you like me to bring you back from London?'

Kathy paused to dab thoughtfully at a vermilion blodge, and consider.

'I'd like' she said finally, 'Prince William. Giftwrapped. It's high time I had a toyboy. One whose wealth or fame can never eclipse my own.'

She laughed, and Shivaun thought what a different woman she was now to the one she'd been a year ago. What different women they both were.

A few days before she was due to depart, Patrick took Shivaun to a baseball game. She'd never been to one before, and didn't understand a single stroke of it, but the atmosphere was great fun and she was in high spirits when they went back to Lowell, furnished with a Chinese take-out and a bottle of wine. It was their last weekend together, if only temporarily, and they felt tenderness between them, glowing affection.

'So,' he said as he set the food out an plates, 'have you decided which job to take when you come back?'

'Yes. The one in Martha's Vineyard. Another stroke patient, a bit older this time, but I've talked to her family and I like the sound of them. They wanted me to start as soon as she's out of hospital but I explained about Marina, so they've got a temp in the meantime. I drove down to Martha's Vineyard the other day to take a look around . . . it'll be great to stay by the sea, in a small place. I think Azalea's right about me not being cut out for big cities.'

She bit into her chow mein, giggling as it slid off the chopsticks, and he looked at her with what seemed to be relief.

'Yeah. The Vineyard's lovely. You'll like it there. Pity it's so far from here, though. Nearly a hundred miles.'

'Mmm . . . about the same from Gloucester, too. But that's nothing on American roads. Except that I won't have Marina's car anymore, I'll have to get one of my own.'

He poured some wine and thought very briefly. 'Let me get you one.'

'What? Buy me one, d'you mean? Are you mad?'

'Oh, Shivaun, cars aren't nearly as expensive here as they are in Ireland, it's no big deal. I'd really like you to have a nice one.'

'I would too! But Patrick, I can't let you do that. It's far too – too *major* a gift. I appreciate the offer, but – no. Thank you, but no.'

'But—'

'What?'

'Oh, nothing. I just thought I'd like to – to mark the moment, that's all.'

'What moment?'

'Your decision to stay in America. Until very recently I was afraid you might not. Now that you are, I feel so relieved! I love you, you know. I really want you in my life, if only you'll ever have me in yours.'

Earnestly, intently, he looked at her over his barely-touched food, and she was nonplussed. What exactly did he mean? Surely that – that wasn't a *proposal*, was it? It sounded more like a plea.

Fiddling with her noodles, she gazed into them.

'Yes. I will have you in mine, Patrick. I'm not sure on what basis, in the long run, but for now I – we – we seem to be making each other very happy.'

'Yes. You're making me incredibly happy, anyway. You've changed my whole life.'

'Hah! For the better, I hope?'

'Very much for the better. If there's anything I can do, any single thing to help you settle in here permanently, you have only to ask. Paperwork, taxes, anything . . . maybe your house in Ireland?'

She was deeply touched. And slightly puzzled. 'What's my house got to do with it?'

Vaguely, he waved a chopstick. 'Well, if you're going to be living here, there's no point in keeping it, is there? Why don't you sell it and then, since you insist on buying your own car, you can have anything you like, maybe a jeep or a convertible? You could probably buy your own little apartment in Martha's Vineyard too, although I hope you'll be spending as much time as possible here with me.'

'But Patrick, accommodation goes with the job, just like it did at Chederlay. Besides, selling my parents' house would be a kind of radical thing to do. I can't let Alana have it rent-free forever, especially considering how she hasn't even kept in touch, but I'd rather give her a choice of renting or else get new tenants. I think of that house as a kind of security blanket, you know, just in case I ever did change my mind and want to go back to Ireland. Azalea and Kathy both seem to feel I might, some day, although I don't want to think that far ahead myself for now.'

He looked both dismayed and apprehensive. 'Shivaun, I would be devastated if you ever did change your mind. I've reached the point where I can't imagine life without you. I want . . . I hope . . . that if you'll only be patient with me, we might be able to talk about getting married one day.'

His face was so full of eagerness, and yet anxiety, it rent her heart. But why did he want her to be patient, as he put it, for what? And how could they talk about marriage, until they'd talked about whether they wanted to adopt children, or any of the other things they had not yet talked about? More and more every day, she was falling in love with him. But still she knew so little about him – not about the man he was now, but the man he had been before. The man who had run away from himself, was still running, didn't trust himself to father children or think they'd want him.

Pushing away what remained of her meal, she sipped some wine and thought about what he was saying to her, about every implication.

The offer of a car was so generous, so endearing . . . and yet so big a gesture, she felt the weight of it, the commitment it suggested. Selling her house would be a serious step too, an acknowledgement that there was no turning back. For her this trip to England was merely an enjoyable diversion, but to him it seemed to mean much more, demarcate a certain point. He was not asking her to marry him outright, tomorrow morning, but he was making it clear that he longed to do it as soon as – as soon as what?

For a while she sat looking out the window, nursing her wine, watching the sky spread out in great crimson streaks, soaking up the light until it turned amethyst, purple and finally black. She was aware of the long still silence, and that he was watching her, but he did not speak, did not interrupt her train of thought. So much was unspoken, there was so much yearning in the air, she felt it around her like velvet mantle.

Finally, she looked at him, and smiled tenatively. Quietly, gravely, he took her hand across the table.

'Shivaun.' His voice was like a breeze whispering in an elm. 'What are you thinking? What can I say to make you share my life? Tell me, and I'll say it. Only please tell me.'

Putting down her glass, she gripped his hand in both of hers.

'Yes, Patrick. I think it is time you told me. I need to know the truth, and I need to know it tonight. About why you had a vasectomy, why you want me to be patient, why you left Ireland and never went back – I want to hear all of it. Everything. Now.'

She felt the tension gather in his hand, spread out to his whole body, immobilising his features as if they were made of glass. He blanched visibly, but he didn't flinch, faced her squarely.

'Yes. You have every right to ask, Shivaun, and I knew that some day you would. I've been trying to prepare for it, hoping that it might not come so soon . . . and it might not have, if you weren't going away. If I didn't feel I had to say everything I have said, so that you'll know how much I want you to come back. Since you want me to tell you now, I will – but – only if you're absolutely sure.'

'I'm sure.'

'All right. It's a long story and I have to warn you, it will distress you. It may frighten you, horrify you as it horrifies me. It – it may even destroy us, if you feel you can't handle it. All I ask of you is to remember that it happened at another time in another place, many miles and years ago, and that I was a different person then. But it has formed me, it has moulded and haunted my every waking moment. If I live to be a hundred, I will never stop regretting it. But I have paid for it, Shivaun. I promise you I have paid – maybe not yet in full, but if I lose you, I'll pay more dearly than I ever knew was possible.'

Taut, verging on terrified, she fought for control, dreading what she was about to hear. She couldn't have continued without hearing it, but now it sounded like the hiss of a snake, coiled and writhing within Pandora's box. Oh, God, why had she opened it? When he stood up, she gasped, recoiled as if he were lunging at her. But he walked around to her side of the table, and put his palm very gently on her shoulder.

'Let's leave all this, and go upstairs. I want you in my arms when I tell you, I want to feel you so alive and vibrant beside me . . . you can hit me if you want, you can scream and shout and abuse me till the cows come home, throw tantrums, punches, missiles, anything. Just so long as you promise to hear me out, and not run away from me?'

Shivering, she stood up and let him encircle his arm around her waist, draw her towards the stairs . . . but suddenly she wished this were happening somewhere else, that she had chosen a safer location, not this house where she was alone with him. Until now she had always sensed him to be a strong man – but what if he turned that strength on her? If he had done something terrible once, could he do it again?

On the stairs her knees almost buckled, her legs jellied under her so that he had to steady her. But his touch was firm, and frank.

'Don't worry, Shivaun. Please don't be afraid. I've often

heard it said that confession is good for the soul, and I think this one will be good for mine. You're the nemesis I always knew would come one day, and I deserve every penance you can hurl at me. If you feel nervous, and I can understand why you would, then why don't you call Marina or Azalea, now this minute, and tell them where you are, who you're with? Would that help?'

Tersely, she disengaged herself from his grip and drew resolute breath.

'Azalea and Marina already know I'm with you. So do Dorothy and Joe.'

Faintly, he smiled. 'Good. They'll know where to send the ambulance, then, after you're through with me.'

But the small levity didn't help. She really was worried. But determined to see it through, because there could be no future if she didn't. Only now did she realise how bound up her life had become with this man's, how much he had come to mean to her, this stranger who had got so close. Every drop of blood was pulsing in her body, every inch of her skin was tingling as they went into the bedroom, and he switched on a small lamp. But then her fingers wouldn't work, she fumbled with her clothes until he came to her, and helped her with them.

'You are so beautiful . . . I love you so much . . .'

He was breathing into her neck, his hands were warm around her, but her nerves were quivering, stretched to snapping point.

'Don't, Patrick. Not now.'

Instantly he released her, but not before she saw the yearning in his eyes, and the sadness. Silently, he waited for her to get into the bed, lifted the duvet over her, undressed and got in beside her.

'Am I – am I allowed to put my arm around you?'

She had to think about it. But he looked so pleading, so acutely unhappy.

'All right.'

She must sound begrudging, she knew, even hostile. But

this, whatever it turned out to be, was of his own making. Bracing herself, she waited.

'I – I—'

Drawing breath, he faltered, and looked searchingly at her. 'I don't know where to begin.'

'Why don't you try the beginning?'

Biting his lip, keeping his arm around her but rolling over onto his back, he lay staring at a long shadow on the ceiling.

'I – Shivaun, I was only a boy. A thick, lonely, bull-headed boy out in the wilds of Monaghan. We were a poor family in a poor country, we had none of the things everyone has today, no sports facilities or cultural resources, no counsellors or even communication, sometimes the only person you'd see in a week was the postman passing by. No books, no travel, no glimpse of a better, richer life. It was a vacuum, and nature abhors a vacuum.'

'What do you mean?'

'I mean that I left school early, as you know already, to help my parents on their farm. I wanted to stay on but they needed my input . . . it meant giving up not only my studies but my friends. Our house was five miles from the nearest village, out in the fields, very isolated. Nobody ever came near us. Nobody except Aidan Cleary, who came cycling up the lane one day – he had to get off his bike, I remember, because it was so rutted. He'd come to buy a couple of chickens for his mother, who knew my mother needed the money. When I said I'd have to get my father to kill them for him, he laughed at me. He said I was a sight for sore eyes, a hulking great sixteen-year-old who couldn't strangle a chicken. I suppose he was right. It was just something I'd always avoided having to do.'

'Did you do it then?'

'No. I gave him a shove and said he surely couldn't do it either. So he did it, right there and then. Just grabbed two hens and throttled them.'

'Uhhh.'

'Yeah, well, that's part of rural life. The only thing that impressed me was the way he did it, so decisive, no ifs or buts about it. I thought he was quite the lad. Younger than me, but a real man. I told him that the next time he wanted chickens, I'd show him. I'd wring their necks in a flash.'

'And did you?'

'Oh yes. I did. And a lot more besides. When he came back a week or two later, I got talking to him. He offered me a fag, which I accepted and nearly choked on. But I smoked it. Down to the dregs. He laughed and said I looked like a pixie pulling a pipe, but that maybe I'd make a man some day yet.'

In the semi-darkness, Shivaun waited.

'So I told him I was a man, as damn good as him any day, and he laughed again. Said that men in these parts did a sight more than smoke fags and kill chickens. I asked him what he meant. He said he meant that real men got off their butts and joined in the fight.'

'What fight?'

'I didn't have to ask him. I knew what he meant. The fight against the British, in the North, the border was only twelve miles from our house. I suppose I was being conscripted, but I didn't realise it at the time. You don't when it's a kid barely your own age who's doing it. Anyway, he clapped me on the back and said he looked forward to seeing me again, on Friday night to be exact, in the barn behind Gerry Kenny's farmhouse. The barn where meetings were held.'

'Jesus, Patrick, you didn't—'

'I did. Of course I did, Shivaun. It was the only way to survive. I didn't think too much about it, I just told myself that if I didn't go Aidan Cleary might never buy another chicken off us, and that if I did go I might meet a few lads, make a few pals. I didn't have any brothers, only sisters, and I'd no school mates any more. I was desperate for any male company around my own age. So I went. I drank my first beer and I swore left, right and centre, uttered every word my father would've walloped the arse off me for saying at home. Most of them I'd never even heard before, since we didn't have a television, but I learned them all that night. Learned, and remembered, and played the hard man. And puked my guts up on the way home.

'After that, there was no going back. You *couldn't*. Once you went the first time you were in and that was the end of it. I'm pretty sure in retrospect that some guys wanted to get out, were scared shitless, but they didn't dare. Nobody did. Nobody was too sure what might happen if they tried. So we all went along to the meetings, regular as clockwork, good little lads . . . good little soldiers, eventually. I learned how to use a gun and how to lie through my teeth. I even learned some of the history I'd missed out at school – selective bits, that made me think maybe I was doing the right thing. That I was *definitely* doing it. I became quite a young convert. Almost a zealot, with that fire in my belly unique to young males, especially when they have access to weapons.'

'But for chrissakes, didn't your parents—?'

'Suspect? Yeah. I'm sure they did. But I never knew whether they approved, or were afraid to intervene. They never said a word either way. It just seemed to be tacitly accepted, part of Monaghan life for a local lad. And there were perks, too, enough rewards to keep us motivated. For the first year or more I actually enjoyed it. I had mates, and a bit of status with them, because I was a good shot. Not that I ever shot anything more than a tin can or some flying object, for target practice.'

She was hugely relieved. 'Oh, Patrick, thank God. I thought you were going to tell me—'

He tightened his arm around her. 'No. I never shot anyone, Shivaun. I did something infinitely worse.'

Their eyes met in the dark, and she was electrified.

'What, Patrick?' She could barely whisper. 'What did you do?'

Screwing his eyes shut, he carried inexorably on.

'I joined a unit. The time had come, and I accepted it. Became a full-fledged member of the IRA. A soldier of destiny. The only problem was, you had to prove you were worthy of the honour. You had to undertake a mission, and not screw it up.

'My mission was to plant a bomb. Not a huge one, not the

kind that'd massacre half a town the way the one in Omagh did. Just a little one. I tried to convince myself it would just make a big bang, do a bit of window damage and give the Brits a good fright. But then I was told where it was to be planted – in a litter bin, in a shopping centre, outside Boots the Chemists. I made the point that the location sounded a bit indiscriminate, but I was told that Boots was a legitimate enemy target, and to shut up.

'So I – I shut up. I knew what might happen if I didn't. The only concession I got was the time of the explosion – just after nine in the morning, when not many people would be out shopping yet. I worked on persuading myself that nobody would get hurt, that Boots would only have a wee insurance claim and that Boots were British anyway, the infidel invaders and repressors of our fourth green field. I ninety per cent convinced myself. Meanwhile, transport was arranged, and on the day – it was a Wednesday – I was driven over the border. Easy peasy: just drop the plastic bag in the bin, stroll away and get picked up in the same car ten minutes later, with plenty of time to spare before the bomb went off. Nobody except my comrades-in-arms knew where I was or what I was doing, I'd be home in time to have a late breakfast and help dip the sheep.

'I made a damn good job of it, Shivaun. I didn't panic. I planted the bomb, walked away, sauntered round the corner, my hands were so steady I was even able to light a cigarette. I took a few puffs, kept on walking, reached the rendezvous and got in the car. I didn't even know the name of the driver – nobody ever did, in case. He just looked like an ordinary Joe to me, as I did to him, two guys in an ordinary car with a pretty girl in the back. Girls were brought along a lot, for cover, that sisterly innocence. For hero-worship and suitable reward, sometimes, although I don't know whether this one was meant to be mine, or had any idea what I'd done.

'I didn't know myself, until I went down to the pub that night, to see the news on telly. Then I found out exactly what my achievement was, what a great success it had all been.

'I'd blown the leg off a twenty-eight-year-old woman, and killed her ten-month-old baby in his buggy.'

Chapter Fifteen

Dawn was breaking, and the sun sliced like a scalpel into Shivaun's salt-streaked face, feeling as if it were lifting the skin from the bone. All night she had wept, as had Patrick, from the core of his being and the depths of his soul. Everything gushed from him, a torrent of remorse, until he was pumped bone dry.

'Her name was Emily Thomas, and her little boy was Kenneth, known to everyone as Kenny. There were pictures of them both. She was small and kind of delicate-looking, with blonde hair that turned in just under her chin. He was chubby, round-faced, with dark eyes and curly hair, cuddling a Snoopy toy in the photo. I wondered whether he'd been holding it when he died. I – I can't describe how I felt. As soon as I saw their faces and heard their names, they were branded on me, I knew I would never forget them as long as I lived. They weren't "targets" any more, they were a mum and a kid, and I'd wrecked my own life every bit as fully and irrevocably as I'd wrecked theirs.

'All the guys thought I was great, a real cool hero, it made me sick to hear the things they said. All I could think of was blood and gore, Kenny dying and Emily losing her leg. I went into a kind of daze, hardly eating or sleeping, going to no more meetings, not caring what happened. I was numb, a zombie.

'About a week later, out of the blue it seemed, my father came to me one day and asked me whether I'd like to go and spend the summer with Uncle Gerry in America. Uncle Gerry was his brother, he'd emigrated decades before, way back in the fifties, and I knew very little about him except that he was a gardener. But I had to get out. Not because the police were after me – it was in the days before security cameras and there was no sign of anyone suspecting me – but because I couldn't live in Monaghan any more, with the IRA or with myself.

'So I went to Uncle Gerry, a teenager off on his summer vacation, and I spent that first summer in Boston, mowing people's lawns and helping him tidy up their gardens. It was a hot summer, but I felt as if I were packed in ice, frozen with horror. It didn't fully sink in for a long time, I just kept my head down and lived quietly in Gerry's family, trying not to think about it. But then one day an envelope arrived. I can still see it, a lightweight blue air-mail envelope with those little stripes around it, and an Irish postmark that nearly floored me with fright. There was no letter inside, just a newspaper clipping. It was a report of Kenny's funeral, and it said that Emily had asked for the funeral to be delayed until she was out of hospital and could be there, in a wheelchair. I wondered whether she'd get an artificial leg, or ever be able to walk again . . . Kenny's dad was in the photo this time too, a big strong steel welder called Jack, and Kenny's brother Brett, who was six at the time. Jack was holding him by the hand at the graveside, behind Emily's wheelchair, and they all looked as if they'd had the life crushed out of them.

'I hid the clipping and spent days thinking about it, wondering who had sent it. Obviously it was someone who knew what I'd done and where I was – maybe even my own father – but to this day I don't know for sure. That's one of the reasons I've never been able to go back to Ireland, Shivaun. Somebody over there knows . . . somebody who sent me another clipping a year or two later, about the Thomas family leaving the North and moving to Waterford, a few miles from Dunmore East. Someone who's never said or done anything, but seems to be watching me. Much later, shortly after I bought this house in Lowell, a third envelope arrived here, with another very small cutting pasted onto paper – a death notice for Emily Thomas, aged thirty-nine, who'd died in Waterford. It didn't say what she had died of. All I know is that she never had any more children, because it said "wife of Jack, mother of Brett and baby Kenny (deceased)". That was when I made up my mind that I would never have any children of my own, because I didn't deserve any. I – I felt I was poison. I accepted that I'd always be alone, an outsider, never normal or happy, holding my own child in my arms. I couldn't bear to have what Emily and Kenny had been robbed of, to start one family when I'd finished another.

'Meanwhile, Uncle Gerry taught me all he knew about gardening, and I earned enough from it to put myself through horticultural college. College is fun for most young guys, but I never enjoyed a single day of it, because I was always looking over my shoulder, waiting for a hand to fall on it. No hand ever did fall, but in a way that made it worse, there were days when I wanted to simply go home, confess and go straight to prison where I belonged. I've never had the courage, but I still think – or did think, until I met you.'

Pausing, Patrick looked at Shivaun, but she did not reply. After a glass-brittle silence, he continued.

'But it makes no difference. I've done prison, here in America. I've made money and a few good, trustworthy friends, I have everything I could materially wish for, but I've never been happy. Never allowed myself to be, until now, and I've never been free. Sometimes I've lain here in this bed for hours, wondering what Kenny would be doing if he were alive, what kind of man he'd be at nearly twenty, whether Emily was medically unable to have another baby or couldn't stand the thought of replacing him . . . I've gone halfway crazy, seeing their faces over and over and over.

'I've also tried to make amends, as far as anyone could. I've put all my free time into the kids you've seen hanging around here, kids the same age as Kenny would be now. Not just as a gesture to his memory, but because I don't want any other kid to get into the kind of trouble I got into, enticed into crime or violence for lack of any other outlet. If my parents had paid more attention, had more resources, not been economic hostages . . . if I'd been able to stay on at school . . . if there'd been decent sports facilities, transport, anyone to take an interest . . . if, if, if. All I can do today is my best, for other people's kids. It'll never be enough, though. There was only one Kenny Thomas and there'll never be another. Every time I see a Snoopy toy or cartoon, it hits me like a hammer to the heart, I think of him lying there in his grave. I will think of him until I'm in my own.'

Tears were coursing down his face, flowing freely into the pillow, but Shivaun lay against hers like a statue, twisting the sheet in her hand, her eyes dark and empty as caves.

'Shivaun?' He touched her arm, and thought it felt like marble. 'I'm sorry. I am so sorry! I will always be sorry! Always!'

'Yes,' she breathed, 'I think you always will be, Patrick.'

Wrenching himself upright beside her, he brushed the tears off his face and the hair off hers, took her chin in his hand and turned it so that she was forced to look at him.

'Do you? Do you hate and condemn me, as much as I hate and condemn myself? Is there no way to break out of this prison, after more than eighteen years? Can I never earn a pardon?'

Her eyebrows moved a fraction. 'Perhaps you should have gone back and given yourself up. You'd have felt better, I think, for a stretch in jail, and have long since been released. But you'll never be released from yourself, will you? Nor from whoever sent you those cuttings, either, that person out there who knows who and what you are. Your conscience, following you all the way across the Atlantic . . . maybe even in person, some day. It could be your father, or one of your former comrades, maybe that girl who was in the getaway car . . . Ireland is such a small country, Patrick. There's always someone who knows something. It's like a spider's web, all connected, all sticky.'

'Yes. And now you know too. The relief of telling someone at last is – is indescribable. If you want, you can go to the police, Irish or American, it doesn't matter, and turn me in. If I thought it would earn your respect, or your forbearance, I'd gladly own up and do jail. *Gladly*, if it would all be over and finished with then, if it would wipe the slate clean and give me a fresh chance, with society, with myself and most of all with you.'

'But' she said simply, 'nothing will give Kenny a fresh chance, will it? Or Emily, either. They're dead.'

His face contorted, his voice rose almost hysterically. 'I know they are! I *know*! That's my punishment! How long will it go *on*? Shivaun, I can't bear much more of this, sometimes I think I'll lose my mind – I even found a priest one day, confided in him and talked to him many times. He was understanding and he was comforting, said all kinds of soothing things about God's love and great compassion, but if God can love me, why can't I learn to love myself again? And now – Shivaun, have I lost all hope of your love, too? Have I?'

His pain hit her with the force of *Titanic* hitting the iceberg, all the loss and suffering irrevocably under way.

'Patrick,' she said, 'have you ever thought of contacting Jack or Brett Thomas? I know it might be much harder than a few lousy years in prison, but has it ever occurred to you that an apology might mean more to them than any prison sentence?'

'Yes. I have thought of it hundreds of times, Shivaun. But their loss was so great, even greater than the loss I face now, if I lose you, all hope of you. What can I say to them? It would almost be an affront, maybe even the easy way out. If I could go to them and prostrate myself, grovel for their forgiveness, I could walk away feeling cleansed, virtually heroic. Even if they had me jailed, there'd be a definite end in sight afterwards, I could look forward to the luxury of what the Americans call closure. But do I deserve that luxury, when death is eternal? I certainly never felt I deserved it, not even when I started wanting it, after I met you. I didn't know whether you were my salvation or my punishment . . . oh, God, Shivaun, I tried to warn you! You pulled me like a magnet, but I tried to resist, make you resist – if only we'd had the strength, either of us, to walk away from each other!'

'Patrick, you were the one who should have had the strength. I knew nothing about any of this. It was up to you.'

'Yes. It was. But you – you were like the sun rising after decades of darkness. You were daylight, the future. Is there no hope that we can get past this, and have a future? If you want children, if you think I'd ever be worthy of fathering them, I'd try to get this vasectomy reversed, or I'd adopt . . . you're adopted yourself, you know how much it might mean. I'd do anything, Shivaun. Anything. Please let me try.'

Oh, God. Dear God in heaven. Basilisk-eyed, she stared at him.

'Patrick, it would be like having children with Jason Dean.'

He should have known, he thought wildly, he should have known he would never get past Jason Dean.

'But Jason Dean might be sorry too! A completely different person now! I've tried to tell you this before – Shivaun, for your own sake if not for mine, let *go*! Move on!'

His plea was jagged and it caught at her heart; she wished desperately that she could do it, go that extra mile into a bright, liberated future. But when she had tried, what had happened?

She had ended up here in the arms of another Jason Dean. Another killer. Her heart splintered as she looked at Patrick, divined every atom of his anguish. And then, tears leaping to her eyes, she wrenched her arm from his grasp, raised it and hit him with the flat of her hand, with superhuman force across his face.

'You bastard! *Bas*tard! I thought you were tomorrow but you're only yesterday, you're a living lie! Have you really the faintest idea what you've done to those people? *Have* you?'

'Yes' he replied, facing her, waiting for her to hit him again, giving her full time and space to do it. She did not do it, but he kept his face raised. 'I know what I did, Shivaun. I know what I did to them.'

'Did? It's not only what you did, it's what you're doing, continue to do every day! For them it's still in the present, it's ongoing, it's not over and done with, it's part of their lives! It's today and tomorrow, it's every day they have to spend without each other, it's forever!'

'No!'

'Yes! It's Brett Thomas growing up with a disabled mother, no brother to love or play with, it's Jack Thomas pushing his wife about in a wheelchair, it's Emily dying before her time, maybe from the physical or mental injuries you inflicted on her. It's Jack losing his wife, never having Kenny or another baby – it has no end! None, until they're all dead themselves and you're dead as well!'

Like a detonated mine Shivaun exploded into a paroxysm of weeping, hammering at Patrick with her fists, tearing at his hair, scratching his skin with her nails, screaming.

'And you thought I could love you! You let me think it, knowing what Jason Dean did to me and to my family! You let all that happen, because you thought *you* could move on, have the love and the family you denied to them! But you'll never have any love or any family, Patrick, not from me, and you'll never have peace either. There'll never be a day that you won't see some little boy in his buggy, some dad playing with his son, some happy couple laughing together – but it will never be us. You needn't worry that I'll ever go to the police, though, because there's nothing more they can do to you, is there? You did it to yourself, the day you killed that child!'

Incoherent with fury, she pushed him away and threw herself face down on the mattress, weeping violently, possessed with pain, sorrow so great it seemed to flow from some cosmic source. He looked at her, and then he lay beside her, burying his face in the pillow to weep with no less agony, with even greater heartbreak, because he knew now that whatever hope of a future she might have, he had none at all.

Some time later, time that seemed to have no measure, Shivaun raised her aching body, sat up and looked down at Patrick inert beside her, his face white and empty as a shell. For one sliver of one second something flashed through her, seared every nerve ending and left it sealed. And then, naked, she got up and went to the curtained window, stood looking out through the muslin veil on the daylight outside.

He stirred and turned, opening his eyes to gaze upon her face and body, her hair flaming where the sun was licking it. After a moment he stretched out his arm to her, and his eyes seemed to stretch with it.

'Shivaun' he whispered, hoarsely. 'Shivaun.'

She padded over to him, leaned down and touched her lips to his mouth, leaving them there until he twitched to life, his body responding and his tongue reaching, searching for hers.

Then she stood up, and turned her back on him.

Three turbulent days later, at thirty thousand feet over Newfoundland, Marina reached forward to accept a Scotch for herself, vodka for Shivaun who was still looking spiritually savaged.

'My first whisky,' she mused, 'since my stroke. Or my "little episode", as Steven calls it. I hope some day I'll be able to look on *him* as just a little episode.'

Stirring herself, Shivaun sat up, raised her glass and saluted Marina. 'You will,' she said in a voice that had a ring of iron, 'you've made a start already. Leaving him for England took guts, and it was your first step away from him. Christ, Marina, aren't men bastards? There's something wrong with them. The whole bloody lot of them.'

Marina eyed her, still stunned by what Shivaun had told her. 'Well, most of them are way more trouble than they're worth, that's for sure. D'you know, Shivaun, I sometimes think having had that stroke might actually have done me good. I don't want to waste any more precious time on anything or anyone that *is* a waste of it. And I don't want you to waste yours, either. You'd have had a lifetime of grief with Patrick Nulty, you know.'

Sinking a shot of vodka, Shivaun nodded, conscious that she was still in a state of shock. 'Yes. I know I would. And yet . . . God, Marina, if only you could have seen his face. He was so devastated, so sorry, desperate to make amends. In spite of everything he's done, I pity him.'

'Do you?'

'Yes. I actually do. As he says himself, he's a different person now. He regrets, he repents, he's genuinely done everything anyone could to construct a decent life, not just for himself but for the kids who are as vulnerable as he once was. If it wasn't for this terrible thing, a crime he committed so many years ago, I think we might have stood a real chance of making it together. If only we didn't know that our happiness would have been stolen from those who had first claim on it. If only I could have accepted the idea of never having children, not even adopting, because they'd always have reminded us of Kenny Thomas. But they would have, every day of our lives, and I think Patrick would have been strangled with guilt, in the end.'

'Would he?'

'Yes. He knows he can never have or enjoy anything the Thomas family didn't have or enjoy. He's serving a life sentence. You – you won't change your mind, will you, about going to the police?'

'No. There's no point, is there? He's already paying the price, will pay it over and over again for the rest of his days. There's nothing to be gained. He can continue to work in my garden, stay friends with Azalea, nobody need ever know anything.'

'I thought you might want to fire him.'

'Well, I could. I could ruin him, if I were vindictively inclined. But I don't think unemployment would serve any purpose, would it? He's better off working. Especially with seven employees to consider.'

'Why did you hire him in the first place, if you never liked him?'

'Because he was a good gardener. He had a knack for making things grow. I never had much social contact with him, only a little after he made friends with Azalea – then, there was something about him that made my spine shiver. But it was always just a vibe, he never said or did anything out of line. I did wonder why he'd left Ireland so young and never gone back, but – but I only ever had some hunch, never any evidence. I'm just so sorry you had to be the one to find it.'

With effort, Shivaun struggled to master her emotions. 'I'll never forget the shock of it, Marina. Never forget his face, his voice, his tears . . . I think he really did love me, and knew he'd lost me. But at least he had the courage to tell the truth.'

'Yes. How dreadful if he'd lied, and you'd found out too late. Shivaun, it – it wasn't too late, was it? You hadn't—?'

'No. I hadn't fallen in love with him, Marina. Not deeply, not quite . . . but I'd become very fond of him, more than fond. I'll never know what held me back.'

'Your instinct held you. Always trust it in future, before you trust a man.'

'If I ever do! We're not very lucky in love, are we, you or I?'

'No. If we had any sense we'd pack it in and give up – I would anyway, at my age, although you're too young. I want you to live to fight another day, bring your children to visit me at Chederlay just as you promised.'

'I hope I will. But don't hold your breath, because it's going to take me a while to get past Patrick. I – I wish I'd been kinder to him.'

'Kinder?'

'Yes. When I found out, I went berserk. I even hit him. But afterwards I wondered whether I could have found it in me to be more . . . you know, apart from this one horrible thing he did nineteen years ago, he's such a good, decent guy. He works hard, he's giving and caring and – and so lonely. So empty, so lonely. It must be terrible for him, and now it's going to be even worse.'

'Yes. If he loved you, it is. I think his strength of character will be severely tested. But yours sounds as if it might be strengthening, expanding.'

'Does it? How so?'

'In the way you can see both sides of him, the good and the bad. You never saw anything good in Jason Dean, did you? He was simply evil incarnate.'

'Yes. He was. Now I – well, I still despise what he did, but I . . . wonder . . . maybe he's haunted, too. Maybe he's trying to get away from the ghost of Jimmy Reilly, and never will. Anyway, I'm going to try to do what Patrick said I must, and let go of him. Ivor used to tell me that too, only I never thought I could do it.'

'Do you think you can do it now?'

'I don't know. But – Marina, did I tell you about the letter?'

'No – what letter?'

'A young lad came to Chederlay this morning while I was upstairs packing. One of Patrick's employees. He had an envelope for me, wouldn't give it to Dorothy, said he was under orders to put it into my hand. So I took it, and when I opened it there was a second envelope inside, as well as a note. The envelope was addressed to Jack and Brett Thomas, c/o Dunmore East Post Office, and the note was from Patrick, asking me to mail it for him from England.'

Marina drained the last of her Scotch. 'Really? What do you think is in it?'

'I can't be sure, but I think it might be an apology. Not that any apology can help Emily or Kenny, but maybe it can help Jack and Brett.'

'I see.'

Momentarily, Marina's attention appeared to wander, she gazed at the film screen and other passengers in front of her. Then, looking thoughtful, she turned back to Shivaun.

'Well, it could be that no apology will make a whit of difference to them. They might tear it up in disgust, or not care, or God knows what. But – Shivaun, would it help you, do you think, to find out how they feel? If you knew, would you find it easier to decide how you feel about Jason Dean?'

Shivaun frowned, and gazed at her. 'Marina, I – yes. I think maybe it could help. Not just me, but Patrick too. Obviously he won't expect any response from the Thomases, but if by any miracle he got one, it might help him enormously. If it was positive, that is.'

'Then why don't we find out? When we get to England, we could make a few phone calls, see if we can track down the Thomases – they might simply be listed in their local phone book, the Irish operator would give us their number. If so, we could make an appointment to see them.'

'But how? Marina, we're not even going to Ireland! Even if they were listed, who would I tell them I was, how would I explain?'

'You'd explain that you had some news for them concerning Kenny and Emily. I'm sure they'd see you to hear what it was. If they agreed, we could go over to Ireland and you could meet them, give them this letter in person and find out what they make of it.'

Shivaun sat back, and thought about it. 'Marina, that would be wonderful. It's a great idea. But we only have a week in England and—'

'And two days of it were pencilled in for shopping, fun stuff. Let's scrub that and go to Ireland instead. It's only a short hop, isn't it?'

It was. Vaguely Shivaun thought that there might even be direct flights to Waterford from London . . . and if she went to Ireland she could visit her house in Dublin too, see Alana and find out how everything was. But—

'Marina, would you really do that? Give up your fun in London to come on a wild-goose chase with me?'

'Of course I would – only, if we do go, then you must be prepared to face whatever you find. These Thomas people might turn out to hate the man who killed Kenny and crippled Emily, they might abuse you, want to know where you got this letter . . . you'd have to brace yourself for anything and everything.'

Shivaun drew a deep breath. If anyone had ever come to her on Jason Dean's behalf she'd have given them a very reluctant hearing – yet, if they'd come bearing an apology from him, she'd have been very glad to get it. So glad that she might – just might – even have accepted it? At the very least, it would represent a form of what Patrick called 'closure'. After all these years, someone else could have the one thing she'd always wanted, and never got, from Jason Dean.

'Then – then I will brace myself, Marina, and I will do it. If you're sure—'

Marina smiled. 'Yes, darling girl, I'm sure. Anything that could give you any peace of mind, any hope of putting the past behind you, is worth a shot. So tonight, when we get to our hotel, why don't you start making a few enquiries, and see whether you can find Jack Thomas, or his son? If Ireland is the little warren of gossip you say it is, it shouldn't be monumentally difficult.'

The Cotswolds were gorgeous, but Shivaun took only fleeting note of the little hills and villages, the quaint houses and sense of history, even the stone church that Marina, with her clients, was converting into a family home. All she could think of was the unexpected prospect of visiting her own home, and the Thomases in Waterford.

The enquiries operator gave her Jack Thomas's phone number, and she dialled it with bated breath, fully expecting to be rebuffed. But the voice that answered sounded open and normal, and she plunged in.

'Mr Thomas? Is that Jack Thomas, father of Brett?'

'Aye, it is. Are you looking for Brett?'

'No, I – well, I'm looking for both of you. My name is Shivaun Reilly, I'm calling from Adbaston in England, but if you'll agree to see me I'm hoping to come to Ireland at the weekend.'

'See you? About what? Who are you, Ms Reilly?'

'I – I'm a nurse. I'm in England with a patient, a friend, but I – I have something for you. A letter.'

'A letter? Well, I don't know why you'd be writing to me, but why don't you post it?'

'I didn't write it. I'm just carrying it for the person who did. It – it's about your late wife and son. About Emily and Kenny.'

There was a stunned silence.

'Emily? And Kenny? But they – they died years ago, Ms Reilly. I'm sorry, but I really don't understand—'

'Mr Thomas, this letter is from the person who—' Oh, God. 'The person who planted the bomb.'

Quaking, she held her breath, waiting to be told to burn it. Or worse. Down the line, she could hear Jack Thomas breathing heavily, almost thinking aloud, baffled but fascinated.

'Have I got this right? You have a letter from the man who killed my son, and destroyed my wife? Or was it a woman? We never knew who did it.'

'It was a man. A man who is unspeakably sorry, and has regretted it ever since. I haven't read this letter, but I think it contains an apology. If you'll let me, I'd like to give it to you in person, and talk to you about it.'

'*Talk* to me? Are you a friend of this man's? Do you know who he is, where he is?'

'Yes. I do.'

Another lengthy silence. When Jack Thomas spoke again, his voice had changed, hardened and chilled. But it was not abusive.

'Then – then we better had meet, and talk. When were you thinking of coming?'

Finally they settled on Friday evening, at seven when Brett could be there as well, because Jack was sure he would want to talk to her too. Shivaun proposed meeting in a hotel or a pub, but Jack said no, she was to come to his house, and gave her directions. This was not the kind of conversation to be conducted in public.

Hugely relieved to have got so far, Shivaun thanked him, hung up, and then made another call. There was no answer, but a voicemail asked her to leave a message.

'Alana, it's Shivaun. I'm in England with Marina and I'm going to Ireland at the weekend. I want to see you. Please keep Saturday night free and be at home. I'll be staying overnight and so will Marina, we're going back to America on Sunday but I need to see you first.'

The week seemed to crawl by, and during it Shivaun was plagued by unending thoughts of Patrick, spiked moments of pain and rage followed by waves of sadness, continuing shock as if she'd been punched, and was still reeling. How could she have been taken in, how could she have let such a man get so close to her, close enough that even now she could see his face, his eyes full of love for her, she could hear his voice and feel his strong body in her arms? Sometimes she shuddered, sometimes tears washed her cheeks, and she felt an enormous void within her. Try as she might, she could not believe that he was intrinsically evil, or that he was capable of ever killing again. She felt that he was, fundamentally, a good man whose life had gone horribly wrong. Irrevocably wrong, sealed into the one split second from which there was no going back. Over and over, she saw his face at the moment at which she kissed him, and left him; it was a face fixed forever in grief, in the loss he knew was so final, so absolute. Loss which, like death, was eternal.

But then other things came to her too, and she turned them over like pebbles on a beach, scrabbling to see what lay underneath. She thought of the night after Marina's party; drunk as she had been, she remembered the cigarette Patrick had produced from his pocket and lit, saying he had given up smoking but still carried them 'for emergencies'. What other things might he have given up, but still harboured for 'emergencies'? Was he a creature of habit, did a leopard ever truly change its spots? He had been hostile to her visit to Britain, too, said he didn't like the sound of Britain . . . at heart, did he still think of it as an enemy? Did he condone the politics of violence, still fight the old fight in his mind or in his secret soul?

Was that why he rejected her criticisms of Ireland? Not because he hadn't been there to see the deterioration in it, but because he didn't want to believe it could happen? Did he still nostalgically idealise the 'old country', even idolise it? Yet he'd admitted it wasn't perfect, wished it had had more to occupy and divert a young boy's energies . . . and still his favourite song was that bitter old lament, 'The Fields of Athenry'. In her mind the pendulum swung back and forth, visiting both sides of him, unable to choose one over the other. It came to her that she would probably wonder forever, never know for sure whether she had thrown away a good, loving husband, or rejected a killer. Even now her blood fired hot with desire for him, but froze when she thought of Kenny Thomas. Baby Kenny, an innocent infant in his buggy.

What would Kenny's father, Jack, be like, and his brother Brett? What would she say to them, or they to her? What if they demanded the information that could locate Patrick, and jail him? Patrick had said he would gladly go to jail, if it would help anyone, but would it? Would she tell them, betray him, or would she protect him?

What if – the thought hit her like a whip – she arrived to find the police waiting, summoned by the Thomases to grill her, force her to divulge everything whether she wanted to or not?

'Jesus, Marina, I could be walking into a trap. Walking Patrick into one too.'

Marina paused over the supper she was eating heartily, glowing after her satisfying day out in her wellies and hard hat, up on a scaffolding in the autumn sun. Shivaun thought she looked decidedly eccentric now, in British tweeds worn like a theatrical costume, to suit the scene.

'That's a thought. You could. Are you willing to risk it, or do you want to just mail the letter after all and not go in person?'

Shivaun pushed away her fish pie and considered. 'No. I want to go. I want to find out how these two men feel, how they've been affected by losing the two people they loved. If they've been able to let go, maybe they'll tell me how they did it . . . and Patrick so badly wanted me to do it.'

'Badly enough that he'd condone what you're planning to do now? Even if it gets him arrested? He can't really want that, Shivaun, or he wouldn't have asked you to mail that letter from England. He doesn't want anyone to find him.'

'No. If it can be avoided, he doesn't. If I'd truly loved him, totally loved him, I'd never gamble his freedom . . . but I am going to gamble it, Marina. I have to, if I'm ever to have any chance of freedom from Jason Dean. The Thomases could be the key to the prison cell.'

'They could, one way or another! So long as you feel you can live with the consequences, whatever they turn out to be.'

'If the Thomases want Patrick to go to jail, then they have the right to pursue him. Pursue the justice they've been denied for nineteen years.'

'Yes. Well, for everyone's sake, we must hope they're not vengeful. I'm sure they were once, but it's been a long time . . . maybe they've learned to forgive, and let go.'

'Maybe. There's only one way to find out.'

As the plane swung in over the Wicklow mountains Shivaun craned her neck to see the view, and was forcibly struck by it; Ireland looked so lovely under the slivers of light striking down from between the clouds, soft, peaceful, revelling in every shade of green from lime to jade, gilded with autumn bronze. Although she had not been homesick in America she was suddenly homesick now, aching to see and touch her country, hear its voice and see its smile. Although she had no family here she felt she belonged, and was coming home.

Home! The word quickened her blood, and she looked around her as she got off the plane, smelling the grass immediately, dazzled with delight. But Marina was brisk, businesslike.

'Now, where do we pick up the car?'

They found the rental desk, got the car and were almost instantaneously killed when Shivaun, distracted by a surge of pure unexpected joy, drove off on the wrong side of the road.

'Left, Shivaun, *left*!' Marina shrieked just in time for her to avert the oncoming lorry, which missed them with inches to spare. Shaken, they pulled in to recover themselves, and Shivaun laughed giddily.

'Christ, that was close. Sorry, Marina.'

'Look, just for God's sake concentrate, OK? I know you're a bit euphoric to be here, and petrified about meeting these people, but now that we've got this far I would like to see it through.'

Resolutely Shivaun concentrated, but was nonetheless seduced by the countryside as they drove off through it, leaving what passed for a main road to wend their way along even smaller ones, hedged with blackberry bushes so thick they brushed the sides of the car. Here and there they saw tractors out in the fields, harvesting the last of the crops, clouds of seagulls hovering overhead.

'This is very pretty' Marina conceded, admiring a ruined ancient castle. 'Not what I'd expected at all, after everything you told me.'

'Oh, I was talking about Dublin. This is much nicer. But I wish there were some signposts – you'd better get Jack's directions and read them out to me.'

Marina read them, but it didn't help much; they got lost numerous times before, eventually, turning up a narrow lane with grass growing in the middle of it.

'This can't be right. It looks very remote.'

But even as Marina spoke Shivaun spotted a chimney, and then the rest of the Thomas house came into view, a long thatched cottage enclosed by a courtyard, with climbing roses in front and a wide green meadow behind. Pulling in, she gazed at it.

'I think this is the right one. We're here.'

Marina eyed her sidelong. 'OK. Get a grip. At least it doesn't look as if it's bristling with cops.'

It didn't. But Shivaun felt prickles of apprehension, her palms sweaty on the steering wheel. Evening was falling and the air was clammy, completely still.

'Two cars. Jack's and Brett's, I suppose.'

'You hope! Oh, Shivaun, don't worry. It will be all right, everything will unfold as it's meant to unfold. I get good vibes here.'

'You are going to come in with me, aren't you?'

'Yes, if you want me to.'

'I do. Come on, let's go . . . go for it.'

As soon as they opened the car doors a barking dog came racing out of nowhere, a big Alsatian with ferocious fangs, but Marina stared it down imperiously.

'Stop that, you silly creature, go find your owner and tell him we're here.'

The dog hesitated, and a man emerged from the cottage, tall and commanding-looking, with thick grey hair and very direct, charcoal-grey eyes.

'Good evening, ladies. Don't mind Steamer here, he's only for show. You must be Ms Reilly and—?'

Marina thrust out her hand. 'Marina Darnoux. How are you, Mr Thomas?'

He looked at her quizzically, and in spite of everything Shivaun smiled; Marina's saffron ensemble, shot with scarlet, was vivid as the sunset, her bearing majestic. Jack Thomas scratched his head.

'To tell the truth I don't rightly know how I am. I've been addled ever since I got your phone call. Don't know what to make of it.'

Shivaun stepped forward. 'I'm Shivaun. It was me who phoned you.'

'Yes. Yes. You'd better come in.'

He led them inside, and they glanced at each other in surprise; the cottage was much larger than it looked, a square tiled hall leading into a sunny, substantial living room with a gleaming wooden floor, its comfortable furniture arranged around a big fireplace in which a stack of wood and peat was burning cheerfully. From the depths of an armchair, a younger man stood up and greeted them politely, but guardedly.

'Hello. I'm Brett Thomas.'

He looked like his father, had the same thick hair and upright stance, deep grey eyes and fresh appearance. But whereas Jack was wearing country cords and brogues, a mustard-coloured waistcoat under a tweed jacket, Brett was sharper in a navy suit, white shirt and red silk tie. Around Shivaun's own age, he sounded cordial, but his aura was slightly wary.

'Please. Sit down.'

Chairs were moved about, closer to the fire, and Shivaun sat facing Brett, Marina facing Jack. For a moment there was an awkward pause, and then Jack cleared his throat.

'You must have had a long trip. Would you like some tea?'

Before they could answer he got up to make it, leaving Brett to entertain them while he went into a kitchen which, from what they could see of it, looked airy, modern and well equipped. Interested, Marina looked around her.

'Vernacular architecture, mid-nineteenth century I'd say, but gutted and renovated interior . . . what a charming house.'

'Dad did it' Brett replied. 'He's good with his hands. He used to be a welder up North, but when we came down here he switched to kitchen fitting. Good call. There's a huge demand for new kitchens these days.'

'Is there?'

'Oh yes. New houses too, new everything. Old Ireland's dead and gone, it's with O'Leary in the grave.'

Marina frowned, but Shivaun recognised the line of Yeats, although she couldn't say which poem it was from. Brett sounded crisp and articulate, and she wondered what he did.

'Do you work locally?'

'Yes. I'm a solicitor. Just qualified last year. I'm with a group practice in Waterford city.'

A solicitor. Shivaun shuddered inwardly, more amazed than ever not to see policemen emerging from the woodwork.

'And – and do you live here? In this house?'

'Yes. Can't leave old Dad on his own.'

Dad didn't look old at all, he was fit and healthy in stance and complexion, around Marina's age. But Brett sounded a little protective of him.

'And you're a nurse, Ms Reilly, is that right?'

'Yes. Please call me Shivaun. Marina is – or was – my private patient. She's an architect.'

'An architect, eh?' Jack called from the kitchen. 'She'd make her fortune around here!'

Marina laughed as he came in with the tea tray, resplendently piled with sparkling china on a white linen cloth. 'I have my own practice in Massachusetts. Are you interested in architecture, Mr Thomas?'

'Oh, aye. I've learned a lot about it since I got into the kitchen fitting business. People are building some beautiful houses in these parts.'

'In traditional style, I hope?'

'Aye. Some.' Pouring the tea, he handed round cups with a courtly air.

Shivaun knew that Marina usually took lemon in hers, but on this occasion she accepted milk without a murmur, and looked around the room again, eyeing its thick walls.

'This really is a fine house. Solid, dignified . . . I like it very much.'

Jack grimaced. 'Thank you. Enjoy it while you can. We'll be moving soon.'

'Oh? But – why is that?'

'Because of the bloody bypass. They're building one alongside the far end of the field – out there, look.'

He gestured at the window and they all looked, horrified, at the quiet green field, its silence unbroken except for a carolling blackbird. Immediately, Shivaun felt something coil inside her.

'A bypass? They're building a bypass *there*?'

'Yes. Well, they have to build it somewhere. It's badly needed.'

'But your house will be destroyed!'

'Aye. We protested, we did what we could, but it was no use in the end. The work will be starting in November, and we'll be lucky to get tuppence for our little cottage.'

Marina looked aghast, and Shivaun leaped to her feet, went to peer more closely out the window. 'But that's outrageous! They can't do that!'

Jack started to explain that they could, but Brett intervened.

'Dad, let's not get started on that. These ladies came here to discuss something else entirely.'

Simmering, reluctantly, Shivaun sat down, and drew a long, deep breath.

'Yes. We came – at least I did – to give you this. I hope you won't find it too upsetting, but I'll understand if you do.'

Opening her bag which lay on the floor, she extracted Patrick's letter, addressed to the two men care of the local post office. Brett sat stock still, holding his teacup almost defensively in front of him, but Jack reached to take it. Quietly, he studied it, examining the typescript.

'Why did you want to bring it yourself? It would have reached us through the post.'

'Yes. It would. But – look, why don't you open it first? Read it, and absorb whatever it says. Then I'll tell you why I wanted to bring it in person.'

Silently, his face closing over in some way, Jack held it for a moment, saying nothing, glancing at his son. With visible distaste, Brett nodded.

'All right.' Instead of ripping it open he got up, went to the mantelpiece, located a paperknife and sliced the top of the envelope neatly across. As he took out the two pieces of paper inside, Shivaun saw that his fingers were shaking, and realised her own were too.

Patrick, she prayed, this had better be worth it. This had better be everything that these two men need, and deserve.

Time felt suspended, they all sat forward and clasped their cups as Jack read the first page, and stared at the second. Then, without a word, he passed them both to his son.

Brett was ruddy-faced, like his father, but he paled as he perused the first sheet, flinched when he looked at the second. Then, his mouth tightening, he handed them both back to his father.

'This is yours, Dad. All yours. I want no part of it.'

'But Brett—'

'None! He's said his piece. Only we'll never get to say ours, will we? The man's a common coward. If he had the guts to come to us in person, I'd ram it down his throat for him.'

Holding the pages, Jack considered, and Shivaun could see

the effort he was making to control the sudden wet gleam in his eyes. Eventually, after a laden pause, he sighed.

'But these ladies – young Shivaun here – she's come in person. She knows who he is and where he is.'

Brett stood up, and faced her with frigid, barely-contained fury.

'Well then, Ms Reilly, when you get back to your friend, please tell him from me that he isn't worth the time of day. Tell him I hope he rots in hell for what he did to my mother and brother, and that I will never forgive him. *Never.*'

All but spitting the words at her, he turned on his heel, marched out of the room and slammed the door behind him.

The sound seemed to echo down all the years, all the way back to the exploding bomb, and Shivaun sat speared with shock. Beside her, Marina was very deliberately saying nothing, but radiating sympathy for Jack Thomas as he struggled to master himself. Finally, looking profoundly sad, he passed the two pages to Shivaun, and she read them.

Although the envelope had been typed, she was taken aback to find that the letter was also typed, devoid of handwriting, unsigned, completely impersonal. Despite everything he had said, Patrick had covered his traces. His words were brief and simple, but in the subterfuge to which he had resorted she could hear his voice in them, and was relieved to hear them sounding sincere, ringing true in her ear.

Mr Thomas, senior and junior—

I killed your son, your brother. I planted the bomb that stole his life and destroyed his mother's. I cannot begin to tell you how sorry I am, and I can never forgive myself. I loathe what I did, and wish it could be undone.

It will be of no comfort to you to know this, but I can only pray that it may be of some value. The enclosed is a very small gesture, which is not intended to be conciliatory, merely constructive.

Please try to forgive me some day, not for my sake but for your own. I am not worth the waste of any more lives.

Shivaun held the letter, stared out the window, and read it again. Then she lifted the second piece of paper. It was a bank draft, for an enormous sum of money, made out in euros to Jack Thomas. For a split second, she wanted to throw it onto the fire.

Money! As if a human life could be measured in it! But it was the only currency Patrick could deal in, failing the courage to come here and talk to Jack Thomas himself. For several suspended seconds she sat looking at Jack, his head buried in his hands, trying to imagine how he must feel. After nearly twenty years, the healing scar had been ripped open, and he sat immobile, speechless, hunched in pain. While she debated whether to speak, or leave the moment untouched, Marina quietly got up. Going to the teapot, she poured him a fresh cup, and sat on the edge of his chair beside him.

'Mr Thomas.' Gently, she touched him on the shoulder. 'Here. Drink this. It's hot. It'll help.'

Looking up, he took the cup from her, managed a grateful smile.

'Thank you.'

While he drank it Marina took the letter from Shivaun, read it, and surveyed the bank draft. Raising her eyebrows, she measured her words before speaking again, very softly.

'So. It is an apology. He really is sorry.'

Yes. Sorrow hung in the air like a lantern between them, and Shivaun knew that Patrick really was. He had meant this money to be a mere token of his shame and sincerity, not at all the affront it was turning out to be, to Brett at any rate. He had not returned to the room, and it was impossible to gauge how, or what, Jack was feeling.

But then Jack raised his cup, with visible effort, and drank some tea, struggling to pull himself together.

'Tell me, Miss – Ms – Shivaun, do you know this man well?'

'Yes,' she said frankly, 'I do.'

'Well enough to believe that he truly is sorry?'

She met his gaze. 'Yes, Mr Thomas. Well enough to believe that he truly is.'

For a time he was silent again, turning to look into the fire, thinking, pondering. When he faced her again, she was struck by something in his eyes, some deep calm depth she had not seen before.

'Then, if he tells me so, I will believe him. I have no reason to trust him, but I will choose to do so.'

Leaning forward, she touched his hand. 'If you can do that, Mr Thomas, I promise you your trust will not be misplaced. I give you my word that he is wholly, profoundly sorry for what he did, and that he has paid for it ever since. Is still paying for it.'

Jack gazed at her. 'Is he? In what way?'

'In – in ways a boy of eighteen could never have foreseen. He's nearly thirty-seven now, but he's still haunted. Still alone, because he can't have children, not when he stole your child from you. Can't marry, because I – I can't marry him. I'm the first woman he ever allowed himself to love, to hope for happiness with, but I think he knew from the start there was no hope.'

'You – you're his girlfriend, then? Not just – *a* friend?'

'No. Not just a friend. We were becoming much closer than that. But when I found out what he did to your son, to your wife, I couldn't go on with him.'

'But you tell me yourself that he's sorry.'

'He is. He's done everything in his power to build a new, better life, to become a different man. He contributes time and money and all his resources to steering other kids out of trouble. But he still murdered your son. My own father was murdered, and I cannot forgive a murderer. I'm trying to, but I just can't. Not completely, not even when he says he's sorry, as – as this man has done.'

She was startled when Jack suddenly got to his feet, and stood frowning at her.

'But you must.'

'I – what?'

'You must! Whether or not you get an apology is irrelevant. A luxury, not a necessity! I don't know who killed your father, but – was it a man?'

'Yes. A young man. A drug addict.'

'When did it happen?'

'Six years ago.'

'Then, if you have not forgiven, you have lost six years of your life! If you do not forgive, he will kill you, as surely as he killed your father! He will own you, squeeze the life out of you!'

Paling, she sat stock still, and Jack's voice rose. 'Forget him! Forgive, forget! My son has never been able to do either of those things, and it is destroying him! That's why I agreed to see you, let you come here, because I hoped, I prayed – it seems I hoped and prayed in vain. Brett can not, will not forgive. But you're young too. I cannot bear to see another young life consumed, poisoned, wasted. If I can't convince him, you must let me try to convince you.'

Transfixed, Shivaun stared at him, impaled on his gaze, stunned by the ferocity in his voice. He was a stranger to her, and yet she felt he knew her, knew things she did not want to admit she knew, deep in her heart, herself. He had been through everything she had been through, he alone had the right, and the authority, to say what he was saying.

Calming himself a little, lowering his voice, he ran his hand through his hair, waved the other in the direction of the door through which Brett had disappeared.

'My younger son died instantly and cleanly. My older son is dying slowly, bitterly, painfully. I have watched his soul withering since he was six years old. For his sake I refused to let mine wither, refused to recriminate, kept going for him as much as for myself. *More* than for myself. He was just a little boy then . . . now he's a man, but he has not grown one inch, in his soul. His heart stalled the day his brother died. He has never let sunlight into it since. But – but you're a nurse! You must surely know that healing is possible!'

Biting her lip, she said nothing.

'You must! Life has to go on, or there's nothing left! If I thought it would help, I would even say to you, marry this – this man, this friend of yours, whoever or wherever he is! Do whatever it takes, but go forward!'

Behind him, she was vaguely aware of Marina, still poised on the edge of Jack's chair, drinking in every word, her attention fixed on the man's broad back. Outside, the sun was sinking slowly to the west, casting one last long glimmering ray across the meadow. Around her the room felt like a tableau, fixed in time, a scene she knew would be part of her for the rest of her life, eternal as a diamond.

'But – Mr Thomas – I have tried. Other people have told me what you're telling me, but—'

'But nothing! Just do it. Tell me you will let go, tell me you will not become what my son has become. Your father would not want his child to shrivel as mine has shrivelled.'

Abruptly, from nowhere, a childhood memory flashed into Shivaun's mind. Jimmy, standing in a garden somewhere, holding a long tendril of some plant in his hand, maybe clematis, touching its frozen bud with his finger. A spring frost had almost, but not quite, killed it, and she could hear his voice as clearly as she could see him in his old corduroys, tenderly gathering it up as he reached for some implement.

'Nearly gone. But where there's life there's hope. This species is a fighter.'

The memory vanished as suddenly as it had come, she had no recollection of what he had done next or whether the plant had survived. But, without knowing it until now, she had stored that moment in some chamber of her heart, and Jack Thomas had dug it out.

Her throat clenched, felt seared as she looked up at him.

'No,' she said, almost inaudibly, 'my father would not want that.'

'No parent would want it' he said, and sagged without warning back onto his chair, his voice lowering as if he were talking to himself. 'If Emily could see what Brett has become, she would be heartbroken. She would grieve almost more than she grieved for Kenny.'

They looked at each other, and silence flowed like a river between them. In the room, there seemed to be translucent, ghostly space where Brett had been, and Shivaun knew that he would never forgive Patrick, never live or let live for as long as his brother was dead. Brett Thomas's future was her future, if she did not espouse another.

At length, she spoke. 'Mr Thomas?'

He seemed drained. 'Yes?'

'Don't you want to know who killed Kenny? His name, or where he is now?'

Wearily, but adamantly, Jack shook his head. 'No. I do not want to know anything about him. Nothing at all, that Brett might prise out of me, and take to the police. It's too late for police, or prison, or anything this man might learn from prison. From what you tell me, it sounds as if his life is already ruined. I'll tell Brett that, and it will be some comfort to him. For myself, I don't want vengeance, or retribution, or anything to do with this man. I once hated him, but it was love Brett needed in his life, not hatred, so I let it go. If anything, all I feel now is contempt. Some small contempt, for this cowardly man who sends me money with an anonymous note. That's all.'

She was amazed. 'Is it?'

'Yes. I'm nearly fifty years of age. I don't have enough time left to waste on cowards, or killers, or memories. You know, Shivaun, life is not infinite.'

As a healthy young woman of twenty-five she felt invincible, felt that life was infinite. As a nurse, she knew that it wasn't.

'Then – then I wish you great joy in the years you have left, Mr Thomas. And I hope you'll have many of them. I – I wasn't expecting to meet someone so forgiving.'

He grimaced, and she felt the unspoken message in his face: what choice is there, at the end of the day, for me or for you, for anyone who has been bereaved? If we've been forcibly robbed of those we love, we just have to get on with whatever, or whoever, is left. Regroup, and rebuild.

Out of the blue, in the shadows where she had been silent for a long time, Marina stood up and spoke as if breaking a spell.

'Mr Thomas, may I ask you a question?'

Clearly Jack had forgotten her, and now he roused himself. 'Yes, ma'am. Certainly you may.'

Marina paused a moment. 'If you sell this house, or are bought out of it by the authorities to make way for this bypass, where are you going to live?'

Somewhat taken aback by the change of subject, he blinked and frowned. 'I don't exactly know yet. I'd like to stay in the area, but—'

'It's a lovely house. I'd greatly enjoy the challenge of designing you another one as nice, along the same lines.'

'I beg your pardon?'

'If you'd be interested, that is. I normally charge a fortune for my work, because it's exceptionally good, but it would give me great pleasure to do this as a labour of love. I've never done Irish vernacular before, so you'd be a bit of a guinea pig, but in return I'd undertake the experiment for free. This wretched cheque you've just received should more than cover the cost of materials, as well as buying the land.'

He gaped at her, as did Shivaun, and then a smile creased his ruddy face. It was, Shivaun thought, a dignified face. Dignified and honest and warm.

'Well, ma'am – I don't know what to say!'

'Good. That's settled then. But only on condition that you stop calling me ma'am. My name is Marina.'

It was Shivaun's turn to sit in silence, distracted by her own thoughts, while Jack got up, hesitated briefly, and then turned in the direction of the kitchen.

'Well, Marina, in return for such an offer, the least I can do is offer you another cup of tea?'

Marina beamed. 'Thank you. That would be lovely. Of course, the offer depends on how your son feels about it. I'd want to design a house that you'd both love living in.'

From the doorway, Jack turned to face her. 'It is my great

sadness, Marina, that my son does not love living, here or anywhere. I've tried for years to change that, to persuade him that he should be enjoying all the things Kenny never did. He should be doing double the living, not half. But he doesn't see it that way, and to be frank I don't think he ever will. It's his choice, his life, and finally nobody else can live it for him.'

Marina glanced at Shivaun, and then back at Jack.

'No. He's a grown adult, and he must make his own choices.'

Shivaun remained where she was, thinking about Brett, waiting for him to reappear. She wanted to talk to him, to persuade him of Patrick's sincerity and find out whether he could accept that the apology was genuine. But he did not reappear.

Chapter Sixteen

'Marina Darnoux, you are a brazen slut and I am ashamed of you.'

Marina grinned out the car window at a herd of cows. 'Is that so.'

Shivaun battled the urge to laugh, and clock Marina the punch she deserved. 'Yes it is! You came *on* to that man! That nice, quiet, decent gentleman!'

'Mmm. He is rather nice, isn't he?'

Shivaun swung the car round a tricky turn, bouncing over a pothole big enough to incarcerate a hippopotamus; evidently the local council was composed of layabouts. Why wasn't a team of workmen out here this minute, filling it in?

'I'll tell you what he is! He is a respectable widower, whose son was killed by your gardener! Have you no decency, no shame?'

Marina's grin widened. 'None whatsoever.'

'As for you, you're barely halfway out of a disgraceful affair with your doctor!

'Oh, no. I think I'm more than halfway out of it now, actually. As they say, what doesn't kill you will cure you.'

'But you're not cured, that I can see, you're lurching from one to the next—'

'I'm not lurching. I've thrown away my stick and am walking quite normally, thanks to my excellent medical team.'

Shivaun walloped the steering wheel. 'Mar*ina*—'

'You know, Shivaun, you have the most vivid imagination. I offer to design a house for someone, and next thing you have me leaping into bed with him. You're nuts.'

She burst out laughing. 'I must be, to have got so entangled with you! I thought I was taking on an invalid, not a scheming, sex-mad trollop!'

'Puh-leez. Mind your manners. I'm still bankrolling you, you know. Besides, that's no way to talk to the grandmother of your future children. Not if they want to swim in my pool.'

Having made her point, Shivaun subsided. Despite what she was saying she was sure Marina understood what she was thinking: that Jack Thomas was more than just a nice man. He was an intelligent, generous, admirable survivor of personal tragedy, who'd never let himself be corroded by bitterness or self-pity. If he struck up a friendship with Marina, and she with him, it might be very enriching for them both. The three thousand miles that lay between them would be no object to Marina, and Shivaun couldn't remember when she'd last seen her looking as carefree, as cheerful and youthful as she looked this morning, en route to Dublin to meet Alana, another stranger to her. How would Alana be, a year on? Still desperately dieting, chasing after men, drinking and partying, with that needy aura still about her? Well, Dublin was only a few hours away now, they would soon find out, and Shivaun was looking forward to whatever incarnation of Alana it might be.

But instead of moving on to Dublin her mind went back to Waterford, to last night's meeting with Jack and Brett Thomas. In the end they had lingered for hours, not left the cottage until nearly midnight, after a long, wide-ranging talk and a glass of Jack's Midleton Reserve whiskey for Marina, graciously offered by Jack in a little cut-crystal tumbler. There was, she thought, something faintly refined about the man; despite his widower's life with his bachelor son he dressed neatly, kept his house clean and fresh and his standards up. Many men in his circumstances might have gone to pot, let it all go to hell, but Jack was clearly stronger than that. Perhaps he felt he owed it to the memory of his dead wife to live as she would have wished him to live, as they had done together?

But he was right, undoubtedly, in thinking that Emily would have been deeply grieved to see her son, Brett. When they'd first met Shivaun had thought Brett looked like an attractive man, crisp and debonair; but now all she could remember about him was his face, twisted with bitterness as he read Patrick's letter and hoped 'he rots in hell.' Perhaps it would give him some satisfaction to know that Patrick was, in a manner of speaking, rotting in hell – but would it change anything? Would it bring Kenny back? Would Patrick's misery enhance Brett's life?

No. Although it was Jack who had spoken to her, implored her to forgive and forget Jason Dean, it was Brett who had finally convinced her that she must do it. Brett was living proof that she had to, unless she wanted to become like him. And she did not, she saw with clarity, want to become like him.

Poor Brett. Although he had not come back into the room, never rejoined them at all, she didn't hold his churlishness against him. Rather she felt sorry for him, not only for what he had lost but for what he could never regain – peace, and serenity, and happiness. In those mere five or ten minutes she had spent with him she had sensed profound emptiness in him, a lost soul storming inside a shiny shell. He had a good career and good looks, youth and health, an expensive car and, probably, lots of girlfriends. But he was not in possession of himself; he was and always would be the property of Patrick Nulty.

She was not – *not* – going to be always the property of Jason Dean.

At that moment something snapped in her soul. She felt it as cleanly, as sharply as if a knife had severed it: the thread that tied her to Jason. In one bright exhilarating flash it was gone, and she was free.

'Marina!'

She shot her a dazzling smile, and Marina turned bemused. 'What?'

Shivaun was so elated she swung the car off the road, pulled it in and threw her arms around Marina beside her.

'Thank you! You're beautiful, you're wonderful and I love you! Thank you!'

Baffled and wry, Marina accepted her embrace, flipped down the sunshield mirror and fixed her dishevelled hair with her fingers. 'I'm sure you're right, darling girl, I am indeed beautiful and wonderful, but what exactly did I do to get such a hug at this precise moment?'

'You sent me Brett Thomas. Going to visit the Thomases was your idea. You – you liberated me.'

'Did I really? From what?'

'From myself. From prison. From becoming what Brett has become. It was like looking in a mirror. A mirror onto the future, that showed me what I'd look like tomorrow, if I didn't let go of yesterday. So I am going to let go – of Jimmy and Jason, and even of Viv. I loved my parents dearly, but they're dead, they're gone. And Jason Dean is gone too. I don't care any more where he is or what he does or who he is. He can't hurt me any more, can't scare me or dictate who *I* am. They're all ghosts, and they're all gone. You're my new Viv, and I love you to bits.'

Her smile was huge, and Marina returned it in full, albeit with a rare hint of a blush.

'That's quite a compliment, darling girl, and quite a challenge too. I know how highly you rated Vivienne Reilly, and how much she meant to you.'

'She meant the world to me. She adopted me. And now I'm adopting you.'

Marina laughed, her face full of vivacity, and squeezed Shivaun's hand. 'Then I'd better call Azalea, and tell her to put an announcement in the *Boston Globe*. "To Marina Darnoux, the daughter she always wanted." I'd say that'd get the gossip going round the dinner tables of Massachusetts.'

'Yes,' Shivaun grinned, 'and give Steven Hunt the fright of his life.'

For the remainder of their journey to Dublin Shivaun was all chat, giving Marina a running commentary on the changing landscape around them, on what history she knew of it, and on the scandalous way Ireland was run.

'See that house? A bigshot politician lives in it. Fancy, isn't it?'

Marina surveyed the house, and raised an eyebrow. 'Mmm. Very elegant. Georgian, undoubtedly. I do love those old houses – they're too austere to be beautiful, in any lush kind of way, but they have such class.'

'Yeah. Unfortunately the politician has no class whatever. He stole the money for that house from the taxpayer. Just thrust his hand into the public pocket and lifted what he needed. What's more, he still got re-elected at the next election. People are absolute fools, gluttons for punishment.'

'Often they are. But it's not exclusive to Ireland, Shivaun, it's global. We have plenty of corruption in the States too.'

'I know. I love America, Marina, my experience of it this past year has been terrific, but I have to tell you I hate your gun laws. Absolutely hate them with a passion, can't believe a kid of six for instance could get hold of a gun and kill a little girl with it. As for your immigration laws – they're pretty tangled, huh? The Pilgrim Fathers would have trouble getting in today, especially if they were starting out from Cuba or Turkey or—'

'Or anywhere that doesn't have lots of money! Politics are all about money, really, in the end.'

Shivaun nodded. 'So it seems. Yet some politicians seem so convincing, so moral and inspiring when they're starting out . . . Jack Kennedy for instance, I can remember Viv telling me how alluring he was, but how disappointing in the long run. Power really does seem to corrupt.'

Marina concurred – and, suddenly, looked at her sidelong.

'Shivaun, tell me, how does it feel to be back in Ireland?'

She beamed. 'It feels very good, Marina! Whatever mess we might make of it – look at that horrible mast up on that hill – it's still a beautiful country, don't you think?'

'I do think. The towns don't look like much to write home

about, but the fields and hills, the crops and animals . . . it feels so slow, so – so creamy and dreamy!'

Shivaun giggled. 'That's it, right enough, creamy and dreamy. It can be good fun though, too. I wish I had time to take you to a nice pub with a fire and some music, meet some people and have a bit of craic.'

Marina blinked. 'Crack? Cocaine? Moi?'

'No, not that kind! Craic is just laughs and chat. People aren't quite so – so earnest as they sometimes are in America. Here, we love winding each other up and taking the mickey. We don't take anyone or anything too seriously.'

'Really? But you seem to take some things quite seriously, Shivaun.'

'Oh, I just get revved up when I see certain things. I react like Pavlov's dog, start barking at litter and dirt and bad management – the health care system is a prime example, Bart Simpson would make a better job of it.'

'H'mm. Or maybe Shivaun Reilly.'

'Huh?'

Marina smiled. 'I sometimes think you should go into politics yourself, Shivaun. Haven't you ever thought of it?'

'No, I – well, other people have said I should. But I'm a nurse. I have work I love.'

'But maybe it's all part of the same thing, all to do with caring . . . tell me, are you looking forward to your new job in Martha's Vineyard?'

Shivaun mulled on it. 'Yes, I guess . . . but only up to a point. It certainly won't be as much fun as working with you has been. I suppose I was partly looking forward to it as a way of staying in America and being near Patrick – Jesus, Marina, I was this close to falling in love with that man. *This* close.'

She held her thumb and forefinger a millimetre apart, and Marina nodded.

'Yes, I think you really were. But I'm so glad you didn't. How are you feeling now?'

'I'm feeling – mixed emotions. Sadness for him, anger,

revulsion and . . . and still some completely perverse attraction. Sex is so incredibly damn dis*tracting*!

Marina grimaced wryly. 'Tell me about it. It's the most expensive commodity in the world, and we've both been fools for it. But at least we haven't been trapped. How much worse if either of us had got what we thought we wanted.'

Slowing the car as it joined up with a traffic jam, Shivaun sat back and draped her forearm over the steering wheel. 'Christ, would you look at this mess, do these traffic planners travel by gondola or what . . . you know, Marina, I don't think I'll forget Patrick in a hurry. In some way he has become a little part of me. There was both good and bad in him, and I'll just have to assimilate the whole lot. More good than bad, on balance, even if the bad bit really was a major shock.'

'It was an awful thing to discover. Absolutely terrible. But at least he took your mind off Ivor Lawlor.'

'Mmm . . . but, d'you know, that's the funny part. I never saw him as a substitute for Ivor. They were too different. Ivor was so much younger, his values and attitudes were nothing like Patrick's, he – he was a lot easier to love. He was changing, though. I wonder what on earth he's doing in Spain, and how he's getting on.'

'Don't wonder. Just assimilate him, like Patrick, into your memories, and look to the future.'

'I will. You should look to yours, too, and give Jack Thomas a call soon. I'd say he might be a bit shy about calling you.'

'Yes! Why is it that men are always so afraid of me? I don't bite, I don't chop them up and eat them on toast for breakfast.'

'No, well, actually, I didn't get the impression that Jack Thomas was a man to be easily intimidated. I just sort of felt that he wouldn't want to intrude on your life, or anyone's. He had a kind of natural – what? – humility about him.'

'Right. Just like Steven Hunt.'

Pleased to hear Marina able to joke about Steven, Shivaun saw both men in her mind's eye, the one glossily polished, the other ruggedly natural. Any outsider would say that Marina was far more socially suited to Steven, but Shivaun felt exactly the reverse; there was something much more solid, more durable, about Jack, that might ground Marina even as she kept the airlines in business.

'There it is.'

Marina looked to where Shivaun was pointing, and saw a semi-detached house of the architectural variety she detested, solid but dull, brightened only by a cute little garden which, on closer inspection, harboured several cans and candy wrappers.

'I'll kill those kids' Shivaun swore as automatically as if she'd never been away, 'I'll string them up and beat the daylights out of them.'

'Politics' Marina laughed for the second time, 'it's definitely the career for you, Shivaun.'

She grinned back, but for a moment she did stop to think about it: instant, huge fines would fix Ireland's litter problem overnight. If she had the power to impose them she would, and do something about education too . . . traffic . . . crime . . . how did you get into politics, anyway? And why was she wondering, when she had a new job to go to in America, another patient to nurse?

For a few transfixed moments she stood wondering, tasting the word politics for the first time on the tip of her tongue. Her regard for most politicians verged on contempt, but not for every last one of them. There were just enough honest, visionary ones to save the species from complete damnation, men and women who thought the world could be better, and fought fairly to make it so. How they survived the temptations around them, the bribes, corruptions and power struggles, God only knew . . . but they hung in there, and it dawned on her that hanging in there was something she had done well for the past six years. She had hung on to her loathing of Jason Dean. But now Jason was gone from her life, and she had a lot of tenacity to redirect. Direct into something more worthwhile, more constructive . . . ? Of course nursing was constructive, but nurses were undervalued; if she had her way they'd be far better paid and given much more say in the way the health system was run.

If, she thought! If I was minister for health—! The ludicrous thought made her laugh aloud, and Marina peered enquiringly at her.

'Well, if it's this house you're laughing at, I can see why! Not that I'm not delighted to visit your family home and flattered to be asked, but really, if I got hold of whoever designed this street I'd have him taken out and shot.'

Shivaun went to swing luggage out of the boot. 'No, it's not this house. However unexciting it may look, I grew up happy in it, and it's still home. I'm home, Marina.'

Again Marina looked at her. 'Are you?'

'Yes. I might sell the house eventually, move all the memories to a place of my own – but you can't sell your roots. Whatever Ireland is today, whatever muddle or mess might meet us inside this door, I still feel like I'm coming home.'

Marina studied her nail polish. 'Where the heart is, huh?'

Shivaun thunked down the bags in the porch. 'Yeah. I guess. It's only now I see it I realise it . . . and understand what Viv meant when she used to say that if you ran far enough you'd meet yourself coming back. In some weird way I feel I am about to meet myself. Not the old Shivaun, but the new one.'

'Then I hope you'll like her when you do! I'm still very fond of the old one.'

'Oh, well, she'll still be around, sometimes . . . hell, where are my keys?'

As she rummaged for them there was a click, and the front door swung open. Standing in its frame was Alana Kennedy; or someone who used to be Alana Kennedy. Someone who still had her madonna-blue eyes and rosy hue, her blonde hair, grown back from lemon to its natural buttery hue and tied haphazardly back from her glowing face. Someone who looked girlishly young without make-up, buoyantly happy and massively pregnant.

They gasped at each other, and Shivaun heard words whistling from her lips like steam from a kettle.

'Alana! You – you're *pregnant*!'

'Yes! I am! And you're home!'

Squealing with delight she embraced Shivaun, drew her in and then stopped, staring over her shoulder.

'Hey! You must be Marina? Come on, come in!'

Bouncing gleefully at Marina she embraced her too, and propelled everyone into the living room where Shivaun stood thunderstruck.

'But – who – how—?'

Alana waved an airy arm in the direction of the armchairs, and as she sank astonished into one Shivaun thought Alana looked like one herself: soft, cushiony, rounded and shabbily comfortable. Once a glamour puss, poured into tight new outfits, painted and varnished, Alana was now wearing denim dungarees, with an old white T-shirt and Scholl sandals. Gape as Shivaun nakedly did, the huge bump in the middle of the dungarees did not disappear; on the contrary it loomed large as the hill of Tara. Shivaun sat breathless, utterly lost for words.

'Cup of tea?'

Shivaun nodded, while even Marina sat immobile, wondering what to say. There hadn't been any mention of a baby. Clearly Shivaun had known nothing whatever about it.

Alana vanished into the kitchen to make the tea, leaving the door open, and when Shivaun found her voice she called out to her.

'Dare I ask –' oh, Jesus – 'dare I ask who the father is?'

She wouldn't have been any more amazed than she already was if Alana replied that she hadn't the slightest idea. But Alana's voice floated back to her, sounding absolutely blissful.

'Fintan.'

Shivaun wrinkled her forehead. 'Fintan? Who?'

'Fintan Daly! God, Shivaun, you've only been away a year, you can't have forgotten our neighbour next door?'

Mistily, the memory came back to her; the freckle-faced Lothario who used to wave to her when she came home from work in the evenings, who was famously known as Five-A-Night-Fintan, because so many women used to flit in and out of his house. And now, evidently, Alana was flitting too. Or had flitted, at least once.

'You mean—?'

'Yes!' Beaming ecstatically, Alana came back into the room bearing a tray of tea things, and plonked it down on the coffee table. As if from outer space, Shivaun noticed a deep gash in the table . . . other things out of kilter too, in some odd way she was too dazed to analyse. The house felt as if it had been – something.

Alana ducked out again, got the tea and returned to pour it, kicked off her Scholls and flopped majestically onto the sofa, which sagged and puffed under her.

'Fintan and I' she said beatifically, 'are getting married.'

'Married?!' Shivaun's voice echoed like a thunderclap. 'But – I – when – why—?'

'Why? Because we love each other. At Christmas. After Butterball here is born. He's due next month.'

Suddenly Shivaun gathered her wits, swallowed some scalding tea and spluttered with laughter. 'I meant, why didn't you tell me? Alana, what is going *on*?'

Wriggling into a more comfortable position, Alana flushed faintly, bit her lip and then beamed again.

'Well, I may as well come clean. I've behaved disgracefully since you went away.'

Shivaun eyed the bump. 'So I see.'

'No. I mean – before that. After you left, I – well, um, I sort of – uh. I crashed your car.'

Oh, God. She'd seen it out in the drive, but not noticed anything amiss with it. 'What happened? Were you hurt?'

'No. But I was petrified you'd kill me. So I took it to a garage to get it fixed. At the garage I met a mechanic called Brendan and I got . . . sort of . . . mixed up with him.'

'But – Brendan? I thought you said Fintan—?'

'Shivaun, wouldja give me a chance, and I'll tell you everything! I got involved with this guy, Brendan McLaughlin, and he persuaded me to have a party. Here, in your house. I thought it would be fun, but it turned out to be a nightmare. He invited zillions of people and everything got completely out of hand. So out of hand that, er, well, somebody called the police.'

'Police!?'

'Yeah. When they arrived, everyone scarpered, including Brendan, because . . . well, there were drugs involved. I ended up out on the front lawn in my new dress, freezing and snivelling, crying my eyes out. And next thing there was Fintan beside me, making me put on his sweater, giving out blue bloody murder. After the police left he marched me into his house and read me the riot act. Told me I was a complete moron, which was bang on exactly right. I just suddenly knew it was, felt as if I'd been slapped across the face and woken up, knew for sure I'd totally screwed up with both Brendan and Ivor—'

Shivaun flinched, and frowned. 'Ivor? Lawlor? What's he got to do with this?'

Alana's gaze bounced briefly off the floor, and then back at Shivaun. 'I'll tell you in a minute. But anyway, I'd only done it because – because I was so lonely. You were gone, Ivor was gone and now Brendan was gone too. I felt so miserable, I cried buckets and – and then Fintan was just so sweet. He stopped giving out to me and said I could stay the night in his spare room, told me he'd help clear up the mess the next day. And he did help. He was wonderful.'

The painter. Jim the painter, who'd unaccountably said Alana didn't live here and he was merely freshening the place up. He must have been repairing the party damage, as Shivaun had suspected . . . remembering that phone call, she felt as if she were grasping one small piece of a very large jigsaw. Which piece was Ivor, where did he fit into it?

Inexorably, clearly determined to get everything off her chest, Alana continued. 'And then, after that, I gradually realised that I'd found the right man at last. Here virtually on my own doorstep. Fintan and I became friends – not lovers at first, just friends, until we realised what idiots we'd been, chasing after everything that moved when all we'd wanted was here under our own noses. It simply clicked with us both one night and – well, that was the night we made Butterball. We've been living together ever since, next door in Fintan's house, because I didn't want to do any more damage to yours. It's all fixed though, honestly, it looks OK, doesn't it?'

Her eyes widened in their eager way, and Shivaun thought yes, everything did look OK, if not entirely familiar. Smiling back, she felt herself warming to the friend who'd always been so lost, but now looked so anchored, almost earth-motherly. Instinctively she knew that Fintan Daly, and Butterball, were what Alana had long wanted and needed, were making her happy in a way she'd never been before. Exhaling a sigh of mixed pleasure and lingering surprise, she sat back and surveyed Alana speculatively.

'So you're going to be a mum!'

'Yep. I can't wait. Neither can Fintan. We're so happy, it's only now I can see how unhappy I was before. That's why I behaved so badly – Shivaun, you're going to be really mad at me, but I hope after that you might be able to forgive me.'

'Oh, Alana. If the car and the house are fixed, then there's nothing to forgive. I'm delighted for you. But why didn't you tell me all this before?'

Again Alana lowered her lashes and studied the floor. 'Because . . . well, for one thing, I didn't want to say anything about Fintan in case I jinxed the whole thing. I wanted to wait until we were really settled and sure of each other, see how things would take. With my track record, I was afraid at first it would all go wrong. It was only when the baby was confirmed, and Fintan started talking about marriage and prams and stuff, that I started to feel comfortable about telling anyone. Even now, I don't want an engagement ring or anything, I simply want to let things . . . evolve. Quietly, peacefully.'

Shivaun laughed. She'd always seen Alana Kennedy as the kind of girl who'd get triumphantly engaged with a diamond as big as the Ritz, dazzling rings around everyone.

'Well, I must say, you've changed, Alana, in more ways than one!'

'Yes, I have, for the better I hope. You'll see why when you meet Fintan. I'll cook lunch tomorrow for all of us, if your flight's not too early?'

Jolted, Shivaun glanced at Marina, who had left them to talk without interruption. Flying to America tomorrow suddenly seemed aeons away, she was only barely adjusting to being home.

'Our flight's not until evening, Marina, is it?'

Marina, who seemed lost in reverie, looked up. 'No. Anyway there's no rush, we can change it if you like.'

Shivaun grinned at Alana. 'This woman spoils me absolutely rotten. This woman, Alana, has become like a mother to me, and I have you to thank for having found her for me.'

Alana looked startled, but Shivaun continued blithely. 'The minute we met I knew we were going to be great friends. Going to America was a great idea, and it was yours. I don't know what put it into your head, but it was brilliant. I've had an absolutely fantastic year.'

Looking extremely pleased, and faintly relieved, Alana smiled. 'I can't wait to hear all about it. I'm sorry I've been so out of touch, but I really needed to keep a low profile for a while.'

'Mmm. That's OK . . . I needed to make new friends anyway. And I did. I must tell you all about Azalea and Kathy and—'

Patrick. Should she tell Alana about Patrick? Perhaps. But not yet. Not until she sorted out the skeins of the story, and was sure how she felt about each strand, about the safety of the man who had entrusted her with his incriminating, haunting secret. Swiftly, she deflected the conversation back to Alana.

'But what was the other reason, Alana?'

'Huh?'

'For not telling me about Fintan or the baby? You said being sure was one reason, so there must be another . . . you said something about Ivor, too. What did he have to do with any of it?'

For a few taut seconds Alana was silent. Then, heaving herself upright, she put her hand on her back and smiled her old smile, the one that had so often stopped Shivaun from throttling her.

'Yes. I did say something about him. But it's kind of – complicated. Why don't you and Marina get comfortable first, shower and change after your drive from Waterford? We can chat later, over dinner tonight, I've got in some beautiful fresh fish for us all.'

'Have you? It'll be nice to eat at home, after all the restaurants we've done lately!'

'Yes, that's what I thought. At least my cooking's one thing I don't have to apologise for!'

Shivaun smiled fondly at her, and put her hand on her arm. 'Alana, you don't have to apologise for anything. Really. If everything is OK with you now, then it's OK with me.'

With fleeting, almost childlike gratitude, Alana smiled back, and said no more. Somehow she had managed to clamber over the first hurdle, but she quailed at the prospect of surmounting the second. Shivaun looked wonderful and was in great spirits, there was something fresh and renewed about her, but the next bit of news was going to blow her right off her feet.

Alana went to a lot of trouble preparing dinner that evening, encouraging Shivaun to not only eat but drink too; wine seemed to be flowing like the Liffey, in bemusing quantity even though Alana was drinking none herself.

Shivaun grinned fondly at her. 'You trying to get me drunk?'

'Oh no,' Alana replied hastily. 'I just thought we'd celebrate your return. Besides, that wine is perfect with this fish . . . I went out to Howth to get it specially, fresh off a trawler. I hope you like it – and Marina too?'

Marina, who'd been letting Shivaun do most of the talking, about America and their recent trip to England, paused, frowned and put down her fork.

'A trawler, did you say?'

'Yes – why, isn't it all right?'

'It's delicious' Marina assured her politely, but her voice trailed off, sounded somehow distant. Surveying her, Shivaun frowned in turn. 'Then what's the matter, Marina?'

'Nothing' she asserted, but something clearly was. Studying her plate, she spoke quietly, absently. 'I just . . . suddenly . . . remembered something.'

'What?' they asked in unison. Glancing at Shivaun, Marina hesitated, studiously concentrating on the fish without touching it.

'It was a long time ago. At least fifteen years, maybe sixteen . . . it was a fishing boat, setting sail out of Gloucester. Nobody noticed or thought anything of it, since trawlers are part of Gloucester's furniture. Only this particular boat wasn't going fishing at all.'

'No? So where was it going?'

'It was going to Ireland. All the way across the Atlantic, from my country to yours. It was called the *Marita Ann*. Instead of carrying nets and gear, it was carrying guns and ammunition. About six or seven tons of them, as I recall.'

'Blimey' Alana gasped, and Shivaun paused, fork aloft. 'Wow, Marina, what a memory you have! I remember that too – not the details, but the name. The *Marita Ann*. It was on the news on television, and the reason I remember is that Viv went mad over it, kept saying how awful it was and how many people could have been killed. But I was only a kid, didn't really know what she meant.'

'She meant exactly that,' Marina stated with certainty. 'The weapons were for the IRA. But they never reached their destination. Somebody tipped off the Irish coastguard, and when the *Marita Ann* sailed into Irish waters she was arrested. She'd been meant to rendezvous with some other ship, I forget its name, which was to take the weapons into a harbour somewhere off the south Irish coast. Instead, the police confiscated everything and, as your mother said, hundreds of lives were saved. I don't know what happened to the crew, but

I guess they went to prison somewhere, depending on whether they were Irish or American or a mix of both.'

Absorbing the story, Shivaun sat mulling on it until, out of the blue, a tremor shot through her like quicksilver.

'Marina,' she breathed, 'have you any idea who tipped off the police?'

'No. Everyone in Gloucester was agog to know, but nobody ever found out. Nobody ever found out who masterminded the plot, either. All I know for sure is that there are two people, possibly still in the area today, who took huge risks. One, obviously, was a fanatical supporter of the IRA, and the other took the chance that the IRA would shoot him if they knew he'd informed.'

Shivaun's gaze locked with Marina's, and they both paled as the story sank in, thinking simultaneously of Patrick Nulty. Had he been one of those two men, and if so, which? Dizzily, Shivaun wondered how many people would have been killed by seven tons – *tons*! – of guns and bullets, and sat stock still.

Not realising the significance of the tale, Alana wondered at the sudden silence that had descended on the table, and attempted to divert it.

'Well, what a weird thing to think of, Marina, after all this time!'

'Yes' agreed Marina, looking hard at Shivaun until, resolutely and adroitly, she regained her poise and smiled at Alana. 'Isn't it funny the little things that can trigger old memories. It was your fish – you're a wonderful cook, Alana.'

Happily, Alana purred. 'Thanks for saying so. I'm quite looking forward to playing the housewife for a while after the baby is born. I enjoy cooking and I think I'll enjoy Butterball, too, bottles and nappies and all.'

Shivaun recovered her composure, and forced herself to concentrate. 'What maternity leave do you get – about three months, isn't it?'

'Fourteen weeks. But actually I've decided to take a career break. A long one, because I want to be with the child until he starts school.'

'School? But he'll be five then – how will you manage, financially?'

'Well, Fintan earns enough to keep the roof over our heads and food on the table. We'll have to give up luxuries, holidays and that kind of thing, but I think it'll be worth it. I want to have fun with Butterball, be around when he says his first word and takes his first step, all that silly stuff I'd hate to miss. You can't have everything, and I'd rather have a secure happy child than a pampered one. He might have to do without the odd Gameboy or PlayStation, and I'll have to do without a new outfit every other week, but hey, how many clothes can you wear, anyway?'

Shivaun thought she must be hearing things. Alana Kennedy seemed to have completely reinvented herself. But she must be heading for thirty now, which was old enough to know what you were doing.

'D'you know for sure it's a boy?'

'Yes. I had a scan. I even have a photo of him!'

Suddenly Shivaun thought of something. 'Did you ever hear anything more about Kilo Finnegan? Or Stan?'

'Nothing about Kilo, which presumably means no news is good news. Stan is still working at that school, caretaking and happy as Larry.'

Shivaun was pleased. At least something good had come out of the Kilo episode, which had been the cause of her break with Ivor Lawlor. Poor Ivor . . . looking back on it, she had been consumed by her nursing career, not given him a fighting chance against all those babies.

'I think you're doing the right thing, Alana. Take a career break, enjoy being a mum and a wife. It'll surely give you as much joy as any of the things the extra money could buy.'

'Yeah. They're only things. I used to shop till I dropped, but now I know that shops don't sell what I was looking for. I can't believe I've found a smashing man and am going to have a family. But since I am, I want to give them priority. Of course it wouldn't suit everyone, some people would blow their brains out if they had to stay home with their baby, but I want to. It's time to stop and smell the roses – even if this species is Fragrance of Nappy!'

Beaming, she refilled Shivaun's empty glass and Marina's, and for a while the meal continued amiably. Trying to push her jangling thoughts of Patrick to the back of her mind, Shivaun reminded herself that she would speak to him when she got back to America, tell him about the Thomases' divided reaction to his letter and . . . and maybe mention Marina's memories of the *Marita Ann*?

He could not have been behind that plot. She was sure – nearly sure, almost sure – that he could not. He was plagued by the death he had already caused, and would never hate any human being enough to kill again. If he had had any hand in the saga of the *Marita Ann*, it was far more likely that he had been the informer, the saviour of countless lives. If she could get the truth out of him, if he had done that at huge risk to himself, she felt she could make peace with him.

Peace! How precious it was, with others and with oneself. But no matter how hard Patrick tried to attain it, she wondered whether he would ever find it within himself. Time had taught Jack Thomas to forgive, she could forgive, society could forgive, but she did not think Patrick Nulty could ever forgive himself. Not wholly, not ever. As he said, he would carry the memory of Kenny Thomas's grave to his own.

Unless he was a liar of blinding proportions, and a hopeless recidivist. If he was either, or both, of those things, then he could have masterminded the *Marita Ann*, could still be a steely nationalist, well capable of killing again. Well capable of lying to a woman when he wanted her. Well capable of anything.

The thought iced her limbs, and she fought to remind herself that he had voluntarily told her about Kenny Thomas. He would never have told her if— would he?

She was sure to within a hair's breadth that he would not. Amongst all the grains of truth in his story, only one single grain continued to itch and scratch stubbornly. Yet its effect was out of all proportion to its size, it rubbed her heart raw, and she knew it was the reason she could never go back to him, never love him even if he had sunk the *Marita Ann*, redeemed himself at a truly heroic level. As she looked at Alana's glowingly happy face, she thought how deeply, how tenderly love changed people, and how much Patrick was missing. The thought afflicted her in some way, saddened her into long speculative silence. Could love of many people ever equal love for just one, even if you laid your life on the line for it?

'What's the matter, Shivaun? You're very quiet.'

She roused herself. 'Oh, nothing, Alana. I – I was just thinking about going back to America.'

Alana flinched slightly, handed around some desserts, and then took a deep breath.

'Before you do, I have to tell you about Ivor. I wish I didn't have to, because it's a terrible confession, but I do. Marina will be horrified, and you're going to be absolutely livid. But I—'

Discreetly, Marina glanced in the direction of the door. 'If it's anything you'd rather I didn't hear, I can take my dessert through to—'

Alana sighed. 'No. Never mind. I'm sure Shivaun will tell you anyway. Besides you'll be going back to America, you won't have to see me again. Which is just as well.'

'Alana,' Shivaun said firmly, 'for God's sake, whatever it is, just spit it out! I can't imagine what you're on about, but it can't be all that bad, Ivor isn't even in the country—'

'Yes,' Alana said woefully, 'he is. That's why I have to tell you.'

Shivaun felt the colour empty from her face. 'Ivor is in Ireland?'

'Yes. In his mother's house only five minutes away. He wants to see you. He came here specifically a few days ago to ask whether there was any news of you, and I told him you were coming this weekend, and he nearly exploded with excitement, made me promise to – oh, God. Shivaun, I – I set you up.'

'What?'

Alana groaned, and her eyes gleamed with threatening tears. 'I sent you to America. Deliberately, because I wanted you out of the way. I – I wanted Ivor for myself.'

'You – Jesus *Christ*!'

'I thought I was in love with him. I'd been mad about him for years, totally infatuated. So I found your job with Marina and encouraged you to take it. The very night you left, I invited Ivor here to dinner in your house. I invited him lots of times. And then one night I – threw myself at him. We had a dreadful row. Not only because of that, but because he found out that I—'

Her voice cracked, and Shivaun gripped her wrist. 'You *what*?'

'I'd pretended you didn't care about him when I knew you did. I told him you never asked for him or mentioned him after you went to America. And then he found a postcard you'd sent, saying how much you missed him. He went completely ballistic.'

Shivaun tried to speak, and choked on the effort.

'He stormed off, but he came back again a few days later to ask for your address in the States. He insisted I give it to him. So I – I gave him a fake one.'

Such anguish, such pure fury surged up in Shivaun that she thought she was going to faint. Either that, or hit Alana, break her jaw. Or both. So Ivor had tried to contact her, after all! And Alana had stopped him, let her think he didn't care, didn't love her in the least! And that was why Alana had told her he'd gone to Australia, instead of Spain . . . her mind whirling, Shivaun sat staring at her, her body coiled like a whiplash.

'Go on. Tell me the rest of it. All of it.'

Tears spilled over Alana's eyelashes and ran unchecked down her cheeks.

'Apparently Ivor wrote to you several times, Shivaun. At the wrong address. When you didn't answer, he came to believe that you didn't want to hear any more from him. That you were finished with him for good. I let him think you didn't love him and I let you think he didn't love you, I – I wrecked everything between you.'

'Yes,' Shivaun breathed, 'you certainly did. I broke my heart over Ivor, Alana. And then, because I thought he'd rejected me, I got involved with somebody else. Somebody who could have destroyed my whole life. You have no idea what you have done.'

Fiercely, Alana nodded, her tears splashing the table. 'Yes! I do know what I've done. When I met Fintan I discovered real love, discovered just how precious it is and – and that was another reason I stayed out of your way, didn't keep in touch. I couldn't bring myself to tell you I'd found happiness when I'd ruined yours. I know you and Ivor had broken up anyway, but he never intended it to be permanent, he was just restless—'

Suddenly Shivaun was restless too, so wildly agitated she could no longer sit at the table, and jumped to her feet.

'Marina, I – I have to go out. I'm sorry, but I – oh, Jesus! Oh, Ivor!'

Racing out into the hall she grabbed her jacket, flung it on and ran to the door, vanishing into the night with a slam behind her.

At the abandoned dinner table, Alana collapsed in torrents of tears, and Marina gazed at her with a mixture of fascination and utter revolt.

'Well,' she said at length, 'so you're Shivaun's best friend, huh? You're the one she gave her car to and let stay in her house, rent free? God above, I don't want to think what she does for enemies.'

Shivaun's legs felt jet-powered as she flew to Ivor's house, thinking wildly, urgently, of the time she had telephoned it to ask his mother to give him her number in Gloucester. So. Alana wasn't the only one who wanted to keep her away from him. Cynthia Lawlor, who'd always been so coldly distant, had clearly had a hand in this outrage too.

Sprinting up the path, she hammered on the front door so hard the glass vibrated, until Cynthia's outline appeared and it was flung open with scandalised speed.

'What is—?'

Shivaun barged past her into the hall. 'Where's Ivor?'

The woman registered righteous distaste, but there was a glimmer of nervousness in it too, that said she knew the game was up. Shivaun had found her out.

'He's outside' she retorted with no attempt to dissemble. 'In the garden shed, making something.'

'Right,' Shivaun glared icily, 'I'll go get him myself. Oh, and for the record, Cynthia, you are a loathsome, despicable, miserable bitch.'

Leaving her gasping and twittering, she shot through the house, out into the garden and down to the shed, where the light was on. Wrenching open the door, she hurled herself inside, and stood gasping at Ivor.

Gasping not only because she could barely breathe, but because the man who whirled round to confront her was so completely, utterly different to the Ivor she'd known and loved all her life. That Ivor had been young and smooth, groomed and clean-shaven; this Ivor was older and adult, with no boyish softness to him whatsoever, deeply tanned, bearded and muscular. Nothing, only his eyes, told her that this was really Ivor Lawlor.

But it was, and his eyes blazed with such pure burning joy she was seared by it, engulfed as he gathered her into an embrace hot as a furnace, kissed her so long and hard she thought her lips would combust. It was a kiss that covered hundreds of days and thousands of miles, a kiss to last a lifetime.

When he let her go she reeled up against the wooden wall, and wondered that it did not burst into flames. Every bone in her body felt like an ignited torch. In turn he stood staring at her, speechless. The silence glowed like a pyre of ashes.

And then he drew away, stepped smartly back. 'Sorry,' he hissed like a doused coal, 'gut reaction. You caught me by surprise.'

'Ivor—'

'Alana said you were coming home, but I didn't expect you to come here. You look great. The new hairstyle is beautiful.'

There were traces of acid in both his look and words, and in a flash she saw that he had suffered. In all the time they had been apart, it had never occurred to her that he might. The break had been of his making – hadn't it?

'Well,' she said slowly, 'I'm not sure that you look great. But you certainly do look different.'

She let her eyes run the length of him, taking in the sun-tinged hair roughly knotted in a ponytail, the darkened skin and callused hands, veins firm in the underside of either forearm. The eyes that had once been so youthfully clear now had depth in them, and the former Ivor would never have worn these battered jeans, this tattered T-shirt with smears of oil or grease on it. The former Ivor would never have looked at her as he was looking now, cautiously yet challengingly.

'What on earth' she said wildly, lost for words, 'are you doing?'

She waved an arm at the wood and tools around him, and he smiled with faint irony. 'I'm working,' he said factually, 'I'm a carpenter.'

'A – *car*penter?'

'Yeah. A carpenter just back from Spain, on his way to someplace else.'

Oh. She felt punched. 'Where?'

'Dunno. Anywhere out of suburbia, anywhere I can have my own workshop and make what I want to make.'

'What do you want to – make?'

'Furniture' he said simply. 'Not money, except as an optional extra. Just furniture.'

'What put – what put this into your head?'

'You did. You and a guy called Miguel Garros and, incredibly, my mother. She asked me to make shelves for her one day, nagged me into doing it, and now she's absolutely furious at the result. Not that I care. I won't be living here.'

She had to talk to him. She had to, right now, because he looked ready to vanish before her eyes.

'Ivor,' she started in a flurry, 'your mother—'

'Shivaun,' he cut across her, 'damn my mother. I want to know about you. Why the fuck did you never write to me?

Never, not even once, after we'd been together for twenty years? Huh?'

He leered accusingly at her, but she sensed pain behind the accusation, and hardly knew where to begin. The old Ivor would never have sworn at her like that, never sounded so rough and unvarnished. A flicker of anger flared in her.

'Because' she retorted, 'I didn't know where the fuck, as you put it, you were! That's what I'm trying to tell you! Your mother – and Alana – they kept us apart – I thought at first you were in Australia – I never got any of your letters—'

Searching for coherence, she floundered, and in that fleeting moment he had it, saw it. 'You never – but I wrote – Alana gave me . . . no! Shivaun, she *can't* have gone that far – it crossed my mind, but I didn't think even she – *Jesus*!'

Volcanically, he erupted with anger, leaped forward as if on his way to murder Alana. But she grabbed his arm and pinned him.

'Ivor, shut up and listen. Just listen, OK? I never wrote to you because I thought you never wrote to me. You said you wanted a break from me and when I didn't hear a damn word from you after that I – I thought that was simply your polite painless way of saying you never wanted to see me again. In retrospect I couldn't blame you, because I'd been so wrapped up in my nursing and my problems – Viv and Jimmy and Jason Damned Dean – that I'd screwed us up. I wanted to marry you, but for selfish reasons, all the wrong reasons. I'd taken you for granted and made a complete horse's ass of our entire relationship. But when I went to America I did miss you. I missed you like crazy, even when pride tried to persuade me I didn't. I missed you so much I even phoned your blasted mother to give her my phone number so she could give it to you. But she never did give it, did she?'

'No' he said, white under his tan. 'She never did. I'll never speak to her again for this.'

'Well, whether you do or not, Alana was the one who gave you the wrong address. She's just made a full confession, because – well, not only because she could see what was coming, but because she regrets what she did. She's in love with Fintan Daly now and – she told me what happened—'

Ivor froze. Alana had told Shivaun how she'd been infatuated with him, how she'd come on to him – and how nearly, how very nearly, he had responded? Even now he could feel it, that falling-over-a-cliff feeling.

Alana Kennedy was not the only one harbouring dark secrets. In a burst of desperate candour, he rummaged in his mind, and flung his own forth into the light of day.

'Yes! I did nearly sleep with her! And more than that, I actually slept with two women in Spain – one was just a passing fling, but the other was – Shivaun, I've been living with an Australian woman. Sleeping with her not just once, out of loneliness, but systematically, out of lust. Sheer, stupid, galloping lust. I make no apologies for it. But I want you to know the truth.'

Standing back, standing upright, he waited. Either she would hit him, berate him, kill him, which would be fine; or she would not care, not give a damn. Which would be unendurable, and truly kill him.

For a moment she said nothing, taking it in, gazing so fixedly at an awl lying on the workbench that he wondered whether she was going to stab him with it.

And then she laughed softly.

'Thank God for that. I'd be worried about a red-blooded man of your age who stayed celibate for a whole year. Tell me, did love play any part in this, or were you just a prisoner of your ungovernable hormones?'

Relief made him laugh wildly, gush with gratitude. 'I was absolutely determined to break away from the woman who'd abandoned me for America and didn't even answer my letters. I was anybody's. But no, I wasn't in love. Sex is a lot easier to find than love, it seems. We broke up before I left.'

'I see. Then you'll understand how it is . . . I broke up with the guy I was sleeping with too, just before I left Gloucester.'

It was absurd. It was completely illogical, insanely unfair, but he was furious, wildly jealous and wounded to the quick. He'd infinitely prefer her to have stabbed him with the awl, straight through the heart.

'You . . . were . . . Shivaun, tell me you weren't.'

His voice spiralled to a whisper, but hers stayed steady. 'I was. Just like you, I was determined to seal my break with my ex, move on – and I was seized with lust, too. Something that very nearly grew into a lot more than lust, and would have if I'd let it.'

He was shattered. And yet he somehow felt as if he'd been snatched from the jaws of death.

'But you – you didn't let it?'

'No. For reasons that have nothing to do with you, I didn't.'

There was a twanging, reverberating silence. What does she mean, he howled within himself, by reasons that have nothing to do with me? Does she still love me, or not? I still love her, she's the love of my life and I was a fool to have ever – but I had to! How am I going to make her understand that I *had* to spend that year away from her, away from Ireland, and become a carpenter? What does she make of my becoming a penniless carpenter, and what did this other bastard do for a living – excavate diamonds?

Swinging himself up on a ledge, he sat looking at her, as nonchalantly as he could. 'So. You had a fling. Well, that's OK, you're young and red-blooded too—'

'Ivor,' she interrupted, 'I'm not asking you to understand, or forgive, or anything else. I'm simply telling you. And what's more, a "fling" isn't exactly the right word to describe it. I was – I was attached to him.'

Attached? What did that mean? He looked down, and the ground seemed miles away. 'So, who was he, then? This – uh – attachment?'

'He was Marina's gardener. He has a landscaping business in a town called Lowell. He's Irish and his name is Patrick. We met on a skiing holiday.'

Landscaping. Skiing. Money. And why is she still talking about him in the present tense?

'When did you last see him?'

'About two weeks ago. I'll probably be seeing him again when I go back, or talking to him on the phone at least. We have some – unfinished business.'

'Go back?' he repeated blankly. 'You're going back?'

'Yes. With Marina, my boss. She's at home with Alana. We're leaving tomorrow. However, as she doesn't really need nursing anymore, I have a new job to start. Another stroke patient, in Martha's Vineyard. But . . . in the long run, I'm thinking of maybe changing careers, as you've apparently done.'

'You wanted me to!' he protested, 'and you were right! I *was* turning into a suit! Now I haven't a penny, but I have a vocation—'

'That's just it,' she smiled inscrutably, 'if your calling is carpentry, I'm delighted you've had the imagination and courage to follow it. And now I'm beginning to hear politics calling me.'

He roared with laughter. '*Politics?* Shivaun, are you mad? They'd eat you for breakfast!'

'Yeah, well, maybe. But at least I'd have novelty value. I'd be an honest politician. Hell, Ivor, there's surely a vacancy!'

Oh, Christ. He could see it already. First it was the babies, next it would be the constituents, grabbing at her time and attention, yowling, shrieking, demanding. She'd be out there banging on about hospitals, taxes, planning, pollution, while once again he— a sharp image sliced his memory, of that protest march years ago, the day she'd gleefully got herself arrested. And then he thought of Justine Adams, who never gave a damn. At a stroke he was felled, absolutely demolished with love for Shivaun Reilly.

But – 'Where would you go into politics? Surely you don't know enough about America—?'

'Oh, no,' she said airily, 'and I probably wouldn't even be eligible to stand for election. Not unless I lived there permanently and applied for citizenship. But America is the business of Americans, Ivor. And Ireland is – is my home. Where I belong, in the long run.'

He jumped down off the ledge, and seized her. Seized her

two arms in his hands so hard she yelped. He never wanted to hurt her again, but neither did he want her going back to America, especially not if some bloody bozo over there had 'unfinished business' with her. Shivaun Reilly was *his* girl and that was all about it.

'Shivaun,' he shouted, 'apart from the carpentry, this entire year has been a nightmare. A nightmare of cold and starvation and separation and misery, chaos and confusion, meddling mothers and lies, misunderstandings of every conceivable kind. I've had enough. I want things sorted out, here and now, between us. I want *you*. I love you and I want to marry you and have eighty-seven kids with you, be with you until we are a thousand years old. Am I making myself clear?'

He was making himself crystal clear. As she looked into his face it opened up like a vista, and the old Ivor was bright as day in it, the Ivor she'd loved since she was four. The Ivor she was born to be with, the only part of her past she wanted, longed to take into her future. As if he had taken up his hammer and hit her with it, she was knocked senseless with love.

Snapping her arms free of his grip, she put them around him and drew him to her, laid her face on the old, familiar chest. She could hear his heart thundering in it.

'Yes,' she murmured, 'you are.'

It wasn't enough. He had to have more, have the full picture. Lifting her chin with his finger, he stared intently into her eyes. 'Well then' he breathed, 'will you have me? Will you marry a scruffy obsessive carpenter who hasn't tuppence, who wants to live in the back of beyond, sawing and drilling and driving you round the bend?'

She laughed, and looked at him. 'That depends.'

Depends? 'On *what*?'

'On how you feel about marrying a wannabe T.D. who'll be out causing trouble night and day, dashing up to Dublin for Dáil meetings, canvassing voters, leaving you home to mind the kids – if she ever gets time to have them – while she writes papers and makes speeches and holds clinics and generally drags the family into one hassle after another.'

He thought about it. And shuddered. And beamed. 'I'll hate it. But I wouldn't have it any other way. I'll hate it nearly as much as I love you.'

'Then I guess we're stuck with each other. The first twenty years were only the start. You're going to live to regret this, you know.'

He knew he was. Her crusading spirit would be like a rival lover, endlessly fighting him for her. But he'd fight back. He knew now that he could fight, as he knew so much else about himself. He could fight for what he loved as hard as it took, for as long as it took.

But he wasn't fighting now. He was in her arms feeling as if he'd been born in them, and she in his. Gathering her closer, deeper, he inhaled the scent of her hair, melted into the softness of her skin, ran his hands over her body as if it were a map in braille, directing him to where nature had always meant him to be.

His fingers felt like molten gold, and she shuddered. Patrick Nulty had had this effect on her too . . . but she had not loved Patrick. Not only because of what he was, but because of what he was not. He was not Ivor Lawlor, neither her foundation nor her future. Seizing Ivor with sudden swirling love, raging rivers of it, she knew they had reached a milestone, and that their paths would never diverge again. She could trust him with her future, and her trust would never be abused. Nor would his, in her; her young, frightened birth parents had run away and left her, but she would never abandon this man, never relinquish their family or their destiny.

Sliding her hands under his ragged shirt she pulled him back where he belonged, and looked around the dusty concrete floor as they sank together onto it.

'Do you think' she murmured into his ear, licking it, 'it might be a fitting punishment for Cynthia if she were to find us fornicating in her garden shed?'

His reply was incoherent, but she did not need to hear it as they reclaimed possession of each other, of the life that belonged to them alone.

* * *

Six months later, on a glinting, gusting spring day just before Easter, Shivaun stood knee-deep in wild daffodils, shielding her eyes with her hand as she scanned the field for Ivor. Some day part of the field would be a garden, and already some of Jimmy's transplanted cuttings were starting to take. Wrapped in wet sacking and newspapers, they were the only thing she'd brought to this small, tranquil Kilkenny village after selling the house in Dublin; apart from Viv's gold earrings, she had let everything else go. Even her job in Martha's Vineyard had gone, to the temporary nurse already in possession of it, and in place of everything she had renounced Shivaun felt a billowing sense of liberation. The only things she was holding onto today were the few essentials she needed, love, friendship and a growing sense of purpose. As yet she was a long way from carving out a niche in politics, but she was burrowing into local life, getting to know the people and the concerns that were of interest here, thinking that rural resettlement might well be one of the cudgels she would eventually take up; in their wildest dreams neither she nor Ivor could envisage ever living in gridlocked suburbia again. For years Irish people had traditionally migrated to cities, to where the jobs were, but now in the age of the internet there was no reason why the jobs should not start coming to them. Even Ivor had a website for God's sake, he made his furniture here in the barn at the end of the field and you could buy it online from Dublin, Dallas, anywhere.

Decentralise! Downsize! That would be her platform when she finally stood for local election, as an independent candidate; live on the land around you, invest in it, don't leave it! Why should people commute hours to work, or hospitals or other amenities, when the amenities should be coming to them? More than ever she opposed the policy of a handful of huge hospitals, massive scattered schools, top-heavy cities and denuded rural villages, and she was ready to raise her voice even if it was a lone one. Whether she had the faintest hope of election, or people would think her eccentric like Viv, she didn't know, but she did know some like-minded souls, and meanwhile she was living, savouring, each day as it came. The sale of the house in Dublin had yielded sufficient funds to buy the cottage and survive for some time to come, supplemented by freelance nursing and the occasional sale of one of Ivor's tables or cabinets. But the sale of these solid chunky pieces never gave him as much pleasure as the making of them, and she was still absorbing the change in him, the new contentment, fulfilment and inner strength. He loved his work, but never worried about it; if people liked it, great, if not he'd get on with it just the same. He was a much looser, happier, more rounded man than before, resilient and philosophical, and Shivaun found him freshly interesting, stimulating. Hard as their year apart had been, it had drawn them much closer together, and they were communicating at a much deeper level. Whenever they travelled in future, they would travel in tandem and travel light, unencumbered by any of the baggage they had jettisoned.

She knew she'd have his full support if she wanted, now, to find Jason Dean and challenge him. She could track Jason down in Dublin and make sure he knew the full import of what he had done, discover whether he was the least bit sorry for it, and Ivor cheerfully offered to beat the guy senseless if she thought it would help either one of them. But Shivaun refused Ivor's offer, and all further thoughts of Jason Dean; he was ancient history and no longer mattered to her. Either he was guilty and suffering, like Patrick, in his own private hell, or he was too worthless to waste another thought on. Like Ivor, Shivaun was a much happier person these days, and determined to enjoy the new young life they were building between them.

Meanwhile, where was Ivor, right now? Banging away in that old barn of his, she supposed, when he'd promised to put new window frames into the house. She knew he'd made them, but they were lying in a heap somewhere along with still-packed wedding presents and assorted debris; the only things installed so far were a vast bed and an equally vast painting by Kathy Shreve.

'Ivor!' she yelled, and eventually her voice carried to him on the breeze, luring him forth from his lair with his jeans spattered in wood shavings. Pushing up his eye shield, he squinted at her against the flashing sun.

'What can I do for you, Mrs Lawlor?'

She waved an envelope and thick white card under his nose. 'You can start packing.'

'Oh. Right. Well, my mother did say this marriage would never last.'

Laughing, Shivaun remembered the day of it, at Chederlay just before Christmas. Ivor's mother had attended as if it were a funeral, and she was the chief mourner. In fact the chief mourner was Patrick Nulty, who had not been at it at all.

Alana had not been at it either, because she was at home nursing her hefty, noisy newborn son, and Ivor had been delighted to hear she wasn't coming. But Shivaun had insisted on inviting her, on the basis that she didn't want to start her married life holding a grudge against anyone. Yet she was relieved when Alana declined, and Azalea could be her bridesmaid instead. I'll always be grateful to Alana, she thought, for having found Marina and sending me off to explore America, explore myself; but it's a good thing she's busy with her own family now, because I never want her next to or near Ivor ever again. He needed to experiment with other women, as I needed to discover other men, but now we both know who we are and what we want, and it isn't Alana, or Patrick or Justine. All we want is our work and our friends and each other – well, almost all.

Grinning, she thrust the card into his hand. 'No. I'm not throwing you out just yet. I'm merely giving you notice that Marina has summoned us to attend her – er – ceremony of commitment. On May 19, at Chederlay.'

Ivor read it, and laughed. 'Well, well. So Jack Thomas is to be catapulted from Dunmore East to Gloucester after all. He didn't stand a chance.'

'He didn't put up much of a fight. Anyway they're both fishing villages, he's so mad about Marina he probably won't even notice he's moved. He couldn't go on flying back and forth and neither could she . . . here, look. She's put a little note in with the invitation, says the designs for the house in Dunmore are going ahead, but they'll be using it for a holiday home. So we'll be seeing a lot of them – hopefully of Azalea and Kathy as well, because Marina is keen that it be used as much as possible. I'd say Kathy will love painting there, and Azalea will bring Jeff with her – what with their trips over here, and ours over there, we'll be able to stay in touch and have lots of fun.'

Ivor was delighted. He knew how much Shivaun's American friends meant to her, and wanted her to keep them.

'So, what'll we give Jack and Marina for a wedding present? Is this to be a big gig, are you going to be matron of honour or something?'

'No, I don't think it's that kind of wedding . . . knowing Marina, it'll probably be performed by a druid or shaman or something, and then we'll have sushi and Morris dancing and tarot readings out on the lawn.'

Ivor, having got well acquainted with Marina, thought he wouldn't be in the least surprised. For their own wedding, she had worn a sari and carpeted Chederlay in rose petals flown in from Florida. She was crackers, but she was very special to Shivaun, and for that he had taken a great shine to her. In turn, she had embraced him eagerly, drawn him in just as Viv Reilly had done, all those years before.

'Still, I'd like us to give her something – something unique. What on earth do you give the woman who has everything?'

Shivaun wrapped her arms around him. 'You give her a piece of hand-crafted furniture by Ivor Lawlor.'

'But Chederlay is full of furniture.'

'Yes. There isn't a stick of it, though, in this new house down in Dunmore.'

'Oh – OK! What'll it be, then? May 19 is only six weeks away, I'd just about have time to do a dining table or a dresser—'

'Would you have time to do a bed? A big yummy bed like ours?'

'Yes! And Marina is French. I could make her a bateau lit.'

'Beautiful. That'll tide her over then, until it's time for the Christmas present.'

Christmas? Ivor groaned. Surely Shivaun couldn't be thinking about next Christmas already? He still had agonisingly mixed memories of the one before last, that icily lonely day in Seville when he had made a crib; a beautiful crib that he had later allowed Miguel to sell to some total stranger.

'Shivaun, that's ages away. Let's not cross our bridges before we come to them.'

'OK. Still, that's when we'll be giving Marina another present. Something else she'd like to complete her happy household. Fortunately, you've already made the first part of it, so you'll only have to do the second.'

'Huh?'

Mischievously, Shivaun snuggled into him, and grinned. 'Mmm. Of course you'll be busy for now with the bateau lit, but later . . . Ivor, d'you know how to make one of those whatsits?'

'Which whatsits?'

'Oh, you know . . . one of those little cradle things, on rockers, that you put babies in.'

He gazed at her, long and hard, and then a smile spread across his face like liquid wax on wood, and he folded his arms around her.

'Yes, Shivaun. I think I might just know how to make one of those.'